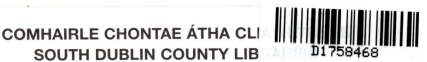

FRANCIS STUART
Artist and Outcast

Kevin Kiely

The Liffey Press

Published by
The Liffey Press
Ashbrook House 10 Main Street
Raheny, Dublin 5, Ireland
www.theliffeypress.com

A catalogue record of this book is
available from the British Library.

ISBN 978-1-905785-25-4

Printed in Spain by Graficas Cems.

CONTENTS

Acknowledgements

There are many people with whom I discussed Stuart's novels and related matters in my youth: Dermot Bolger, Rory Brennan, Terry and Dorothy Brennan, Paul Brittain, Ces Cassidy, Lar Cassidy, Olga Cox, Anthony Cronin, Ronan Downs, Mary Drake, Ashling Drury Byrne, Paul Engle (Iowa University), Jasusc Glowacki (Iowa University), Frank and Pauline Hall, Denis and Christine Hickey, Aidan Higgins, Fred Johnston, John Jordan, Michael and Shelley Kane, Katherine Kavanagh, Rita Kelly, Desmond Kiely, Faustine Kiely, Tom McGonigle, Dan MacMahon, Marie McQuaid, Augustine Martin (UCD), Michael and Tess Moore, Eamonn Moorhead, Mary Morrissey, Caitriona Murphy, Tom and Liz Nally, Peter and Mary Nazareth, Austin Nolan, Don Nolan, Helga Novak, Evanna O'Boyle, Conleth O'Connor, Matt O'Dowd, Nuala O'Faolain, Timothy O'Keeffe, Michael O'Loughin, Mattie O'Neill, Eoghan Ó Tuairisc, Elizabeth Peavoy, Lucille Redmond, Anne Rowland, Maurice Scully, Ronan Sheehan, Tommy Smith, Gary Snyder, Antoinette Spillane, Gerard Stafford, Rosita Sweetman, Mary Timmons, Colm Tóibín, John Vaughan-Neil and Eva Zadrzinska.

In 1997, the year this project began, new associates came on the horizon, some of whom gave of their time for interview purposes, advice and council: Jeremy Addis (Books Ireland), Gary Ansbro (Department of Foreign Affairs), Lez Barstow, Ciarán Bennet, Ciaran Benson, Joanna Boulter, Terence Brown (TCD), Anna Buggy Stuart, Andrew Carpenter (UCD), Clare Carpenter, Philip Casey, Frank Cass, Bernadette Chambers (Department of Foreign Affairs), Christine Clear, Dr Maurice Craig (TCD), Caitriona Crowe (National Archives), Gerald Dawe (TCD), Rosemary Dawson, Mary de Rachewiltz, Ted Dolan (RTÉ), Geoffrey Elborn, Mannix Flynn, Roy

Foster (University of Oxford), Peggy Fox, Maeve Friel, John Gery, Brendan Graham, Finola and Daniel Graham, Maurice Harmon (UCD), Anne and Geraldine Haverty, Martha Henry, Sean Hughes, Lisa Hyde, Anthony J. Jordan, Orla Kaminska, Ivan Kelly (personal advisor), Brendan Kennelly (TCD), Adrian Kenny, Robert and Ashling Law, Dr Inge Leipold, Orla Lehane, Paul Lenihan, Bernard and Mary Loughlin, Brian Lynch, Sinéad MacAodha (Ireland Literature Exchange), Brian McCarthy, Sheila McCarthy, Anne McCartney (QUB), Bill MacCormack (University of London), Tom MacIntyre, Jonathan Manley (Taylor & Francis), Emily Mitchell Wallace, John Montague, John and Nuala Mulcahy, Ger Mulgrew, Hayden Murphy, Tina Neylon (*Irish Examiner*), Geraldine Nichol, Ambrose and Christina O'Connor, Ulick O'Connor, Jim and Mary O'Donnell, David Pierce (York University), William Pratt, Robert Rehder, Anne Richardson, Kay Sheehy, Piet Sluis, Ian Stuart, Imogen Stuart, Miho Takahashi, Catherine Tierney, Bob Welch (University of Ulster at Coleraine), Nick and Deirdre Wollaston, Joseph Woods and Helen Wynne (University of Canterbury).

Others deserving of gratitude are The Jonathan Williams Literary Agency; the Arts Council, which provided a two-year bursary at a vital stage of the project; Patrick Villiers-Stuart for residence in the Ardenza studio-apartment from 1997 onwards; a couple (who wish to remain anonymous) for the use of their cottage, "Shangri-La" in Drummin, County Mayo over many years; my partner, Maeve McCarthy; David Givens and the staff of The Liffey Press; Deirdre O'Neill for editorial advice and bringing the book into its prepublication format.

The letter from Ezra Pound to Francis Stuart on page 177 appears by kind permission of New Directions, New York.

Once again, I acknowledge Francis Stuart who read early drafts of this biography.

"If luck comes to his aid he [Stuart] will be our great writer." — W.B. Yeats to Olivia Shakespear (Letter, 1929)

"Just read [The] *Great Squire*. It's a great book. Iseult is right about your genius. Am just writing out of the excitement of reading it." — Maud Gonne MacBride to Francis Stuart (Letter, 1939)

"In speaking to you from Germany I do not pretend to know any more about the war, in its military and strategic aspects, than you at home do; but from here at the hub of Europe I am in a position to get a clearer idea of it; of something in the nature of a world revolution, the great dividing line in history, a vital change upon the face of life." — Francis Stuart broadcast from Irland-Redaktion, Berlin, 29 March 1942

"Whatever the motives for my coming here, and they were complex and far from pure, I've begun to realise that it's here in the company of the guilty that with my peculiar, and if you like, flawed kind of imagination, I belong. The situation I've involved myself in, however disastrous for my reputation, and perhaps because it is disastrous, gives me a chance of becoming the only sort of writer it's in my power to be." — Francis Stuart, *Black List, Section H*

Introduction

COMMENTATORS AND CRITICS OF FRANCIS STUART tend to fall into two extreme groups: those who revile him and those who support him. The former group believe he was anti-Semitic in his pre-Second World War writings, and automatically rushed to support the Nazi cause: hence his decision to broadcast from Berlin for the Third Reich. As Oscar Wilde said, "The truth is rarely pure and never simple", and so it is with Stuart.

This introduction gives an account of my friendship over twenty-three years with Francis Stuart. It might seem that I am in a compromised, even biased position having been his friend; very few people have had my privileged access.

It is true that the commentary on his life and writings comes from our conversations over many years. To me he was a rare confidant and an extraordinary person to engage with in discussion. After striving to complete the task that Stuart set me, namely to write an account of his life with reference to his works in it, some may see me as being his supporter rather than an objective critic. It is also better to state at the outset that I do not agree with a definitive gloss on any writer; I prefer to make up my own mind about Stuart and to give the reader the same option.

I have tried to tell the truth as I see it and give all sides in the various controversies and scandals relating to Francis Stuart. I do not expect both factions relating to Stuart to agree with me. I have heard people on one side call Stuart a politically naïve person and a bit of a saint. Others see him having been compromised in much the same way as Ezra Pound was, who broadcast on Rome Radio during the Second World War in support of Mussolini and the Fascists. Pound was indicted for treason but never brought to trial. Stuart's wartime activities put him in the same treasonous situation as Pound or William Joyce ("Lord Haw Haw") who was hanged by the British for his broadcasts from Berlin. Stuart's situation requires a lot of clarification before anyone who does not have the full facts should decide whether he was an outcast or a traitor.

I FIRST MET FRANCIS STUART IN THE AUTUMN of 1977 at National University of Ireland, Galway, where he was giving a talk to a group of young writers before a public debate on "The Writer and the Politician". He was over six feet tall, had white hair, a bulbous nose and deep-set eyes. Apart from the occasional gentle smile, his expression conveyed utter distance. He was 75 years old, but looked fit, even robust, for his age.

Students and staff at the university knew that Stuart was as controversial and scandalous as Wilde, Synge, Yeats and O'Casey. The writings of John Broderick, Kate O'Brien, John McGahern and Edna O'Brien had not reached the same levels of public controversy. The moderator of the workshop, Anthony Cronin, seated me next to Stuart at the post-seminar lunch, but suggested that we should not rile him with awkward questions. Someone picked up the reading matter I had, *Collected Poems* by W. B. Yeats; it was not a book to wave in Stuart's face, Cronin admonished. Maud Gonne, the object of Yeats's greatest love poetry, had a daughter, Iseult, who became Stuart's wife in 1920. Yeats was infatuated by the Gonne women, and had proposed marriage to both of them at different times. Both had refused him.

Little did I know that this lunch would be the start of a friendship with Francis Stuart that would last over the last 23 years of his life. When given the chance, I mentioned reading his then most recent novels, *A Hole in the Head* and *Black List, Section H.* No one at the table spoke about his Berlin period or the controversial broadcasts. Instead, the conversation touched on Stuart as a young writer, when he had co-edited a pamphlet, *Tomorrow* (1924), which became the subject of scandal and derision in Ireland, and also the banning of some of his pre-war novels by the Irish Censorship Board. *Memorial* was impounded by the Irish customs and was given to the censors for examination in 1973. *Who Fears To Speak,* one of his plays, was withdrawn before opening night at the Peacock Theatre, Dublin in the same decade, because it was adjudged to be subversive.

"The Writer and the Politician" proved to be a lively topic for debate. In his introduction, the head of the English department mentioned Yeats, who had presented Stuart with a Royal Irish Academy prize for *We Have Kept the Faith,* his first book of poems in 1924. Yeats said on that occasion: "If luck comes to his aid, he will be our great writer." The head of the department then outlined Stuart's life other than art and literature. He was the squire of a Gothic castle in County Wicklow, a title he would lose because of his broadcasts from Berlin for the Nazi regime. He met a student in Germany, Gertrud Helene Meissner and their relationship effectively ended his marriage to Iseult and estrangement from his son, Ian and daughter, Katherine. Before and after his years in Berlin there were periods of imprisonment, drinking, gambling, drifting, reading astrophysics and theology and, not least, his passion for the world of horse racing.

Henry Francis Montgomery Stuart was born in Australia in 1902, of Northern Irish parents. His father committed suicide when Francis was four months old. By the time he was in his early thirties, Stuart had become a successful novelist. *Pigeon Irish* (1932) was reviewed on the front page of the *New York Times Book Review* as "an out-of-the-ordinary work of fiction", while Victor Gollancz, one of his publishers, said of Stuart, "He is not really a novelist at all, but a poet philosopher. He is incapable of approaching a novel as a piece of craftsmanship, to be undertaken for the pleasure of the craft (or to pay the rent): he must be conveying his vision."[1]

With the reissue of his masterpiece, *Black List, Section H,* in 1975, Roger Garfitt insightfully commented in the *London Magazine*: "There are still critics who feel that Stuart's move to Berlin in 1940 prejudices everything he has written since. I would argue precisely the opposite: that to questions raised by that decision, to the questions Stuart himself raised when discussing *Black List, Section H,* the character and quality of his work since then provide the only sufficient answer." The head of the English department quoted this and closed his welcoming speech by saying that he was eagerly looking forward to Stuart addressing his chosen theme of the evening.

Stuart began by saying that he could speak only about the writer, "whereas politics and the politician use a familiar language degrading the rhythms and meanings of common speech. Literature is taught as something apart from the business and struggle of living, as something for leisure hours and discussion in literary societies, almost never as one of the few methods of exploring the eternal problems of life and death." [2]

Stuart spoke of the literary artist blossoming in the isolation that the French novelist Gustave Flaubert recommended. He said that he was acquainted with "fidelity to failure"; "that to be an artist is to fail, as no other dare fail", [3] a phrase of Samuel Beckett's. Dante had echoed a similar sentiment in the *Paradiso*, as did Michelangelo and Shakespeare in some of their sonnets. He concluded that the writer "bears it out even to the edge of doom". I revelled in Stuart's lecture and made a few notes, hoping that I would be able to meet him once more.

After the seminar, Stuart's novels became my obsession. Those that I could not get in the public library I read at the National Library, Kildare Street, Dublin, not in order of publication but as the titles caught my attention – *Pigeon Irish, The White Hare, Glory, Try the Sky, The Angel of Pity*. His novels set in Berlin, including *Victors and Vanquished*, were so vivid that I assumed they must be based on experience. *Things to Live For: Notes for an Autobiography* (1934) evoked scenes from Stuart's twenties; the chapter entitled "Night-Flight" seemed familiar. I had among my books a prose anthology from my schooldays and, sure enough, "Night-Flight" was in it. I wrote to Stuart (through his publisher), sending a copy of a magazine that I co-edited – *The Belle* – mentioning our brief meeting in NUIG, and was delighted to receive a reply with an invitation to a garden party at his house:

> Dear Kevin Kiely,
>
> Thank you for your letter and for the copy of *The Belle*. I think your editorial that comes direct from the heart, or psyche, is moving. Of course, as you say yourself, such writing demands responsiveness and sacrifice (of preconceived ideas) on the part of the reader conditioned by the usual jargon. I remember the seminar in Galway last year with pleasure and affection, and, as you mention, we did not have much opportunity to talk personally.

I can still recall the Stuarts' house on that first visit: the creaky gate that would not close properly; the front garden with sunflowers reaching high above the bay window; Madeleine Stuart's distinctly German accent and how she opened the door holding her pet rabbit in her arms.

On that first occasion I met writers, editors, journalists and others, such as a monk who had left an enclosed order for his partner and a striking-looking woman studying Eastern mysticism. There were people from the world of horseracing, a state psychiatrist from the Central Mental Hospital (the high walls of the asylum could be seen from the Stuart's front gate) an ex-prisoner and a jockey. Some of the guests were like characters from Stuart's novels. I got to know others on various occasions at the Stuarts' house, such as Elgy Gillespie, Nuala O'Faolain, John Mulcahy and Nuala O'Farrell, John Feeney, John Jordan, Lucille Redmond, Jim O'Donnell and his wife Mary O'Donnell, and Katherine Kavanagh, widow of Patrick Kavanagh.

The first time I went to a restaurant with Stuart was in an art gallery. He ordered salad and wine and was quite taken by the waitress. "She has the most beautiful dimples," he said discreetly. I had not noticed a dimple. "No," Stuart insisted, "the dimples at the back of her knees."

Madeleine and Francis had the aura of lovers. They enjoyed great ease in each other's company, despite the pressure of being hosts. Madeleine was neither fussy nor bourgeois. The house was spartan in its furnishings. The only echo of Germany was a photograph of Madeleine in her school uniform. Gertrud Helene Meissner, whom Stuart always called Madeleine, was actually Polish. There was also the intrigue that Stuart had met her in Berlin and ultimately left his first wife and two children for her. Everyone at these parties seemed to have scanty details about how Stuart had met Madeleine, so I was curious to know more and would find out the full story in time.

She was a lively and passionate woman in her sixties when we met. Her teeth seemed to shine as she laughed, and what a laugh! Stuart was in her conversation endlessly, or "Frawn-cease" as she called him. His doings never ceased to amuse her. She thought he should be called "Saint Francis". One often felt an intruder in their love nest, except that to attempt to leave their company prematurely was difficult since they enjoyed visitors so much.

Just before my first visit, they had been entertaining a previous caller who was on day release from the nearby Central Mental Hospital. This incident eventually found its way into Stuart's novel *The High Consistory* (1980). I discussed his novels with him. This was what I had come for, and it was deeply satisfying to be at an exclusive seminar with Stuart. Such treasured conversations would go on for years.

He was highly practical about the artist's calling, which was an obsession that I could unburden to Stuart: "You have to make the best of it," he advised. One had a destiny. This sounds like stoicism, but Stuart understood that if the dream was of such a compelling nature, you had better obey. "Reality," he remarked, "is nothing if not our most intense imaginative concepts of it." He often used the phrase "a model for reality" and judged art, science and literature in terms of it being a good or true model for reality. However, he was not a dogmatist in this theory; he tended to have definite theories on most aspects of life, but never felt these to be valid for everyone. Early on I formed the opinion that he was not someone who believed in collectivism or, indeed, in any "ism". He was strikingly singular in character and expected the same from me as a novice writer. He questioned whatever was popular in science, politics, the arts and life in general, preferring to engage with any valid individual vision which he would rigorously test and then either accept or reject.

He was very cautious when discussing mysticism. However, it was one of the subjects which cemented our friendship. I was desperately seeking for certainty and stability for whatever inner chaos was my lot at the time. To my great relief Stuart discussed such matters instinctively and understood people in terms of how they coped with "inner disturbance and turmoil". Life *in extremis*, anxiety, fear and terror were his preserve. To sit with him for any length of time and mention one's inner conflicts was to have such conflict put in perspective and harmony. This was more than a consolation and I knew it early on in our relationship. He had read mystics from pre-Christian times to the Middle Ages, from Buddhism and Sufism to the Kabbalah and Hasidism. He was familiar with Plotinus, Meister Eckhart, Dame Julian of Norwich and many others. Looking back I am sure that he refrained from mentioning too many books in case my reading would lead to destruction rather than to some fruitful individuation and my emergence into maturity as a writer. He would often caution me about lives of people he knew or had read about that moved towards disaster whether by their own volition or through their fate or destiny. He had a special ability to forecast some public lives. For instance, he once mentioned that Lady Diana Spencer might well be doomed because of her marriage into royalty and what he had heard from media news and gossip columns. He did not blame the house of Windsor, rather her lifestyle and what he perceived to be her brimming chaos. This was in the 1980s. He was proven correct by her untimely death in a car accident in Paris.

My life during this period (the late 1970s and early 1980s) was one of concentrated study and having Stuart to call on for discussion added to the adventure. I was not wealthy by any means, but frugal living and part-time employment allowed me to continue my pursuits.

In his twenties and thirties, two figures captivated Stuart's imagination – he wrote of them, "after the autobiography of Saint Thérèse of Lisieux, the story that made the greatest impression on me was the life of St Catherine of Siena".[4] I would in time read these two life stories and find the latter saint more personally interesting. One of my pursuits as a budding writer was to frequent second-hand bookshops and soon a copy of Williamson's *Letters from the Saints* caught my eye at 30 pence. In this were three key letters by St Catherine, most notably where she writes of administering to a friend at his execution.

On one occasion when I visited Stuart I had been reading Maslow's *Religions, Values and Peak Experiences* because of my search for an explanation for strange personal experiences. While Stuart asserted the difficulties of interpretation and meaning, he said that ultimate understanding was personal. Time and memory, if they did not alter the experiences, would reveal their significance or otherwise. He spoke without much enthusiasm for "the spiritualism dabbled in by Yeats, Maud Gonne, AE and Hester Travers-Smith" (his own one-time landlady in Dublin).

We discussed poetry and literature with great pleasure but not *ad nauseam* since I felt that our growing friendship might not survive on literature alone. Whenever he mentioned Yeats, Maud Gonne and that circle, I plucked up the courage to ask about them. Stuart said he had been chastened by argument from his early years with Yeats, Iseult Gonne and her mother, Maud, and sometimes pretended not to have read as much as them. This was a pose of primitive ignorance and innocence, he claimed. His terms of reference were as wide as Yeats's even if he did not always like to display such knowledge; he said that such literary talk was excessive. I never minded when he quoted multiple references and, on the occasions that he quoted from whatever book he was reading at the time, it was a delight to me. Somehow, I always got the impression that the ghost of Yeats was hovering somewhere when a bookish discussion began and Stuart would sometimes nip it in the bud. He did not want books to be the departure for an evening; they had to be artfully percolated into the conversation. I was fascinated and inspired by his insightful remarks, such as his comments about Gogol's *Dead Souls* being one of those prophetic novels that shows where a country and its people were heading to at a particular time in their history. When he spoke passionately about literature, Stuart rarely disparaged it. He believed that, at its greatest, the printed word from a true artist evoked and responded to the deepest needs of the individual from the spiritual realm to wellbeing, prophecy, inspiration and, not least, excitement and entertainment.

The only person I ever heard him vehemently disparage was Maud Gonne: "That woman was forever acting in her own melodrama." I got the impression that Mrs Georgie Yeats (W.B. Yeats's wife) was an ally of Stuart's. She once told Stuart that Yeats put her nerves on edge and that was why she drank whiskey. Stuart thought she was the kind of woman who might have suited him. When I suggested, "More than Iseult?" he became silent. Stuart never spoke about Iseult except with kindness, but it was clear that he found it very difficult to talk about her until we discussed my writing a book about his life and work, at which point we had to discuss her fully.

What amazed me was how much he regretted Yeats's publicly praising his collection of poems, *We Have Kept the Faith* (1924). He claimed that such exposure was anathema to his poetic talent and he hated Yeats for embarrassing him on that occasion. Stuart's poetic output was stifled and sporadic. He blamed Yeats for this and did not publish another collection of poems until *Night Pilot* (1988). He considered himself a spoiled poet and while he saw this as being "a useful fastness for an assault on poetry", he had a creative division within himself, in that his best prose shows the mark of the poet. The formal poetry that he wrote was extremely allusive for him. It goes without saying that this was a lifelong crisis: "not having buckled down satisfactorily with the muse" was his phrase during one of our discussions about this matter.

Once when Yeats called on him at his home in Laragh Castle, County Wicklow, Stuart lit a fire in the dining room so they could sit in comfort. There was rather a long silence, broken by the older poet calling Stuart by his first name. "Harry, I fear the fire is going out," followed by a long moan. Stuart was perplexed because the flames were blazing, the logs giving off crackling sparks. "Harry," Yeats repeated rhetorically, "I fear the fire is going out in my imagination." When I asked Stuart if he had responded to this, he said. "Oh, I don't remember, nor do I want to." He did revere Yeats as a poet but also seemed defensive about him and found it sometimes unsavoury to gossip about "those writers from the Celtic Twilight". "A good name for them," he would chuckle. I think he meant that they were working in a bad light!

Madeleine's favourite poet was Rainer Maria Rilke whom she read in the original German; she was full of insight about his poetry and always keen to take the book off the shelf and read out some favourite lines which she would translate for us. She was emphatic that you could not translate Rilke effectively. In this, she was a purist. She knew her Rilke love poems and sonnets, and often repeated simple phrases over and over, *weil ich rühme* (because I praise). German poetry was her tradition she told me, "because it deals with everything: love, nature, life, death and God." Stuart's roots went back to Keats, Shelley, Blake and Emily Brontë. He disliked many poets: "Dante – a tedious moralist. Baudelaire – a sentimental Catholic. T.S. Eliot – a Sunday morning vicar". He half-admired Ezra Pound, but only his *Pisan Cantos*, where for the first time the poet "had found essential humility" evoked in certain passages such as "What thou lovest well remains/The rest is dross" and "Pull down thy vanity/How mean thy hates/Fostered in falsity,/Pull down thy vanity".[5] Pound was a subject I usually had to delicately inject into the conversation, since the poet had had a love affair with Stuart's first wife, Iseult. Stuart preferred poets such as Auden and David Gascoyne to the modernists.

Long before meeting Stuart I discovered that he had enemies who reviled and insulted him in print. Some people would leave an event in protest if Stuart began to speak, or would gossip about him and Madeleine within their hearing. If Stuart was mentioned in company, derogatory remarks might ensue, such as "that unrepentant Nazi collaborator", "Hitler-worshipping maniac", "Kraut lover", "anti-Semite" and other slurs. His best-known novel, *Black List, Section H,* was once referred to as *Black Shirt, Section Hitler* in my presence at an undergraduate party.

A journalist friend of mine knew that Stuart and I were acquainted, and asked if she might do an interview with him. She was calling in a favour from me, so I wrote to him in order to have the evidence of a reply:

> In general, as you may imagine, I'm not very keen on these as they seem to serve little purpose except satisfying superficial curiosity ... [if] it's a matter of the usual gossipy platitudes, then best tell her politely that I'm some sort of eccentric recluse!

I received another letter after Stuart had discussed his frequent public condemnation with me:

> Dear Kevin,
>
> ... God knows there are "foes" enough around without inviting them in and pouring out one's heart to them. Still, I believe, as it says in the Psalms, about delivering those whom the Lord protects from the snares of the hunter, that we are saved from the machinations of our enemies and, what are worse, those who pose as well-wishers with hard and malicious hearts.

The first time I asked him what it had been like in Germany during the Allied bombing raids, Stuart replied, "There would need to be thunder and lightning and peacocks on the glass roof of the porch, in order to set up the scene." Stuart and Madeleine did not tell me the fascinating story of their German odyssey sequentially, but over the years the pieces began to fit into place. The story infiltrated their conversation and was the trauma of their lives, along with imprisonment by the French in the immediate post-war period when Madeleine was mistaken for a Nazi spy of a similar name; she was later reprieved. I never heard the Stuarts make anti-Semitic remarks. Madeleine was in her twenties during the war and was fearful for her and Francis's lives. Their aim, like the minority of people in Berlin, was to survive the war. They never hatched plans to flee the city during the Nazi reign. Such a venture would have put them at risk and ended in almost certain death since everyone was carefully herded through excessive documentation, sporadic screening and searches for identity papers. To be a fugitive in Nazi Germany was fraught with extreme danger of death on capture. If I was to sum up my impression of their wartime experience, I would say it was one of fear. Their countenances changed when talking about those times; a grey pallor entered their faces and, if they were able to laugh about some rare happy occasion from that time, it was usually some close encounter with fearsome authority or a lucky escape from death.

They had a map (printed in Berlin) of Europe, the Mediterranean and North Africa, with borders marked off showing what was under German Axis occupation in 1942. I asked Stuart was there a feeling at that time that Germany would make further conquests? He shook his head. They had witnessed the decreasing national euphoria compounded after the Battle of Britain (September 1940), the entry into the war of the United States (December 1941) and the Russian campaign, culminating in German annihilation at Stalingrad (January 1943). Stuart said that Hitler was a tyrant whose military prowess was extremely limited. He attested to how common gossip was in Berlin about the frustration of generals in conducting their campaigns. The military genius of Heinz Guderian, Erich von Manstein and Hermann Hoth was not fully utilised – this was gossip he had heard on various occasions. Stuart debunked many war films and the historical legacy of a preening Nazi regime expecting to conquer the world.

He and Madeleine spoke of the nightlife of Berlin, a brothel in Giesebrechtstrasse known as "salon Kitty", used by the higher military ranks, and of how Nazi society was rigorously stratified. The Allied bombing raids and the constraints of rationing, the queuing even for a bottle of schnapps, soap shortages, poor hygiene and hunger, which approached near starvation in their case as the war progressed. Madeleine showed me ration books stamped with the German insignia and mentioned that she had known the marching songs of Horst Wessel since her schooldays. She never expressed any opinion about Hitler except to say that he had outlawed divorce. I took her anxiousness at the mention of his name as fear and never found that if I had recourse to mention him that she glowed with admiration or longing like Germans in newsreels of the Nazi period. Although the Hitler era for Madeleine and Stuart was a shared memory, it resided very much in the past. It is supposed among their detractors that the Reich was somehow an alluring source of debauchery, perversion and evil that they revelled in. If this was the case it was never apparent to me and my account of their Berlin period does not cater for such excess, but reflects the actual situations that they witnessed.

☙ ☙ ☙

AT FESTIVE TIMES OF THE YEAR, SUCH AS Christmas and Easter, the Stuarts maintained a peaceful atmosphere. At Christmas, Madeleine would have a tree with candles in holders on the branches. A prayer or a few verses from the Psalms were part of her ritual. When she lit the candles, she would insist on putting out the electric light. Stuart and she did not like bright lights. Madeleine would make Christmas cards for their cats and the rabbit. They had a fish that grew to the ripe old age of 30, according to Stuart. This was kept in a long glass tank and lavished with love like all their pets.

The year my first novel, *Quintesse* (1982), was published, Stuart was having a celebratory dinner for the Penguin edition of *Black List, Section H*. It had been reviewed in the London *Observer* under a headline "A Portrait of the Artist as a Young Nazi". Stuart asked if I had seen the review. When I said I had, he added, "I've been the subject of much abuse, some of it for my novel about H." He admitted that much of his fiction was autobiographical. He felt that imagined plots, circumstances and the invention of major characters made for bad fiction. The closer every element was to life, the better for his purposes as an artist. He was not positing a law. When I cited incidents depicted in *Black List, Section H*, he said: "I am H the central figure; his events are my events." I cited the passage, "Things that should have bound them – nationalism, religion, literature – were stumbling blocks between them." This referred to Stuart and Iseult in the novel. Did it refer to the actual situation between them? As far as he was concerned, yes.

Over the years I received many inspiring letters from Stuart, such as the following in brief extract:

> Dear Kevin,
>
> ... It is in gardens, one or two in particular, that we are sometimes overcome by the sort of pain that leads to as much insight as we are capable of, the pain simultaneously increasing the capability. Precious are invisible blossoms,
>
> In affection, Francis.

And another:

> Dear Kevin,
>
> ... From long passages in *Quintesse* and from personal contact I always assumed you could, and perhaps would, write some original and imaginative fiction, poetry too ...
>
> ... Let me know if you would like us to meet, both for old times' sake and the future's.
>
> Love from Francis.

In 1994 Stuart's post-war novels, *Redemption* and *The Pillar of Cloud*, were republished. On a visit to Stuart at Christmas 1996, he and I decided that, instead of writing an article on *Redemption* and *The Pillar of Cloud*, I would write his biography. We drank a toast to the collaboration, sipping his favourite Black Bush whiskey. So began an intense series of interviews between us over the remaining years of his life.

As I began an early draft and showed it to him, Stuart was in deep controversy (yet again) because of his membership of Aosdána, the Irish state-subsidised academy of writers, artists and composers. Máire Mhac an tSaoi, the distinguished Irish language poet, proposed a motion at a meeting of Aosdána in Dublin Castle in 1997 demanding that Stuart resign from Aosdána. She was impelled to suggest this because of an interview he had given to a Channel 4 TV programme.

In his nineties, Stuart was made a *saoi* of Aosdána for his contribution to the arts. *Saoi* is an Irish word meaning "wise-elder". It is a lifetime achievement award bestowed by Aosdána on certain members and has been awarded also to Samuel Beckett, Seamus Heaney, Benedict Kiely and Anthony Cronin. Stuart accepted the honour, remaining somewhat confused as to whether he approved or disapproved – typical of his stance as an outsider – a position which the playwright and novelist, Thomas Kilroy did not accept, finding its expression of individualism merely "consoling to the society of liberal aspiration".

I made many visits to Francis Stuart during these controversies, but it was a difficult time, since the newspapers discussed Stuart, Nazism, anti-Semitism, and definitions of collaboration. He was classified with Waugh, Huxley, Lawrence, Eliot, Pound, Wyndham Lewis and Graham Greene, who had made openly anti-Semitic comments in some of their writings. Stuart was virulently condemned by public figures such as Conor Cruise O'Brien, Máire Mhac an tSaoi, Christabel Bielenberg, Val Mulkerns, Ronit and Louis Lentin, Brendan Barrington, Liam Carson and Aidan Higgins. Anthony Cronin, John Montague, Dermot Bolger, Hugo Hamilton, Paul Durcan, Ulick O'Connor, Eavan Boland, Declan Kiberd, Michael D. Higgins and Jeremy Addis among others defended him or at least from letters to the newspapers at the time and other writings appeared to be pro-Stuart. However, it is not strange to find writers and commentators who once might have defended Stuart suddenly change their stance towards him. One such is Jerry Natterstad who wrote a short book about Stuart published in 1973 and later recanted on his favourable assessment.

Stuart won a libel action against *The Irish Times* two years after "the Aosdána furore", arising out of Kevin Myers's comments in the same newspaper that he had "volunteered to serve that enemy of civilisation" – Nazi Germany. Myers expressed reservations, if not disgust, along with others, at Stuart having been honoured by Aosdána, since "beyond any shadow of a doubt he was a collaborator of the Nazis".

Stuart's radio broadcasts from Berlin remain the major controversy, along with his going to Germany and lecturing there, having taken up the offer to visit the country as a foreign writer months before the outbreak of the Second World War. The intent with which he ensured his return to Berlin, after the war had begun, and how he managed to travel when restrictions were everywhere in Europe, has been the subject of widespread interpretation.

Because his writings are heavily autobiographical, I asked him about the safety of such a critical method, but he assured me that the paradigm of his life's events are in the novels. This has to be so, since writing was the main business of his life. He often expressed reservations about writers whose whole life is their writing and who find little time for living. Being a writer does not excuse him his failings as a human being, but Stuart the man was and remains condemned. The legacy of his work as an outcast witness remains controversial since many believe he was not an outcast at all.

Allied bombing destroyed the file on Stuart at the Irish Legation in Berlin. Duplication of documents meant that copies were safe and sound at the Department of Foreign Affairs in Dublin – this bulky file was a valuable source, substantiating what might otherwise be unverifiable beyond Stuart's letters, diaries and my interviews and recollections of our conversations.

This biography presents the facts of Stuart's life as they were available to me; further facts may come to light, but I have been fortunate to have had access to vast primary sources, not least Stuart himself. There is a portrayal of the women in his life, his children, intimate friends and contacts, and a brief analysis of the writings based on our conversations. Into his late nineties, Stuart's memory for events in the distant past was phenomenal. The controversy as to whether or not his work is anti-Semitic is analysed. Stuart's final period produced five novels, a novella, and a handful of poems. To have known him throughout these years was an enriching experience.

This is not an *apologia pro vita sua* – the ideal situation being to pursue balance in the interests of objectivity while avoiding hagiography. However, influenced by his ideals of refraining from being judgmental and striving for a sense of neutrality, my aim is neither to defend nor condemn but to present the evidence as accurately as possible. I have been advised by writers who read early drafts of this book to make myself an equal part of what follows, and to outline our relationship in atmospheric detail. However, false modesty apart, I do not see myself as having had an exclusive friendship with Stuart in the last twenty-three years of his life. Throughout those years, as people say, we both had "lives of our own". Our special friendship was intellectual, visceral and spiritual.

We met at his house in Dundrum, usually in the sitting room but occasionally in his study. Sometimes he and Madeleine laid on a meal and always offered me a drink, usually wine or whiskey. Stuart and I also met at other locations in Dublin, and places in Ireland, as friends: man to man, or rather, elder to young man, but we never travelled together or spent more than a few nights under the same roof in the company of our wives. However, our one-to-one meetings were intense, always of a long duration, and we often regrouped within the same week to continue the discussion and deliberations. What follows, you can be sure, is based on what Stuart said to me, but I have verified certain facts and events of his life and sources in common with his novels and other writings. The atmosphere of our meetings was not one that requires elaborate description. Of course, we walked in public parks, met in galleries, ate in restaurants, drank in cafés and bars, went on car journeys, attended a few theatre performances, but this book does not require a chronology of my life – such would be a pompous distortion to what follows. If I do not constantly allude to the fact that behind every phrase and sentence is my relationship with Francis Stuart, this is in the interests of mawkish repetition. Nor do I continually allude to the backdrop, the clothes he wore, the weather, the season, for the sake of conciseness and unnecessary meandering. My exclusive purpose is to explore Stuart to the utmost of personal insight, vouchsafed by he who entrusted me to write a book about him – not provide an extended piece of colour journalism.

When I first met Stuart I was spiritually needy and remain so. Over many years of meetings with him I finally reached the conclusion that such neediness was an invaluable possession. There was balm in his companionship. I often asked myself what I really thought about him. This book is an attempt to answer this question.

I would be dishonest if I denied that Francis Stuart was a great friend. If I can understand fully all that he conveyed through his life and work, I tend to believe that he is not gone but is somewhere in another dimension. It may be said that he spent his life in a search for the Absolute or God, consulting different models of reality in religion, literature, art and science. At another level I strongly believe that what he shared with Yeats was an aversion to being "political", but admit that, like Yeats, he cannot avoid being classified according to certain political proclivities. Stuart witnessed the evil and the good of his century; despair was never his mood with me over the period that I knew him. Instead, he nearly always gave me a sense of hope and abundance and this rich legacy still astounds and perplexes me.

Part One

1902–1938

1

The Australian Tragedy

In our conversations, Stuart was always dismissive of his background and forebears. He had no complex about it, but I got the impression that he had shaken off the emotion of family ties in adolescence because of the unique circumstances of his childhood. I often thought he was unduly harsh about this because he had, by any comparison, illustriously wealthy forebears on both sides of the family and was nurtured and even indulged by his aunt, although less so his mother.

However, behind this remained the scandal of his father's death. Both the scandal that the family felt, and the event itself, left an indelible scar on Stuart's psyche and is a key factor that cannot be omitted from an attempt to understand the man and the writer in all his complexity. The first few months of Stuart's life have a Gothic scenario to them that give credence to the notion that infants are capable of subliminally absorbing the fallout of such family tragedies. Stuart's ancestors receive lengthy entries in various family histories of County Antrim, such as Amanda Shanks's *Rural Aristocracy in Northern Ireland*. His first cousin, Amy Stuart, published a family history, *Three Hundred Years in Inishowen.* In Burke's *Irish Family Records,* which first appeared in 1899 as *Burke's Landed Gentry of Ireland,* Stuart's father is stated as having died childless while his mother is accredited thus: "had issue, one son", without naming Francis Stuart. These omissions and inaccuracies are inexplicable or else mere human error, hardly a conspiracy of silence. With all the focus on his pedigree, in connection with Antrim in particular, it is intriguing to discover that Stuart was not born in Northern Ireland.

His birth certificate, registered in Townsville, Queensland, Australia, bears the names Henry Francis Montgomery Stuart, born 29

April 1902 in Stagpole Street. His mother was Elizabeth Barbara Montgomery, known as Lily. In Sydney, less than four months later, his father Henry Stuart committed suicide. The death of Stuart's father, aged 49, is a salient biographical fact that at the outset focuses attention away from the son.

Henry Irwin Stuart was born in 1853 at Ballyhivistock, near Dervock, County Antrim. His father was Captain Charles George Stuart, who had succeeded to the family farm in 1826. His forebears were of Scottish-Presbyterian origin. Charles, at 23, married Maria Christina Creery. They had two daughters, Isabella and Elizabeth, and eight sons. The eldest, Charles McDaniel Stuart, took over his father's land agency and was assisted by the fifth son, Alexander. Another son, Leslie, became rear admiral in the Royal Navy. William was a civil engineer in Canada on the Canadian Pacific railway, and also for the Mexican government. The other four sons: Henry and James (twins) and Wallace and George worked in the Australian bush. In their twenties, the twins went to Australia and began work at a sheep station owned by Sam McCaughey. McCaughey, an Antrim neighbour, had emigrated and become wealthy. He needed two jackaroos who could run the Rockwood station, 300 miles inland from Townsville, which is on the coast. Henry and James grazed more than 10,000 sheep. They rode vast distances on horseback in the course of their work as grazers; and as overseers they looked after fencing, hiring and firing. Stuart only mentioned the scantiest of details about his forebears in Australia. The subject did not seem to interest him at all, but my research left me feeling that he had dissociated himself completely from his brief months in Australia, even imaginatively. In many ways, his first months of existence were to him as if they had never happened. He would shrug at whatever details I revealed, since he knew little. What follows in this chapter was remote to him, except for the central event: the tragedy of his father's suicide.

Rockwood was an area bigger than County Sligo. By the 1880s there was a boom in sheep farming, prices rose and the Stuart brothers shepherded a flock numbering 100,000. It was not long until they bought a sheep station of their own and, in 1884, they were made Justices of the Peace in Tangorin, near Townsville.

Henry (Stuart's father) returned home to Northern Ireland for his mother's funeral in 1898. He met Elizabeth Barbara Montgomery, Lily, who was living two miles away at Benvarden. She was 23 years old and Henry was 45. Her parents had died in 1893, leaving her older sister, Janet Maude, to run the house, along with her two brothers, Francis James and John Alexander, who inherited the farm that was larger than that of their Stuart neighbours. The two brothers rose to the rank of captain and major, respectively, in the Royal Irish Rifles.

Lily and Janet had been taught at home by governesses. Their father, Robert James Montgomery, was the local Justice of the Peace, High Sheriff and a captain in the Dragoon Guards who served in the Crimean War; a keen huntsman who rode, was a good shot and eventually died of alcoholism. When John, the eldest son, took over the farm, he resolutely maintained his father's Loyalist tradition to the British Empire. John married, but it was an unhappy union and he became dependent on his sister Janet. Always something of a tomboy, Janet defiantly smoked a pipe and grew in sympathy towards the politics of Southern Ireland and Irish Nationalism. However, her uncle, Field Marshal Sir George S. White, was famed in military history for relieving Ladysmith during the Boer War, and yet his son, Captain J.R. White, would sever family traditions and join James Connolly's Citizen Army in Dublin in 1913. Later in life, J.R. (Jack) White wrote a memoir entitled *Misfit*. Still, it was a surprise to everyone when Janet left Benvarden for a house in County Meath long before the marriage of her sister, Lily.

It is said that Janet might have made a better partner for Henry. Nevertheless, Lily and Henry married on 28 January 1901 in Derrykeighan Parish Church, Dervock. Two days earlier in Coleraine, at the offices of James Semple, Solicitor, they had signed an indenture including a clause granting Lily a sum of £5,000 in the event of her husband's death. [1] The honeymoon couple went to London, sailed for Brisbane and then made the thousand-mile train journey to Townsville, which was a developing seaport at the time, before going inland to Rockwood. Henry and Lily joined his two brothers, their wives and children to form a little colony of Stuarts at the sheep station.

A year later, when Lily was pregnant and near her time, she went to the nursing home in Townsville. Family legend has it that a bat flew into the delivery room, a bad omen to the superstitious. Lily returned with her baby son, Henry Francis, to Rockwood. That summer unusually high temperatures were recorded, above 120° F.

Henry and James began moving their herds to high ground near the coastal regions of Queensland and lost thousands of sheep in the Federation Drought of 1902.

Suddenly, Henry underwent a transformation. The first cause of his mental imbalance may have been sunstroke. It was well known locally that grazers "not able to endure such acute, long-drawn-out anxiety become mentally deranged".[2] Henry's breakdown was also caused by the drought and the huge losses in their sheep herd. James wrote home to Antrim, and his eldest brother Charles arrived in mid-August. It was a major family crisis.

It is not known exactly why Henry Stuart killed himself. There is no death certificate available, which compounds the mystery. One is tempted to suggest a cover-up by his brother James, a Justice of the Peace, but there is no proof of this. What is known is that Henry had tried to stab himself with a kitchen knife weeks before his admission to Callan Park, a private asylum in Sydney. Another brother, George, witnessed this and the deterioration in Henry's mental and physical health while they resided at the Aarons Exchange Hotel. He arranged for him to be examined by two physicians from Macquarie Street in Sydney who agreed on a diagnosis of "profound persecution mania".[3] Henry was committed in July, under the Lunacy Act, by the sanction of his wife and brothers. He believed that his brothers wanted to kill him and that one of the doctors, Dr Shildon, was going to torture him for some wrongs he had done. The report includes evidence from Herbert Laidlaw, the asylum attendant. While under his care, Henry made three further suicide attempts by trying to thrust a comb down his throat, bashing his head off a mantelpiece while being moved to a special ward, and stabbing himself in the abdomen with a scissors. Laidlaw listed Henry's somewhat favourable response to opium treatments and a last sighting of him with the bedclothes over his head. It is justifiable to rule out total insanity because he was "capable of calculating the right moment to outwit his attendant".[4] Henry Stuart hanged himself from a gas pipe, with a rope made from a bed sheet, in the early hours of 14 August 1902 at Callan Park Asylum. The *Sydney Morning Herald*, the *Telegraph* and two other newspapers reported the incident.[5]

Henry Stuart ended his life in part due to feelings of union with "evil" and self-persecution. Evidence based on the accounts of the Sydney physicians at the inquest pointed to an aberration of the mind, a temporary psychosis. What had forced him to the decision to end his life? Nothing; at least, nothing one knows of at this remove. James, George and Charles attended their brother's funeral and the Christian burial at Waverley Cemetery in Sydney, which was allowed through the compassion of a vicar. This might imply the prior refusal of a Christian burial in Townsville. Lily Stuart did not go to the funeral. Geoffrey Elborn, in his book on Stuart, *Francis Stuart: A Life* (1990), an interim biography published during the life of its subject, posits marital infidelity on Lily's part. There are no facts to support the theory that Henry Stuart killed himself in a fit of jealousy or because he might have doubted the paternity of his newborn son. Besides, the likeness between son and father from photographs is unmistakable.

The facts as given here, which I showed Stuart, were known to him only in his eighties, while much of the material about his father was new to him. When I asked whether he had ever sought information about his father's breakdown and suicide, he always replied that he did not ever officially try to discover in records or reports what had happened to him. When I queried him as to why, he admitted that imagination had filled in many of the gaps; the mystery obsessed him with varying degrees of intensity at various times, but ultimately he wanted to wait for some revelation that would unveil the mystery. Perhaps he lived with partial knowledge of the circumstances, I suggested, and had laid it to rest. To this he shook his head. "No, I haven't laid it to rest," he said. It was, I believe, a central trauma in Stuart's life.

In December 1902, Lily made the long journey home to Ireland with her infant son Henry Francis, affectionately known as Harry, and his nurse, Nellie Farren. Originally from Bournemouth, Nellie Farren had gone to Brisbane as a domestic, where she became engaged to a man who later abandoned her. Charles did not accompany them, nor did any of the brothers, instead, James Stuart-Moore, a nephew of Henry's, was their travelling companion. Still devastated by her husband's suicide, Lily remained in her cabin throughout the voyage. Even when the Governor of Gibraltar came on board and offered sympathy to the widow and her child, she was inconsolable. Back in Ireland she told her family that Henry had shot himself. The Stuarts explained to neighbours that Henry Stuart had died in

Townsville for fear of bringing any attention to the tragedy in Sydney.

It is significant that Lily was never thereafter invited to visit any of the Stuarts. They may have blamed her and obviously did little to console her. Lily soon moved away from County Antrim, with her son and Nellie Farren, to live with Janet in Shallon, County Meath. This move was made out of necessity by Lily, and also meant, to some extent, adopting the Irish Nationalist South. Furthermore, Janet had converted to Roman Catholicism. Lily would do the same. Young Harry's formative years were lived in the care of three women, in a comfortable cottage on the banks of the Boyne. While he was cosseted by Nellie Farren, the faithful nurse whom he called Weg, and Aunt Janet, his mother's role was very different. Lily kept an emotional distance from her son. He was a living reminder of the Australian experience. She needed time to recover from the shock of Henry Stuart's suicide, and Janet was on hand to give her the support she needed. Nellie Farren bonded with the growing child and relieved the mother of his otherwise clinging nature. Stuart's dependence on Nellie was increased because of his mother's indifference. A later comment by him is telling, "My mother lived her own life and neither then nor later had I any very close bonds with her. She never resented my preference for my nurse and the latter became, in all but name, my mother."[6]

As soon as Stuart could walk he developed a love of nature. Aunt Janet's garden became his world of flowers, plants and vegetables. He watched birds and was deft enough to stalk hares, rabbits and other animals without frightening them away. Janet kept chickens, which he took to with some excitement. In his twenties he would become a chicken farmer and win an award for egg yield. On walks as a child he was escorted to the banks of the Boyne and the sight of horses in distant fields amazed him – they would become a lifelong passion. Regular and lengthy holidays with Uncle John in Benvarden occasionally included a visit to his Stuart uncles in Ballyhivistock. The local river is called the Bush and gives its name to the whiskey distillery in the beautiful village of Bushmills. No wonder that Stuart's favourite tipple came from this place.

Benvarden had been in the Montgomery family since 1797. It was a vast, rambling mansion with 16 bay windows, 12 bedrooms and a lower floor of various rooms including a 26-foot long ballroom.

Above the entrance-hall of the house's central section was a balustered elliptical light well, and below ground level a wine cellar. The garden and grounds, set on two acres, accommodated a porter's lodge. The Stuart's Ballyhivistock House, built in 1826, was a more modest but still substantial two-storey residence, with attic windows in the gables and three bay windows. The Stuart uncles, Charles and Alexander, made him feel isolated, if not stigmatised, he told me, and he was often happier to return to Shallon. Hence, subliminally or otherwise, Stuart's political formation was dominated by the Southern Nationalist rather than the Northern Loyalist tradition. This was also his first experience of being an outsider between his mother's people and his father's, as soon as he was old enough to register the distinctions.

Stuart knew nothing about the events of his father's death and had discovered very little by the time he was in his teens. One item of furniture, a wicker chair, had been brought on the long journey from Australia and this became the sole object of his fascination once Nellie told him about its origin. He had no knowledge of being fatherless until the topic would surface in the kind of questions that children ask each other in the schoolyard. He told me that his father was a secret about which he knew little, so he could never say anything on the subject.

He did not have any formal schooling in County Meath. It may be too dramatic to suggest that the father's death gave birth to the son as a writer, or to suggest that, in the event of knowing so little, he soon invented or fictionalised a father for himself. Stuart would later write four novels in which a character or characters commit suicide. Aunt Janet first taught him to read and encouraged him to write and praised his efforts. Her library in Shallon was substantial. One of his memories from early childhood is of Nellie telling him to sharpen his pencils. Later on, in his early teens, she encouraged him to write a story in an exercise book. The copperplate handwriting runs to 13 pages about the melting down in the fire of a lead rabbit that magically thereafter takes the hero on a series of bizarre adventures. The story is dedicated to his mother. One of the nursery rhymes he learnt by heart suggests that it might have been written by himself or one of his devoted minders:

Henry Francis Montgomery Stuart
Is a highclass-sounding name
But he spilt the broth all over the cloth
And his knickerbockers the same.[7]

A child who has no recollection, neither sight nor sound, of a father, is apt to invent one. It was Stuart's conviction that the power of imagining is increased through extreme experiences and pain. Childhood experiences can, in certain circumstances, provide the necessary pain. Still, the innocence of childhood cannot understand the simple truth that one inherits traits and features of one's father. He formed an image of his father while subconsciously being a part of his father already. Imagination is a great power bestowed on a child. Stuart's fiction comes from a mysterious combination of personal experiences and an imaginative comprehension of those same experiences. Without imagination, reality might be called the mere cold facts. Stuart called imagination a very dangerous faculty because it can imagine anything.

The experiences of his childhood meant that as an adult his relationships with children were strained; he could not relate to them very well. They made him nervous, he admitted. Children have little or no part in his fiction. He rarely discussed childhood and when he did, implied to me that it was the part of life that he had shrugged off. He admitted that as a teenager he longed for adulthood and this is borne out in the fact of his marriage at the age of seventeen.

He wrote about his father in the 1970s, revealing how little he knew: "The circumstances of his death in a mental home soon after my birth have never been clear to me. Nobody spoke to me of him as I grew up. My mother was always silent on the subject. I think he died from alcoholism, though it is possible he killed himself during a fit of alcoholic depression."[8] However, the mysterious father would remain an enduring obsession. Stuart believed in fate with regard to his own life, and the loss of his father heightened this belief. It may seem strange that he never revisited Australia, the place of his birth and the scene of his father's traumatic last days. The father would come to represent the outcast for Stuart in his life and writings. He revealed to me that he took on this paternal legacy in reaction to his own childhood and lived in fidelity to the outcast. This explains why his novels depict extreme situations where the human spirit may be easily broken. In many of the novels the main characters are in crisis. The crisis may or may not be resolved. Many writers and artists who were outcasts also feature in his writings, such as Keats, Blake, Van Gogh, Dostoevsky and Mandelstam. The crucifixion of Jesus and the suicide of Hitler form part of his writings. Many of Stuart's detractors would say he fell in love with Hitler. His relationship with Jesus will be explored in more detail later. However, Stuart never set himself up as a guru and denied that he was a mystic. As a writer, he eventually became dubious about "art" and fine writing; and used language with expert suspicion as if it were borrowed, flawed and brittle. His mature writing style is reluctant and dissenting.

Early in 1909 Lily decided it was time to move from Shallon and rented "a house with a seaview" in the fashionable Dublin suburb of Monkstown. There is no record of the exact location except for Stuart's vague recollection. A fixed yearly annuity from the estate of her deceased husband maintained the household. The 6-year-old Stuart began attending nearby Rathdown School. Living in Monkstown meant that he began to discover the south side of Dublin, but all this ended in 1912 when he was sent to a preparatory school in England. He would spend only a year at Bilton Grange in Warwickshire. Significantly, he wrote a poem about the *Titanic* disaster that was headline news at the time.[9] When he went to Bilton Grange, Lily naturally dispensed with the services of Nellie Farren who returned to England. He missed his mother and registered a double shock in the loss of Weg (the name he gave his faithful nurse), as well as the initial confrontation with boarding school.

He was very lonely at that preparatory school. Meanwhile, Lily, on one of her infrequent visits to Antrim, began an affair with Henry Clements. Clements, who had been a cowboy in Texas and Mexico, was much older than she. He was handsome, irreverent, a drinker and a gambler. Lily fell for him and they went to Chester, away from prying gossip in Antrim, and married in 1913. Stuart's persistent letters to his mother had the effect of persuading her to remove him from the school in Bilton Grange. However, she was too preoccupied with Clements to have Stuart join them. She wrote to Nellie Farren who agreed to bring him back to their house in Bournemouth, where they had an emotional reunion. Lily found another school for her son. He would recall those days in a novel written in his eighties, *The High Consistory*, and the crying scenes which heralded his departure from his nurse, "For those with neurological systems that function on a larger proportion of interior, or self-induced, stimuli than normal, daytime dreaming is equally vital. Being distracted from this at boarding school was, I believe, what made it so unendurable".[10]

Stuart had three more years at various preparatory schools, one in North Wales and another in Kent, before he was sent to Rugby with its library tower, pseudo-Gothic buildings and the schoolhouse triangle. He entered Rugby late into the school year. In January 1916, Rugby school was little more than another lugubrious institution to the 14-year-old Stuart. The day began at 5.45 a.m. with a cold bath. Then there was a short lesson before breakfast that consisted of porridge, dried haddock, tea, bread and butter. Stuart began as a lonely boarder whose schoolwork was below average.

He went on another short holiday to Nellie Farren at Bournemouth and this coincided with the 1916 Rising in Dublin that he read about in the newspapers. He was amazed by the events and the "rebels", as his fellow schoolmates called them. Stuart had an intuition that the rebels were "outsiders", but the concept of outsider was not a word in his vocabulary at the time. However, when he showed Nellie the newspapers, *Daily Sketch* and the *Graphic*, she said, "Don't leave those terrible photos in my room overnight; those criminals!"[11] Stuart said to me that he felt her reaction was similar to the reactions of others on the few occasions when his father's name was mentioned. By deduction, he presumed that his father might have been a criminal. Stuart did not experience any emotive nationalism concerning the 1916 Rising, he admitted, but what registered with him was that the leaders were executed by firing squad. He was afraid to ask Nellie whether or not his father had been executed. When it came to asking his mother any such question, he became terrified and found himself unable to speak.

I always found Stuart insightful about upheavals such as war or insurrection, as in the case of the 1916 Rising. He understood the urge towards violent revolution in humanity, the inevitable outcome of war in certain circumstances, and, while he did not condone it, he knew from experience how incidents could spiral into bloodletting and slaughter. The whole phenomenon of violence, from murder to world war, was a subject he could discuss with keen analysis and it is no surprise that such subject matter plays a major part in his fiction.

Clements and Lily travelled, while Stuart, hoping to please them, tried to settle into Rugby. He increasingly lost contact with his nurse and became accustomed to the already limited relationship with his mother. Clements adopted the role of stepfather, but secretly hated his stepson. He found him a burdensome child and a "milksop". Stuart felt afraid of Clements and later commented: "He didn't like the influence of my nurse ... I didn't get on with him".[12] Stuart's first summer holiday from Rugby was spent in a car hired by Clements with Lily's money. They toured the coast of North Wales. It was not a good holiday for the youngster in the company of an estranged mother and a hostile stepfather. Meanwhile his school progress was abysmal year after year. He developed some self-reliance, but steadily became damaged emotionally and psychologically. In moments of disparagement he told me that Rugby was an excellent pre-school for prison life. He had little aptitude for the defiant military exercises that were part of the school curriculum. These were widespread throughout public schools at the time, while England was fighting the Germans in the First World War.

Stuart's other school holidays with Clements and Lily were at various rented houses in England. Clements drank, caroused and gambled on the Stock Exchange with Lily's finances until Janet confronted him. After some months he ran off with a woman from Portrush, a maid employed by Stuart's Uncle George. Janet helped Stuart to write an angry letter to Clements, who was in a hotel in London recuperating after a heart attack. Clements never returned and Lily did not seem to mind. She had at least not lost all her inherited money since "Clements had been unable to touch her income from capital held in trust".[13]

Identity began to intrigue the growing boy who, of course, had no memory of his infancy in Australia, a remote continent which seemed so far away as he looked into his school atlas. While he languished at Rugby, moodily stewing through study periods, playing games half-heartedly, two of his cousins (James Maitland Stuart, 19, and Charles Maitland Stuart, 18) both gave their lives in the First World War. Shortly before his own eighteenth birthday, Stuart would marry the daughter of Maud Gonne, an ardent and notorious nationalist. Not only that, he would smuggle guns for the Irish Republicans and be interned for his part in the Irish Civil War with de Valera's anti-Treaty faction. He would also be hailed as a poet whose first published book earned for its youthful author a distinguished award at a public ceremony in Dublin.

Stuart began to tolerate what would be his last year in Rugby, with the help of school friends: "A Jew and a Pole; we made a little group, and it was good."[14] There was always fear of a birching for poor schoolwork, so he began to do a modicum of study and avoided punishment. Although he did not excel in any subject, his conduct was never undisciplined because of a shy, introspective temperament. He spent his final summer holiday with Aunt Janet in Ballybogey, County Antrim, returning via Bournemouth to visit Nellie Farren before going on to Rugby. He read some of Ezra Pound's poems for the first time at Bournemouth. Secretly he felt that he would become a poet himself and had begun to dabble in rhyming verse. On this point he was assured that the calling to be a writer had come clearly and unconsciously. He became absorbed by the new movement in poetry founded by Pound and its influence on W.B. Yeats. At Rugby he could not avoid hearing about Rupert Brooke's poems since one of the masters was Brooke's father, and other famous poets were connected with the school, such as Matthew Arnold.

Unlike Stuart, his school chums had found no excitement in the 1916 Rising, whereas the Russian Revolution of November 1917 fired their imaginations. They were excited when they heard about the poets, Yesenin and Mayakovsky, both of whom supported the revolution with zeal and later committed suicide. Stuart became attracted by other Russian writers, such as Tolstoy, whose novel *Resurrection* captivated him as being one of the first books "to grant him the magical experience of art". Aunt Janet bought a copy of Joyce's *A Portrait of the Artist as a Young Man* for Stuart. It became a model for his best-known work, *Black List, Section H,* which is a substantial critique of that novel.

Long before the First World War ended, Stuart had had enough of Rugby and formed a negative attitude towards the school, not least because of a housemaster who repeatedly called him "eccentric". The school's final evaluation of him advised his withdrawal because his reports were "fair to middling" and at worst simply "bad". Lily and Janet saw that he had become headstrong but also too accepting of the school's dismissive attitude, and they reluctantly permitted him to leave Rugby.

H.O. White, a fellow of Trinity College, Dublin, began to tutor the young man at the request of Aunt Janet in the hope that he might enter Trinity. Despite White's efforts, Stuart never obtained a place in college. Janet showed Stuart's poems to White, who saw little merit in them. White had some acquaintance with the poet, painter and mystic, George Russell (AE) who was from County Antrim. AE had a small regular coterie of callers, usually on Sundays in Rathgar, Dublin, where he lived with his wife and two sons. He was to be probed for a second opinion on Stuart's poems. Russell never published any in *The Irish Statesman*. Stuart appeared in the letters pages of the weekly journal in 1924, "No movement, either in life or art, has ever sprung or been moulded but gradually from within". Already he was beginning to expound in loose fashion, elements that would become part of his credo as a writer.

Stuart told me his first impressions of AE – an egomaniac, revelling in a scrapbook of press cuttings about his recent lecture tour of America. The Sunday evening soirée at AE's began with what Stuart saw as an unpromising start when the self-absorbed host introduced him to the gathering as "Mr St George" – the name of a US millionaire industrialist. With hindsight, this might be seen as a comic scene, he reiterated to me on recounting the evening which would change his life.

Stuart was much taken by a 25-year-old woman who had just arrived to chat with Russell's two sons. He thought the woman was Yeats's beloved who inspired his poetry, especially in *Wind Among the Reeds*. She was not Maud Gonne but Iseult Gonne, her daughter who would become Stuart's wife. On that first night they were not even introduced.

2

Yeats, Maud Gonne and Iseult

WHENEVER YEATS ENTERED OUR CONVERSATIONS it was usually through my questions about the great poet and Stuart would become sombre, if not slightly defensive, with such interrogation. There is a limit to Yeatsian anecdote and as I have matured, my need for it is less. But at the time my appetite was voracious for first-hand gossip about the writers and artists that I idolised, many of whom Stuart had known. In the 1970s when I knew Stuart, Yeats scholarship was plentiful with various publications and books appearing on a regular basis. There were emerging Irish poets and established poets at the time, but Yeats still reigned supreme as a colossus of Irish poetry, both in Ireland and elsewhere, especially in the United States. Stuart was only a footnote, or at most gained brief mention, in Yeatsian biography and that was largely because of his marriage to Iseult Gonne and the fact that Maud Gonne was his mother-in-law. He had no antipathy to this situation, but did feel that the same information was re-used about him, mainly from the Gonne–Yeats letters, Iseult's letters and other sources that he felt were manipulated unfairly by Yeats scholars and biographers. I never found that he was envious of Yeats's stature as a literary figure. Stuart did not have any apparent rivalry with other writers; rather he had a stolid patience about the progress of his own work. His life and career proved the fact by his early success in the 1930s followed by revilement, rejection and neglect after the Second World War until his re-discovery in 1971 with the publication of *Black List, Section H*. His sense of place in literature was assured and while he was never bombastic on this matter, his presence, utterances and convictions made his position clear.

Stuart alluded to Yeats's melodramatic personality during our discussions, his domineering presence and booming voice, his continual literary discourse and pondering of questions about poetry, art and literature as if there was nothing else to life. Stuart believed that Yeats had a highly affected personality, yet he respected him as an artist. However, because of their unique relationship and its complications, he never liked him, and admitted that he never could – the possibility of a friendship with Yeats was not a reality and for this situation Stuart blamed Yeats's utter self-absorption. Stuart criticised Yeats for being a spectator of life and felt he was not a participant. When I first heard this it struck me as being unjust, but in order to advance our friendship I did not voice this opinion since I wanted to hear more.

Much to his annoyance, Stuart's early manhood was spent in the company of Iseult and her mother, Maud Gonne (hereafter Gonne), with Yeats in the background. In some respects this powerful and eminent coterie launched him onto the Dublin literary scene in what was a significant cultural renaissance in Ireland. In retrospect, Stuart rejected the idea that it was a good start for him as a writer. In fact it may well have delayed his progress, according to his deepest instincts. I felt ultimately that Stuart had been damaged by Yeats and Gonne, and not least Iseult, except he was loath to admit it and would become silent if I persisted in such questioning, neither denying nor agreeing with me. His encounter with them was a fatal initiation for a young artist, a bad twist of fate in some ways, extremely difficult for a 17-year-old from his troubled childhood and background.

Yeats would, in turn, propose marriage to Gonne and her daughter on many occasions, even after Iseult had married Stuart. I was sceptical about the truth of the latter assertion of Stuart's, considering the fact that Yeats married three years before Stuart married Iseult. It is well documented that Yeats had "happily" married Georgie Hyde Lees; how could he still hanker after Iseult? But according to Stuart he did. How did Stuart, fortunately or otherwise become so involved with Iseult, Gonne and Yeats?

Gonne was born in 1866 in Aldershot, England, a fact that never prevented her becoming an ardent Irish Nationalist. When she was four years old, her mother, Edith Cook, died of tuberculosis. Edith Cook was part of the London Cook empire that made their money in the drapery business. Thomas Gonne, a captain in the British army, was transferred to the Curragh in Ireland, taking with him his two daughters, Maud and Kathleen. As a young woman, Gonne had a reputation for being celibate among many suitors as she moved in London and Paris society. After her father's death in 1887 she inherited a large fortune and found a French lover, Lucien Millevoye, grandson of the poet Millevoye. Her references to Millevoye when she was in Ireland were always secretive. Millevoye told her that he hated the English because they had vanquished his hero, Napoleon. He suggested that she might free Ireland as Joan of Arc had freed France. Such adoration fuelled and inflamed Gonne's passion for Ireland and Irish nationalism. She wrote impassioned anti-British articles for Arthur Griffith's nationalist weekly the *United Irishman*. Millevoye, became editor of the influential newspaper, *La Patrie* and was a gifted orator.

Besides Nationalism, Gonne's other fervent beliefs were in Catholicism and reincarnation. Along with AE, she joined the Theosophical Society in Dublin to study esoteric religions. As a supporter of the doctrine of reincarnation, she believed that a son of hers would be the reincarnation of her father. She had a son with Millevoye, named Georges, who died of meningitis before his second birthday. She hoped to resurrect the soul of their dead son. In the memorial chapel at Samois where he was buried, she conceived with Millevoye a daughter, who was born on 6 August 1894. The legendary conception of the child was matched by her mythical name, Iseult Germaine Lucille.

Iseult's early schooling was in a convent at Laval where her mother had been received into the Catholic Church. She was the only child there and was instructed by the nuns and allowed to roam in the vast Carmelite gardens with its central fishpond. Gonne had a baby alligator delivered to the convent for her daughter. When she left the convent, Iseult was cared for by an elderly widow, Madame Bourbonne, at Gonne's house in Paris. Millevoye visited and brought his daughter lavish gifts. He fell in love with a French chanteuse and Gonne ended her relationship with him. Gonne married the Irish Republican activist, Major John MacBride, in 1903, ignoring the protests of her nine-year-old daughter who took a dislike to MacBride. Iseult would later tell Stuart that she sensed MacBride was perverted and claimed that he made sexual advances to her and exposed himself to her during periods of drunkenness. This allegation, reported by Stuart, has met with dismissal and outrage from some MacBride commentators. Iseult resented her mother for marrying MacBride. Maud Gonne had first met him in Dublin and then two years later in Paris in 1902, after his return from the Boer War.

Gonne's sister Kathleen begged her to marry Yeats who had fallen madly in love with her on their first meeting in London. Gonne's marriage to MacBride was doomed, despite the birth of a son, Seán (Seaghan). The brief marriage ended in a judicial separation that was widely reported in Irish newspapers. MacBride envied her admirers and hated himself for living off her, and, on one occasion, while drunk, kicked her repeatedly. The Gonne–MacBride separation was granted in favour of her being awarded custody of the child and the immorality charges against him were disproved.[1]

W.B. Yeats had long before this fallen hopelessly in love with Maud Gonne. Stuart would grin at the mention of this famous love affair and often did so, stating that both people would obviously not have suited each other. He felt that if they had married it would have been a highly fraught and contentious situation. When Yeats proposed to Gonne, and he did so on many occasions, her refusal marked the beginning of their "mystical marriage". She remained the central muse of his love poems and was categorical in telling him, "I have a horror and terror of physical love."[2] This may have been a polite refusal of his advances. He was more than willing to write and dedicate *The Countess Cathleen* to her. She would take the lead in his next play, *Cathleen Ní Houlihan*. According to a letter she wrote to him, it seems they had at least one night of sex together. However, Yeats in his *Memoirs* would recall her antipathy to sexual intercourse. In *Black List, Section H* Stuart makes a scathing comment to the effect that she filled the emotional void of her life through nationalist politics, "having failed in her relationships to her three men" (Yeats, Millevoye and MacBride).[3] Need there be further proof of Stuart's disdain for her?

In Ireland, Gonne presented Iseult in public, not as a daughter, but as an adopted niece. The subterfuge had its effect on Iseult and may have explained why she always referred to her mother by the pet name, Moura. Gonne insisted that her daughter never called her "mother" when in Ireland. Iseult lived with a sense of illegitimacy and this was something she found difficult to speak about. In Paris, aged 15, Iseult began joking that she would marry Yeats – "Uncle Willie". Yeats suggested to Gonne that, when Iseult came of age, they might marry. Gonne did not protest. Meanwhile, Iseult's schooling continued in another convent at Caen and her half-brother, Seán MacBride, went to the Jesuit school in Passy. Their summers were spent at a large villa, "Les Mouettes", in Colleville, Normandy, a gift from Millevoye. The house became a menagerie of animals, including many dogs. One was a Great Dane called Dagda. Yeats used the name of Iseult's Persian cat, Minnaloushe in a play entitled *The Cat and the Moon*. Yeats doted on Iseult, entranced by "her archaic smile". Stuart told me that Iseult had a formidable intellect, more than he was able to credit her with during their troubled marriage.

When MacBride was executed at Kilmainham Jail in Dublin for his part in the 1916 Rising, Gonne was in Paris and wrote to Yeats: "Those who die for Ireland are sacred."[4] When he showed her an elegy, "Easter, 1916", written about the Rising, she thought it was not worthy of his genius. It would become one of the most notable poems that he ever wrote. She had already told Yeats about MacBride's alleged violent dipsomania which he mentioned in the poem, referring to the major as "a drunken, vainglorious lout". Yeats brought Iseult to meet Bernard Shaw; she was silent until Shaw spoke of writing to the English newspapers about the leaders of 1916 executed in cold blood – "entirely incorrect" since "they were prisoners of war". Iseult, perhaps imbued with her mother's patriotism more than her own, agreed with him. Stuart firmly believed that Iseult was the underling of her mother, but my own impression from the facts and research contradicts this somewhat.

By the age of 19, Iseult had become more strong willed and broke free from her mother's shadow. In 1911, the artist Joseph Granié painted a portrait of her as an angel. She sat for two portraits by AE and for one by William Rothenstein. When Yeats brought her to London, Thomas Sturge Moore, the artist and poet, thought her "very lovely to look at". Iseult spoke to Stuart of seeing Isadora Duncan dance at the Trocadero in Paris many times. This background of hers fascinated Stuart, however much he admitted that it made him feel insignificant when he was young. He often said to me that Iseult knew so many people in Dublin, London and Paris at that time; he knew no one of that sort and wondered why she had bothered with him. He never believed that she could in fact have loved him and doubted her declaration of love. Yeats introduced Iseult to Rabindranath Tagore, and she began studying Eastern literature with

Devabrata Mukerjee, who fell in love with her. She hated Mukerjee, a nephew of Tagore, who taught her the rudiments of Bengalese, and chastened him with an account of her first proposal of marriage from the French writer Jean Malyé that she refused in 1912. She left Mukerjee and went to Dax, a spa at the foot of the Pyrenees, to shake him off and recover her lost nervous energy.

Yeats sent her *Gitanjali* (meaning "song offerings") by Tagore, who would win a Nobel Prize for Literature. She began translating Tagore into English, but became distracted from completing her version of his work, *The Gardener*. Arthur Symons, the critic, found her "strangely exotic" and dedicated his *Colour Studies in Paris* "to the adorable Iseult Gonne". Symons, who had a considerable reputation as a decadent poet, was never predatory and she spoke highly of him for the rest of her life, according to Stuart. His best work would be in criticism, such as his masterpiece *The Symbolist Movement in Literature.* Stuart had access to Symons's books, usually in signed first editions, but admitted that his interest was limited. The torrent of available books from literati could be overwhelming to him and, as a young man, he feared they could stifle his first efforts at writing. In order to maintain his sense of being a writer he could not absorb Yeats and his milieu, except on his own terms, whereas Iseult could read at will and did so. She was far better read than he, which he freely admits in *Black List, Section H*.

Symons knew about her private life, concealed from her mother, which included vagabondage, selling family jewellery for money, smoking hashish and renting a room in the Rue Lénore as an act of independence. Whatever about hashish smoking, which also appealed to Maud Gonne as an experience and is mentioned in her autobiography *A Servant of the Queen*, Symons heard from Iseult about the difficult relationship with her mother. This is supported by Stuart, and conflicts with the account of his son, Ian, who claims that Gonne and Iseult were very close. However, that was at a later stage in their lives.

One significant incident in Iseult's life prior to meeting Stuart completes this portrait of her as a young woman. In July 1917, Yeats arrived at Colleville for what would be an emotionally fraught summer. First, he made a marriage proposal to Maud Gonne in the same manner as the previous year and, as before, she refused him. Asking her permission, he proposed to the 22-year-old Iseult, who also refused him, just as she had done a year earlier. No wonder he began to find their villa "a big ugly house on the sea beach". Iseult was more interested in asking his opinions of her prose-poems. Yeats's Olympianism did not extend to encouraging her efforts. He had disappointed her by not editing the poems; and he did not give any attention to the essays she had drafted on Huysmans and D'Annunzio. His encouragement, if given, might have enabled her to fashion them better. Even with gentle hints from Gonne about Iseult's progress as a writer, Yeats remained preoccupied with himself. When he suggested that Iseult and he edit an anthology of French Catholic poets, she was diffident. This was a diffidence that Yeats had detected with regard to her own work. In a telling comment she told Yeats that "with spectators in the soul no one can write sincerely". Her own impossible standards would seem to render her as a pure writer, but one who could never feel able to publish.

Iseult's better nature came to the fore and, being fluent in French, she helped Yeats to read the French poet, Francis Jammes. Yeats was also immersed in thinking out the early stages of his most esoteric book, *A Vision,* but, when he explained his theory about the *Anima Mundi* (world spirit) to Iseult, she was sceptical and confided to her black-covered notebook thoughts of morbid introspection and moodiness verging on despair. Her philosophical searching kept her interested in listening to and talking with him. As a couple their speculations diverged and not only age separated them: she was approaching 23 and he 52. Iseult got extremely upset when Yeats proposed marriage a second time. Her refusal was a categorical "no".

If neither Gonne nor Iseult was going to marry him, he was going to try elsewhere. Iseult felt guilty about the refusal and was greatly confused. Days later Yeats was in England, having accepted an invitation from Mrs Tucker and her daughter, Georgie Hyde Lees, a 24-four-year old art student who was in love with him. Georgie and he were members the Order of the Golden Dawn, a secret society involved with ceremony, symbolism, Hermetic philosophy and the ancient Jewish mysticism of the Kabbalah. Mrs Tucker thought her daughter too young for Yeats, but Georgie accepted his proposal of marriage. When Yeats announced the engagement, Lady Augusta Gregory was delighted; Gonne also, and Iseult in time became friends with Georgie, relieved that the poet had found a wife at last.

After the marriage, the couple shuffled around from one place to another in a bizarre and protracted honeymoon and eventually settled in Stone Cottage, inviting Iseult for Christmas. Stone Cottage was near Colman's Hatch in Sussex and had been rented by Yeats as early as 1914 when he and the American poet, Ezra Pound, shared it. Pound had at that time just married Dorothy Shakespear, the daughter of Olivia Shakespear, a former lover of Yeats. Stuart was never judgmental about this, but understood at a deeper level that such philandering and affairs could take their toll in terms of energy, guilt and suffering as well as the excitement and pleasure in the early stages.

In the new year, 1918, Yeats said he would find a job for Iseult – something that would suit her intense intellectualism. At every opportunity he showed her off to his friends, such as Lady Cunard, Bernard Shaw and the young fireball poet, Ezra Pound. Pound became smitten by Iseult. He asked her to be his part-time secretary, complaining about having to type on his Corona. It was a pompous excuse for a poet who wanted to lure and seem alluring to a woman he fancied. When Iseult was not typing for Pound, she lived at Woburn Buildings, London, where Yeats rented rooms above a cobbler's shop for his wife Georgie and himself. Iseult and Pound became lovers when Maud Gonne was unable to chaperone her. Pound was 11 years older than Iseult. She wrote Pound many letters, but he tired of her eventually. When she boasted of the affair to Stuart after their marriage, he became enraged in passionate jealousy and found the truth of her relationship painful to accept. For years he doubted it and, finally accepting the facts, felt that it was ultimately damaging for him in his dealings with Iseult, making him seek revengeful encounters with other women. He was too young to forgive this love affair from her past, secretly hated her for it and the situation added to his sense of not being equal to her other lovers, especially Pound. The reaction for a young man and writer sounds reasonable, but for Stuart, the seeds of dissent and disharmony between him and Iseult had been sown. Stuart's comments about Iseult to me were delivered in what I call an "extended state of emotion" giving the distinct impression that there was much unfinished business between him and his first wife.

As Maud Gonne got older, she liked to be seen in public with Iseult, even though she was eclipsed by her daughter's beauty, according to Stuart. Gonne's former sexual restraint in bohemian circles did not become Iseult's mode of living. Iseult indulged herself; she wore exotic clothes, smoked through a cigarette holder and was seen at parties with a Persian cat which, in the distance, looked like a fur-scarf around her neck. She moved away from Woburn Buildings when Yeats got her a job in the library at the School of Oriental Studies. She shared a flat with Iris Barry who also worked there. When Iseult realised that Barry had been Pound's mistress, she felt rather foolish. Pound ended his affair with Iris first and then with her. Pound would later refer to her in *The Cantos* (CIV). Iseult met Wyndham Lewis through Barry. Stuart was convinced that Iseult must have slept with Lewis also, such was his possessiveness about Iseult decades after the time she knew Lewis and Pound.

Yeats wrote poems for Iseult: "To a Child Dancing in the Wind", "Two Years Later" and "To a Young Girl". In "To a Young Beauty", without naming her, he acknowledged her creative worth:

> Dear fellow-artist, why so free
> With every sort of company,
> With every Jack and Jill? [5]

Stuart and Iseult had been aware of each other since AE's "Sunday Night" in Rathgar. They met for the second time at Maud Gonne's house in St Stephen's Green. Immediately, he was again entranced because of her beauty and her French-accented English. She would retain her "foreign" accent all of her life. Stuart was living nearby in a mews flat off Fitzwilliam Street, where his live-in landlady was the spiritualist, Hester Travers-Smith. H.O. White, his "sometime tutor", had recommended him to Hester Travers-Smith as a suitable tenant. Stuart disliked the spiritualist gatherings, but they were at least a break in his solitude. Aunt Janet and Lily had gone to Antrim and he began his pursuit of Iseult.

While he could not abide Maud Gonne's melodramatic posturing, he was bewitched by Iseult and accepted an invitation to their cottage, Ballinagoneen, in Glenmalure, Co Wicklow, with a young captain who had been fighting in France. She told them the cottage was the one referred to as "Baravore" in J.M. Synge's *The Shadow of the Glen*. Gonne had bought it with the proceeds of the house in Normandy. Stuart hiked south into the Wicklow hills with Captain Purcell, searching for the cottage. Little did he know that the long trek would be momentous. The cottage, secluded at the end of the valley, was situated beyond a waterfall. The cottage, with its red iron roof, is now a hostel and remains much as it was when Stuart and Iseult lived there. Across the precipitous slopes are Glendalough. The setting compares to any alpine region: it is suffused with natural beauty. Stuart stayed for a few days, having helped with planting apple trees. Purcell later told Stuart that, while alone with Iseult, he had kissed her.

When Stuart got a chance for a walk with Iseult on his own, he showed her his copy of Yeats's *Responsibilities*. She quickly flicked through the book and found a poem written to her and he read it aloud. Iseult entranced him with talk, in her French-accented English, of Yeats, Shaw, Synge, Lady Gregory, James Stephens, Ezra Pound, Arthur Symons, Wyndham Lewis, James Connolly, Arthur Griffith and others whom she had met. When he heard about how the 1916 Rising had touched their lives through Major John MacBride, he could only reflect on his discovery of the events in newspapers, while staying with Nellie Farren in Bournemouth. Iseult had read a lot, including Dante, and was knowledgeable in matters of literature that were beyond him. Suddenly, he felt embarrassed at mentioning his own furtive attempts at writing. She had also produced more writing than he, had travelled more extensively, had been a nurse to wounded and dying soldiers from the First World War in Normandy and heard the artillery and other rumblings from the Western Front when he was a mere public schoolboy.

Iseult was friendly with the playwright Lennox Robinson. Yeats hoped that Iseult would marry Robinson. He too had fallen in love with her. Robinson was almost her own age – a lively and gifted character, appointed by Yeats as manager of the Abbey Theatre and author of two fairly successful plays. Georgie Yeats found him a suitable drinking companion on occasions, according to Stuart. Robinson was known to be never far away from a copious supply of whiskey and often carried a supply in his briefcase, Stuart told me. He was at that time engaged in writing a comedy, *The Whiteheaded Boy,* which has become a masterpiece of Irish theatre along with others such as *Drama at Inish*. However, Iseult turned down Robinson's many proposals of marriage and he married Dollie, the daughter of Hester Travers-Smith.

Iseult considered Stuart as her future husband, but Gonne firmly disapproved even though the couple made a striking and singular pair. When Iseult discussed her plans of marriage with Yeats, he effusively agreed, perhaps out of guilt for his previous preying on her. Iseult was by any standards a beautiful-looking woman and Stuart was a handsome young man, especially tall like his Stuart uncles. Gonne thought Stuart had a fine head of wavy hair, sandy in colour that would turn to snowy in his later years. Iseult, whose male company had always been poets of the first rank, made it her destiny to marry a poet. There were deeper reasons too. She wrote to Yeats mentioning Stuart's naïvety and declared, "he is a blessed angel". Further expanding the complicated triangle of their relationship, she felt that Stuart was Yeats's spiritual child and added, "there are times I wonder even if you might be his real father". Iseult and Stuart could also share what their past lives had in common: the experiences of having stepfathers and losing their natural fathers. Millevoye had died in 1918 and when Iseult read an obituary in London, she entered a period of grief. When she talked about Millevoye, Stuart was able to tell what little he knew about the death of his own father which "was shrouded in shame and mystery".[6]

Similarly, she and Stuart had gone through lengthy periods of institutional schooling, only having contact with a parent and relatives seasonally. In Iseult's case, having left the cloistered life of a Carmelite convent, she had become in some ways a casualty of bohemianism, wilfully adopting it as her mode of life after the strictures of her unusual schooling. Stuart said to me that Iseult's childhood and adolescence were too extreme. Millevoye was a remote father, whereas Gonne was a larger-than-life mother who was a chaperone to her daughter (publicly "her niece") in society, denying her freedom. Iseult may have seen him (Stuart) as the solution to achieve independence from her mother and a new start, Stuart admitted.

Early omens for the relationship were not good. Within whatever harmony they achieved, they discovered deeper divisions. Stuart could not match her erudition and reading, which irked him as a budding writer. When he was reading de la Mare's poetry with great enjoyment, she scoffed, saying it was second rate. Her past life sounded almost fictional to him. They had religious differences, not of a sectarian nature but of a more profound sort. Iseult was undergoing a spiritual crisis for most of her life, Stuart said. Their quarrels over theology were tragic because of pain mutually suffered and inflicted. These quarrels are mentioned in *Black List, Section H* as centring on the fundamental tenets of Catholicism: the Resurrection of Jesus and the Assumption of his Mother into Heaven.

When I referred to his novel of 1981, *The High Consistory*, where Stuart castigates Ireland as "this island of priests and prams",[7] he assured me that he said such things to upset Iseult and regretted it later in life. He often said that he had so many regrets about her when he thought about their marriage. She had read some of the Catholic mystics, and Stuart would follow her example and struggle in succeeding years, attempting to reconcile Christianity with his own belief structure. They unwisely buried these divisions, but not before Iseult, in a psychic premonition, told him: "I'm the willow rooted on the river bank and you're the black swan gliding past".[8]

She had fallen in love with Stuart and, realising his antipathy to her mother, suggested a trip to London. Stuart resented Gonne for calling Iseult "Ma belle animal" and "my lovely niece" and expecting to be called "Madame" by him. They went to London the same year of their first meeting, 1919, and rented a room on Tottenham Street. A part of London – Fitzrovia, Bloomsbury and Soho – that Stuart would frequent many times in his life. After a few weeks, Stuart recalled, he thought Iseult's talk about free love was bravado. In actual fact, he had no sexual experience with a woman and, in their early sexual fumblings, accused her of the negation of sensual pleasure. He disagreed violently with her view that sex was only for procreation purposes. Iseult told him that she had latterly recoiled from his advances largely because of previous experiences with lovers that, in retrospect, had repulsed her. Soon they discovered that they were sexually incompatible. Although he felt heartbroken about this, he still loved her but he didn't know how to surmount the problem of her restricted sex drive.

Stuart said that he had rarely engaged in masturbation, finding the practice a shock to his nervous system rather than a release, as he would reveal in *A Hole in the Head*. He claimed to have some sexual experience during adolescence with his cousin Stella, Wallace Stuart's daughter, and exchanged letters with her and another cousin, Maida who was the daughter of his Uncle James (Stuart). Innocent enough physically, but otherwise very passionate, he added.

On their return from London before Christmas, Gonne was relieved to see them and underwent a change from her earlier negative opinions about the relationship. A visit was arranged for Stuart's uncles and also Lily, his mother, to meet with Iseult and Gonne. The visit was uncomfortable to say the least, according to Stuart. Neither of Stuart's uncles would speak up for him as a potential husband and went so far as to suggest that he may have inherited mental instability from his father. Gonne reported this to Iseult after the meeting and also that the uncles were critical of the Montgomerys, especially Stuart's grandfather, Captain Montgomery, who had died of alcoholism. The uncles could also detect Gonne's political affiliations in Iseult when they met her briefly and were disapproving. Stuart did not know exactly what she said, but it must have revealed some republican sentiment. Lily's meeting with Gonne went better. Lily approved of marrying her son into a family of reputable distinction and wealth. Gonne was made fully aware of Stuart's past and his father's suicide, but said nothing to him about it, he recalled. Such a subject would have been beyond her vocabulary, he added with derision.

Stuart began rooming with Lennox Robinson before the wedding. After following a course of instruction, Stuart was received into the Roman Catholic Church in January 1920 at University Church, St Stephen's Green, Dublin, and received First Communion on 15 March (he had been brought up a Protestant). Lily, who had converted to Catholicism after returning from Australia, did not have her son instructed into the Catholic faith as a boy. It was never a conflict between Stuart, his mother or Aunt Janet, also a Catholic convert. Stuart's Roman Catholicism or otherwise will be explored later.

The marriage on 10 April was a subdued occasion. Stuart was weeks away from his eighteenth birthday and Iseult was 25 years old. Lily attended the wedding, along with Aunt Janet, Maud Gonne and a few friends including Helena Maloney, a sister of the Irish patriot Kevin Barry, at University Church. Mr and Mrs Stuart left for the boat train after a simple wedding celebration. Lennox Robinson saw them off at the station, en route to London. Even Robinson knew about Stuart's past by then and soon Lady Gregory would know by the next letter arriving at Coole Park from Yeats. In a letter to Yeats, Maud Gonne wrote: "The marriage is a tragedy & I don't like to speak or think of it."[9] The letter continues: "His family are a queer lot from Antrim who, though well connected, have drunk themselves into degeneracy. He has a talent of a queer morbid kind, but no education & no power or will to work. He gives you an example that college is unnecessary when one is a genius."[10] Stuart would later comment on this period of his life in *Black List, Section H.* In the novel the central character is referred to as Ruark, Henry and H, but is obviously based on Stuart. When everyone regards H as neurotic because of his background and the manner of his father's death, he is defiant, "only by what they called his neurosis becoming more profound could he write the kind of poems that might lessen his isolation, or at least fully reconcile him to it."[11]

So Yeats and Gonne hovered in the shadows of Stuart's and Iseult's lives almost like characters from the legendary myth of Tristan and Isolde. Iseult's name and life followed a mythic pattern. Tristan (Stuart) has the wound from birth – the father's suicide. The name Tristan suggests the melancholy attributable to poets, except that Stuart's maturing personality eschewed any prolonged morbidity or despair. In the myth, Iseult nurses Tristan's wound. King Mark might well be Yeats, entrusting Stuart to carry on the art of poetry. Gonne would have happily played the role of the Queen of Ireland and of course was mother of Iseult. Stuart and Iseult drank the love potion that wears off – in other words, however over-used the phrase, they fell in love or were in love for a time. Adventures take Tristan away from Iseult, as with Stuart. In the legend, Iseult remarries but is reunited with his Tristan, who dies with her, but this was not to be the life history of Stuart and Iseult.

Lady Gregory was glad to see Iseult married. The artist Sarah Purser told Iseult that she had less sense in marrying a poet than her mother who rightly refused to marry Yeats. The young married couple soon enough entered difficult emotional terrain. Iseult's seven years of seniority might not have mattered if mutual harmony had been achieved. They fought over everything, including money. Stuart's mother was giving him £350 a year, while Iseult received £100 a year from Gonne. Stuart felt that Iseult and her mother should pay the rent on their first flat in Ely Place. When they moved to another flat in Fitzwilliam Square, the relocation annoyed Gonne. The flat became a refuge from Stuart for Iseult when he was difficult. Otherwise when she grew restless she left Stuart in the cottage in Glenmalure.

As it happened, they faced Iseult's pregnancy after emotionally fraught scenes. Yeats witnessed the difficulties throughout the early part of their marriage. He wrote to Lady Gregory, "the young man is a sadist - one of those who torture those they love, a recognised lunatic type."[12] On one occasion, after an argument, Stuart went into a frenzy and set fire to gorse dangerously close to the cottage, then he brought Iseult's clothes from the house, flinging them into the flames. Was he trying to cause her death? The burning of Iseult's dresses may have been subconscious revenge for her previous sex life. He admitted to me that their relationship was so fraught as to be doomed. She in turn broke his plaster heron - a legacy of art classes at Rugby. Stuart stole first editions of books that Yeats had inscribed to Gonne and sold them at a good price.[13] There were reconciliations, one of which in the early stages of marital disharmony had produced their first child.

3

Soldier and Poet

AFTER THEY HAD BEEN MARRIED FOR 11 months, a daughter was born. Stuart admitted to me that it shook him to the core of his being. Dolores Veronica was born on 9 March 1921 at Gonne's house in St Stephen's Green. Stuart was weeks away from his nineteenth birthday and, with the pre-marriage hullabaloo caused by his uncles, he was gradually discovering basic details of his father's suicide from Iseult, told to her by Gonne. The reality of this event also took its toll on him. Now a father himself, he worried that heredity might take over and that the birth of a child bring on some temporary insanity. The birth had the effect of forcing him into the Fitzwilliam Square flat in Dublin, away from the intense solitude of Wicklow. He had begun to feel nervous alone in Wicklow, brooding on his father's last days and the act of suicide itself. There was the agonising situation that he still did not have a direct account of what happened. His father had committed suicide in an insane asylum – these were the bare facts he possessed. He felt deep foreboding, but this, he said to me, was in retrospect and tempered by memory. Omens to some degree ruled his life: about people he knew and himself. If he had had a bad omen at this time of his life, he would have been more right than he could have imagined.

Iseult and Stuart braced themselves in the initial weeks of parenting, divided as they were. Having a flat in Dublin and the cottage in Wicklow implies a wealthier lifestyle than was actually the case. Besides, Gonne had only given them the cottage on loan. Both husband and wife were aspiring writers and had begun to publish in a little magazine, *Aengus,* Iseult being obliged to publish under the bias of the time as "Maurice Gonne", although she had been published under her own name in the *Irish Review*. To give its full title, *Aengus: An*

All Poetry Journal appeared in four issues between 1919 and 1920. Stuart was the editor except for the first issue which was edited by H.O. White, the man who had tutored Stuart in the hopes of getting him into Trinity College and who would later become professor of English there.

Stuart's most recent poems were written for the ballerina Tamara Karsavina, 20 years his senior, who had captured his heart, but they never got beyond a chaste kiss during the time when he pursued her in London while selling a necklace of Iseult's. The necklace was a Montgomery heirloom and wedding present to Iseult, but that did not stop him handing it over for cash in a pawnshop. He felt that this action, bred of necessity, might have been influenced by his reading Russian fiction at the time.

Iseult had written an essay on mysticism entitled "Veil of Veronica" about the woman who, reputed to have wiped the bleeding face of Jesus on his way to Golgotha, finds the imprint of his face on her veil. This explains why she gave her daughter the name Veronica. Stuart suggested the child also be christened Dolores and did not attend the christening because of the fraught situation with Iseult. The name and the events surrounding the birth of their daughter seem doom-laden.

When Stuart would not encourage Iseult's efforts as a writer, she asked Lennox Robinson to look for a publisher for her prose-poems and essays under the uninspiring title, *Dreams*. Stuart and she found it difficult to accommodate the fact that both of them were writers. He readily admitted this when I suggested it to him, but added that he could not see how it affected them adversely. In this, I differed from his opinion. Gonne wrote to Yeats, begging him to encourage Iseult. Gonne was also distraught about her son, Seán, who had been imprisoned in Mountjoy, having been caught in the Black and Tan curfew late one night. No publisher was found for Iseult's work nor did Yeats give much encouragement. Instead, Yeats tried to give Stuart advice on marriage which the young man shrugged off with the fitfulness that often accompanies youth. Of course, another bad omen, Stuart admitted to me, since this was his first meeting with Yeats. Then, Yeats visited Iseult and recommended her to the care of Dr Bethel Solomon, master of the Rotunda Hospital, who knew Oliver St John Gogarty well. Solomon had her sent to a nursing home. He also interviewed Stuart so as to set Gonne's mind at ease.

Lily wrote to Gonne about reconciling Stuart and Iseult, but she had heard about the death of Henry Clements in London in August and was not in good spirits. The meetings of Yeats and Dr Solomon with Stuart had some effect on the young husband and father because Iseult received an affectionate letter from him soon after. Iseult was invited to Benvarden in County Antrim in September and by November the Stuarts were reconciled in their flat. Stuart told me that he felt that he had to try harder and work things out with Iseult for the future.

Whatever about the reconciliation, Stuart was suffering because of the bad relationship with his mother-in-law. Both Iseult and he found themselves in the kind of crisis that heralds a first child into a marriage that is showing signs of major problems. However much he ridiculed Gonne, Iseult was capable of enduring an amount of criticism about her own mother. Stuart felt alienated from his newborn daughter (a portent of his future failure as a parent) and went to the cottage in Wicklow. He was beginning to long for freedom from the whole family set up, and when he was reunited with his daughter and Iseult in the flat in Fitzwilliam Square the domestic situation did not improve. Perhaps his age may exempt him, but Stuart was a frivolous husband and expected Iseult to be his housekeeper. She was not used to domestic chores, let alone minding a baby. Stuart, impressed by Lennox Robinson who had a motorbike, bought one to relieve his boredom and to get away from the baby's crying. Baby Dolores was also proving a troublesome child for Iseult, which made the difficult transition to motherhood more of an ordeal. When Stuart was not speeding here and there on his motorcycle, he was studying Keats's life and poetry and trying to write more poems. After much study he found a misprint in Keats's poem "Teignmouth". He wrote to the *Times Literary Supplement* in London about the error and was proved right by the scholar Sidney Colvin. In line 75 of the poem the word "love" should have read "lore". Yeats and Lady Gregory were impressed, he remembered.

The War of Independence had come to an end in July of 1921 after two and half years of guerrilla warfare between the IRA and British forces with the dreaded Black and Tans having entered the fracas in January 1920. Stuart and Iseult had given up their Dublin flat in May and returned to the cottage in Wicklow. Iseult felt that she and Dolores might benefit from country living away from the city.

Whether in city or country, the baby was sleeping badly and in fact had developed meningitis. Iseult left Wicklow suddenly for St Ultan's hospital with her daughter, but nothing could save the child. Dolores Veronica died on 24 July 1921. Gonne's niece, Thora Pilcher said that "the light died in Iseult at this time". Stuart was equally devastated at the death of his four-month-old daughter. He was alone in Glenmalure trying to write and awaiting a permit for his motorcycle when he received the news by telegram. One reaction would be the privately printed poem "To Our Daughter", an effort to explain his absence from her christening to Iseult.

Of interest are Stuart's comments 50 years afterwards:

> It is the ignominious or obscure deaths of the victims, the vulnerable, among whom I see both my father and my baby daughter, that I try to – I won't say atone for – but celebrate in my work as the kind of events that are of vital significance in man's inner development. [1]

Gonne wrote to Yeats, "We buried it in a very beautiful place in Dean's Grange Cemetery, from where the mountains look quite near. The tiny grave is among the roots of a very old yew tree. Iseult's husband only came after the child was dead. He seemed very moved." [2]

Stuart wrote about the death of Dolores in *Black List, Section H* and in *Things to Live For* where the child is transposed to a boy: "Opening his small arms to life even when life was death."[3]

Yeats believed in astrological prediction, as did his wife Georgie who had a premonition about the child. He wrote to Lady Gregory: "Georgie said months ago that it would not live … it is well that a race of tragic women should die out." His comment sounds callous and also prophetic of Iseult's future life. After the funeral, Stuart and Iseult went to Lough Dan in County Wicklow because she did not want to return to the cottage in Glenmalure. She spent Christmas between Wicklow and her mother's house. Stuart was undergoing a period of hibernation and confusion, which he clearly recalled for me from vivid memories. Otherwise it was a period of chaos and grief, he added, and for the first time grief for his father. I noticed that Stuart's processes of recall could be extended by providing him with basic facts, and he would get lost in remembering details that he had seemingly forgotten far beyond my barest promptings. Much to Yeats's and Gonne's relief, the young couple in mourning were brought closer together. In consoling Iseult, Gonne was reminded of the death of her son, Georges, who died before his second birthday and whose booties she kept throughout her life.

In an effort to dissipate the funereal gloom among the disparate family, Gonne promised to take them on a holiday in Europe in the spring and said she would pay for everything. Gonne, Iseult and Stuart toured the cities of Nuremberg, Dresden, Prague and Vienna. The journey was as sad an event as the reason for their departure, Stuart told me, sighing in recollection. Gonne became hostile towards Stuart because of his frenzied conduct in the recent past: his overwhelming tears and sorrow on seeing his dead child coupled with indifference to Iseult's labour and the birth. Gonne became convinced that he was syphilitic as John MacBride had been. So Stuart told me.

In Munich, Stuart found the season of Wagner's operas beyond his appreciation and the galleries unsuited to his grief; otherwise he would have indulged his passion for paintings and sculpture. In any event, as he admitted to me many times, his appreciation of music was always limited. Walking alone in Munich, he noticed a poster of his fantasy woman, Tamara Karsavina. The prima ballerina was on tour. He harangued Iseult who wanted him to stay with them and instead went off in pursuit of Tamara. It is easy to condemn him for abandoning his grieving wife to pursue Tamara. Iseult did not seem to object when he told her where he was going because their marriage was already an open one, due to mutual disharmony and not least their diverging sex drives. The lowering of sexual libido after giving birth and then losing an infant was not something that Stuart understood and said so in our conversations. Iseult can be said to have suffered sexual harassment before she met him, Stuart implied to me.

In Prague, while Stuart cavorted with his muse, Iseult was the third party in the *ménage à trois*. He would produce his best love poems for Tamara, imitating the poet John Keats, whose beloved was Fanny Brawne. Stuart became the self-conscious poet luxuriating in his flighty, flirtatious beloved and the ballerina was used to the role from previous lovers. In her dressing room at the Coliseum in Munich, she confided to her young admirer: "If I didn't go through despair, my dancing would lose its expressiveness. No one would pay to see it. So, you see, I live on my despair."[4] Stuart, in discussing such youthful romantic adventures, always seemed quite proud of himself because as a poet it showed proof of his recklessness and daring by associating with an international ballerina. This was his logic.

Stuart's poems to Tamara are imitative of Keats and Yeats; the Yeats before *Responsibilities*. Perhaps the first meetings with Tamara were more satisfactory and from these comes the best poem, "For A Dancer, II":

> You were a young fountain, a mad bird
> And half a woman, a secret overheard
> In a dark forest,
> Setting the trees alive, the leaves astir.
> You were my joy, my sorrowful you were! [5]

When they returned from Europe, Iseult went to stay with Lily by the sea at Bettystown, Co Meath. A fond relationship was growing between the two women. Soon Gonne summoned Iseult to the house in St Stephen's Green for two reasons. Gonne was moving to Roebuck House in the Dublin suburb of Clonskeagh, having recently co-purchased the property with Mrs Despard. They hoped to set up a jam industry because of the extensive gardens and outhouses. Dublin wits referred to them as "Maud Gone Mad" and "Mrs Desperate".

The Civil War broke out with the occupation of the Four Courts in June 1922. Earlier in January, the Anglo-Irish Treaty, signed under duress in London, was debated in the First Dáil in Dublin and ratified by 60 votes in favour, to 58 votes against. From the latter, the anti-Treaty faction was formed, led by Éamon de Valera. Gonne was pro-de Valera and entered into the anti-Treaty frenzy against Michael Collins. Collins had been empowered to establish the Irish Free State (Saorstát Éireann) by signing, as head of the Provisional Government, an agreement with Winston Churchill for the transfer of power from Britain 26 of the 32 counties of Ireland.

Gonne heckled Stuart whose political views were neither fervent nor formed in either the pro- or anti-Treaty camp. For a 20-year-old poet, Stuart was strangely apolitical and emphatically attested to me the fact that he was always so. Iseult began nursing the wounded from the anti-Treaty faction and Stuart helped her for the sake of harmony. Soon Lily joined them at Roebuck House. Then, it was as if Iseult and Gonne decided Stuart would become a Republican and, passively, he complied. He joined the Irish Volunteers, Company B III. His soldiering was farcical, according to his various accounts in our conversations; he was always dismissive of it but his outlook on life matured during the Civil War. On a gunrunning episode to Belgium for the IRA, when he collected a shipment of weapons, he also bought condoms in a plan to advance the mediocre sexual activity of his marriage. Again, this might seem insensitive after his wife's loss of a child.

As a Republican volunteer taking part in a hold-up of the Wexford train on one occasion, he had an insight as the action was taking place. The mission lost its excitement for him when some of the passengers shouted "Up the Republic! Up de Valera!" He was unable to revel in such belligerence and suddenly became uncertain of the de Valera cause. Nor did he support de Valera's ideal of an ultra-Catholic Gaelic state. Stuart also took part in a skirmish in Cork. He was arrested on 9 August 1922, by a Free State lieutenant, during an incident when his unit had seized an arms cache from a train in Amiens Street station, Dublin. After being held in Wellington Barracks for a few days, he was herded on to a prison train with others, many of whom were pistol whipped by their captors. This was a story he often repeated to me because he was terrified during the events on the train. He would spend six months in Maryborough (Portlaoise) Prison. His description of the death of Collins in *Black List* shows that the shooting of General Collins is greeted with cheering by the internees at Maryborough Prison. Stuart acknowledged that it was based on this outburst of joy from the prisoners which significantly catches the divisions between both sides in the Civil War.

After some weeks, one of their leaders, Commandant Joe Griffin, organised a fire in the prison cells. Stuart and the others were punished by being left out in the yard for days and then returned to the cells to inhale the pervasive burnt atmosphere. Hammocks were provided since the bedding and mattresses had been destroyed. Food parcels arrived for Stuart and his cellmate, Basil Blewett, and by coincidence each received a copy of Dostoevsky's *The Brothers Karamazov*. For Stuart it was a perfect setting in which to study one of the greatest novels ever written. It not only passed the time, but it became his textbook; and a book that ensured me a continuous entré into his company, once I mentioned I had read it and valued it highly. On being transferred to the military prison at the Curragh, known as Tintown, he found other literature that had been smuggled in and came under the influence of Joseph Campbell, fellow anti-Treaty prisoner. He read some of his poems to Campbell who noted in a diary the young poet's recitation, "the faint murmur of his voice à la Golding and Ezra Pound" and that Stuart talked of "Ezra's dressing gown, beard, one gold earring in ear",[5a] a reference to Pound's appearance as reported in Yeats's gossip from the London literary scene, and also Stuart's obsession with the American poet. Stuart was skinny at the time, looked sickly, tubercular and was declared unfit for work and, along with other idle prisoners, read and discussed the writings of Pearse, Davis, Mitchell's *Jail Journal*, Connolly's *Labour in Irish History* and especially the essays of Fintan Lalor, he told me. He was released the following year, 1923, shortly before Christmas. He had been incarcerated for 15 months. Stuart, near the end of his life, spoke of Collins with considerable awe and, when asked to sum up de Valera, said angrily to me on one occasion, "de Valera was an utter phoney, a nobody".[6] His opinion of de Valera changed at various times throughout his life. Stuart had an obsession with rulers, leaders, kings and despots and enjoyed telling their life's events and about the women whom they pursued.

Stuart's arrest during the Civil War, signed by General Richard Mulcahy as described in *Black List* is at variance with the earlier account in *Things to Live For*. For his own fictional purposes he did not want to glamorise H, the hero of *Black List*. The description of the firing squad at Maryborough prison is more vivid in *Things to Live For* than in *Black List* and is a good example of his early writing style:

> There were tears streaming down the face of one of the boys from under his shut eyelids. There was the rain on their faces too but I saw the tears. When the soldiers fired he put up his hands to his chest and tore at his coat as though he wanted to open it. He swayed forward without falling. His coat came open with the buttons ripped off and the blood ran down his hands. Then he fell on his knees with his head bowed over the other boy who had fallen sideways, his face in a pool. Joe had fallen back against the wall but his feet were still on the ground and he was choking with blood and spittle coming out of his mouth and his face turned dark. The other boy fell from his knees and the two boys lay one across the other. The sergeant put his gun to the side of Joe's head and fired four or five shots into it. The side of his head was torn open; then he

> fell sideways with his shoulders slipping down along the wall.[7]

Stuart often referred to this event. I distinctly felt that he replayed it in his mind almost endlessly searching for some detail he had missed. Like any soldier he said that kinship with those who had died, including by firing squad, remained part of his private meditation and remembrance all of his life. The soldier in Stuart rested uneasily with the artist, not knowing who took more risks in life. He had a passionate respect for anyone who put their life on the line. Discussing such matters his imagination unfurled itself in splendour and eloquence; his talk was never sentimental. In fact, I often thought that this voice was different from the tone of his novels, but it was equally mesmerising to me as a young man. When he freed himself of tormented recollection over fallen comrades if we happened to be drinking wine or whiskey he would raise his glass and say "saluté", "touché" and "l'audace"; only very seldom did I hear him utter the Gaelic, "sláinte". Whichever toast he made, he would chuckle to himself before putting the glass to his lips. This was also a ceremonial signal that the subject of the conversation would have to be changed. He might turn his gaze on me and say, "What have you been up to? How is your life going, at all, and your writing?" In my turn I was expected to balance our conversations with much detail and news. Stuart was by no means a solipsistic deliverer of endless monologues. When he paused and went silent I would have to marshal my best lines to maintain our dialogue while being aware that my interlocutor was vastly older and more experienced than I in my twenties. The fact that our friendship continued was a source of delight to me and I never suffered anxiety about its longevity since we had found a mutual ease long since our first meeting.

His friendship with a fellow soldier, Jim Phelan, the sort of character engaged in life's shadow side, would prove a strong influence during the Civil War. Phelan (1895-1966) served long sentences in prisons at Maidstone, Dartmoor and Parkhurst for armed robbery and other crimes, up to the late 1930s. He was the author of prison literature including *Lifer* (1938) and *Jail Journal* (1940). In *Black List* Phelan is called Lane. He knocked the Yeatsian glow out of me, if I ever had such a glow, said Stuart. Stuart, I could see, was deeply influenced and fascinated by Phelan. I also believe and asserted the point in conversation with him that the Civil War made him long for a complete declassé kind of companionship and fixed his mind on not being solely an artist dedicated to art alone. Stuart never liked to be classified or "boxed in" but agreed to elaborate and advance a discussion. In conversation with Stuart, Phelan criticised Joyce, Synge, Yeats and Shaw as writers in smoking jackets and shiny waistcoats, wearing monocles, pince-nez and such. Telling me this, Stuart would beam with smiles and laughter. Lane demanded that a writer be one of the condemned, an outcast – this to Stuart was instantaneously alluring. It fitted his own emerging sense as an artist and at one remove, this merged with his image of Henry, his father or at least the identity that he had given his father as the outcast of the family. In a perverse sort of way, Stuart believed and assumed this genetic heritage with a devout personal passion. He absorbed what he wanted from Phelan while in Tintown Prison Camp and they lost contact after being released.

Stuart would go on to write two "Civil War" novels, *Pigeon Irish* and *The Coloured Dome*. These novels preserve his immediate reactions to the Civil War, a decade later. The months in prison became the young man's university of real life. He had greatly benefited from reading Dostoevsky and began to write a novel. His meeting and discussions with doctrinaire Republican revolutionaries like George Gilmore and Peadar O'Donnell widened his outlook further, he said emphatically. This was typical of Stuart's pride in his affinity with such men and his equally proud backward glance at having shared his youth with them under the strictures of captivity. Stuart elaborated for me that these gunmen knew that, since 1916, a "new" Ireland must be more than an idealistic vision. He proclaimed that during his time in the Curragh prison, it was the likes of Ernie O'Malley and Seán Tracy who were spoken of as genuine guerrillas rather than Dev or Collins. By 1923, the possibilities of some utopia faded into come-day go-day democracy in Ireland, according to Stuart, whose sense of defeat was marked with disgust and who said that he was neither pro- nor anti-Treaty. 1916–23 would remain for him and others the unprecedented era, since every political advance and reversal for modern Ireland can be traced to those seven years of revolution. Stuart, like some from that time who did not settle into constitutional and political structures, believed that a great epoch had not come to full fruition. However, also like many utopianists, Stuart was never truly able to outline what his ideal Ireland should be or upon what it should base its political philosophy, state craft and infrastructures. Late in life he would write a novel on this theme entitled *Faillandia*.

A prison term of 15 months with all its pain and frustration did catapult him on to the poetry scene. Iseult crusaded for her poet husband with Yeats who had been made an Irish Free State senator in 1922. AE had turned down a senatorship and Gonne disapproved of Yeats's acceptance of Cosgrave's offer of a seat in the Irish Senate. The following year, W.B. Yeats became a Nobel Laureate. Stuart's collection of poems, entitled *We Have Kept the Faith*, was printed in a small edition. It was funded by a prize of US$100, which had been awarded to Stuart in April 1923 while he was in prison, from Harriet Monroe of *Poetry*, the Chicago magazine influenced by Ezra Pound, William Carlos Williams, Robert Frost and Yeats. The prize money had been donated by Edith Rockefeller McCormick. Of course, he was proud of this achievement and saw it in mythic terms, but soon got disillusioned because it did not merge with his solitary experience of being a prisoner. Many of the poems came from an earlier phase of his life.

On his release from Tintown Prison Camp, Stuart was far from impressed by the thin book, bound in cardboard with a cloth spine, the title affixed by label: *We Have Kept the Faith, H. Stuart*. Prison experiences had tempered the previous egotism of the young man. Some of the poems included had appeared in the magazine *Chapbook*. He was physically debilitated after taking part in a hunger strike that had lasted for 11 days before his release and none too happy to be recuperating at his mother-in-law's, in Roebuck House. However, he could not complain since Gonne's pleas to various Free State leaders had brought about the amnesty that led to a general release of anti-Treaty prisoners.

The news of Yeats's Nobel Prize, awarded in November 1923, was still big literary gossip in Dublin, and Iseult saw to it that he received a signed copy of her husband's poems. Robinson also received an inscribed copy "To Lennox from Harry Stuart Xmas 1923". F.R. Higgins, Yeats's poet friend, had organised their publication from Oak Leaf Press of 13 Fleet Street, a general advertiser and wood printing company that had also printed *Aengus* and the opening issue of *To-morrow*. The poems officially appeared in January 1924.

This period of Stuart's life takes up a number of chapters in *Black List, Section H,* which I discussed with him on many occasions. For me this was a useful way of getting him to talk about the 1920s. I will highlight a few key passages from the novel which Stuart brought to my attention as significant concerning his beliefs as an artist and the disagreements with Yeats on such matters. He told me candidly that these chapters evoked the period as seen through his eyes. In the text nothing was invented and the dialogue was reproduced from memory. In fact, when I attended some M. Phil. seminars at University College Dublin in the 1980s given by Stuart specifically on *Black List, Section H,* he often repeated that for H in the novel one could easily substitute the author.

In *Black List* the dinner table scene with Yeats comes after H's release from prison and the publication of his poems. It can be read as a subconscious parody by Stuart of the dinner table scene in Joyce's *A Portrait of the Artist as a Young Man*. He agreed with my reading of the novel in this manner, but as will be seen he had issues with Joyce as a writer and a human being. Yeats listens to H who claims that:

> If some one somewhere writes a book which is so radical and original that it would burst the present literary set-up wide open, that writer will be treated with a polite contempt by the critical and academic authorities that will discourage further mention of him. He'll raise deeper, more subconscious hostility than sectarian ones and he'll be destroyed far more effectively by enlightened neglect than anything we would do to him here.[8]

Of course Stuart may not have used these exact words, but on release from prison he felt a certain edge in his relations with the great poet, realising that he had endured and prevailed, whereas Yeats had not gone through similar experiences. Yeats listens and asks: "You believe that the artist is bound to be rejected? You equate him with the prophet?"[9] Stuart recalled that Yeats's wife Georgie "drank like a fish" and remembers seeing her on one occasion walking around Merrion Square wearing mismatched shoes. She had obviously gone shopping for drink, he added. She would remain for the rest of her life "a bottle-a-day" woman.[10]

At dinner on another occasion with Yeats and Georgie, H says, "It's the writer who's one with his work, and doesn't create it as a thing apart, as a beautiful artifice outside himself". [11] Later on, alone with Iseult in their bedroom, H cannot sleep due to nervous exhaustion. As he thinks about the discussion with Yeats, he believes:

> Not only had the poet failed to merge his life and his art (the classic intellectual situation, perhaps) but the style of his living was so formal and unspontaneous that it was in constant opposition to the increasingly disreputable spirit that was inspiring much of his later poetry.[12]

Even though H is aware of being "a nobody in the literary world addressing a Nobel Prizewinner", there is the impression that he feels Yeats has sold out to the established Free State, and that a poet must not do this. Otherwise, Stuart writing in his sixties mocks at H, "Not a shot fired in the civil war, not a blow landed in the Tintown 2 tournament, not a French letter worn in a bold sexual bout! He, caster of doubt on all kinds of things from the Irish Literary Renaissance to Iseult's right to pronounce moral judgements, at least knew what it was like to have doubt cast on himself!"[13]

The structure of *Black List* only permits a restricted portrait of Yeats. Stuart told me that another of his reservations about Yeats as a writer was his glorying in the lover rather than the beloved, which he considered to be a fault of some of Yeats's love poems. He would temper this criticism by commenting that Yeats's "generosity toward younger writers, which he showed by never failing to praise those of us with whom he felt some kinship, however slight". Whenever he was negative about Yeats in my company he always managed to say some positive things about him. In retrospect I regret having made Yeats such an obtrusive ghost in our early meetings, but this would change, thankfully, for Stuart I'm sure, as time passed in our friendship.

George Moore's *Hail and Farewell* certainly gives a more savage portrait of Yeats than Stuart's portrait does in *Black List*. Both writers reveal an upstage posturing persona of Yeats's and this has ensured that their versions of literary history have been seen as countercultural in intent. One is glad to have varying accounts when it comes to the literary history of this significant period. Ulick O'Connor's *Celtic Dawn*, which also deals with the period, quotes the opinion that "a biographer is an artist who is on oath" and puts forward the view that to tell the truth and even shame the biographical subject is vital.[14]

Black List as literary history maintains a high level of scrutiny and subversion. Any autobiographical novel tends to keep the reader constantly suspicious and alert for self-aggrandisement and falsehood on the author's part, hence Stuart's portrayal of the central character as an unglamorous anti-hero. When Yeats wrote the autobiographical *Dramatis Personae* he paid Moore back with a revengeful and amusing portrait. Stuart is not mentioned. Yeats refers to Iseult and, disparagingly, to Stuart in a poem, one of the last he wrote, *Why Should not Old Men be Mad?"*

> A girl that knew all Dante once
> Live to bear children to a dunce.[15]

Yeats's wife confirmed for the critic, Norman Jeffares, that the girl is indeed Iseult and Stuart the dunce. Stuart replied in a poem *Remembering Yeats,* "And why – though why not – had he called me a dunce?"[16] This is an unspiteful riposte to Yeats's censure since obviously no writer wants to be labelled a dunce.

Just as Stuart at the age of 21 was being adopted into the literary establishment of Ireland, he was privately rejecting nearly all of its members. I was somewhat shocked at this because when I met Stuart the Irish Literary Revival fascinated me. The movement, with its writers, poets and artists, was central to Irish publishing with a huge input from the academic presses of the United States and, to some extent, England, while in Ireland the newspapers and media constantly featured Synge, Yeats, Gregory, Joyce and their contemporaries. Stuart's personal stance with regard to his elders came in part from the experiences of prison during the Civil War and his early reading. Like H, Stuart demanded that literature should "be plucked directly from the tree of life" and he found this incompatible with living in a literary milieu which early on he began to loathe. He wanted "to keep clear of literary circles". This was also the milieu in which Iseult had striven to make a literary career for herself. Stuart believed that the hothouse effects of such a milieu were not conducive to literary creation. His ambivalence towards the literary scene was a considerable step backwards for a young writer, some might think, whereas most writers would immediately consider their advancement carefully. Stuart's antagonism towards Yeats, and on many occasions inherent hostility, encountered a level of patience in the older poet. Yeats easily detected Stuart's refusal to be of good cheer with him since the young writer's deepest conviction was that he was against almost everything Yeats stood for.

Stuart's seriousness as a budding writer can be validly gauged in such a stance. He emphasised to me that he was determined to write outside any Irish Literary Revival influence and in part, from his background, felt he might too easily fit into the mould. For many, Stuart remains identified as an Anglo-Irish writer. He is in some manner, but not totally. When many in Dublin felt privileged to have Yeats as a colleague, Stuart was wary of close friendship with the famous poet. He said that being honoured by Yeats and the Academy had, at a subconscious level, adversely affected his own poetic output. Stuart did not want to fawn on Yeats like Seán O'Casey who, before he fell out with Yeats would indulge the poet's whims and walk endlessly around Merrion Square until Yeats recovered his energies and invited him back into his house to continue whatever discussion he had suddenly interrupted. When, in 1927, O'Casey's *The Shadow of a Gunman* was a riotous success at the Abbey Theatre, Gonne would widen the gulf in her friendship with Yeats because he defended the play publicly with its gloss on Republicanism. Iseult adopted her mother's militant Republicanism and her literary values, and disliked the subversive works of O'Casey, Synge and Joyce. Stuart said that Iseult's literary opinions did not influence his own in the slightest. Stuart also heard O'Casey's invective against Yeats behind the poet's back on a few occasions.

Two plays by Stuart would be presented at the Abbey a decade later which shows how much he was by then absorbed as something of a playwright, certainly as a poet and soon as an eminent young novelist. Outrageous as it might seem, he had very little time for members of Yeats's coterie such as Lady Gregory and Oliver St John Gogarty, remaining stolidly pugnacious about them. Similarly, Stuart did not bother to re-establish even an acquaintanceship with the likes of AE once their initial meeting at Rathgar proved mutually unpleasant. In a certain sense he deliberately kept himself to himself, and in telling me this expressed full justification. I do not want to give the impression of him as being pompous. He did not want to get embroiled with the "old guard", as he called them. However, the idea of his living an isolated existence is far from the truth. When he made efforts at friendship with fellow writers and artists, he was quite choosy if not largely ambivalent about the outcome. Yet, he would soon have a friend who would prove a significant connection for his early novels in the influential London publishing arena. When it came to women, once he had overcome his youthful shyness and intense vulnerability, his attitude was very open, he said with an ironic grin.

4

Pamphlets, Poultry and Mysticism

BESIDES HIS NEEDS FOR SOLITUDE, STUART looked for gaiety and diversion after his time in prison and through Iseult met Cecil Salkeld, the artist, poet, playwright and illustrator whose mural triptych *The Triumph of Bacchus* can still be seen on the walls of Davy Byrne's pub in Duke Street, Dublin. Among the figures depicted are Mícheál MacLiammóir, George Bernard Shaw and Myles na gCopaleen. He had attended Dublin's Metropolitan School of Art and was one of the few artists of his era to spend years at the Kunstakademie in Kassel, Germany. His mother was the poet, Blanaid Salkeld. Cecil Salkeld became a friend and neighbour in Wicklow in 1924, when the Stuarts settled in Glencree, and instantly noticed their problematic marriage. Once, when Salkeld visited Iseult in the cottage, she was distraught because Stuart had left after an argument, having locked their food in his room and taken the key. Early on in the year 1924, Stuart gave a public lecture under the auspices of Sinn Féin and Darrell Figgis. Figgis had intrigued him ever since they had been introduced on meeting by chance in the Sinn Féin offices: in fact, Figgis almost knocked him down with his ebullience that Stuart later felt was a false brilliance. Still, Stuart's recollections of Figgis were always those of an admirer for an idol. Figgis was a living legend to Stuart who never lost his fascination with such a person.

Figgis organised the Howth Gunrunning with Erskine Childers prior to the 1916 Rising. He became a fast friend of G.K. Chesterton while working for the publisher, Dent, in London. He had many friends in Dublin, including AE, Arthur Griffith and Michael Collins who appointed him acting chairman of the committee that framed the Irish Constitution in 1922. The young Stuart was enthralled whenever he met Figgis thereafter, not least since he was a poet, novelist, literary journalist and political polemicist, the author of scholarly works on Milton and Blake as well as a notable study of Shakespeare. When Alice Stopford Green suggested to Figgis that Stuart give a lecture, he enthusiastically agreed. Stuart did not want to disappoint Figgis, who limped in to hear him speak. He had lost a leg as a soldier in the Civil War fighting on the pro-Treaty side. Stuart's mingling with such notables as Figgis and Stopford Green, both pro-Treatyites, reveals that even at a young age political affiliation had never been a big issue for him.

By all accounts the lecture was not much of an event and the text reveals a hasty attention to his topic, "Nationality and Culture". He made sure that the sentiments were Republican, and avoided any controversial comment in the wake of the Civil War by remarking that the GPO and the Four Courts "were levelled by English guns". In calling for Ireland to remain no longer a colony of England, he concluded, "it is well for us to remember again after what seems so many years the meaning of, and exult in the name of, Sinn Féin."[1] A year later, Figgis shot himself in London. It was a shock to Stuart as the news filtered back mainly through gossip, as did news of the death of Figgis's mistress, and the suicide of Figgis's wife two years before her husband's. The sorry saga was a final intense confrontation with reality for Stuart in the aftermath of the Civil War, forcing him to make sense of what had happened, especially since Figgis was a relatively young man at 42, and seemed to have so much to live for. When I asked him if he had any premonition as to whether Figgis would die by his own hand, he said that he could not honestly say "yes" or "no".

In the spring of 1924, Cecil Salkeld held a party at which Stuart met Liam O'Flaherty and recalled being struck by his piercing seagull-blue eyes. When O'Flaherty asked about his writing, Stuart replied that he had sent a manuscript that he had begun drafting in prison to an English publisher who returned it with the comment that he should first learn to spell. The working title was "The Sweat of the Martrys" and he had misspelt "Martyrs". O'Flaherty recommended the novel to Edward Garnett, at the London publishing house of Jonathan Cape, who read it and found it faulty.

O'Flaherty was a drinker and womaniser with a Hemingwayesque swagger. He became the ideal racing companion for Stuart who was as obsessed with horses as his new friend. He had fought in the First World War and wrote about it in *The Return of the Brute*. Best known for his Civil War novel, *The Informer*, he is mentioned in Stuart's *Things to Live For* working on a novel, *Skerrett* at the Royal Hotel in Glendalough. He also appears as Seamus Arrochar in Stuart's *The Coloured Dome*. O'Flaherty soon got to like Stuart, six years younger, and, when not in his company, wrote him letters about carousing, womanising, betting, travelling and, of course, writing. O'Flaherty was ever anxious to pursue "any fresh cuties on the horizon".[2] He liked Stuart, the tall young man who was a former Republican soldier and a new poet on the scene, but it was an uneven friendship. O'Flaherty's many parties would provide Stuart with a London bohemia to augment the, at times, less satisfactory Dublin one. In *Black List* he appears under his name and introduces H to a solicitor who says that legally the marriage with Iseult could be annulled since he had been under the age of 18 at the time. Meanwhile, Stuart awaited a legal opinion but was more concerned with his writing than his marriage.

Yeats, as a Free State Senator, sensing an opportunity to institutionalise the Arts, prepared to set up an academy. Funnily enough, Stuart's membership would be deplored in a letter to Yeats from H.O. White, his former tutor. White was sticking by his opinion that Stuart was a dolt. A few years later the professor of French at Trinity College, Dublin, Rudmose-Brown, protested at Stuart's membership of the Royal Irish Academy, which had not deemed the writer Lord Dunsany worthy of the honour. Dunsany of Norman-French ancestry lived in a castle in county Meath. Stuart told me an anecdote about the Black and Tans raiding the castle when his Lordship was away in London. They took bottles of his favourite port and other items while the butler waited in the large entrance hall. As they were leaving, he said to them, "Who shall I say called?" It was an anecdote that Gogarty used to tell.

Stuart was duly honoured with a crown of bay leaves, the time-honoured symbol of poethood. Yeats spoke to the crowded assembly that included Iseult, Maud Gonne and Cecil Salkeld. He compared Stuart, as a poet, with Oliver St John Gogarty, "His genius, if genius it be, is the opposite of Dr Gogarty's". The ceremony took place as part of the Tailteann Games at Ballsbridge on 9 August 1924, when Stuart was 22 years old. His book *We Have Kept the Faith* had been selected by Russell, Robinson and Yeats who conferred the Royal Irish Academy Award which is written of in quasi-comic detail in *Black List*. Patrick J. Tuohy was awarded a medal by Sir John Lavery

RA for his portrait of James Joyce's father, John Stanislaus Joyce. Stephen McKenna declined to attend; a medal honouring his translations of Plotinus was accepted for him by the robust G.K. Chesterton. Stuart found Chesterton's Catholic triumphalist tone overbearing, never spoke well of him and did not like his writings, which I found discordant with my own views. Our discussions naturally ran into disagreement about literary and other matters occasionally.

Stuart, of course, was honoured by Yeats's public endorsement of his talent. Still he felt he had betrayed his friend from the Civil War, Jim Phelan, who was emphatic that the poet must be a figure of dishonour and an outcast so as to achieve a higher degree of perfection for his art and for his life. Phelan would remain a guiding star of Stuart's inner credo for the artist. The power of this doctrine over Stuart gave it the necessary personal resonance that made it an unshakeable belief. When I asked about it he mentioned another source for the concept of the outcast – the Russian writer Vasili Vasilievich Rozanov's book of aphorisms, *Solitaria* and his study of Dostoevsky, *The Legend of the Grand Inquisitor*. Rozanov's impish belligerence appealed to Stuart.

Lennox Robinson became disgruntled over his involvement with Stuart's magazine, *To-morrow,* which caused a breach in their friendship. The magazine lasted for two issues in August and September, 1924. Maud Gonne was among the contributors, with F.R. Higgins, Joseph Campbell and Cecil Salkeld providing illustrations. *To-morrow* published Yeats's "Leda and The Swan", a poem which offended because of its eroticism, and Robinson's "The Madonna of Slieve Dun", the story of a rape victim, Mary, who believes she will become the mother of Christ for his Second Coming. O'Flaherty contributed the story "A Red Petticoat" and Iseult a prose piece entitled "The Poplar Road". Due to the public furore in the press over the contents of the magazine, Robinson dissociated himself from *To-morrow* "never dreaming it would raise such a storm" as did Stuart's co-editor, Cecil Salkeld. The controversy led to Robinson's dismissal as Secretary of the Carnegie Library Committee. The magazine was sold from A.J. Leventhal's bookshop in Dawson Street, Dublin, and sold out its first issue. An extract from the editorial by Stuart and Salkeld shows their youthful pugnacity:

> We proclaim that we can forgive the sinner, but abhor the atheist, and that we count among atheists bad writers and

> Bishops of all denominations.... What devout man can read the Pastorals of our Hierarchy without horror at a style rancid, coarse and vague, like that of our daily papers?[3]

It was widely rumoured that, after the second issue of *To-morrow* (which had to be printed in England because of censorship problems), W.T. Cosgrave intended to have it suppressed.

Yeats had proclaimed his belief in Stuart's future as a writer, based on a few poems and an essay on the Silesian shoemaker and mystic, Jakob Boehme, whose dense esoteric book *Mysterium Magnum* would engage the young poet during his study of the mystics. In my twenties, I asked Stuart whether I should read this book, which I had found listed in the catalogue at the National Library of Ireland. He was non-committal about recommending books, but did point me in the direction of some over the years. By this time I was making up my own mind on such matters and went ahead and read Boehme.

Despite marital difficulties, Stuart and Iseult tried to overcome their differences while living in Glencree. The Campbells became their closest friends in the valley. Joseph Campbell had penned the popular song "My Lagan Love" and was a member of Pound's Imagist group of poets, along with T.E. Hulme, F.S. Flint, Hilda Doolittle and Edward Storer. Stuart's career as a poet was about to be ended just as it had begun to be recognised. He did not find favour with the Imagists and this, coupled with an inability to produce more poetry, caused him to stop writing verse almost completely; poetry would remain a sporadic and infrequent creative process throughout his life. Yeats's estimation of Stuart was very different from that of Pound's who felt that "the worst that could be said was that he was not yet a good poet".[4] Iseult thought highly of her husband's poetic gift but was disappointed as time went on and he began exclusively to write prose fiction. It was yet another source of division and discord. She had been used to the company of the poets, yet as a writer herself realised that the process could not be forced. However, secretly she expected Stuart not only to be a poet, but to be *her* poet.

Iseult began growing herbs and vegetables as well as trees, shrubs and flowering plants. She would become a considerable gardener throughout her life. Stuart built a hermitage that is detailed in *Glory*, a novel from this period. The hermitage, or more accurately the hut, comprised seven sections, including an A-shaped tarred-felt roof. Stuart set it up under a granite rock that overhung a corner of their garden for maximum shelter from the Wicklow weather. He moved Iseult's books from the house to his hut and explored them in a daily ritual of reading and contemplation. He read Blake, Keats and more Dostoevsky. When Yeats sent Iseult a copy of *A Vision* early in 1926, Stuart read it first in a chilly politeness knowing he had pre-empted Iseult's reading of it. For a while they achieved harmony in their daily lives – including going to Mass together and taking the mountain route over the slopes to Glendalough – and might have seemed an ideal and united couple to locals. When Stuart wanted to escape the solitude and Iseult for a day, he drove his Opel Darracq to Dublin, which was less than an hour away.

The effects of his reading are borne lightly in the early novels. While he avoided the literary scene in Dublin, he re-established his love of horse racing and began to bet. He had, as a youth, first placed a bet at a meeting in Bellewstown with his northern uncles who were regular attendees at race meetings. He never went fishing, hunting or shooting and instead became immersed in the communal sport of horse racing. For Stuart, horse racing reflected a paradigm of life and one wonders at his restraint in never writing a complete novel about riders, jockeys, owners, trainers, bookies, tick-tackmen, racegoers and the whole spectacle. In *The High Consistory* (1981) the central character prays to St Thérèse of Lisieux for a glimpse of the winner's name on the eve of a big race meeting. The use of horse racing is not a trivial matter in his fiction. It involves a layer of meaning for reflection and absorption, particularly revealing how fate, chance and certain conditions produce different results. Horse racing becomes involved with a character's fate, will and destiny. Just as there is good and evil in existence there is also good and bad luck, often in matters of life and death.

His own foray into horse ownership was a natural progression. Iseult was someone to whom horses were almost zoo-like creatures; functionless on the landscape and remote from her consciousness. She disliked his betting, especially the accumulator method which will be mentioned later with regard to one of his novels. Stuart was thrifty because of his background and never betted huge sums of money in any event. Neither was the world of racing the totality of his world view. He bought a horse, a two-year-old, Sunnymova (Iseult suggested the name) and he hired a trainer. In the autumn of

1926, Sunnymova was entered in the flat season at the Phoenix Park races in Dublin. Stuart backed his own horse, a rank outsider at 20/1. The horse was among the bottom weights in the race, ran well over five furlongs and was beaten by a neck.

In his hermitage in Glencree, Stuart searched for a correlation to the mystical side of his psyche by reading Evelyn Underhill's, *Mysticism,* a substantial anthology of jottings from many mystics with interpolating commentaries. It was also a particular favourite of Gonne's. Stuart studied the Letters of St Paul, *The Autobiography of a Saint* by St Thérèse of Lisieux and the writings of St Catherine of Siena, whom he yearned to have known: "To be with her must have been to live behind the veil that never lifted." Late in life he wrote a long essay about his esoteric explorations, in part theological, in part scientific, entitled *The Abandoned Snail Shell* (1987). In *Things to Live For* there is a telling remark: "Hermits have made more adventurous lives than soldiers or gamblers. One can open one's arms to life more widely in a cell than anywhere else perhaps." He defined mystical experience as paradoxical and yet being "most personal in which the personal consciousness is in a sense lost ... To believe that God speaks to us is not necessarily mystical but is probably delusional".[5] This is derived from the Spanish mystic John of the Cross's *The Living Flame of Love:* "Faith is darkness to the intellect."[6] And also "God's purpose in bestowing corporal visions is not that a person desire and become attached to them".[7]

A marriage fraught with disharmony and stress needed periods of absence; Stuart would retreat within the walled perimeter of the cottage to his hermitage, allowing himself and Iseult vital hours away from each other. Leaving aside the age gap of eight years, from what he told me I felt that the couple were diverging almost from the first night they met. Stuart himself, with hindsight, consistently confided to me that the marriage was a good marriage as marriages go. However, I realise that he did not want to malign Iseult's memory. It may not be unfair to say that she took a chance on him. She seemed determined to marry a *littérateur* since such unions were part of her milieu. Although Stuart had married passively, he was also as much in love with this beauty, Iseult Gonne, as fascinated by her.

Lily was with them at the birth of Ian, a son born 5 October 1926. The healthy child was baptised in the church where his parents had been married. Stuart and Iseult had attended the wedding of Seán MacBride and Catalina Bulfin in the same church the previous year, in January 1925. Ian is mentioned in *Black List*: H "was unexpectedly delighted with the baby and proud of how it responded to him".[8] The use of the word "unexpectedly" is revealing.

Lily came to live in Glencree and became a wonderful grandmother, as if her better self had emerged from the traumatic life she experienced as a young widowed mother in Australia and in her flawed marriage to Henry Clements. She had not been impressed either way by her son's poems, their publication or his forays into the literary world. According to Stuart she feared he might expose through his writing some of the dark past she wished to forget. Instead she blended with Iseult, bonded with her grandson and found a new life. Stuart experienced fatherly pride but felt shut out by his wife. Iseult doted on her son Ian who would always be her favourite child.

The domestic scene of mother, grandmother, father and baby son meant cramped conditions in the cottage. Gonne, "Madame", solved the problem miraculously, as only an injection of money can in such a situation. She sold Ballinagoneen cottage in 1928 and bought them a castle. Well, at least it looked from a distance like a castle but as Yeats and Georgie had found out ten years previously with their castle at Thoor Ballylea in County Galway, there were practical problems. Whenever I mentioned the castle I quickly surmised that he did not want to be reminded about it too much. The castle was the setting for many scenes that are part of the Stuart myth, but I strongly associate it with Iseult. My first visit there was in the 1990s since somehow I never wanted to intrude before then because of his diffidence about the place. When I did gain some access, at the present owner's behest, my scrutiny was total and absorbed, including the garden and extensive outhouses.

Laragh Castle, a stronghold of the 1798 rebellion, would become the model for the castle in Stuart's *The Great Squire,* his final novel published before the Second World War. Laragh Castle may in the fullness of time be restored as a Francis Stuart museum since it is a listed building. The castle resembles a simple church-like structure with an imposing turret and a prominent porch and is on a byroad off the Laragh road that slopes into Glendalough village in County Wicklow. The castle is crenellated at turret top and atop the second storey. The outhouses were obviously vast in their heyday, comprising the one-time soldiers' quarters and the sturdy enclosure known as the prisoners' yard. The castle is surrounded by ten acres of sloping landscape among many beech and elm trees. Through the stone archway at the end of the entrance lane is St John's Anglican Church. Shortly after Stuart, Iseult, Lily and baby Ian moved in, they converted as much of the outhouses as were necessary for laying sheds for hens, purchased a copy of *Poultry Encyclopaedia* and set to repairing the enclosing high wall. Stuart traded in his old car for a new Peugeot 201 saloon.

After the initial excitement, the castle had feasibility problems, but still they were pleased with its romantic medieval look. Their setting resembled that of many of the Anglo-Irish who lived isolated lives in the emerging Free State, except that the Stuarts were Catholic gentry. Stuart could have cultivated the image of being Anglo-Irish with some justification in respect of his Northern Ireland ancestry; however, in point of fact such identity did not interest him, he admitted. To see him as a novice novelist, horse breeder, chicken farmer and bohemian is closer to actuality, he said to me, though he always disliked the term "bohemian", finding it disreputable by association with some writers and artists whose work he disliked. He had very definite aesthetic tastes; there was nothing personal usually in his castigation of certain writers whom he divided into two groups, either "encouraging and inspiring" or "offensive and disreputable".

Lily soon came to be known as "Mrs Clements" in the village and enjoyed making acquaintances with local people whom she could drop in on for a chat and a cup of tea. She would regularly set off after breakfast, having unlocked the chickens from the laying sheds, and go into the village to post a letter to Janet or get a few groceries, with the intention of meeting up with anyone and everyone. In this respect she was more outgoing than Iseult who, locally, gave the impression of being the lady of the manor. The Stuarts had a gardener who helped Iseult in season with the cultivation of vegetables and especially fruit trees. A housemaid was engaged to cook and clean.

On more adventurous occasions any of the household could have a day out in Dublin which was a pleasant bus ride by the recently established St Kevin's Bus Service. The journey began uphill from Laragh through Annamoe valley, Roundwood, past the Roundwood lakes to the heather-clad Calary plain, then ascended between the Little and Great Sugarloaf mountains until finally arriving at the seaside town of Bray before entering the outskirts of the city.

There was a turret room in Laragh Castle with a deal floor that Stuart made into a study and here he generally wrote in the mornings.

The main section of the castle had two floors: the upper one had a large bedroom and two small bedrooms. The ground floor had a kitchen, a large living room and two small rooms, one of which served as a playroom for Ian when he became a toddler. Very soon after moving in, they discovered an infestation of rats and Stuart got a shotgun to control the situation. He shot many rats and claimed that there was one he would not kill, having mis-hit the creature so many times that they had got to know each other. With three adults it seemed that they could easily become efficient and economically self-sufficient from horticulture and chicken farming. They often consulted with Aunt Janet in County Meath because of her vast experience with poultry. Stuart would in time rear prize-winning pullets, sell the eggs and the chickens far and wide and hire a farm manager, Hilda Burnett. By 1930 he would win a silver medal in the Department of Agriculture competition at the Royal Dublin Society "for the pullet non-sitting-breed having the highest winter record of first grade eggs". This particular hen's laying had been monitored over a year during which time it had only failed on four days to lay an egg. The award gave him satisfaction long afterwards and he was always happy to fetch it from a drawer to show me the large medal on a ribbon.

Meanwhile, after consistent study of the mystics, he wrote an essay that he subsequently destroyed. However, he went on to publish some of his findings in a pamphlet, *Mystics and Mysticism* (1929), referred to already. It is a sharp contrast with his life as poultry farmer, battling to avoid loss of fowl through disease and discussing with Miss Burnett how to increase egg yield. Yeats arrived for a holiday and seemed fascinated by their life in Laragh Castle but, in correspondence to others, said he found Stuart self-absorbed. Stuart told me that the older poet's intense intellectualism and literary talk made him uncomfortable as usual, even in his home. Yeats as a guest could not curb his instinct for talk and interminable discussion. Yeats always loved being in full flight of conversation and Stuart was inclined to shut him down with ponderous silences. Stuart said that he might have enjoyed his company more if he could have indulged in ordinary small talk, but Yeats seemed incapable of this. However, Yeats would champion Stuart's early novels unreservedly. Nevertheless, the two writers were growing further apart. It may sound ungracious, but the less Stuart saw of Yeats the happier he was living in Laragh Castle, while Iseult always looked forward to his visits.

5

Pilgrim, Novelist, Hedonist

According to Stuart's recollections of the spring of 1930, "Madame" and Iseult set off for France to visit the grotto and the spring at Massabielle, near Lourdes, with him tagging along out of curiosity. He had studied the accounts of the 15 apparitions of Bernadette Soubirous, the 14-year-old who had a vision of Mary, the Mother of Jesus, and who would die at the age of 35 from asthma, in an enclosed order of nuns. He read Bernadette's story, written in "the pure, near-manic clarity that accompanies states of possession experienced by poets, mystics, and madmen, and which he himself responded to obsessively".[1] According to Stuart she may have been visualising the experience of her own hidden self. When he met a crippled girl named Maggie Bradley, who was dying, he found himself drawn to her. He became a *brancardier* (stretcher-bearer) and this experience supplied some elements for his first novel. He would also write about Lourdes in *Things to Live For, Pilgrimage* and *Black List, Section H*.

Much later in the 1970s Stuart would comment in a letter: "My novels are certainly not 'Catholic' novels. That is not to say that I have completely rejected the Catholic Church as have almost all serious Irish writers. As the hero of my last novel says: 'My psyche is *au fond* a believing, not a skeptical one.' "[2] This was a theme that became central to our discussions, though I always felt that his utterances on such an absolute subject were never definitive. In this respect I found Stuart mystical; in other words he attested to something beyond life, some assertion as to the concept of God, using simple rather than pious language in an attempt to convey the heights of his tranquillity. For a chaotic young man this was helpful to me. Some other writers whom I got to know also visited him: Dermot Bolger, Michael

O'Loughlin, Conleth O'Connor and Paul Durcan found the same sanctuary in his presence. He could inject a sort of beatitude into a discussion, yet behind this one felt that there were intense conflicts in his psyche. When I knew him he seemed to have achieved the ability to exude and reach peace beyond his own personal chaos; at least so I presumed in his company. What his other states of mind were I could only gauge from his works and penetrate into these through our discussions.

He was certainly not a modern Joris Karl Huysmans who wrote a bible of decadence, *À Rebours* whose hero is a disillusioned bohemian, so much so that he never leaves his house. Huysmans also set a novel in Lourdes, *Là Bas,* and lived near a monastery at the end of his days, searching for "the art of Catholicism, the mystical. There one encounters extraordinary things about reality and life, frightening states of the soul, battles that the profane have no idea of." [3] This brief aside on Huysmans was typical of my reading at the time which I could share with Stuart at greater length and who would indulge me until he wished to change the subject.

Maggie Bradley touched Stuart deeply, forcing a complete reconsideration of the mysticism which he had read during their days together. He arrived at the conclusion that Bernadette was not a fraud because of her mystical experience and, while he did not know what this meant for him, he was certain that "reality can express itself as well in fiction as in fact". This would become an unshakeable belief for him. Stuart saw language, even ordinary conversation, as multilayered in the way C.G. Jung had explored the subconscious and the collective unconscious. What also appealed to him in accepting Maggie's sincerity of faith was that it had come through her sufferings, which was also true of Julian of Norwich whose *Revelations of Divine Love* resulted from the experience of a near fatal illness. Similarly, John of the Cross had his revelations during a period of debility while imprisoned in a dark cell by his fellow Carmelite friars. His work survived the censorship of the Spanish Inquisition. Also, St Paul of the New Testament, whose mystical experiences are a major written source of Christianity, endured a stigma, "a thorn was given me in the flesh" (2 Cor 12: 7), which is hinted at in his vigorously written letters. Stuart found it impossible to escape the effects of his studies of the mystics. Agnostics would possibly see this as his need for a "Big Daddy" in the sky, having never known his own father.

Stuart, up to the end of his life, remained enigmatic as to his concept of God: "If there is a divine creator let us say that one side of him is extremely ruthless. He has compassion, undoubtedly, but let us just say that his spirit is very complex."[4] He qualified this a decade previously in *The High Consistory* (1981): "Any deity would, I suppose, have to share every intense experience, happy or painful, of each of his creatures to rank as a personal God." His notion of God was shifting and never dogmatic.

At Lourdes, Gonne immersed herself regularly in the bathhouse at the grotto, hoping to find a cure for her rheumatism. Stuart annoyed Iseult by pointing out that Yeats had once written love poems to a woman whose bones now ached. Iseult, for her part, mocked Yeats as "silly old Willie". Stuart and Iseult began to have little time for the myth of Yeats and Gonne since they were too close to them to believe in it. Stuart as usual found travelling with Gonne infuriating and felt desolate with Iseult because of their barren sex life. Yet he accompanied them to a farmhouse at the foot of the Pyrenees in the village of Arrens after they had completed the pilgrimage. Back at Laragh Castle in the turret room, he worked feverishly at what would be his first novel and sent it off to Edward Garnett of Cape in London. Impatient for a reply and worried lest it might even be lost in the post, he followed after it. Unable to muster up the courage to make contact with Garnett in London, Stuart went on to Paris. His sudden splurge into fiction was not inexplicable, as he mentioned to me so many years later. The problem of his recalcitrant and constantly vanishing muse, as I have noted, rather naturally forced him into the novel form. He was also desperate, in the shadow of the milieu of the literary revival, to make his mark as a writer.

I was fascinated when he told me the following account of his visits to Paris at this time, which he vividly recalled. He got a room at the Hotel Terminus, Gare Saint-Lazare. After a visit to the barber for a shave, he went to the Café Dôme on the Boulevard Montparnasse for a Pernod with ice and soda. There he met two young women who later came back to his room at the hotel and for days they indulged in an orgy of drinking and sexual activity. He also began to read D.H. Lawrence and would soon be compared with him by Compton Mackenzie and the critic R. Ellis Roberts. Lawrence believed that sexual experience revealed "the immediate, non-mental knowledge of the divine otherness". The elaboration of his theory goes on:

> And God the Father, the Inscrutable, the Unknowable, we know in the flesh, in Woman. She is the door for our in-going and our out-coming. In her we go back to the Father; but like the witnesses of the transfiguration, blind and unconscious. [5]

The orgy in Paris took place because Stuart's sexual needs were unfulfilled. He felt negatively

> influenced by Iseult's way of keeping the sexual act from impinging too clearly on everyday consciousness. For her it was a weakness, an aberration, best confined to night and darkness, or disguised by musical accompaniment, never indulged in too deliberately but, if possible, slipped into by chance and quickly forgotten.[5]

In the absence of an equally detailed report on her side of the story, one presumes they were sexually incompatible. Around this time, he wondered, "Was there a poison in the sap in his cells that prevented him accepting the natural and humble task of staying with Iseult and, if not loving her with the love that was inner revelation, trying to reassure her?"[6]

In Laragh, before the onset of summer, his novel came back with recommendations for rewriting. Stuart decided to return to Paris via London, calling in on the way to introduce himself to Garnett and elicit any advice about how to begin revision. He told me that he then made a second visit to Lourdes wanting to experience the grotto and spring without the discomfort of Gonne. On the return journey through Paris, he showed the manuscript to the poet and critic, Thomas MacGreevy, who was part of the adulatory James Joyce circle and would become the dedicatee of Stuart's novel. MacGreevy was ten years Stuart's senior. They had first formed an acquaintance while residing at the same lodgings of Hester Travers-Smith in Dublin. MacGreevy would later be a neglected poet in Ireland after halcyon literary days in Paris, and would obtain a sinecure as Director of the National Gallery. He was a close friend of the Joyce's and a kind of servant to Shem, as Joyce was nicknamed by his friends. MacGreevy, residing at the Hotel Corneille, found the manuscript eminently publishable. In any event, he may have liked the evolving Catholic theme that is by no means dominant. Encouraged by MacGreevy's favourable reading of the novel and armed with further advice, Stuart rewrote and resubmitted the manuscript to Edward Garnett.

Garnett's wife, Constance Garnett, translated Russian writers into English, including Dostoevsky whom Stuart had read in her translations. In Stuart's novel, the writing smacks of Garnett's editorial veto. The *raison d'être* being that, if Stuart was deriving his style from Hemingway, why not make it better than pastiche Hemingway. It must be Hemingway as Hemingway might even approve. Hence the writing is finely wrought in his first novel. As he awaited an answer from Garnett, it became apparent that Iseult's writing career had ceased. None of her illustrious male writer friends, except Arthur Symons, had made any effort to promote her. Symons had tried to interest the French critic Henry D. Davray in her work since she had been the central inspiration for Symon's play, *Tristan and Iseult*. Stuart was ambivalent and knew that she had, to all intents and purposes, ceased writing for the foreseeable future.

Stuart had worked all hours to meet Garnett's Olympian standards for the novel. The domestic tension this caused was heightened by his absence while gallivanting in Paris, leaving Lily and Iseult with Ian. The novel, entitled *Women and God*, had ultimately been published through O'Flaherty's recommendation. The print run was 1,500, of which 600 were wasted. Once more Stuart shrugged off domestic responsibilities and decided to leave Laragh for Paris to spend the £50 advance – a lot of money at the time. And spend it he did. He had become obsessed with the French capital. Paris at the turn of the 1920s was still the home of avant-garde modernism. French writers and poets, such as Jean Cocteau, Paul Éluard and the diffuse elder, Paul Valéry, witnessed the comings and goings of long- and short-term celebrity residents such as Picasso, Le Corbusier, Hemingway, Scott Fitzgerald, Edith Wharton, Gertrude Stein, Ezra Pound and James Joyce. The composers Stravinsky, Satie, Honegger and Ravel found common ground in Paris with visiting Americans such as George Gershwin and Cole Porter. The young Sam Beckett would soon rent a hotel room, as Stuart had done, and come up with a first novel, *Dream of Fair to Middling Women*, that would not be published until Beckett found unprecedented fame. They would meet the following year in Dublin.

Now footloose and fancy-free in Paris, Stuart strolled along the boulevards and lounged in his favourite cafés – the Coupole, the Select and the Rotonde – like a character in his novel, and kept company with strangers. One evening in the Café Dôme as he sat nursing a fierce hangover with two Americans while the barman Monsieur Larry served Pernods and Bières Cassis, a thin man of neat attire with thick lens spectacles was writing on a paper napkin at a nearby table. It was James Joyce. Stuart was bashful but one of the American women was loud, if not gregarious, and indicating Joyce insisted that Stuart go over to him. When Stuart reluctantly introduced himself, Joyce was genteel and repeated Stuart's name as if trying to recall something. Then Joyce disarmed his polite intruder by saying he had read a poem, if he remembered correctly, by H. Stuart in *The Transatlantic Review,* a journal edited in Paris by Ford Madox Ford. That said, Stuart's propriety was to leave with cordial greetings as the Americans voiced sentiments of homage. However much over the years I sought further information on the meeting with Joyce, Stuart was always dismissive. I also heard him mention this anecdote at a public lecture and noticed that he seemed quite nonchalant about what must not have been a big event in his life, in that Joyce was not an idol of Stuart's by any means, in fact the opposite.

Years later Stuart had forgotten the dialogue with Joyce, which was not significant in any event, he claimed, because of the brevity of the meeting. Joyce had an encyclopaedic mind and may have recalled the members of the Irish Academy of Letters and, if so, did remember Harry Stuart or more likely H. Stuart. Stuart had not read *Ulysses* at that time except for extracts and had no interest in *Tales Told of Shem and Shaun* and other advance portions of *Finnegans Wake* which were appearing in the Paris magazine *transition*. The fact that Joyce recognised Stuart by name is significant – even psychic. Whether he registered it or not, Stuart was "known" at the time by the famous Irish writers of his day: Yeats, Shaw, O'Casey, Augusta Gregory, George Moore, James Stephens, James Joyce, Pádraic Colum, George Russell (AE), Oliver St John Gogarty, Edward Dunsany, Seumas O'Sullivan and Lennox Robinson.

Stuart went on a mind-expanding drunken spree in Paris, and not for the first time found, in the ethyl of alcohol, drinking insights that he would comment on in his novels. He once told me that he believed that alcohol was a diluted relic of the ambrosia of the Gods. To drink some slowly in moderation was to enter into a realm of sanctity where a different sort of communication with reality might begin.

But, he added, with much laughter, when you return from this stupor you may not be able to remember the messages that you have received. He also believed that the purer and high proof alcohol such as Black Bushmills entered the blood stream and areas of the brain, taking over the body and negating the central nervous system. There followed a kind of possession and unparalleled relaxation where he could think out certain questions that obsessed him. When he spoke about alcohol he sounded like some scientist or doctor who used himself for experiments with a sacred, even dangerous, substance. I admit that some of his theories went beyond my understanding, but made for great talk over a few glasses of cheer.

Back in Ireland, he was late for the birth of his daughter, Katherine Frances, born on 31 May 1931. She would be known as Kay. The death of his first child, Dolores, had kept him furtively away from Iseult during the births of Ian and Kay. It was a reaction to the trauma of the death of his infant daughter but might also be seen as indifference. In *Black List* the children get the most cursory of treatment. Of Kay, he wrote, "Katherine was born and H's novel appeared. The baby girl, darker than Ian, had also a more placid nature and was less in need of H's tranquillising effect".[8]

Iseult and Lily were and would remain the real parents of the children, with Stuart becoming a progressively absentee father. On one level of consensus both Iseult and Stuart would have almost agreed, if they agreed on anything at this period, that their marriage was failing. Stuart would only be able to validate this and overcome it ten years later when he met a woman with whom he would settle into a long and lasting relationship. Iseult was undecided as to what would happen between "Grim", as she called Stuart, and herself. They would never divorce and in reality remained man and wife at a remove that emotionally, and later geographically, increased. Their children would have two parents, two loving grandmothers and Iseult would be their mainstay even though, as her diary proves, she found it emotionally difficult. When I interviewed Ian Stuart, a father himself twice over, his memory of his upbringing was one of goodness and happiness. The same can be said of Kay who remarked in conversation as a mature adult on "her father's apparently wayward life".

Women and God was published by Jonathan Cape in 1931, four months after the birth of Kay. Stuart took a flat in Dublin, away from

Laragh, and indulged himself in much drinking. When I suggested that he loathed domesticity, he shrugged, but admitted they were troubled times for him. "Youth," he added. He was apprehensive about fatherhood and about being an author. At Davy Byrne's, his friend A.J. Leventhal, who had sold the seditious pamphlet *Tomorrow* from his Dawson Street bookshop, introduced him to Samuel Beckett. Other friends, such as Liam O'Flaherty, Arland Ussher, Joseph Campbell the poet, and Cecil Salkeld made up a lively bohemian coterie. When times were dull, one of their harmless pastimes was a game with stamp paper. A competitor would lick the paper, then run and jump as high as possible in an attempt to stick the paper onto the ceiling. Stuart's height often won the day. Other times Beckett's wiry athleticism won, while A.J. (Con) Leventhal was a poor third.

When some or all of them met after a day's racing, and winnings had been good, they would occupy a table at Jammet's on nearby Nassau Street. Beckett never went to the races, Stuart recalled. Here they might catch sight of William Orpen or Jack Yeats, brother of W.B., with a group including Pádraic Colum and Austin Clarke. Stuart was casually acquainted with Colum and they had met briefly in Paris a few times. He attended some of Jack Yeats's Thursday "at homes" at the painter's studio at the corner of Fitzwilliam Square. Otherwise, Stuart and his friends frequented the Hibernian Buttery when dining out and if times were lean, the Dolphin Hotel where its owner Jack Nugent, a portly man, well known for his savage wit and knowledge of horses, dominated the bar. When they returned from dinner and were usually looking for more drink, the heavyweight champion boxer Jack Doyle sometimes joined them. Beckett was never part of these gastronomic excursions, but became a friend of Stuart's. Fate set them on different paths in literature and life. Stuart recalled that Salkeld, O'Flaherty, Leventhal, Doyle and the Campbells were all heavy drinkers at the time also.

Jack Doyle was the kind of person whom Stuart admired because of his risk-taking nature which often ended in disaster. Doyle's disqualification in a fight with Welsh boxer Jack Petersen became one of the high points in his career when crowds gathered in the streets of Dublin waiting for confirmation of the news from White City, London, greeting it with a disappointment equal to the boxer's own depression. Despite this, Doyle, a Corkman, remained a legend, marrying an heiress of the Dodge empire, who soon divorced him. He then married a Mexican actress, Movita. They formed a variety stage act for some years, but she left him for Marlon Brando. According to Stuart, Doyle ended up in dire poverty, but they lost contact with each other in any event.

Stuart remained indifferent and kept distant from other contemporaries of this period such as Peadar O'Donnell who had published four novels. Sean O'Faolain triumphantly sent a copy of his first novel *Bird Alone* to James Joyce who belatedly acknowledged its arrival saying that he read very few novels. Frank O'Connor, whom according to Stuart, Yeats and AE had taken under their wing, had done well with a collection of stories, *Guests of the Nation* and was working on a novel, *The Saint and Mary Kate.* Stuart would retain a lifelong antipathy to O'Connor and O'Faolain, while being less dismissive of O'Donnell because of his revolutionary experiences in the War of Independence and the Civil War.

Among the uncertainties of Stuart's life there were also certainties. He was moving or pushing aside the mantle of fatherhood. He was embarking on a prolific and extremely bizarre career compared to other novelists. And in retrospect from his Berlin Diary of a decade later, he commented on this period,

> Then Laragh. The Poultry. Lack of money that was acute. Beginning to write novels. Working too much. Too isolated and the reaction of hectic plunging into the world. The mad vain search for fulfilment through such people as ...[9]

He then lists the names of women with whom he admits having fleeting but intense affairs, not all necessarily of a sexual nature.

His commentary is accurate: he had become a father, a published author, a bohemian and a runaway husband, but he admitted to me that none of these identities were his real self as it would emerge in later maturity. When he returned to Laragh from his Dublin sorties, he found Iseult despairing of him because she was not resigned to abandonment and part-time desertion. Lily said little as usual. On this occasion there were letters for him from London. Opening them, he found press cuttings from Jonathan Cape. He had foolishly expected rave reviews. As if unknown to himself he had let out a first novel containing a thinly veiled report on the author's present welfare or lack of it. The influences on the book were plainly stamped on the much rewritten sentences. The reviews were bad. The hallowed bible of book reviews, the *Times Literary Supplement*, was almost schoolmasterly in its censure. The young man was dejected. By his own account, he was unwilling ever to write another novel. He would in fact write another 25 novels. His motor car had broken down on the way to Laragh so he wanted to leave almost as soon as he had arrived in order to rescue it. He had become his own mechanic and collected necessary items for repairing the car.

After savouring a domestic scene not to his liking, he returned to his other life in Dublin, moving between extremes of mood, between company and solitude. For many months he went into crisis, he told me, and drank far too much.

6

Some Early Success

STUART'S FIRST NOVEL *WOMEN AND GOD,* which sounds like a D.H. Lawrence title, is stylistically indebted to Ernest Hemingway as has already been mentioned. Another comparison maybe made with F. Scott Fitzgerald since *Women and God* is set among the idle rich who find time heavy on their hands in Paris. They are on "the gaudiest spree" of that period which Fitzgerald named "the Jazz Age". To understand the milieu of *Women and God,* I read it along with other novels of the time: *Women in Love* (Lawrence), *The Sun Also Rises* (Hemingway), *Tender is the Night* (Fitzgerald) and *Vile Bodies* (Waugh). The heroes and heroines of Hemingway and Fitzgerald are doomed to the faded glory of their failed lives, defying death and breakdown with only their courage to assist them. In *Women in Love,* Lawrence's characters leave England for the snowy Alps and are ultimately in love with the icy death of the peaks. Waugh's bright young things are also idle, wealthy and destructive and live up to his condemnatory title.

Laura Caddell, the heroine of *Women and God,* might be at home in any of the above except that her breakdown proves to be some kind of breakthrough. The novel was prophetic of what would happen in Stuart's life many years later, after the Second World War, when he asked Iseult to accept another woman into their household in Laragh in a *ménage à trois.* This I found startling and when Stuart heard my remarks he was not surprised. He said that writing novels involved him in bizarre kinds of wish-fulfilment and augury which was reflected in what actually happened to him later. Naturally, faced with reading 20 and more of Stuart's novels when I got to know him became an exciting adventure because of my obvious fascination with him as a writer.

I distinctly recall reading *Women and God* during a long train journey and noticed that it had few authorial intrusions, as was the fashion of the 1930s, so as to let the characters speak. The scenes take place in less than a week. The events are propelled forward through a well-written framework of dialogue. Also, in imitation of the avant-garde of the time, the novel shows no major events with the exception of Stuart's denouement in the old-fashioned sense when one of the characters is miraculously cured. The novel is cinematic in form after the manner of Bely's *Petersburg*, Joyce's *Ulysses* and Faulkner's *As I Lay Dying*, novels that I revered in my early twenties. The religious orthodoxy of *Women and God* is intrusive in the novel, especially when it is out of character with some of the main protagonists. However, it is true to its author, reflecting the crisis he experienced while contemplating the mystics and spiritual writers. He was enduring the ordeal of painful investigation into life, death, women and God and unable to find inner peace. He reflected the unhappiness of his novel's characters without any of the hope that one them, Elizabeth Bailey had found. As he began to forget about the bad reviews, he registered the danger of lying to one's self in fiction and began to hate his first book.

He was not alone in this: MacGreevy, the dedicatee of *Women and God*, who had only seen an early version, wrote a year after its publication to Yeats: "I hated Harry Stuart's novel. But he took my disapproval like a charitable Catholic instead of a merely faithful one. He's writing very well I think." Stuart was actually writing very well. His next two novels would prove that MacGreevy's comments from Paris were fairly accurate. If one takes into account his father's suicide and his neglectful mother and stepfather, it might be expected that Stuart would become a writer obsessed with father and son relationships. But he never did; nor was he obsessed with mourning and melancholia as a theme. In this respect he is not a Gothic writer, though he did publish one Gothic novel, *The Great Squire*.

As mentioned earlier, Ernest Hemingway influenced Stuart's first novel, *Women and God*. Hemingway's father killed himself with a gun, as Hemingway did in 1961, the year Stuart began writing his best-known and most reprinted work, *Black List, Section H*. While Hemingway might be explained from a Freudian perspective and from Otto Rank's psychoanalytic theories of anxiety and trauma, Stuart is not as easily classifiable. Hemingway's novella *The Old Man and the Sea* is about hooking the ultimate big fish. In the moment of failure, the hero says: "Man can be destroyed but not defeated."[1] The "tough guy" image of Hemingway was modified by his suicide. Stuart has told the present writer that he never considered suicide as a personal option. He was emphatic on this point, but understood how, in extreme circumstances, a person could see such an action as a dire but inevitable outcome. He did not moralise about this situation. The theme, as presented in a few of his novels, will be discussed in a later chapter.

With the commercial failure of *Women and God* Jonathan Cape had such little interest in hearing about his plans for another novel that Stuart began to have serious doubts about his talent as a prose writer. These doubts would remain a constant demon in his writing. Late in life he commented, "I realise my prose is awkward. I don't try to smooth it out. But it expresses for me what Heidegger calls 'the thing to hand'". The influential critic, Frank Swinnerton, had buried *Women and God* critically in the *Times Literary Supplement*. Swinnerton's review is justified in panning the miraculous recovery of Elizabeth Bailey that is too daring a plot device. Without it the novel would be a parable on decadent bohemianism. *Women and God* is not the singular first novel that, say, Wyndham Lewis's *Tarr* is, a book that Stuart admired and recommended me to read and which I too found to be singular. However, Stuart's intentions were honest and his obsession with the sacred and profane in life would not end with the assumed failure of *Women and God*. He recalled, "I found and opened the reviews. Few novels can have had such shockingly bad ones. I had craved for success. It was a knock all right".

Stuart agreed that he had not reached the spiritual peace claimed for some of the characters in the novel. He pursued decadent bohemian paths, well worn by heroes of his youth; writers and poets such as Gérard de Nerval, Arthur Rimbaud and Paul Verlaine. I was reading the novels of Joris Karl Huysmans at the time and mentioned Huysmans' final relinquishment of decadence that came through overpowering feelings of personal and universal evil of which he felt a part but wished to escape. In Huysmans' case there was a dilemma, in the words of a contemporary Barbey d'Aurevilly who saw his life going towards "the mouth of the pistol or to the foot of the Cross".[2] Stuart said that he could understand such a tension as Huysmans', but he had moved beyond such a crisis. Stuart's quest has some similarities to Huysmans', but was never as conventionally orthodox as the reformed Huysmans who was full of personal recrimination if not personal negation. Huysmans became a hermit annexed to a monastery, somewhat like the aging Franz Liszt. Stuart often mentioned William Blake to me. I knew Blake's aphorism "that the road to excess leads to the palace of wisdom" and Stuart, who knew some of Blake's poetry by heart, recited a short poem of Blake's,

What is it men in women do require?
The lineaments of Gratified Desire.
What is it women do in men desire?
The lineaments of Gratified Desire.

There are many different types of religious writer. Stuart adapted Christian terminology for his own purposes. While the influence of the Gospels is felt in some of the novels, it is a gentle influence of the Gospels without a prescribed or rigid theology. He was always careful to emphasise this point. Later in life he wrote a long essay after studying a dissident cleric, Edward Schillebeeckx. Stuart's final novel, *A Compendium of Lovers,* states that "If the Gospels are in a secret or esoteric language, as the cosmos appears to its explorers in mathematical equations, then I could translate it and make an intoxicating story. That was not the difficulty. The problem was to at least make the suggestion that they might be also true not seem to slip into fantasy."[3] When I questioned him about scripture he referred to Maggie Bradley in *Black List.* "Reality was what involved one most," he said. He believed that the Gospels have the impact of reality since they reflect reality, but added that he did not know if they are true. He was never definitive, as I have said earlier, but he was not nihilistic. Nor was he evangelical or fundamentalist; he read the Gospels and the Bible regularly, but not to the exclusion of other sacred books.

Jonathan Cape did not want anything to do with his second novel entitled *Pigeon Irish* – a traditional response even from a reputable publisher when an author admits that his debut novel has produced dismal sales. Stuart's literary agent, Curtis Brown, tried other London publishers and eventually sent it back to him. Through the friendly entreaties of the irascible Liam O'Flaherty, he was introduced to Victor Gollancz. Gollancz was Jewish, based at Henrietta

Street in the bustling Covent Garden district of London, and was proving himself a maverick publisher. He had lured O'Flaherty away from Jonathan Cape. Stuart found the first meeting with Gollancz warm but not very reassuring since he was not offered a drink, he told me. O'Flaherty had told him that the offer of a drink was Gollancz's seal of approval for a new author. Drink or no drink, in due course Gollancz accepted the novel and that was the beginning of an exceedingly fruitful relationship.

He contacted Stuart to ask if Yeats might review the novel. Yeats eventually wrote Gollancz a letter of praise, but did not review *Pigeon Irish*. Some of the letter was used as publicity. The novel was reviewed on the front page of the *New York Times Book Review*.[4] There were also good reviews in English newspapers, including the *Spectator, New Statesman, Nation, New English Weekly, Time and Tide,* and all by opinion-making critics such as Compton Mackenzie and the eminent biographer L.A.G. Strong. The novel was a success and reached a second imprint within six months, earning over £300 pounds in royalties on top of the advance.

Pigeon Irish is unashamedly allegorical, quasi-mystical and based on actual Irish Civil War events when the Four Courts in Dublin were besieged by Free State troops. The leaders of the siege, Rory O'Connor, Liam Mellows, Richard Barrett and Joseph McKelvey, were captured and executed in Mountjoy Jail on 8 December 1922 in reprisal for the shooting of a pro-Treaty TD Seán Hales the previous day. Their execution is passionately deplored, but not in the partisan tone which Civil War fiction usually reveals: being for one side or the other. The execution orders were signed by the Free State Minister for Home Affairs, Kevin O'Higgins. Five years later O'Higgins was shot in reprisal: it has often been imputed that Seán MacBride was indirectly involved in the shooting, but the killers were Archie Doyle, Tim Murphy and Bill Gannon.

Stuart's Civil War in *Pigeon Irish* is at once mythical, factual and futuristic; this might seem overloaded for one novel, but such are the contents. The pigeons talk to each other, which is not very effective, and carry messages of the war's progress. General Frank Allen, the narrator, reads St Catherine of Siena's letters about how she helped a soldier sentenced to death to face his execution with sublime peace. This is a valid detail since the book follows a similar path. A cleric named Porteous makes a prediction for General Allen's future; it will involve "an utter stripping away of all that you value most ... that was to be not an actual execution of the body but the loss of all that was most valuable".[5] Stuart's narration sounds ultra-democratic in the face of anarchy. The discipline of both factions in the war depends on shifting loyalties of command and control. Volatile revolution and incipient civil war are the obvious consequences of too many generals in dissent over the methods for commanding undisciplined soldiers. When it comes to military anarchy, Stuart begins to hate the armed conflict in his novel as shown by the tone of the writing. At least this was what he implied when I questioned him about it.

Iseult was the dedicatee of *Pigeon Irish*. She reserved judgement, saying little or nothing, as did Lily. Aunt Janet gallantly bought a copy and read it. She had always encouraged Harry, who was now becoming better known as the novelist Francis Stuart. The poet H. Stuart would be silent for many years to come after the main flourish of work which came into print between 1924–26 in *To-morrow, The Transatlantic Review, The Chapbook, The Dublin Magazine* and *Poetry* (Chicago). These amounted to 13 poems, representing only seven new poems since the publication of his collection *We Have Kept the Faith*. Around this time, Samuel Beckett would utter a half-truth in a review of *Recent Irish Poetry*: "Mr Francis Stuart is of course best known as a novelist, but he writes verse."[6] When Beckett's comment appeared in print, Stuart had not written any verse for ten years.

Liam O'Flaherty visited Laragh in the spring of 1932 and stayed at the Royal Hotel in Glendalough. According to Stuart, he made a pass at Iseult while Stuart was on a brief overnight foray in Dublin. There were many forays and some of them lasted longer than overnight. O'Flaherty's marriage to Margaret Barrington ("Topsy") was breaking up. O'Flaherty advised Stuart not to rest on his laurels. Leaving a copy of his latest novel, *The Puritan*, he signed it, "To Francis from Liam, may we both take off safe and make a good landing". The pun referred to their recent adventures into flying. *The Puritan* had got a hot reception on arrival in Ireland and was banned by the Irish Censorship Board, evoking letters of protest from Yeats. Stuart was working on another novel, but somehow the theme of the previous one would not leave him alone.

Yeats visited after O'Flaherty had left and also stayed at the hotel in Glendalough. It was June and he was unwell. He stayed for over a month. He told Iseult that the other guests made him nervous, so she offered him a room in Laragh Castle. When a copy of Stuart's new novel, *The Coloured Dome*, arrived in the post, Yeats invited them to celebrate at the hotel. Stuart, less upstaged by Yeats than usual, seemed for once to find concord with the elder poet.

Still, Stuart and Iseult tended to keep a respectful distance from Yeats who was able to be his bumbling self with them or, at least off guard, since he did not expect them to be ardent admirers. He would jokingly rebuke Iseult for marrying the "wild" young Stuart. He boldly declared in Laragh Castle that she should have married him and Iseult retorted, "O Willie, we wouldn't have lasted a year". When Yeats got back to Dublin, he read *The Coloured Dome* with immense delight. He praised Stuart unreservedly to everyone: Lennox Robinson, Olivia Shakespear, and even Bernard Shaw. Yeats seemed to forgive Stuart for marrying Iseult who, he saw, had eclipsed whatever promise she had shown as a writer. Iseult, prejudiced by the times when it was more difficult for a woman to be accepted by any literary coterie, and preyed upon by many male writers and artists, had lain to rest further ambitions of being a published writer. Meanwhile her sporadic search for peace in comparative religions continued in private.

Yeats realised that Iseult had been eclipsed, as it were, by Stuart:

> What an inexplicable thing sexual selection is! Iseult picked this young man, by what seemed half a chance, half a mere desire to escape from an impossible life, and when he seemed almost an imbecile to his own relations. Now he is her very self made active and visible, her nobility walking and singing. If luck comes to his aid he will be our great writer. [7]

Yeats stubbornly saw Stuart as the creation of Iseult, which implied some prejudice on the older poet's part, if not jealousy. By July *The Coloured Dome* was selling well, with its inscription on the yellow dust jacket: "a novel by Francis Stuart, author of *Pigeon Irish* which was so highly praised by W.B. Yeats, Liam O'Flaherty, L.A.G. Strong and Compton Mackenzie." Victor Gollancz had another successful writer on his hands and, sure enough, the novel required a new edition before the year was out.

By then, Stuart was a full member of Yeats's Irish Academy of Letters, and along with the other members attended a special meeting in the Peacock Theatre, Dublin. Gonne was there, lending public support. Meanwhile, Bernard Shaw's wife, Charlotte, was reading Stuart's novel with great delight, recommending it to T.E. Shaw (Lawrence of Arabia, an associate member of the Irish Academy of Letters), and wrote to Yeats: "What a fine book *The Coloured Dome.*" Yeats wrote about it to Olivia Shakespear, "It is strange and exciting in theme and perhaps more personally and beautifully written than any book of our generation".[8] O'Flaherty, in a letter to Stuart, commented: "It's the manner of your writing, the power and beauty of expression, insight into life, that matter to you as an artist and poet."[9]

The Coloured Dome has greater impact than his previous two novels. It was begun in a torrent of activity as he stayed up one night and wrote nearly 40 pages and by then could see the direction of the whole book, he told me. The pared-down style conveys everything essential; it is, as if what strikes a particular character is also made to strike the reader. Well, that is the intention. What is more effective is that he finally stops imitating Hemingway's staccato word-repetitions and other stylistic mannerisms. It is my favourite among Stuart's first three novels and one that he felt gave him a huge surge in going on to establish his pre-War reputation as a significant novelist. Whatever his reservations about *The Coloured Dome,* he always had a glow when he spoke of it and remembered the book as an early breakthrough for him.

The action is resolved within two days as in *Women and God* and *Pigeon Irish.* The central character, Garry Delea, a bookmaker's clerk, is changed through meeting two women, Tulloolagh McCoolagh and Clarice Morrisey. A number of minor characters, including Seamus Arrochar, based on Liam O'Flaherty, Stuart suggested to me, make their entrance and exit without detracting from the flow of the novel. Thomas Osbert is a comic character based on Stuart's flying instructor, Sir Osmonde Esmond, a First World War ace pilot and founder of a flying school in Finglas, Dublin. Esmond, also a TD, became Ambassador to Spain. Stuart made his first solo flight in a De Havilland Moth, almost crashing into a haystack on landing, he told me, with much chuckling over the incident. He occasionally borrowed an aeroplane from Esmonde for flying which he greatly enjoyed. He recalled Esmonde as an eccentric who released a cage of canaries in Dáil Éireann during a speech by Éamon de Valera.

Garry Delea says near the close of the novel, "I have been in prison, been condemned to death, fallen in love with a woman, held her in my arms, heard men shot, found the only happiness, and lost it again".[10] Garry has paid a price for his glimpse of reality and afterwards nothing seems less real than the life of his customer-gamblers who are timid except for one, a Jew. The Jew places a small bet on a 20/1 outsider. With the winnings he puts the lot on the next race and wins again. He continues with this accumulator bet and begins losing a considerable amount – over £1,000 on the final race – and leaves the betting office without any money. The depiction of the Jew is not anti-Semitic; he is shown as an ordinary punter except a particularly unlucky one.

The Coloured Dome outlines the impulsive, the reckless, the prodigal sons and daughters who live for the moment. Their belief in action is religious. Stuart's typical presentation of two women in his novelistic manner has a biblical connotation, however tenuous, based on Martha and Mary, while Garry might be considered a Lazarus figure who finds new life.

Pigeon Irish and *The Coloured Dome* are not the stuff of Irish Civil War or War of Independence novels in a picaresque historical setting, such as those by Walter Macken, Leon Uris and O'Flaherty. Stuart's characters are not easily identifiable as pure Republicans. They are not glamorised, melodramatised or made knights in gilded green armour. He does not proclaim blood sacrifice, as do the writings and the life of Patrick Pearse. The ascendancy figures – the Anglo-Irish – are the main source of fun in the narrative. In these two novels, Stuart moved beyond his obsession with the civil upheavals which had encircled his early manhood. Clarice Morrisey is based on Paulina Caddell, whose husband smuggled arms from Russia to the Irish Republicans and died in the Spanish Civil War. Paulina Caddell later went to Australia with an Irish doctor. Tulloollagh McCoolagh is based on Christabel Manning who also left Ireland. *The Coloured Dome* is dedicated to Christabel, with whom Stuart had a brief, tempestuous relationship.

7

Rejection by Gollancz

IN 1932, THE YEAR IN WHICH HE HAD two novels published, Stuart bought another horse, Galamac, for nine guineas at the bloodstock sales in Ballsbridge. He had bought his first horse, Sunnymova, seven years previously. Mick Gleason, a former jockey, was hired as trainer. However, they soon argued over the handling of Galamac, so Stuart hired another trainer who proved to be a better choice. Galamac outran the favourite and won the Dromskin Plate at Dundalk races. Stuart recalled that the win brought out his worst vanity. The celebration party at the racetrack exceeded the cost of his winnings. Ultimately, the experience of victory left him feeling dejected. A further irony arose when he later sold Galamac and the horse began to win races in Ceylon.

O'Flaherty invited Stuart to Galway after the victory in Dundalk. On their journey, O'Flaherty mentioned that he still admired *The Coloured Dome*, but openly expressed his dislike of *Pigeon Irish*, referring to it as "the Puritan Pigeons", but added that Stuart had "a very beautiful soul".[1] Stuart was aware that he had an important meeting the next day in Dublin, but he still got very drunk in Galway. He drove across the country on the following morning, but had to stop the car in mid-journey to vomit violently into a ditch. At Laragh he collected Iseult and managed to arrive for the meeting without being too late.

Stuart had become used to keeping secrets from Iseult. She had made no comment on the dedication of *The Coloured Dome* to Christabel Manning, rightly assuming she was one of his "friends". Their marriage had reached a mutual accommodation and he was able to come and go at Laragh with the minimum of disharmony. He was of course being unfaithful which made him feel guilty, but this did not stop his infidelities. Iseult was capable of shrugging off the facts about her husband's double life and did not confront him. They drove to meet Compton Mackenzie, who learned of another Stuart secret that Iseult knew. He had written a new novel that summer. Prophetic in some ways, it contains a reference to a Nazi demonstrator – a first for an Irish novelist. The word "Nazi" would haunt its author for the rest of his life. That autumn of 1932 Mackenzie looked forward to reading it since he had praised *Pigeon Irish* in the *Daily Mail* as "a novel that swept me off my feet". Stuart, who had just turned 30, had certainly produced a strange novel in *Try the Sky*. It was published in January 1933 by Gollancz who was very pleased with Stuart's blossoming career. The yellow paper cover on the novel boasted a forward by Compton Mackenzie who ranked Stuart with D.H. Lawrence, who had died in 1930, and was being hailed in England after years of hatred, censorship and revilement. "I suggest that Francis Stuart has a message for the modern world of infinitely greater importance than anything offered by D.H. Lawrence, and I believe that in his book he has made his message more easily intelligible than in his previous novels or even in his beautiful poems."[2] In *Black List, Section H* the hero says, "only Lawrence, who was some years dead, might have what H was looking for but, ironically, he hadn't yet got the hang of him".[3] Stuart always expressed admiration for Lawrence's work in our discussions and since I was going through a phase of idolatry over his writings this also advanced our friendship.

The reference to poetry by Mackenzie concerned Stuart being anthologised in *The Golden Treasury of Irish Verse*, which included two of his poems and, as already stated, would mark a silence in his poetic output for many years to come. Meanwhile as a novelist he was being acclaimed along with Lawrence who had become a prophet without peer in the minds of many critics, except perhaps Richard Aldington. Lawrence would soon be rendered canonical by F.R. Leavis. *Lady Chatterley's Lover* was as infamous a novel as *Ulysses* and *Madame Bovary* and the once-scandalous poems of Charles Baudelaire, *Les Fleurs du Mal*. Lawrence had also posthumously been shown to be a considerable poet in the Whitman tradition. Stuart was exalted critically by a highly regarded English novelist, Mackenzie, and such praise found echoes from other writers too. Within months,

Try the Sky went into an American edition from Macmillan of New York, as did his two previous novels.

If *Try the Sky* has a message, in Compton Mackenzie's meaning of the term, it is something to do with the search for the romantic god. Finding the romantic god means that the hero can find peace and security in the world of lovers, away from the pain and sufferings of life. D.H. Lawrence's *Lady Chatterley's Lover* shows the central characters, Connie and Mellors, resurrecting their lives through mutual love of which sensual union is a significant part. However, *Lady Chatterley's Lover* is not only about romantic love, nor is *Try the Sky*.

Like Dick Diver in F. Scott Fitzgerald's *Tender is the Night*, which was published the same year, Stuart's characters in Vienna are reminiscent of the "lost generation", except these people are less bored and more dynamic. A riot is depicted in the novel; one of the insurgents "had on a sort of uniform with a white circle on his arm and a swastika sign in black on the white, so that I knew he was one of the Nazis".[4] The Nazi is pursued by the police and shot. Another of the characters, Dr Karl Graf, turns into a Hitleresque speechmaker to crowds of young lovers as the novel takes off in a flight of fancy in a surrealistic episode. The central character is transported back to Ireland by plane with a faded dream of Carlotta, his lover.

Stuart, in a broadcast from Berlin during the war, referred to the novel and his sympathies for the brownshirts, "as they then were". In other words his sympathies were of that period. By 1933 the Nazis had polled 43 per cent of the German electorate. Hitler became a politician of European importance three years earlier when his party entered the Reichstag, having won 18 per cent of the poll. *The Times*, the *Daily Mail* and *Daily Express* praised his anti-Bolshevik policies. Interviewed by Sefton Delmer of the *Daily Express*, Hitler denied the rumours of a massacre of political opponents: "We have appointed tribunals which will try enemies of the State legally." He was engaged in a series of political intrigues to oust President Hindenberg from public office, unite the army under his leadership and gain a majority over the Nationalists.[5]

Meanwhile, Stuart had entered a treadmill of writing. Behind the scenes, sales of *Try the Sky* were dwindling. Gollancz was preparing to publish another Stuart novel that would be the author's undoing as regards one aspect of his career. Sean O'Faolain would review it negatively in the *New Statesman and Nation*. However, long before the novel was published, Stuart had had his first play performed at the Abbey Theatre in March 1933. Yeats, Robinson and Gonne attended the opening night. Yeats was aloof when Stuart and Iseult thanked him for coming. Gonne would not go over to greet Yeats when Iseult begged her to. At the end of the play the small audience heard Robinson and a few others calling for Stuart to say a few words. He was happy to have forgotten the first night when I asked him. Joseph Holloway (whose theatrical recollections run to hundreds of volumes in the National Library of Ireland) condemned the play, *Men Crowd Me Round,* "that should not have been allowed to be produced in a Catholic city" and its author as "a member of Yeats's Academy of Letters". This latter comment made Stuart aware of the collectivisation of writers that the Academy had instituted. He did not approve of the academy and despised himself for being a member.[6] On this point he was dogmatic throughout the years I knew him and had a stolid unforgiving attitude towards such organisations. I always associated this with his self-professed outsider stance. The topic of academies surfaces later on in discussing Aosdána and Stuart's membership of the assembly and receipt of its highest honour.

Like O'Flaherty, he grew more and more to dislike Yeats. O'Flaherty had despised Yeats from the time of the riot over *The Plough and the Stars* six years previously at the Abbey when Yeats championed O'Casey and his portrayal of the 1916 Rising against the dissenting audience. O'Flaherty, while repudiating political nationalism, revered Pearse and Connolly and despised Yeats "who rose to fame on the shoulders of those men". Stuart, refusing to feed any audiences' vanity, pitched his play *Men Crowd Me Round* beyond a vision of defiant Republicanism at odds with personal ideals of love, and added in some British bigotry to the otherwise "air of artificiality that never ripened into real drama", according to Holloway. Stuart had tried to cause a riot among the audience and forgot about the structuring of his play. Undaunted, he would have two more plays produced before the end of the decade, one in London and the other at the Abbey.

The next two years saw him engaged in furious writing activity. His novel *Glory* was published in August 1933 and because of it he was commissioned to write an autobiography. This, however, gives a false impression of the success of the novel which he planned while passing through St George's Channel on board a liner owned by an acquaintance, Colonel Pole. *Glory,* in depicting a warlord, is a successful leap of the imagination based on a period in history when many dictators such as Stalin, Hitler, Mussolini and Franco came to power in the 1930s. "A monster machine in which printing-presses, aeroplanes, gas-cylinders, guns, all formed a part."[7] Stuart seems fully in tune with the times. He was obviously attracted by the reality of warlords and it can be seen that his fictional paradigm of military power would have a basis in the Second World War some years later. In the novel, Marshal Shang Ya, a Chinese dictator, plans to gas and bomb the world into submission but does not succeed.

Victor Gollancz did not like *Glory* and wrote asking Liam O'Flaherty for his opinion. O'Flaherty was sent a copy and later wrote back, "I don't know what to say about *Glory*. Really, it's a bit too mad to tell the truth. Please say if you like, 'What magnificent extravagance! but I think it's just insanity'."[8] Gollancz decided to drop Stuart from his list. After the publication of *Glory,* Stuart was left in the lurch with no publisher in England or the United States, just as his career as a novelist was becoming well established. His despondency was tempered by a letter from Yeats who found the novel "a masterpiece ... majestic, beautiful, all intellectual passion, perfect in structure, far beyond anything you have done hitherto – but sometimes vile in its grammar".[9]

Glory articulates Stuart's imaginative reconstruction of power-wielding warlords and his fascination with them. His harshest critics may well find in it evidence of his longing for some kind of martyrdom, like the central characters Frank and Mairead in the novel. It has a despairing tone that may account for his going on retreat to a monastery after its publication. His reason was a continuing sense of wanting to become a monk, which would recur periodically throughout his life. He went to Mount St Joseph's Abbey, Roscrea where the present writer first read *Things to Live For: Notes for an Autobiography* in the late 1960s. In *Black List, Section H,* H tells a monk that he is looking for "intimations of a spirit more (at least imaginatively and potentially) perverse than myself, one that has had the experiences I can only guess and tremble at, who bears not only the signs of the stigmata but of the most terrible traumata as well".[10] Stuart wrote this in the 1960s, outlining the life of his surrogate self who has ahead of him the experiences of wartime in Berlin, prison and other deprivations and suffering.

When Stuart returned from the monastery, an eccentric student stayed with him and Iseult for several weeks. José de Ruiloba was attending Trinity College. He was a Hispanic-American and a compulsive gambler. His parents had sent him to study in Ireland, hoping he might give up drinking, a habit he acquired in New York speakeasies during Prohibition. However, de Ruiloba soon grew to love Guinness, a weakness which added to his money problems. Meanwhile, when not pestering the Stuarts, he sent off cables to the United States begging money from his father. Iseult could not get rid of him. Stuart, Iseult and Lily, along with Ian and Kay, pretended they were leaving the castle for a few days and brought de Ruiloba to Dublin with them. That night when they arrived back in Laragh he was waiting at the castle gate. Stuart, through the years, attracted many such waifs and strays to whom he would give counsel and friendship, but he was uneasy about being taken for a guru figure.

8

Cape, Collins, Womanising

STUART TOLD ME THAT HE FELT IT WAS bad luck being dropped by Gollancz, especially when he had taken a chance on a purely imaginative novel with *Glory*. While Stuart had written compulsively he had got used to having the support of his London publisher. Before embarking on a new book he wrote to Jonathan Cape who had published his first novel, *Women and God*. Cape did not want another novel but found Stuart's letter about his life since *Women and God* exciting enough and full enough to suggest that he write an autobiography.

Stuart was very surprised and pleased with Cape's response, but also taken aback since he did not want to write an autobiography. He was, after all, a successful novelist and was unwilling to write about his childhood. Besides, at the age of 30, he saw himself fully engaged with life. However, he then faced the practicality of earning some money and set to it. After many false starts he found a way of shaping his notes for an autobiography. The book became an anthology of some chapters on childhood, a solo-flight in an aeroplane, buying a horse at the bloodstock sales in Dublin, the experiences of a *brancardier* in Lourdes and his reaction to the public reception of *Pigeon Irish,* which influenced a group of people to try to set up a Catholic monarchy in Ireland.

Stuart had found the ensuing controversy during 1932 humorous, which is shown in a comment in *Things to Live For*: "It must be the first time that a novel has ever had a part in king-making."[1] He thought the Catholic Monarchy Society was farcical, he told me. Sir Osmonde Esmonde, whom he satirised in *The Coloured Dome,* hoped to overthrow the government and crown a descendent of the O'Neills as king of Ireland.

A reading of *Things to Live For* can still surprise with its lust for life. Much of the contents have been commented on here already, but there are many intriguing asides:

> In some of my own novels, in *Pigeon Irish, The Coloured Dome,* and *Glory* I have written about men and women who have gone through all sorts of defeat and humiliation and have triumphed in the end. Though, it is a strange kind of triumph. But the greatest triumphs are the strangest in the eyes of the world.[2]

About writing, he says:

> I see no virtue whatsoever in so-called realism as such. The only realism is that of the heart.[3]

Dedicated to Stuart's son, Ian Nicholas, Cape published *Things to Live For: Notes for an Autobiography* in 1934. Stuart told me that because it was well advertised the 1,500 copies were soon sold out. It was reissued in the United States the following year by Macmillan and well reviewed. Jim Carney, secretary to Jim Larkin the Trades Union activist, sent a letter of praise: "I am writing as maybe you know, with a vast experience of life. Thank you for your book".[4]

In London, Stuart visited Joan Haslip, the novelist who had begun a biography of Charles Stewart Parnell and with whom he was having an affair. He went mountain climbing with her in Cumberland, where they stayed in the mountain retreat of Lady Ankeret Howard, a friend of O'Flaherty's. Their affair had been fading and before Christmas, he decided to end the relationship. He returned to Laragh via Liverpool, with gifts for everyone. He was a good part-time father capable of telling stories, wrapping presents, decorating a Christmas tree and the house. His daughter Kay, as a grown woman, would recall her father asking Ian and herself on Christmas Day, "Which did you enjoy the most, the early Mass, the big breakfast, or opening the presents?"

Around this time he was included in *Great Contemporaries* and found his entry sympathetic and understanding. In June of 1935 W.R. Cottmann of the Australian Literature Society in Melbourne asked Stuart for a brief biographical sketch because of his birthplace in

Townsville. Cottmann eventually referred to Stuart and his work on Melbourne Radio.

Stuart's meeting with a London film-maker, Desmond Hurst of Kinnerton Studios, had resulted in screenplay work for him. His first effort at a screenplay was of no use to Hurst. Stuart could not seem to produce a script from Synge's *Riders to the Sea* which satisfied Hurst's changing concept of the kind of film he wished to make. Stuart's next foray into fiction came under the strictures of self-appraisal and commercial viability – he wrote *In Search of Love* within six weeks at Laragh. The book is perceptively critical of the film and publicity industry, at times verging on the satirical in terms of the cinema, merchandising and hype. Dedicated "to all who are in search of love", the novel of 1935 sold well for his newly found publisher, Collins. There are no flights of imagination. No mysticism. No religious quest. Neither does it contain any Catholic soul-bearing of the sort found in *Women and God* or the revolutionary anarchy of *The Coloured Dome* and *Pigeon Irish*. When the novel appeared, Desmond Hurst (who would make a film of Synge's *The Playboy of the Western World*) was persuaded to give him another chance at screenwriting, but Stuart's final treatment of *Riders to Sea* was also rejected.

Much is made by previous writers on Stuart, for instance Elborn and Natterstad, of the speed with which the novel was written, the commercial intention and its failure to hold rank with his other novels. One need not quarrel with this except to say that, however speedy the composition, *In Search of Love* is no better or worse than any populist fiction. It aspires to satire in the manner of Evelyn Waugh's *Scoop,* a novel published two years previous to it, lambasting the world of journalism, although Stuart's comic temperament is not as fully achieved. *In Search of Love* pleased its publishers with two editions, the second in the month of publication. There followed an American edition from Macmillan. The novel is funny in places as a story of rags to riches and fame. For all that, there is no character in it that is not well and truly fit for the pulp fiction gallery of rogues, heroines and caricatures and, coming from Stuart, the book has an awkward feel. I never felt any need to discuss it with him except to remark that his titles have a memorable ring to them. He was proud of his titles for nearly all of the novels but confided in me that he thought one of the best titles for a novel he had heard but never used was *Dante Called You Beatrice*. He recommended me to write a novel using this title, which I did years later, but on completing it I changed the title to *Excess Road*.

Meanwhile at Laragh, Stuart had been finding the routine of poultry farming hard work for little profit or joy. Furthermore, Miss Burnett had quit as manager of the farm and married a doctor in 1935. Stuart had had enough, he said recalling the torpor of the time. Soon poultry farming ranked amongst his hobbies; he had always brought some expertise to everything, including motorcycling, flying and especially the horses. He had not flown for years and the motorbike had been sold long since. He sold the Peugeot and bought a six-cylinder Buick tourer. Ian was eight years old and attending school, and Kay was 4. The children had a well-regulated and loving childhood that included visits to and from Aunt Janet and also Madame MacBride. In time, bonds would grow between Ian and Kay and the MacBride grandchildren, Tiernan and Anna, the son and daughter of Seán and Kit.

Around this time I visited Laragh Castle for the first time. I found it a magical setting, as well as an impressive structure, but I was unable to gain access. The locals told me that the owners were away, and I was reluctant to disturb their privacy by going back too soon. I told Stuart of my visit and as we reminisced about the trees and the ruins of the outhouses and discussed the interior of the castle, he began to recollect some fascinating details from the 1930s. He recalled that life at the castle had slipped into a pattern which was very much dependent on the maid to maintain domestic life, since neither Iseult nor Lily was used to cooking on a daily basis. Iseult rose for breakfast in her dressing gown and tended to make a long affair of the meal. She was a picky eater, as is often the case with habitual smokers. Lily, who was called "Ninny" by her grandchildren, would go to the shop every other day, usually for cigarettes for Iseult, who smoked anything but preferred Craven A and Sweet Afton. Lily bought plenty of matches because Iseult was always forgetting where she had left them. They got on well, fortunately for the children's sake; however, it was Lily's money that was the main source of income. This had been arranged as an accommodation between the lady of the house and her mother-in-law. Lily was suited to village life but had become something of an anomaly, like the Stuarts themselves, to the locals. She was a small, squat woman who went around Laragh in an oilskin coat and sou'wester hat. It was sensible gear to combat what she called "sheets of rain", but it made her a source of gossip. Similarly, her Northern accent was almost foreign to some of the locals. Iseult's pronounced French-accented English, along with Stuart's long absences from the castle, made them seem like outsiders. Iseult was rarely seen in the village and her life followed the cloistered conditions of her childhood and adolescence. In season she gardened with the help of a local to do the heavier work. She adored flowers and bedecked the rooms with them when her mood was good. Otherwise she was happily obsessive about cultivating vegetables, while the fruit trees provided the means of making jams.

Stuart, and his mother in particular, gave the appearance of being very religious. Lily went through periods of daily Mass attendance as well as on Sundays with her grandchildren in tow. She could not abide inattentive or misbehaved children in church. Ian and Kay were subjected to the strong Catholic upbringing of the 1930s. Bible reading was not part of the household practice; however, on pilgrimage days, Lily would dress the children in their Sunday best and they would walk through Glendalough. She was known to be intrusively social if she happened to go to the hotel or local teashop. In the village she made friends with Church of Ireland and Catholic folk, feeling quite at ease and happy to accept any and every invitation. Conditions inside Laragh Castle almost precluded regular "at homes" because of the damp walls and the impossibility of warming the place up, as well as Iseult's reserved nature which tended to the introspective and depressive. However, Iseult did strike up a friendship with the Bartons, rather surprisingly since Robert Barton was one of the pro-Treaty signatories, whereas Gonne strongly disapproved of this alliance with "political undesirables".

Stuart had not reaped a lot financially from his novels and was unsure about how to hold on to Collins, his publisher, especially when the house rejected his next offering of an overtly religious novel, *The Angel of Pity*. It was written for Iseult as a kind of peace offering for their tattered marriage. Much later, a year before she died, summing up many of their sorrowful times, she wrote to Stuart: "It nearly broke my heart that you had dedicated it to me." Iseult and Stuart had the kind of personalities that are deeply obsessed with the quest for God (or ultimate meaning). So similar were their strong convictions and deeply held beliefs that the divergences were painful for each of them. He acknowledged this as I probed deeper and deeper into his life.

Meanwhile he decided to dedicate *The Angel of Pity* to Iseult and wondered if it would ever get into print. He brought the novel to London and met O'Flaherty, who was staying at the National Hotel, Bloomsbury, basking in the post-launch glory of his autobiography, *Shame the Devil*. The book had been brought out by a small publisher, Rupert Grayson. Among other news, Stuart reluctantly disclosed his anxieties about his own novel and told O'Flaherty that it had been inspired by Joseph O'Neill's *Day of Wrath*, an apocalyptic account of a war to come. There were many such novels of the mid to late 1930s giving prognostications of what another war would be like with even more destruction and more sinister death-dealing weaponry than the First World War. O'Flaherty suggested that Stuart submit it to Grayson through his agent A.D. Peters. Soon *The Angel of Pity* was accepted and announced as "philosophy written as fiction". Yeats intended writing a preface, but illness prevented him. I found it very difficult to find a copy of *The Angel of Pity* since Stuart had mislaid his only existing copy, but eventually found one in the National Library, where I read it over two days.

The novel is a daring adventure in imaginative writing and yet found few readers on its first appearance. One of them was Captain Basil Liddel Hart, the military historian, whose help was instrumental in rescuing Stuart from prolonged incarceration in prison after the war. Stuart's argumentative friend, Harold Stroud, could not get through the new novel at all. Stroud was a confirmed Marxist living off a private income, a habitué of the Plough Bar, a corner house on Museum Street and casual meeting place for Stuart with his London friends. The novel was published in the Christmas season of 1935. The front cover by Isobel R. Beard depicted nude swimmers moving upwards along a beam of light. In Stuart's words the book received a "rather cold reception by critics and the general public".

O'Flaherty wrote to Stuart about the novel, having seen a review where it was called "rather odd". He added, "We should worry. One of these days we shall knock them." O'Flaherty was consolidating what would be a lifelong relationship with Kitty Tailer. He had also publicly supported de Valera's economic war with Britain and when reading *Great Contemporaries* (1935), an essay collection by various writers, had seen Stuart's contribution praising de Valera. Dev was called a "democratic genius" and further lauded as, "still the strongest force in Ireland because he has shown himself in 1916 and in 1922 capable of going his own way towards the goal that he sees, whether the people whom he loves follow him or not". Dev's anti-Tea campaign led to Fianna Fáil's imposition of five shillings import tax on a pound of tea. Fianna Fáil, having gained power in 1932, would not lose it until 1948. One must assume that Stuart was pro-de Valera in this period, but I was rather loath ever to mention the leading Irish Statesman to him because of his predictable dismissive reaction.

The Angel of Pity has a charge in the energetic prose similar to that of D.H. Lawrence in *Fantasia of the Unconscious*. In the latter, Lawrence pours forth in fluid prose a "philosophy of immortality". *The Angel of Pity* is a daring attempt to write a "fifth gospel" after imagining a global war where "misery and slaughter was only the hysterical outburst of despair".[5] For Stuart it is the closest he gets to achieving a tract of nihilism. It can also be seen as a world vision of devastation that breaks him down in the face of nature obliterated. Humanity's power for destruction is exposed but without his usual hints that supreme power is not solely in human hands. He also loses the strength shown in previous novels, derived from the splendour of the natural world and its proximity to the vast cosmos.

The Angel of Pity is compelling about the reality of suffering, similar to Christian terminology and esoteric Buddhism, and manages to propel itself forward oracularly without becoming too homiletic. The prophetic novel appeared four years before the outbreak of the Second World War. "From battles in which hundreds of thousands are killed right down the scale to the fashioning of a nest or a doll's house, all is made to serve the mysterious purposes of the infinite love."[6] This for some may be an unsatisfying mysticism. *The Angel of Pity* is too dogmatic and didactic for its own good. Stuart agreed with me, and said it is "a very flawed novel". He forbade its republication in the 1950s. Perhaps Iseult was right after all to repudiate it at the time of its first publication. When I read it first in the National Library of Ireland in my twenties I found it compelling but re-reading the novel in preparation to write the biography, I was somewhat disappointed.

In January 1936 in London, Basil Liddell Hart wanted to meet Stuart who was involved at the Arts Club Theatre with an adaptation of the novel *Glory*. Stuart invited Liddel Hart to see the play. The actress who played Mairead O'Byrne was Margery Binner. Margery and Stuart were having an affair that is portrayed in *Black List, Section H.* At the time Stuart had some unfinished business with another woman, Honor Henderson. He had met Honor through Liam O'Flaherty. She was a daughter of Lord Kylsant, former chairman of the White Star Shipping Line of *RMS Titanic* fame. Honor knew influential legal people and obtained a speedy divorce from her husband. She took Queen's Counsel's advice about Stuart's marriage and discovered that he could get an annulment on the grounds of having been underage. As Stuart toyed with the idea and almost went through with signing the necessary papers, Honor got cold feet and called off their wedding. In retrospect Stuart told me that his involvement with Honor revealed a desire to do anything to end his marriage officially.

He contradicted this on another occasion and said that he did not want to marry Honor, or to end his marriage. This may well be true since faced with the option of an annulment he took no definitive steps to bring it about. His marriage was not untypical of the Ireland of the time because of the prevailing hegemony of Church and State which would be set forth in the Irish Constitution of 1937. Long before the Eucharistic Congress in Dublin in 1932, the Irish Southern State had courted Vatican approval. The Vatican remained vague about recognising the Irish Free State until the State proposed setting up a Catholic constitution. Vatican dogmatism was politicised in the 1930s, especially when faced with the spread of Communist ideology throughout Europe. In Italy, the Lateran Treaty severed Church–State relations so the Vatican craved dominance elsewhere and would slowly recognise Franco's Government in Spain, but only in return for his allegiance as it had done with de Valera's. This Catholic supremacy in the Irish state would become a subtext in Stuart's next two novels but by then, as Europe faced the Second World War, his life would change dramatically as he left Ireland for Germany.

Meanwhile, Stuart fell in love, after a fashion, with Margery Binner. She was a music-hall star and he found it exciting to watch her in his play *Glory* and enjoyed staying at her flat. When Margery decided they should become engaged, she publicised it in a way reminiscent of a scene from *In Search of Love,* where a new restaurant was being opened. She collected as many celebrities as she could and an account of the party was written up in the press, including photographs. Margery respected wealth more than character and celebrity more than talent, according to Stuart, and had a taste for the artificial, if not the superficial. A neighbour in Laragh happened to see the photo in an English newspaper and brought it to Iseult who was shocked and upset. Stuart arrived back in Ireland to begin his next novel and there were bitter marital scenes. With some scorn, Iseult told Stuart that he was in search of love wherever it might be found. She said that she thought he was pathetic.

He was firmly settled with Collins publishers and tailored the next books to suit their needs. These books only require cursory reference here and set up the immediate backdrop to Stuart's years in Berlin. These were the last of the Laragh novels and one would explore the theme of sexual infidelity. One of the novels, *The White Hare,* had a special significance for Stuart, who as a child was always intrigued by any sighting of a hare. As a schoolboy in Monkstown he had written his first story about such a creature. Later, at Tintown internment camp in the summer of 1923, he made a drawing of a rabbit, having spent hours watching them outside the perimeter fence of the prison.

The White Hare sold badly despite excellent reviews. Iseult loved it. The *London Evening Standard* made it their Book of the Month and declared Stuart "a great romantic writer". The *Sunday Times* praised it highly. The *News Chronicle* was almost embarrassingly superlative. It was reissued in the United States and much later adapted for the screen by Littlebird Productions under the title *Moondance,* in 1994.

Despite being regarded as a successful novelist, his pre-war books, he told me bluntly, never earned huge royalties and rarely exceeded the advance, circa £75, half of which was usually paid on acceptance, the remainder on publication. A notable exception was his second novel, *Pigeon Irish,* which was his most successful book commercially. In a perverse sort of way, his lack of commerciality made him feel that he was being true to his vocation as a writer. He emphasised that he was not a wealthy member of the Wicklow gentry. Stuart's earnings, along with Lily's annuity, yielded an average income to maintain the household above spartan comfort. Stuart remembered that there was always a feeling that "financially the wolf was at the door". The seasonal ordeal of living in Laragh Castle in winter with young children made the adults often consider moving, but they could not afford it. It required resilience to endure the harsh conditions during spells of bad weather.

For instance, when Samuel Beckett visited in the autumn of 1936 with George Reavey, the poet and publisher from Paris, they noticed the bleak beauty of the surroundings and the crackling log fire just about warming the damp atmosphere. They were given tea and refreshments and discussed Stalinist Russia, of all things, while Iseult played hostess with impressive grace and suavity. Reavey had an interest in Stuart as a possible author for his Europa Press. However, Collins, the London publishing house, was happy enough with Stuart and wanted to build on the two novels which had been well received on both sides of the Atlantic. Stuart and Reavey never did any business together as author and publisher. Meanwhile Macmillan brought out *In Search of Love* and *The White Hare* in the United States, having seen seven books by Stuart into print.

9

Pre-war Plots

BECAUSE OF ITS SERIOUS SUBJECT MATTER, Stuart's next novel, *The Bridge*, may seem a strange book to dedicate to a 6-year-old child. Stuart dedicated to it to his daughter Katherine Frances. It is a stark depiction of provincial Irish life in Drogheda (re-named Fert in the novel), and marital infidelity, a theme well within the author's experience. Stuart visited Drogheda many times as a child when he lived with his Aunt Janet in Shallon, County Meath; it held a mythical status for him, he said, as it was the first town with which he became familiar. The subplot of *The Bridge* is reminiscent of Compton Mackenzie's *Whiskey Galore.* However, this is to trivialise a book which would go into three consecutive reprints in Berlin during the Second World War translated as *Die Brucke,* and in the year after the war, into Italian as *Il Ponte.*

The Bridge is not a giggly novel of hearty drinkers and head-shaking policemen willing to look the other way over a few kegs of poteen. The smuggling divides loyalties and provides liquor against a backdrop of added confusion. This is not a tale of idle malicious gossip like Brinsley MacNamara's *The Valley of the Squinting Windows*. The novel shows adultery as the last refuge of the desperately unhappy, who, in an effort to dull various pains, actually embrace greater ones. The illicit couple, like the liquor passing in and around the town, are fiery, beneficial, fructifying as well as dangerous and excessive.

It is too facile to see Stuart in the feckless Larry Byrne in the novel and Joanna his lover as a composite of Honor Henderson and Margery Binner, the London actress and friend of Aldous Huxley. Still, the writing of a novel about an adulterer may have relieved Stuart's own guilt over these affairs. He considered *The Bridge* to be one of his artistically successful pre-War novels. However, it was a slow seller for Collins and Macmillan turned down an option for a United States edition.

Collins was willing to keep Stuart on their list, so he began another novel in the book-lined study in the turret room of Laragh Castle. It would be his tenth novel. Secretly, he was unhappy with Collins and felt subconsciously that they were prodding him to produce a certain sort of book, he told me. After a false start he was unable to make any progress at all on the new novel. Suddenly, during an unhappy respite, he abandoned it temporarily and wrote *Racing for Pleasure and Profit in Ireland and Elsewhere* (1937), which was published by the Talbot Press. It is a short book on his general theory about backing outsiders, how to study racing form and the probability of winning and losing. There is also the suggestion that the Irish Derby should cease being run at the Curragh and instead transfer to a favourite racecourse of Stuart's: Navan, County Meath.

Meanwhile his luck was stagnant. He was aware of writing too much, but there was little else he could do. He recalled for me that, in his mid-thirties, overproduction was debilitating him. He went to London in an effort to reactivate the creative principle and continue with his book. London failed him, so he went on to Paris and met Sam Beckett. Sam's hopes were placed in the small publishing house, George Reavey, who was unsuccessfully peddling a novel, *Murphy*. Beckett had published a collection of short stories, *More Pricks than Kicks*, but remained in a publishing limbo. Stuart said that he envied Beckett's exile in Paris but Beckett announced that he would soon be returning to Dublin. Stuart told me how Beckett and he could talk and drink into the small hours of the night in Montparnasse and once felt as if they might in some way be twins, such was their mutual understanding. Stuart added that Beckett could not carouse at his pace so their long nights on the town together were rare. They were to meet again, but not for a long time, by that stage much would have changed in the world.

Julie, the novel Stuart completed with ease on returning, forms part of an arbitrarily linked London trilogy of novels along with *The Flowering Cross* (1950) and *The Chariot* (1953). All set in London, they are true to their time, place and milieu and reflect Stuart's many periods spent there, ranking it with other cities most associated with him and his writings: Berlin, Paris, Dublin and Belfast. The novel reveals a complete leap of imagination and the main characters are convincing, which is not the case in *The White Hare*. Stuart had developed as a writer and would manage to get even further. He had not yet reached the revelations that he would in Berlin about the creation of characters in fiction being "a miracle that only happens very rarely".[1] In the intense atmosphere of Germany he would posit the Olympian ideal that character creation in literature has actually occurred more infrequently than otherwise. He explained this to me as an unconsciousness striving rather than something that could be forced. A novel, he believed, was given to the writer almost like some fantastic dream or phantasmagoria, and part of the great excitement of writing it down was to unravel each link in the chain of the story. Yet he always maintained that what he had written was never totally opaque; the story was like an elaborate parable incapable of paraphrase. Otherwise the result would be a bad novel. He stressed that his theories applied to his own method and were best exemplified in his best work.

In *Julie* the central character of the title decides "to join in the mysterious game that was going on under her nose, the game of making money".[2] The other main character, Goldberg, states his case to her, "I don't defraud the poor and squeeze the last ounce out of them. I go for the rich, Julie; for the insurance companies and for the banks."[3] When Goldberg is jailed for fraud and arson, Julie's life becomes so fraught that she longs for death but does not kill herself. Stuart mentioned to me that suicide is the option of intervening in personal destiny, in other words, that he imagined the Creator adding a suicide clause to life's contract for his creatures and the supreme empowerment which this implies.

Julie is one of Stuart's memorable characters, as is Goldberg. Alfred Knopf republished the novel in New York within its first year of publication in London. Percy Hutchinson reviewed *Julie* in glowing terms for the *New York Times Book Review*: "It will be one of the most widely read of recent novels." Hutchinson praised Stuart's novels throughout the 1930s in the same newspaper and, except for some reservations over *In Search of Love*, he was overwhelmed by Stuart, "half poet, half seer, not to know his work is to neglect the most arresting novelist in many a year … a novelist so far removed from the general run of fiction writers that few of the usual canons apply".

After the publication of *Julie* in the United States, Stuart lost faith in the realistic novels demanded by his London publisher and gambled on another departure, producing a novel which came in part from his *Racing for Pleasure and Profit in Ireland and Elsewhere.* This contained subject matter that obsessed him. Horse racing was in his background and in his blood. As a child he had a particular feeling for animals, especially horses. So had his father and uncles in Dervock, County Antrim. The Stuarts, like some other Irish families had a sixth sense about horses.

His researches led him pleasurably on to reading about Laragh Castle. It was then that he found the central story that seems invented, but actually happened, and was well documented. Besides he had always loved the moment in George Moore's *Esther Waters* when the heroine meets Will Latch and the novel gains a new lease of life from the big race on Derby Day. Stuart's final book before the war, *The Great Squire,* reads like a two-volume novel in the nineteenth-century mode. With hindsight, he told me that it quickly put an end to Collins as his publisher, war or no war. They had accepted him on condition that he did not write overtly imaginative novels. He admitted to me that with *The Great Squire* he was tempting fate in the subconscious hope that they would break the contract. As it happened fate moved far bigger events than that.

In the winter of 1938, as he began to write, following the twists and turns in the novel, he could not have known that his real destiny as a writer was beginning. Nor could he have divined that he would be in Berlin in a year's time. He found domestic conditions were hampering the book's progress, so he moved to the Dolphin Hotel in Dublin. This provided an ideal location for solitary writing broken by controlled diversions of dining out with the painter Beatrice Glenavy, the poet F.R. Higgins and once with Sam Beckett at Jammet's where the food was better than at his hotel but more expensive, he remembered. Meanwhile, he wrote what would be his longest ever novel. It is difficult to establish whether there is any parodic intent on Stuart's part in *The Great Squire*. He considered it strictly as an entertainment and it did find its fans over the years. For his racing friends of the time it satisfied their wish for a Stuart novel about the sport of kings. It is dedicated to "to B.G.", Beatrice Glenavy. Lord Glenavy and his wife Beatrice were both lifelong friends of Stuart.

Gonne wrote to him in glowing terms: "A great book. Iseult is right about your genius."[4] She liked the fact that some of the characters were meant to represent nineteenth-century United Irishmen. The comments were somewhat conciliatory to her son-in-law, but did not make him relent in keeping away from Gonne as much as possible. However, *The Great Squire* need not be highly acclaimed. It is very strange in the context of his total output. At times, it reads as if he had not written it at all, since it has little of his usual style of the period. It is also far too long. The first edition from Collins of Pall Mall was a deluxe production. The cover illustration reproduces a bizarre race between a horse and a pig. Some of the story is based on an actual race taken from Sharkey's racing calendar. The main plot is borrowed from Dickens's *A Tale of Two Cities* except in Stuart's novel one character disguises himself and goes to the gallows to save the other. *The Great Squire* displays its historical research lightly and ends in a dirge of melancholy.

There is something prophetic in the novel, as if by intent, since Stuart would cease to be a husband and father in Laragh and begin to seek his real destiny. Jerry Natterstad finds that "the epithet 'The Great Squire' soon tastes of ashes, and he is led slowly and painfully to an awareness of suffering [...] his newly found humility leads ultimately to a capacity for sacrifice".[5] Stuart's flight into the unknown would lead to a similar nemesis.

It would be eight years before he wrote another novel and by then his life as a novelist would have changed radically. On 16 October 1942, four years after *The Great Squire* had appeared in print, Stuart would write in his diary in Pension Naumann, Berlin:

> I see how all that youthful fire without enough experience makes conceits. My books up to *Glory* were full of conceits, of fancy, not of the imagination that has its roots in life. It was the desire and the necessity that my books should sell more that forced me to earth, more than to life which began a bit in *The White Hare, The Bridge, Julie* and *The Great Squire*, which was not the right motive either. All my books are very imperfect, all are fragmentary, confused and much marred. But some of them are unique attempts in their own way.[6]

Then he lists them with the comment, "books I need not be ashamed of". Much later on in 1947, in a self-congratulatory mood, he adds to his diary: "All must be fact and nothing invented – characters must not be invented. Now at last I know how to write, how to be myself and the long years of uncertainty as a writer are over."[7] By then he had entered a spectacular creative phase by his standards.

By the time I got to know him, he was quite dismissive of his pre-War novels, viewing them as merely formative. When I was preparing to write this book I found his sidelining of these novels impeded my own progress and in a moment of exasperation suggested I leave them out or block them together in a few pages. Then he succumbed and said I should give them equal treatment but they could not be left out; they were as much of his life of the time as anything else he did in the 1930s, a decade which he generally shrugged off in any event. He half-admitted to preferring those later in the decade, all the novels published by Collins except for *In Search of Love, Pigeon Irish,* because of its reception in the press, and *The Coloured Dome* which he affectionately referred to it as his "first scratchings, scrapings and grappling with the novel form", even though it was not in fact his first novel.

In 1938 he began writing a play about a nun, Sister Mairead, who is turned out of her nunnery and finds solace with a family who are themselves in a fix. The notable actress Ria Mooney played the nun and central character in *Strange Guest,* which was presented at the Abbey Theatre in December of 1940. The play was a huge success, even though its plot is quite melodramatic. Mairead breathes new life into the troubled family and restores the fortunes of her order of nuns when a jockey helps her win a lot of money on a horse race. As might easily be observed: a somewhat typical Stuartian plot. Stuart was not at the production because he was not in Dublin; his new life in Germany had begun at the same time. It was left to Iseult to attend the opening night. Perhaps she had an insight into her husband's persistent inner struggle, but did not understand the minutiae of his quest. Joseph Holloway, the theatre critic of the period, did not like the play and criticised Stuart's awkward stagecraft.

Part Two

1939-1949

What would have happened if Hitler, in full consciousness of the calamity he had brought on millions of people and on himself (because at this mysterious level, the decisive events are personal) and accepting his utter humiliation, had bowed himself to the blood soaked rubble and publicly proclaimed his guilt, like Raskolnikov in *Crime and Punishment*. — Francis Stuart, *Faillandia*

Perhaps I was wrong to speak, perhaps it was identifying myself too much with the horrors of Nazism and it was a later realisation of this that made me refuse to speak further. Of course in one sense better I had kept clear of the whole business, but had I done so, had I not suffered I would not have come to my present knowledge. – *The Diaries of Francis Stuart*

10

German Odyssey

I CAN WELL IMAGINE THAT SOME READERS would prefer this book to begin here with what is seen as the core events of Stuart's life, but I feel a loyalty to my friend in that I promised to write about his life and writings. His own arduous writing career, with its fluctuations, advances and setbacks, has given me the inspiration to pursue my task to its conclusion despite minor setbacks and the years of work involved.

Stuart and Iseult made a final visit to see Yeats at Riversdale House in Rathfarnham in 1938. Yeats would soon leave for England and eventually end up in the Hotel Idéal Séjour at Cap Martin, Monte Carlo. Iseult found him shuffling about in slippers and complaining about old age. He had written about Iseult, Maud Gonne and his wife Georgie in *The Only Jealousy of Emer*, a play that reveals what he felt about all three once you unravel who is based on whom. When Yeats spoke to the Abbey Theatre audience after a production of his play *Purgatory*, he said it contained "his own convictions about this world and the next". He died a few months later in January 1939, having spent days in bed writing a contents list for his *Last Poems*. He sounds triumphant in a final letter to Lady Elizabeth Pelham: "I have found what I wanted. When I try to put all into a phrase I say, 'Man can embody truth but he cannot know it.'" Stuart would mark his passing, critically: "He never came to complete utterance because he never himself reached that point of inner truth. And how far was this because his later life was too comfortable and easy?" As I have pointed out, the Gonne–Yeats–Stuart–Iseult foursome was always a troubled one.

For many what follows is their only interest in Stuart's life – the Berlin years – how and why he went. In fact, Iseult Stuart set in motion her husband's German odyssey. Ian Stuart told me that Iseult may have longed for a temporary separation from him to ease the domestic strife. The trip came about through Helmut Clissmann of the German Academic Exchange Service in Ireland, who knew of Gonne's pro-German sympathies. Ewald Heinrich Helmut Clissmann, to give his full name, was born in Aachen in 1911, a German diplomat in Dublin who married a Sligo woman, Budge Mulcahy. As a friend of Iseult's, Clissmann arranged Stuart's lecture tour through connections in the Deutsch Akademie, Berlin. Clissmann was, like many Germans worldwide in the 1930s, serving his country while in exile. He would also be associated with Stuart in Berlin and again in Ireland in the 1980s. Stuart told me about being a visitor at the German Legation at Northumberland Road in Dublin in 1938 and also at Edouard Hempel's private residence in Monkstown. Dr Hempel, the German ambassador to Ireland, was a good friend of Gonne's, Iseult's and Seán MacBride's. These occasions were informal, according to Stuart, and not particularly entertaining, more in the category of Sunday afternoon social visits. Hempel, who had taken up the post of German Ambassador in 1937, also courted figures such as Yeats whom he visited that year, presenting him with an inscribed copy of a collection of propagandising essays entitled *Germany Speaks*.

When I knew Stuart he was not all that enamoured by any pomp and circumstance, position or social standing. In fact, the opposite could be said to be true; he might often assume that rounds of society dinners, parties, gatherings of media, political and public figures in the arts, film and entertainment were only ever as invigorating as the individuals involved. I often suggested that he had done his own share of hobnobbing and still did when I knew him, but he sometimes expressed loathing of what he called the social and society scene. He far preferred a private party with intimates or to meet people who interested him and many public figures held no interest for him.

Iseult approached Clissmann before *The Great Squire* was published in February 1939 to discuss a visit for her husband to Germany. She had, like Stuart, become complaisant about his steady profusion of novels: the aftermath of their publication, the arrival of the second half of the advance and then the waiting for reviews and later on, sales figures. Taking up his wife's idea of going to Germany

Stuart's mother and father

Henry Irwin Stuart, who went insane and took his own life

Stuart at Rugby, one of three public schools he attended

Stuart as a young man

Maud Gonne, her son Seán (MacBride) and daughter Iseult

Laragh Castle – Stuart wrote most of his pre-war novels in the turret room

Iseult, Katherine (Kay) and Ian, Laragh 1939 – Stuart had this photograph in Germany during the war years

Róisín Ní Mheara photographed by Stuart in Berlin, 1941 – their brief relationship was tempestuous

Herman Goertz, German spy

Hitler on parade in Kaiser Allee, Berlin, 1942 (photograph taken by Francis Stuart)

Stuart with Frau Piening and Madeleine,
Dornbirn, 1945 – Stuart was on his way to Paris

Stuart and Madeleine reunited on release from prison
by the Allies, Freiburg, August 1946

Stuart and Madeleine (left) meeting Ian and Kay (right) after the war

Stuart reunited with his son Ian after the war

Stuart in Paris, 1950

Madeleine, Stuart and Ethel Mannin,
London, 1951

Stuart and Madeleine on the day of their wedding, London

Last photograph of Iseult, at Laragh Castle

might seem like another instance of Stuart's passivity, but he was also quite glad to go. When I asked if he was passive in terms of Iseult and Gonne, "Hopelessly so," he replied. Hence his flights from the domestic hearth and home? "Yes," he agreed.

Lily had no pro-German sympathies but certainly Iseult was influenced in such matters by her mother, while Stuart may receive the benefit of the doubt about strong pro-German leanings in 1938. He shook his head on this matter, saying that he had no loyalty to any country in Europe but favoured France and Russia because of his passion for some of their literature. However, it needs reiterating that Gonne and Iseult can be accurately portrayed as typical of a minority of Irish people with staunch Republican ideals who were also pro-German simply because they were anti-British. Seán MacBride supported Saor Éire and had gone on the run along with other top IRA officers after the suppression of its newspaper *An Phoblacht* in 1931. In 1936, he was made Chief of Staff of the political wing of the IRA opposing de Valera and Cosgrave, but he had no left-wing tendencies, unlike other IRA activists Peadar O'Donnell, Charlie Gilmore and Frank Ryan.

Meanwhile the *bête noire* of Stuart's life, Hitler, led the *Volk* (the people) to serve his will for power. In our discussions of Hitler, the basic facts of his life emerged: his being a dropout arts student in his teenage years and living in doss houses after being a First World War corporal and *meldegünger* (courier). When I told Stuart that I felt a phoney intellectualism permeated the pages of Hitler's self-published *Mein Kampf* (my struggle) which displays a violent hatred for Jews and a wish to conquer Europe, he said he had never given more than a brief glance at the book and that was long after the war in London in the 1950s. Propaganda and turgid drivel, was Stuart's response to his brief perusal of *Mein Kampf*. I suggested to Stuart that Hitler is sometimes incorrectly classified with Friedrich Nietzsche, who was not anti-Semitic but whose sister, Elizabeth Förster, allied herself with the Nazis in order to fund Nietzsche's posthumous reputation as a philosopher. Some biography of Nietzsche or other provided me with this background and I had also read Alan Bullock's standard biography of Hitler and Stalin. Stuart responded that Hitler had no interest in Nietzsche or any philosophy.

I probed him on other aspects of Hitler. Hitler's mass appeal had a sexual dimension, I suggested, he was a sex symbol to German women. At this Stuart agreed, but laughed. Hitler had no great involvement with any woman, he added. He had an affair with his niece, Geli Raubel, who died aged 23. His jealousy reached psychopathic levels beyond her endurance. Her death, using his revolver, was claimed to be suicide but only Hitler knew the facts and used his power to cover them up. Raubel had a sexual affair with his chauffeur, in order to escape Hitler's perversity. Stuart had read something about this too but was not that interested. He continued saying that Hitler seemed to have found companionship of a sort in Eva Braun, but he presumed that he never experienced sexual bliss or received the spiritual healing of sex. He may have shown public affection for children and his dog Rolf, but these came from his false self, according to Stuart, like his taste in art for sentimental painting and marshal band music. Any comment I ever heard Stuart make about Hitler was derisory and negative. He often said that Hitler was an evil incarnation.

Stuart admitted that during the first months of the Second World War he thought of Hitler as "a kind of blind Samson who was pulling down the pillars of Western Society as we knew it, which I still believed had to come about before any new world could arise".[1] This is fairly categorical in its revolutionary intent. It even tacitly admits to accepting violent revolution. Incidentally, it echoes George Russell (AE) in support of Jim Larkin and the Dublin Lock-out in 1913 who proclaimed in a famous letter to the industrialist bosses, "It is you who are blind Samsons pulling down the pillars of society". Stuart also thought of Hitler "as a great destructive force, not a constructive one". However, long after the war, when writing to Jerry Natterstad, Stuart clarified his views on Fascism: "It has never seemed to me that anyone of imagination and psychic complexity could be a fascist."[2]

Stuart told me that before he left for Berlin in April 1939, he was awaiting a reply to a job application from the *Daily Express*. His own opinion of that year was that he wanted to go anywhere away from Laragh. The *Express* turned him down. What if they had not? Would he have been in London during the war in the company of Edward R. Murrow who broadcast during the Blitz to America? Or would the *Daily Express* have sent him to Berlin? Obviously, this can only be speculation. What follows is a narrative that I heard many times from

Stuart, not because he absentmindedly repeated himself but because I wanted to ascertain the facts as he remembered them.

Stuart arrived in Berlin in April 1939 and celebrated his birthday quietly. He was 37. At the Deutsche Akademie he met Professor Walter Schirmer who had a cheque for him and the itinerary for a lecture tour: Munich, Hamburg, Bonn and Cologne. There was an official greeting party in his honour including a significant meeting in the Englische Seminar with a lecturer, Hans Galinsky, who would prove a valuable contact in the future.

When Stuart was driven to his first venue the next day with the typical punctiliousness of the Third Reich, he noticed that the newspaper *Der Stürmer* contained anti-Jewish propaganda. He later wrote to Iseult, "It is an extraordinary thing to see the busy, fashionable streets of a big city without Jewish faces".[3] During their travels in Europe in the 1920s, when he befriended a Jew in Vienna, Iseult was annoyed and in *Black List*, he contrasts her with the Jew, "humble where she was proud, realist where she relied on abstract principles, revelling in the senses which to her were tiresome. If there was a Jewish idea, which was surely a contradiction, it was a hidden, unheroic, and critical one, a worm that could get into a lot of fine-looking fruit."[4] This latter phrase became a source of much misinterpretation in the 1990s for Stuart. The intent for him, which he explained to me, is that the Jewish perspective on life is keenly aware of the good and evil sides of existence; there is no shirking from a recognition of the dark side of life, either within the self or in others. Stuart's context shows that he is engaged in a critical tirade against Iseult, displaying what he sees as her narrow Catholicism which denies, or would prefer not to acknowledge, the darker sides of existence.

In the spring of 1939 he had to wait until reaching Cologne before cashing his cheque and was invited to dinner by the Direktor of the Deutsche Bank who, though he had never heard of Francis Stuart the writer, was certain that he must be famous, otherwise he would never have been invited to Germany! Back in Berlin he was given a plush apartment and could explore the city, but had to carry a special visitor's ID card. Professor Schirmer personally saw to it that he was wined and dined. Stuart became friendly with Professor Hans Galinsky who would eventually get him a lectureship in Berlin. The professor of Modern English Literature in Trinity College, Terence

Brown, told me that he believed that this was only possible because of the Nazi domination of Academia: Stuart had no credentials or degree for lecturing at any university, let alone one in Berlin.

Stuart relaxed after the lecture tour through Munich, Hamburg, Bonn and Cologne. In every city he had a driver and interpreter. He was driven to the Rhine by Prince Biron von Kürland (who died in the Battle of Britain) and watched an elite squadron of Luftwaffe show off their low flying. Stuart shared the prince's experience of previous flying hours and they enjoyed their day together. These were meetings he always looked back on fondly, even with a residue of the initial excitement. Stuart's antennae and perceptions were mesmerised to some extent during his first visit to Germany. Pre-war Germany has been so much documented that it is unnecessary to elaborate about the re-emergence of Germany in the 1930s and the early Hitler euphoria.

Stuart felt relieved to be away from the domestic scene in Laragh also, and this added to his savouring the high spirits that were palpable in Germany. In Hamburg, when he read the more subversive passages from his writings, a heavily decorated Gestapo Officer walked out in disgust. Stuart quickly realised the Nazi antipathy to his novels.

By the beginning of May he was asked to give some lectures in Berlin, after which Professor Schirmer invited him to return to Berlin as a lecturer for that autumn in English and Irish literature. Letters had arrived with Irish postmarks during his absence from Berlin. His daughter Kay was missing him, especially since her first Communion was imminent and, with the fuss of it all, she had caught a cold. Ian wrote from his private boarding school, St Gerard's in Bray. These notes from his children with footnotes by Iseult made him lonely. He wrote to Iseult and asked her to come over with Ian and Kay. When she refused, he replied with regret about having accepted the job. Iseult's letter conceded that a holiday in Berlin might be a good idea. He then replied to her saying that it was too expensive. At the end of June he wrote of his indecision about staying or going back to Ireland, ending the letter, "I miss you all very much".[5] He could have stayed on in Berlin on that occasion but choose not to do so. I asked him why and he replied candidly that something had made him hesitate. He also wanted to go home to Iseult and the children, and think things out in the peace and quiet of Laragh.

Stuart's letters were under scrutiny from Irish Intelligence since his departure for Germany. While he was away, the Garda Síochána reported details to Irish Intelligence of a visit by Dr Edouard Hempel, accompanied by Gonne, to Laragh Castle. Hempel was also an occasional visitor to Roebuck House, Clonskeagh, Gonne's home.

Meanwhile, on completing his first visit to Berlin, Stuart hoped that Iseult might return with him for the autumn while Ian was away at boarding school. Iseult reminded him that if she travelled to Berlin, someone would have to mind seven-year-old Kay; Gonne was elderly and would not do so. Iseult did not want to leave her daughter with Lily because she felt it might be too much for Lily to run the house and to mind Kay at the same time. Besides, she did not wish to leave her daughter. None of these domestic considerations impinged on Stuart's attending the Midsummer's Festival at the Olympic Stadium which was a pageant of the sort excelled in by the Nazis. The kind of extravaganza portrayed in newsreels of Nazi rallies and Leni Riefenstahl's film, *Triumph of the Will*. He watched 120,000 youths parading against a background of huge swastika flags and bands. In a letter to Iseult he seemed impressed: "Such a spectacle and organisation!" but added, "I am convinced of the unimaginable terror and horror of war."[6] The summer of 1939 was a bizarre time in Europe. It did not take a prophet to know that war was approaching. Even William Shirer, a journalist in Berlin, who had secretly begun making notes which would be turned into a mammoth book, *The Rise and Fall of the Third Reich,* felt the palpable imminence of war and said so in a brief social encounter with Stuart. Nothing came of the plan for Iseult to join him in Berlin in the summer of 1939.

Stuart returned to Ireland in July and half-heartedly tried to persuade Iseult to return with him in the autumn when the university term began. However, he admitted to me that he was much undecided about what to do. During the summer of 1939, he raised a tricolour, and a German flag which he had been presented with before leaving Berlin, on the flagpole of the castle's turret. When the local sergeant called to inquire about the flags, Stuart informed him that the German one was lower than the tricolour. Stuart told me this in a spirit of fun, recalling the scene at the time. He believed that he flew the German flag as mere defiance, signifying his inner turmoil. This is the sort of conduct that comes from disturbance of the psyche, he added.

The expectation of war was everywhere and when it was declared (his son Ian ran to tell him) Stuart would later write in *The Chariot*, "The realisation that it had come at last and for the first hours, at least, there's this sense of release". The German invasion of Poland on 1 September, "Operation White", was bogusly justified by an attack on a German radio station at Gleiwitz near the Polish frontier which was actually staged by the German Gestapo wearing Polish uniforms. The Government in Ireland, with de Valera at the head, immediately went into an overnight sitting which resulted in a declaration of Irish neutrality. Edouard Hempel, German Ambassador, in due course reported Berlin's satisfaction over the neutrality decision. John Maffey, the British Representative in Dublin, realised that de Valera was going to use neutrality in a bid for the reunification of Ireland and the recovery of the six counties partitioned since the Anglo-Irish Treaty of 1921. The IRA declared war on Britain and began a sabotage bombing campaign. When a bomb killed five people and wounded fifty others in Coventry, two IRA volunteers, Peter Barnes and James McCormack, were arrested, tried and hanged. There followed a raid on the Magazine Fort in the Phoenix Park by the IRA and de Valera countered this with the Emergency Powers Act. Meanwhile the Republic of Ireland, and also Germany, feared the forcible seizure of Irish ports by the British.

Stuart firmly decided against Iseult's going to Germany with him. Instead, realising that he might soon be leaving his children, he brought Kay on many trips to various public offices in Dublin while he tried to get the necessary documents for his return to Berlin. She was eight years old. He had brought back her teddy bear from Germany that she had given to him as a "friend" in case he got lonely. The gesture struck him deeply as significant of a daughter giving of herself to the father she loved. It may also suggest subconsciously that she thought he was without any friends. He realised that, if he got the necessary visas, he would be parting for an indeterminate period of time from her, Ian, Iseult and Lily. He admitted to me that events took over since he had no strong will power to make any decision. He wanted to get to Berlin and at other times did not want to leave Ireland at all.

Professor Schirmer had written to him before the declaration of war confirming his earlier appointment as lecturer. When Stuart was issued a passport in October he wrote to the French Consulate in Dublin: "I only wish to pass through France on my way to Switzerland where I am going for reasons of health, on my doctor's recommendation."[7] He was, in fact, lying, he told me. When notified to send on a medical certificate, he did so. He contacted Hilda Burnett, his former farm manager, who had married a doctor. The bogus certificate stated that H.F. Stuart was tubercular and needed to attend a clinic in Switzerland. He desperately wanted to get back to Berlin, he finally admitted to me. Iseult was a perfect accomplice for his plans. They naturally felt anxious about him leaving the children for a war zone. Eventually the 24-hour transit visa for England and France with an entry permit to Switzerland came in the post. He also received a letter from Stanley Kunitz of *Twentieth-Century Authors,* looking for an up-to-date biographical sketch. In the section asking him to list his favourite writers, he noted Kafka, Yeats, Proust, Rilke, Thomas Wolfe, Somerset Maugham and J.B. Priestley. The last two are uncharacteristic choices of his later years, but it is heartening to see Yeats on the list.

In December, the gardaí seized a transmitter bought in the United States with funds raised by Clan na Gael leader, Joseph McGarrity, for use between the IRA and Abwehr II - German Intelligence. Two known German agents, Oscar K. Pfaus and Ernest Drohl, had landed in Ireland and met with IRA chiefs. One day Stuart received an invitation from Jim O'Donovan, an IRA organiser who had gone to Berlin to meet Kurt Haller and set up links with Abwehr II. O'Donovan was pro-Fascist according to Republican activist, George Gilmore. Gilmore disapproved of the IRA making Nazi connections. Stuart went with O'Donovan and met chief of staff, Stephen Hayes, who gave him a message to deliver in Berlin. Hayes did not want German troops landing in Ireland, but gave Stuart the vital message asking for German aid and a German liaison officer to be secretly sent to Ireland to meet with the IRA. This conveys some of the differing factions within the IRA at the time. Iseult sewed the message into the lining of Stuart's winter coat.

It was leave-taking time after Christmas. He did not want to unsettle his children, so as happily as possible he hugged and kissed Kay, now aged 9, and Ian, 14. He vividly recalled for me his boarding the St Kevin's bus outside Laragh Castle and seeing Lily holding Kay and Ian by the hand. Iseult accompanied him on the bus to Dublin. He was desperately sad leaving the children and brought with him a photograph of Iseult with Ian and Kay. Dublin seemed its old self, indifferent to the war in Europe, according to Stuart, as they went to Gonne at Roebuck House. During their stay, they went to visit Hempel's private residence at Gortleitragh in Dún Laoghaire. Gonne's autobiography, *A Servant of the Queen* (1938) had recently been published. The book ends at the time of her honeymoon with Major John MacBride in 1903. While Millevoye is mentioned in the text, he is nowhere acknowledged as Iseult's father. Gonne was also interested in Stuart's trip to Germany since he had met Ruth Weiland on his lecture tour. She was hoping that Ruth Weiland would supervise a German translation of *A Servant of the Queen* but was otherwise excited, according to Stuart with his decision to go.

What Stuart, Gonne and Weiland did not know was that their letters were being censored by Colonel Liam Archer of G2, Director of Military Intelligence based in the Phoenix Park, Dublin. Archer was convinced that Stuart would not go to Switzerland but intended to go to Berlin. Stuart's transit visa had come from the Legation d'Irlande, Paris, having been sanctioned by His Excellency Seán Murphy, the Minister Plenipotentiary. Archer also expected Stuart not to delay in Paris more than the few hours necessary to catch his train.

It was a sad and confused parting between Stuart and Iseult. She said that if the visas failed "he could do worse than spend the war with her". Stuart told me that if she had asked him not to go he would have returned to Laragh with her. As they kissed before he went up the gangplank to the ship at Dun Laoghaire pier, they had to disengage as a rat scurried towards them. Iseult, used to rats around Laragh Castle, shooed it away. Stuart thought of it as a bad omen and remembered news that he had received days earlier about the death in England of Nellie Farren, his childhood nurse. He had also taken her death as a bad omen when he remembered that it was she who told him about the bat flying into the delivery room in Townsville, Australia, on the night he was born. He waved to Iseult with a divided heart, was anxious leaving Ireland yet willing himself to go. At such times when he told me about this leave-taking, he would become silent. I did not dare intrude in such a private moment that had determined the course of the remainder of his life. It was up to him to tell me more, which of course, he did.

On the boat to England his passport and visa were inspected by Irish Intelligence officers who had been tipped off by Archer of G2. This encounter made him rip the seam of his coat lining in a toilet cubicle and retrieve the message from Stephen Hayes of the IRA. Like a spy he memorised the contents. He tore it into tiny pieces, later releasing them into the high winds and the choppy Irish Sea. It is a moot point as to whether Stuart, out of deference to his wife and mother-in-law, intended taking an IRA message to Berlin for the sake of the adventure or in support of the IRA. This action, along with others of the period, has labelled him pro-German if not pro-IRA. His own opinion was that the adventurer aspect came first for him. His action, he said required one to take an overall view and make a complete ideological leap and to see him as the outcast, neutral observer, the novelist and poet rather than an IRA activist. He had to decide, if he reached Berlin, whether he would deliver the secret contents of that message.

In London, as he passed a cinema billboard, a poster for a film, *The Rains Came* starring Myra Loy and Tyrone Power, depicting the stars against a background of monsoons and earthquakes, seemed prophetic. It might not be gentle rain from heaven and there would be little quality of mercy either, he conjectured, as he went on his way. He did not make contact with a former lover, Margery Binner. She had married a producer in the BBC and he decided to leave well alone. After dawn at Boulogne, French authorities scrutinised his passport and visa before he boarded the train for Paris. The city, he said, had an air of expectation like London, but for some reason fewer people in uniforms were noticeable among the civilian population. He had only a few hours to wait for an express train to Berne. Crossing the Swiss border at Basel, as he showed his documentation to the border guard, a photograph of Iseult and the children was scrutinised also. They seemed far away, he told me, sighing. Travel fatigue made him miss the train to Berlin and he got on a local rail line to Freiburg.

He stayed overnight at Freiburg in the Hotel Habsburger and next morning two plainclothes members of the Gestapo in grey raincoats and black fedora hats abruptly came, as if from nowhere, and asked for identification. His passport and visa made them suspicious until he produced the letter from Hempel.[8] The letter relaxed the whole situation. They registered the fact that it was from the German Ambassador to Ireland, but were more impressed by the assignation to meet with Ernst von Weizsäcker in Berlin. Incidentally, von Weizsäcker's son, a nuclear physicist, was working on a German atomic bomb. More to the point however was that Weizsäcker, as Head of the Foreign Office (Auswertiges Amt), was in frequent consultation with Foreign Minister Ribbentrop, Heinrich Himmler and, of course, Adolf Hitler.

It took me many meetings with Stuart to piece together this ensuing chronology of events and sometimes on my return visits to him and he did not always want to be forced back into continuing his account. However, he did honestly tell me everything he could remember while other substantial sources have verified the greater part of his narrative.

11

Friends, Lovers, a Spy

STUART RECALLED THAT HE ARRIVED IN Berlin at night. Everywhere was blacked out. It was January 1940. He felt the immensity of the war for the first time. There is an evocative account in his post-war novel, *Victors and Vanquished*. His first night at the Anhalter Hof was bleak. Without ration cards he could get no food. On the following day, in the Friedrich Wilhelms University, the academic year was functioning at full efficiency. He was surprised to find that he had accumulated a salary payment from his previous visit and was assigned a large fifth-floor flat on Nikolsburger Platz; by any standards a luxury flat, with three bedrooms, a large dining room, parlour, kitchen, bathroom and a balcony/conservatory. He immediately set about arranging for money to be sent to Iseult in Ireland. Days later, he went to the German Foreign Ministry with the letter of introduction from Hempel.

Stuart was summoned to a meeting with Ernst von Weizsäcker, Head of the Foreign Office on 4 February. He asked for a free pass to explore Berlin, but Weizsäcker ignored his question and asked what the mood was in London. Stuart said he could not be a judge of such things at all. As he relaxed, he detected that Weizsäcker might not be a totally committed Nazi. Asked if he had heard Lord Haw-Haw's broadcasts, Stuart replied that a writer friend, Liam O'Flaherty, had said that "Lord Haw-Haw is winning the war single-handedly for Germany".[1] Weizsäcker wanted to know how to spell O'Flaherty and Stuart told him. Did Stuart speak German? No, but he had bought a dictionary and phrase book. Then in the silence that followed, Stuart emphasised his neutrality. He was issued a permit to go where he wanted in Berlin. Finally Weizsäcker asked him if he thought Germany would win the war. "No," answered Stuart. "Nor do I," Weizsäcker replied.[2]

Stuart told me the story of this meeting many times. He would often remark on the German's comment about losing the war. Stuart always seemed incredulous that such a meeting had taken place, yet swore that it had. Before the meeting ended, he said to Weizsäcker that he wished if possible to visit Professor Franz Fromme whom he had met in Dublin. When Weizsäcker picked up a phone and asked someone to arrange the meeting, Stuart said he remained stunned and perplexed at Hitler's Foreign Secretary commenting about the possible outcome of the war in a most extraordinary manner. [3] Looking back, he said that it only stuck in his mind because of the comment about losing the war but as time went on he had developed a whole theory about it, namely that Germany had entered the war with great doubts as to the outcome ending in their favour. This he thought summed up the German feeling at the time – one of nervous and vague optimism. He added that surely Weizsäcker should have been put out by him saying that he did not think Germany would be victorious in the war.

Stuart was driven to Fromme's apartment in a long black Daimler with swastika flags over the two headlights. His initial problem was getting a message to Iseult. Fromme asked him to write a hasty letter and he would have it sent to Ireland in the diplomatic bag, and secretly conveyed to Iseult. Fromme listened to Stuart's verbal message from the IRA and considered its urgency for Kurt Haller of Abwehr. The message from Stephen Hayes requested German aid and a German liaison officer to go to Ireland and meet with IRA chiefs of staff, but was wary about supporting a German invasion. When I asked Stuart to comment on the fact of being an IRA courier, he nodded candidly. There was a part of him that liked this complexity and yet could dismiss it as not very important or crucial in the light of larger events. Meanwhile, the IRA men condemned to death for the Coventry bomb became world headlines, even in Berlin, where it was being used to drum up pro-German support in Ireland. In Dublin, de Valera asked London for clemency, as did Irish-American sympathisers, but the men were hanged.

Fromme contacted Stuart about a meeting with Dr Schobert who worked directly with "Lord Haw-Haw". Stuart was surprised at this and postponed the meeting. Instead he went to the Irish Legation on

Drakestrasse and made himself known to William Warnock. Eventually he could not avoid meeting Dr Schobert and began meeting Haw-Haw (William Joyce), Warnock invited Stuart to listen to Haw-Haw on his radio. Joyce's anti-British speeches met a sympathetic ear from Stuart because of his disgust at the lack of clemency for the condemned Coventry bombers. He was asked for some material for broadcasting by Lord Haw-Haw, but what he submitted was deemed not to be of much use, according to Stuart. He was distinctly hostile when referring to Haw-Haw in *Black List, Section H* and in conversation with me.

On St Patrick's Day, Stuart gave a modest party with the help of William Warnock, the Irish Ambassador to Germany. Also invited was Eileen Walsh, Warnock's secretary. Professor Fromme introduced Captain Hermann Goertz to Stuart the following month. He also met Róisín Ní Mheara through Goertz at some party or other – he could not exactly remember where – but Róisín struck him deeply. He said that he suddenly felt glad to be surrounded by a lot of new friends. Róisín was the adopted daughter of General Sir Ian Hamilton, Commander-in-Chief of British forces at the battle of the Dardanelles in the First World War. She told him that she had met Hitler in the 1930s. Stuart noticed she was pregnant and she told him about the Ukrainian lover who had abandoned her. She did not know anything about her father, and this also drew her and Stuart together. At the time, he explained to me, he always wanted to share that mystery of his with anyone who was sympathetic and this required a person who had some similar experience. The fact that Róisín was a beautiful woman added to the attraction and they soon became lovers.

Róisín moved into his flat on Nikolsburger Platz. Her child was born and Stuart engaged a maid who cooked and helped with the infant. He got Róisín a job translating news broadcasts from English to German because of her greater fluency in the language. Stuart recalled that Róisín Ní Mheara was the most beautiful woman he had ever known and, by implication, that he had ever slept with. One of his many comments on sexuality is revealing: "Behind their seemly façade, women are constructed for the most unseemly and sensational act imaginable."[4] When I asked him about her he said that he was often puzzled about why they had not lasted as a couple. Was it the fact that she had a child? At this he looked indifferent, but I surmised that it might have been a mitigating factor on his part.

Róisín had a lot of spare time as a new mother because of the maid. Stuart recalled her sitting around reading a wartime bestseller *Auf den Marmorklippen* (*On the Marble Cliffs*) by Ernst Jünger. Published the previous year, the novel was a thinly disguised satire on Reich Marshal and Commander-in-Chief of the Luftwaffe, Hermann Goering. The novel contains a horrific evocation of a death camp. Róisín translated passages as she read to Stuart, whose German was improving, though it was not yet up to Jünger's acidic prose. Jünger, who was posted to Paris, became a supporter of the July 1944 plot to kill Hitler. He was declared loyal by General Spiegel and avoided an awful death – hanging by piano wire – the fate of the other July plot conspirators, including Colonel Graf von Stauffenberg whom Stuart had met in 1940. According to Stuart's account, Jünger was dishonourably discharged from the German Army, near the end of the war, as a crank. His literary career went through many ups and downs until his death at the age of 102. When Róisín Ní Mheara returned the Jünger novel, the local librarian was furious and suspicious she had been able to borrow such a book because it had since been withdrawn from circulation.

In the spring of 1940, Stuart met Hermann Goertz again. Goertz was completing parachute training and other instruction with the Corps Brandenburg, a Special Operations Unit of Abwehr II (German Military Intelligence) under Colonel Lahousen. He told Stuart that he was too old to be a pilot at the age of 50 but that during the First World War he had been in the German Air Force. Stuart was further surprised to learn that he had studied Law at Edinburgh and worked as a solicitor in London for four years. On his return to Germany in the 1930s, he was recruited as a spy and sent back to England. In March 1936 he was arrested for passing on information about the RAF. He served three years of a four-year sentence of penal servitude. Stuart recalled the excitement of Goertz after his selection as a spy to go to Ireland with funds for the IRA as part of an advance squad preparing for a German invasion. He had been on holiday in Ireland before the war. Their conversation led to Stuart giving details about Laragh Castle. Stuart realised that he could not give a letter to the German spy for Iseult, but he remembered that he had an Irish pound note among change from buying foreign currency before his departure for Berlin. He asked Goertz to give it to his daughter, not expecting that the spy would end up in Laragh.

Goertz's mission began after many weeks' delay. The plane, a Heinkel, was meant to take him to County Tyrone, but an RAF fighter shadowed them and, when the German pilot shook him off in heavy mist, he shouted at Goertz to bale out. He parachuted down into County Meath. It was 5 May 1940. He spent the first morning in the vicinity of a small town, Kinnegad, having found his equipment and later in the day made it to the river Boyne. Swimming across he changed out of military garb and put on breeches, a jumper and a beret. Having consulted his map he considered that Wicklow was not too long a trek. It took him four days to reach Laragh. He arrived in rags, exhausted and hungry. He did not know that he could have used the US currency notes in his possession. A sense of honour kept him from spending the Irish pound, but it was also his calling card as he stumbled up the laneway into Laragh Castle. It was not long before he convinced Iseult and Bridie, the maid that he had met Stuart in Berlin. Then Iseult sent word to her mother who arrived as speedily as possible by taxi. They were fully welcoming to the German spy. Gonne and Iseult, after making the children swear to secrecy, went to Dublin to get clothes for Goertz in Switzers, leaving Lily in charge. Ian Stuart, who was 14 at the time, was fascinated by Goertz and says he looked like the actor Conrad Veidt (who played a Nazi major in the film *Casablanca*).[5] They both had an interest in woodcarving and here the young Ian found a first mentor in his formative years as a sculptor. They even planned to work together after the war. Meanwhile, Stuart's son and daughter kept the German fed, as he hid in the scrublands around Laragh Castle by day, sleeping at night in one of the outhouses, watchful but none too anxious in the sleepy Wicklow village. However, locals noticed him and telephoned the police.

Soon enough, with the discovery of Goertz's parachute and wireless set, the event became news. Embassies buzzed with activity, especially the British and German ones in Dublin. Iseult was arrested on 24 May with Goertz's contact, Stephen Held. Held was a known IRA man who was having secret meetings with Goertz at the time. Goertz escaped after a chase by gardaí and went on the run. Iseult was taken to Mountjoy Jail in Dublin where she spent five weeks awaiting trial. Her son, Ian, recalled visiting his mother in prison and worrying about her. Iseult got upset seeing him. Gonne kept a stern face with the prison guards and encouraged her daughter to be brave. Seán MacBride, by then a barrister, was barred by legal protocol from defending his half-sister in court. Iseult was tried under the Offences Against the State Act and found not guilty because of insufficient evidence. Stephen Held was of German parentage. In his house in the Dublin suburb of Templeogue, police found the $20,000 that Goertz had brought from England. It transpired that he had also met Goertz in Berlin just after the outbreak of war. They had been meeting in Donnybrook in Dublin since the spy parachuted into Ireland. Held was sentenced to five years' imprisonment.

Stuart's salary was stopped for a while because of press and radio coverage of the Stephen Held–Iseult Stuart case in Dublin. German Ambassador Hempel met with Gonne who pleaded poverty for Iseult and her children. Hempel feared "indiscreet statements" in Stuart's letters and wished to defuse further publicity in Ireland. Stuart's letters were censored by the ABP, Ausland Brief Politzei. Hempel contacted the chargé d'affaires in Berlin at the Irish Legation on Drakestrasse, asking that he allow through money deducted from Stuart's salary for his wife and children.

After her release, Iseult began a relationship with Goertz who became a nightly visitor to Laragh after a number of searches by police failed to trace him. The police presumed that he would not be foolish enough to stay around Wicklow. However, he did. Iseult and Goertz engaged in a love affair while he evaded capture for 19 months. My source for this affair is Stuart who surmised the fact. Ian also said that his mother had become involved with Goertz, and Anna MacBride-White, Iseult's cousin, mentions a liaison between the spy and Iseult in her account *Dante Knew*. Kay would later comment that Goertz "had a profound effect on her mother". Examining the evidence of Ian's comments and Stuart's conjecture, I feel obliged to include this further twist in the tale.

Goertz, alias "Brandy", had a wife, Ellen, and three children in Lübeck. When he was arrested in November of 1941 his identity card had the name Heinz Kruse. He had signed the card "Dr Hermann Kruse". In a statement made to the Irish Secret Service, he naturally had to discuss Stuart, of whom he said: "He had nothing to do with the Abwehr, he was no politician, he had no contacts with the IRA and not much knowledge about them. But he was a genuine Irish patriot and the prototype of those people who later became my friends in Ireland." The *Irish Independent* headlined his arrest, calling him "a German parachutist" rather than a spy. Goertz would prove to be a difficult prisoner, first in Arbour Hill prison then at Athlone from where he persistently sought a transfer to the Curragh Military Prison Camp, which he eventually got, having claimed officer status.

In the summer of 1940 the German Ambassador to Ireland was fully compromised by German spies landing all over the countryside. It did not matter that spies such as Goertz were eccentric and ineffective in funding the IRA to prepare for the remote possibility of a German invasion. Not all that remote, however, since Hitler is recorded as saying at this time: "The occupation of Ireland might lead to the end of the war."[6] A 1941 secret document released in the 1990s revealed contingency plans in the event of a German invasion. When Irish forces could no longer resist, the chief of staff was to advise the Taoiseach, de Valera, who would then decide to invite the British in. The document emphasises that the British military must not cross the border until met by liaison officers from the Irish army. This states the official, pro-British stance which also reflected the majority of Southern Irish thinking at the time, and was expressed in the popular witticism: "Who Are We Neutral Against?"[7]

12

Frank Ryan, Operation Dove

ON 14 JULY 1940, MAJOR RUMPEL (Stuart recalled the name for me) drove himself, Róisín and Frank Ryan, who had recently arrived in Berlin, to a POW camp. An RAF sergeant in the POW (Stalag), near Posen was appalled to see Stuart, an Irish writer, siding with "these vicious brutes". Leaving the camp, Stuart saw Polish prisoners being kicked and beaten by guards. Days later, he arranged a meeting with Colonel von Stauffenberg whose English was perfect, according to Stuart, to ask consideration for the POWs, some of whom were Irish. Meanwhile, he joined in the high life and euphoria of Berlin, as much as his status allowed, but he was still a foreigner in a strange city and certainly not in the centre of things even socially. Róisín Ní Mheara was willing to partner him since she, too, had a taste for bohemian living which was somewhat curbed by wartime restrictions on food and alcohol. Stuart enjoyed a sporadic companionship with the military who would engage him in conversation if their English was adequate. Was he fully aware that he was among the Nazis at this stage? When I asked this, he shrugged affirmatively.

A retrospective comment from *Black List* attempts a partial explanation: "The advantage he had over the ordinary criminal was that in the prevailing conditions it was possible to act in a way that would evoke in his judges the same condemnation as the kind of peacetime crime of which he was incapable." To some of his critics *Black List, Section H* is a novel written with the hindsight of 20 years. Whenever I put this criticism to Stuart, he would say, "It is well known that I spent the war in Berlin. I wrote that novel with imaginative integrity and conviction."

He told me that he sometimes felt self-disgust at abandoning Iseult, Ian and Kay. Still, in the unique atmosphere of wartime Berlin he was earning his living through working at the University and broadcasting, and found that having an affair with Róisín Ní Mheara was preferable to the stalemate of his marriage. He also recalls feeling immensely free and aware of unpredictable possibilities. My reaction to this was never one of moral disapproval, rather a fascination with what he had seen and experienced. Latterly, I accept that anyone who feels that Stuart's actions in Berlin can be seen as siding with the Nazis is justified, but according to my judgement of him over 20 years and more he was not a Nazi sympathiser. The issue of collaborator and traitor is another matter.

He spoke about meeting Ruth Weiland at the Presseklub in Leipziger Platz. She invited him to write on heroes of his native land, so he contributed two articles for *Irische Freiheitskämpfer* (Irish Freedom Fighters) on Casement and de Valera. The tone of the articles is similar to his broadcasts. They also collaborated on a translation of William Maloney's *The Forged Casement Diaries*. Casement, hanged for treason by the British in 1916, had been a servant of the British Crown with the Colonial Service in Africa prior to supporting the Irish Cause that led to his capture. When Maloney refused permission for a German translation, Stuart wrote his own account and this is what Ruth Weiland translated. It was published in Hamburg by Hanseatische in 1940. So began a collaboration with Ruth Weiland which would result in the translation of three of his novels, *The Coloured Dome, The Great Squire* and *The Bridge*, the latter going into three editions from the publishing house, Keil. *Die Brucke* became a well-known novel in wartime Berlin. Copies of the German edition are a rarity because of the aftermath of bombing raids by the British and the Americans. When Stuart was asked what he had written he would cite *Die Brucke* and the other two novels which gave him validity as a writer.

The closing lines of the book on Casement provide another slant on whether Stuart can be seen as pro-German during his stay in Berlin. Stuart had become fascinated by the Irish patriot in the 1930s, and in a letter to the *Irish Press* along with others, such as Bernard Shaw and Peadar O'Donnell, he defended Maloney, whose biography of Casement had come under attack for the veracity of its contents. Stuart denied to me that the closing lines of the book were written by him (translated by Ruth Weiland) in *Der Fall Casement*: "Perhaps one day, no longer lying far away, Irish and German soldiers will stand together before Casement's unmarked grave to honour the great patriot who has done so much to further friendship between the two nations."[1] It sounds too propagandist for Stuart's pen and besides he claimed that he never saw the finished proofs before the book was published in Hamburg. His involvement with the Casement book points to feelings of solidarity with the Anglo-Irish patriot who negotiated successfully with the Germans during the Great War for weapons for the Irish Cause. Stuart's involvement with the Casement book, in my opinion, reveals some sort of pro-German affiliation, if not of the same intensity as that of Iseult and Gonne. There was also the aspect that it involved him imaginatively in arms smuggling, but he told me that with hindsight he never envisaged a German invasion of Ireland and while he tacitly approved of the transport of arms to the IRA he believed that such arms and weapons would not advance their aims during the war.

On his second visit to the Presseklub, Stuart met the American John Cudahy of the *New York Herald Tribune*. Cudahy was a figure he often discussed with me; someone he felt kinship with and to some extent believed him to be heading for disaster. Cudahy had been United States minister in Dublin but was replaced in April of 1940 by David Gray whose wife was an aunt of Eleanor Roosevelt. When Cudahy first arrived in Berlin as a disgruntled journalist, he began advising Hitler about how to keep the United States out of the war (so he had told Stuart over champagne cocktails at the Hotel Adlon). Cudahy was embittered at losing his job in Dublin, according to Stuart, and, having fallen under Hitler's spell, had turned pro-German, securing an interview with the Führer for *Life* magazine in 1941. The American was expecting further invitations to meet with Hitler and asked the authorities if Stuart might go along. In Stuart's mood of daring at the time, it is likely he would have gone to meet Adolf Hitler had the opportunity occurred. He expressed reservations to me about giving the long arm salute, seeing it as expressive of the totalitarian regime which he realised by then was certainly no advance on democratic capitalism, and in fact, was the reverse. However, Stuart never had a meeting with Hitler. Cudahy died in a riding accident in the United States after the war.

Frank Ryan's presence in Berlin is almost as legendary as Stuart's. This was a relationship that he was always reluctant to talk about, but I persisted in questioning him. They were often together but remained wary and suspicious of each other. Ryan had been allowed to escape from the Spanish prison at Burgos in a deal with Franco, the German Foreign Ministry and Admiral Wilhelm Canaris of the Abwehr (German Special Intelligence). The IRA were also involved through Seán Russell, the saboteur, who came to Berlin from the United States via Genoa, where he was met by Professor Franz Fromme who became his interpreter. Long before his imprisonment for involvement in the Goertz landing in Ireland, Stephen Held had also arrived in Berlin to begin organising Ryan's welcome by Nazi officials. Helmut Clissmann, with the special commando unit (the Brandenburg Regiment), attached to the Abwehr, also knew about Ryan whose plight in Burgos prison was international news. General Erwin von Lahousen of the Abwehr called Ryan "a terrorist, a gangster". Clissmann's wife went to Madrid on a secret mission to inform the Irish Legation there about Ryan while he languished in Burgos Prison.[2] Stuart's mingling with these people compounds some kind of intent on his part and makes him look like a supporter or, more accurately, a hanger on of German Intelligence personnel. He admitted to me that the company of such people ensured that he was not cut off from social life since he could not and did not go about on his own in order to avoid the sort of scrutiny that was prevalent at the time.

Dr Edmund Veesenmayer, German Foreign Office "special Adviser" on Ireland, escorted Ryan from Paris after his "escape" from Burgos and became a friend to the Irishman. It was de Valera who had previously made a plea to the Spanish leader to reprieve a sentence of death on Ryan, as a member of the International Brigade in the Spanish Civil War. De Valera did not want Ryan back in Ireland. Franco had kept him prisoner because of his collateral potential and, while there is no documentation available, it is likely that Ryan's escape to Berlin was brought about by promises from Berlin to Franco. Ryan's Republican position was allied to that of Peadar O'Donnell and George Gilmore whose ideology claimed the necessity of a socialist workers' revolution. Ryan was deemed a communist in Ireland for fighting against Franco's Fascists and opposing Eoin O'Duffy's Blueshirts. He was a chameleon figure, a brilliant student at University College Dublin in Celtic Studies and a prize-winning public speaker. He became a Republican polemicist with anti-imperialist leanings, claiming that his politics were neither "from Moscow nor

Maynooth". Like Stuart, he fought on the anti-Treaty side in the Civil War and also took part in the War of Independence. In an academic way, he was better read than Stuart. He was tall like Stuart, and his ears stuck out. He had thick, wavy, black hair and was attractive to women but not at ease with them, according to Stuart. In fact, he frequented places under special privilege through his Nazi contacts in Giesebrechtstrasse, an area of brothels where he could find prostitutes. His ego was insufferable, Stuart told me. His worst trait was a harsh egotism that was grating, he added with disapproval.

Ryan was nearly totally deaf and of no use to the Germans, according to Stuart, but lived in Berlin under the name Frank Rickard in a large gloomy flat on Nymphenburgerstrasse. Still, he was kept as a consultant to the Nazis on Irish affairs, enjoyed great freedom and the special rations of a diplomat. Soon after settling in he met with Seán Russell who obtained Abwehr support to plan sabotage campaigns in Ireland prior to a German invasion. Two previous missions at the planning stage with Helmut Clissmann never came to anything. The mission with Russell was set in motion in August 1940 under code name "Operation Dove". Ryan told this in secret to Stuart, who bought a postcard of a German U-boat and wrote some lines from Mangan's "My dark Rosaleen" across it. He gave the card to Róisín Ní Mheara, told her about the mission, and warned her not to tell anyone. However, Russell died on board a German U-boat in Irish waters and Ryan decided to return to Berlin. MI5 files imply that Ryan may have poisoned Russell because of mutual rivalry, which might explain Russell's acute stomach cramps prior to his death. Meanwhile Ryan waited in Berlin, losing whatever petty authority he possessed, according to Stuart. Stuart and Ryan found each other's company unbearable at times. Ryan, according to Stuart, was continually threatening him in an effort to legitimise his tenuous position. He acted as if he was vital to the war machine but in truth he was a disposable individual to the Nazis and became dependent on Stuart and Róisín Ní Mheara. It was a very uncomfortable triangle, Stuart told me.

Ryan's endless stories of his exploits in the Spanish Civil War did not move Stuart to any political affiliation. Stuart had no strong feelings about Spain around the time of the Civil War, unlike many writers, notably Orwell and Auden. During the Spanish Civil War, Ryan had been badly wounded in one arm at the Battle of Jarama. He told

Stuart about the battle and was disgusted at the deaths of women and children in Guernica in the Basque Country, gunned down and bombed from swooping planes. He had met Ernest Hemingway outside Madrid and they had discussed Hitler's using Spain as a test ground for blanket bombing by sending Franco the German Condor Air Legion.

Franco was the only European leader who gave Hitler the runaround. The Führer had failed to unite Spain with the Axis powers as he had with Italy and Mussolini. Commenting on his diplomatic disasters with Franco, Hitler told Mussolini that "he would prefer to have three or four teeth taken out" rather than negotiate with the Spanish leader.[3]

13

Madeleine

STUART CONTINUED LECTURING TO HIS all-female class at the Friedrich Wilhelm Universität in the Unter den Linden, amongst whom was a 25-year-old student, Gertrud Meissner. She became instantly attracted to Stuart. Gertrud Helene Meissner was born in 1915 in Gdansk, formerly Danzig-Langfuhr, and was living in Lauben where her father, Jan Meissner, died when she was 6 years old. He had been a teacher, and left a widow with four daughters who eventually moved to Berlin in 1936. Gertrud continued her education at a school in central Berlin, the Handelsschüle, where she showed an aptitude for languages. Her results, on leaving school in 1937, were excellent in English, French and Spanish. The family background was Polish, Kashubian-Catholics. Kashubia, a badlands zone better known as the Polish corridor, left a minority of its citizens in a somewhat tribal position. They were seen as neither German nor Polish; in fact, they were viewed as outsiders. Gertrud's eagerness to learn soon led her to a job as a trainee stenographer-typist with the Reichsbank. She was an employee during the period when Dr Hjalmar Schacht was president of the bank, she told me. He was replaced by Walther Funk in January 1939, which brought the Reichsbank under Hilter's control. After two years' service, in March 1939, she was awarded her certificate and continued working until her application for Berlin radio proved successful. This was also her way of getting to university which she entered after matriculation in January 1940. She was delighted to begin studying English, German and Spanish literature at university level.[1]

Stuart was looking for a typist and she phoned offering help. They had their first private meeting together that autumn in 1940 at the corner of Charlottenstrasse, Unter den Linden and afterwards walked up to the Wireless Service building (Rundfunkhaus). Entry to the building involved showing identity to the steel-helmeted SS guards. The ground floor of the Wireless Service building was a pub (*Kneipe*), the Funk-Eck, and a few floors above, in a small office, they set to work translating some of the German news into English for broadcast. Stuart and Madeleine (Gertrud) both recounted this episode for me. This was a duty incumbent on Stuart during his first year in Berlin and it enabled him to send money to Iseult in Laragh. Professor Fromme had offered him the work. Gertrud was already making an income for herself as a translator and knew many of the personnel at the Rundfunkhaus, including Lord Haw-Haw and the writer P.G. Wodehouse whom Stuart never really got to know.[2]

Stuart was still involved with Róisín Ní Mheara. He became friends with the writer Günther Weissenborn and his wife who lived on Nürnberger Strasse. A novel of his, *Das Mädchen von Fanö*, had been filmed with Brigitte Horney, the Hungarian actress, playing the lead. When he and Róisín were at a dinner party with the Weissenborns in their elegant top-floor apartment, among the guests were Horney and Lala Anderson who became famous for her wartime song, "Lili Marlene". This song was a favourite of the Stuarts when I knew them. Stuart also met the Schultze-Boysens, Harold and Libertas. Harold had written poems in his youth, but when Stuart met him he was engaged in a deadly game of infiltration of Nazi institutions with a Soviet Secret Service group, the Rote Kapelle. Stuart was interested in these people because he was planning to leave Berlin for Moscow with Róisín if possible. This fantasy was something he told me in private and it seemed to obsess him long after the event as a lost adventure, possibly even a very different outcome to his life. Harold and Libertas were tortured and executed by the SS. It is highly probable that the Schultze-Boysens may have referred to Stuart while under torture. Stuart was visited by the Gestapo around this time but he had taken the precaution of removing any diary entries that referred to members of the Rote Kapelle. Terror gripped him as he was interviewed by these men from Prinz-Albrechtstrasse, the notorious headquarters of the Geheime Staatspolitzei, known to Berliners as the "House of Horror" because of its torture chambers. He was able to satisfy the Gestapo's questions and they left him alone.[3]

When Róisín discovered the existence of Stuart's new friend, Gertrud Meissner, the two women became rivals. Róisín had independently hired a nurse for her baby, Nadeshka, and began to pursue an acting career with the help of Brigitte Horney. Iseult was often in his thoughts and when the life in Berlin did not prove to be a distraction, he continually missed the children. This he freely admitted to me. He was involved sexually with Róisín but not, as yet, with Gertrud. With her arrival in his life he was repeating a pattern of tiring of a partner sexually and seeking another. It may be too overtly psychoanalytical to trace this situation to his childhood when he was petted by his nurse, Nellie Farren, and also by Aunt Janet. However, the least attention coming from his mother accentuated his anxieties and insecurities, making him fantasise about captivating the love of his mother. Hence for Stuart as an adult, the aloof and perhaps unattainable woman could easily make the docile, loving woman of the moment less alluring: in this case perhaps Róisín lost her magic to the more remote Gertrud.

Getting away from the women he went to Munich during the summer holidays. Róisín sent him a cake and a copy of *Death in Venice*. In reading Thomas Mann he said that suddenly something of value for himself as a writer gripped him in the story, *The Abject*. He would later incorporate this into *Black List* quoting Mann who "renounced Bohemianism and all its works".[4] Stuart, in Berlin, was dipping in and out of one of the most infamous Bohemias of all time. He began to reconsider his literary career from before the war. His alter ego H, during a creative crisis at this time says:

> As soon as a book was placed, alone or with others, in the space reserved for reviews it became an exposed and, in proportion to the degree of its unique quality, slightly ridiculous object [...] such a piece of imaginative fiction, though with its own inherent consistency, wasn't meant to stand up to a public examination by literary accountants.[5]

Róisín wrote to say that she was upset that he had left Berlin. Stuart went on to Vienna and became haunted by memories of Iseult and his previous sojourns with her. He was in turmoil, he told me. Then the plans for going to Moscow were quashed because of Operation Barbarossa – Germany had invaded Russia. Before the invasion began in June, the Deputy Führer, Rudolf Hess, parachuted into Britain to negotiate a peace settlement. Hess was made a prisoner of war. Hitler spent most of that summer at Wolfsschanze, a fortified hideout in the desolate woods of East Prussia. The military campaign in Russia went well for the German advance. Stuart in *Black List* makes a crucial statement:

> To be acclaimed by a sizeable élite in a triumphant Reich as a foreign writer of genius would hardly be a bearable situation. In the case of a German disaster, which even then he didn't rule out, having thrown in his lot with the losing side would certainly turn out to be of immense value in his growth as an imaginative writer. Though being branded a Nazi by those from whom most of his readers would have to come, scarcely argued well for his future, no matter how his work developed.[6]

As a writer he had already discovered that the psyche's secret journey through reality has an absolute need for fiction. The psyche, he said, is "one of the names the mind, looking into its mirror, gives itself".[7]

Up to this point he had experienced some of life's extremes but nothing compared to the crisis of war. He had depicted war in novels such as *The Coloured Dome*, *Pigeon Irish*, *Glory* and *The Angel of Pity*. In Berlin he was under the immense shadow of disaster, and still wishing to write fiction in order to explore its deeper layers. With huge satisfaction and excitement as a novelist, he was living an interior journey as witness in Berlin under the Reich. He always admitted this to me without flinching. The other journey, of which Berlin was the first stage, had been predicted in his book *Things to Live For* (1934) when he longed to be with

> those on the coastline, on the frontiers. With gamblers, wanderers, fighters, geniuses, martyrs and mystics. With the champions of wild loves and lost causes, the storm troopers of life. With all those who live dangerously though not necessarily spectacularly, on the knife edge between triumph and defeat.[8]

On New Year's eve 1940, Stuart and Gertrud went for dinner and wine to a restaurant, Nikolsburger Krug. He had begun to call her "Madeleine" from that night onwards after her second name "Helene", as a term of affection. Madeleine fascinated him, especially with accounts of her first-hand witnessing of the rise of Hitler. Their relationship progressed diffidently until May of the following year when Stuart suddenly expressed deep feelings for her. While he was away in Vienna in the summer of 1941, she tried to concentrate on her studies and on her translation work at the radio station. Secretly, she had fallen in love and called him "Tiger". She was ecstatic and further excited when she got a letter inviting her to Vienna. Her mother was shocked at the idea of her wanting to go to Vienna. Luckily Madeleine did not tell her about Stuart's invitation. Instead, she wrote to him saying that she could not go because of her need to study. When he returned in September, he ended the relationship with Róisín and moved from the spacious flat they had shared on Nikolsburger Platz to Pension Naumann in the same square.

Together again, Stuart and Madeleine went for picnics to the Berlin Zoo and enjoyed rambling in its lush forest. They earned less than 400 Reichmarks a month collectively from the Rundfunk - about £40 at the time. This hardly allowed them to eat at Kempinskis, Zum Krone, the Bristol Hotel or Gerolds on the Kurfürstendamm, Stuart told me mentioning the better places to dine out. For days they travelled by U-Bahn from Kaiserallee-Hohenzollerndamm to the Grünewalde (the Zoo). The weather was glorious that summer as their romance blossomed. On 27 September their sexual relationship began. Stuart was delighted that "she displayed the same impatience as [my] own". Then they arranged private times together, usually on evenings before going to the Rundfunkhaus. However, mutual desire remained the great decider as to when they came together. When he reflected on the happiness found with Madeleine, one of his students (13 years younger) and the fact that they also worked together at the Irland Redaktion, he found himself in a whirlpool of emotion about her. His previous relationships had been with very different women; Pauline Caddell, Christabel Manning, the divorcée Honor Henderson, the actress Margery Binner, the writer Ethel Mannin, and there had been other brief encounters in Dublin, London and Paris. As regards his wife Iseult, he was a serial adulterer. His remark, "I had failed her very much", is included with the mutual lack of "capacity for that passion of love, which Iseult never had and did not believe in". Of course, Stuart must not have fully understood and loved her either. Yeats, perhaps, better understood Iseult's inner depth and recorded it in his book *A Vision* when he recalled seeing her, self-absorbed on the beach at Normandy, and heard her reciting verses she had written with the end line of each stanza, "O Lord, let something remain".

Stuart told me that in his relations with women before meeting Madeleine, he was "in a mad vain search for fulfilment". Had love now finally come to Stuart the philanderer? By Christmas Eve he met Madeleine's mother. Stuart bought Madeleine a ring with a green stone. When her mother asked where she had obtained the ring, she said Lord Haw-Haw (William Joyce) gave it to her. Madeleine was a friend of Haw-Haw's and occasionally went drinking with him. Once during an air raid she stayed behind with him at the Rundfunk instead of going to the shelter, *Luftschutzkeller*. They watched the bombs falling far off, since he assured her that the RAF was not going to bomb residential areas. This was to change when Arthur Harris took over Bomber Command and saturation bombing commenced, according to Madeleine. She never disavowed Haw-Haw's propaganda and helped type some of his anti-British broadcasts. Madeleine had genuine affection for Haw-Haw from what I heard her say of him. She knew his wife, Margaret, and Jack Trevor, the actor, a colleague of Haw-Haw who also broadcast for Goebbels. Margaret's infidelities were well known, Madeleine said. She remembered Haw-Haw's scarred face and that he sounded less nasal than his radio voice, which was meant to be an imitation of the typical English blue-blood aristocrat. His *"Jairmany Caw-ling"* for "Germany Calling" was a bit of an act, according to Madeline. He had a scar from his mouth up to his right ear, the result of a scuffle at a British Fascist meeting in London when he was 18 years old, a gathering that was infiltrated by communists, one of whom slashed him with a razor. According to her, Haw-Haw was proud of this. Not long after meeting Stuart, and because of his influence, Madeleine ceased socialising and drinking schnapps with the likes of Haw-Haw and some of the US broadcasters for the Nazis, such as Constance Drexel, Fred Kaltenbach and Edward L. Delaney. She also spoke to me about Haw-Haw's courage after the war in facing prison and execution at the hands of the British. She kept a press cutting about the execution that was found on her person when she was arrested in Dornbirn in 1945.[9]

14

Irland-Redaktion, Berlin

STUART'S DECISION TO BROADCAST FROM Berlin remains the greatest area of controversy, hence it was something which we discussed at length. It all began in July 1942 when Stuart received a phone call from Dr Hans Hartmann asking if he would agree to broadcast from the Ireland-Redaktion (Irish Service). Stuart told me that Hartmann's phone call stunned him and his immediate response was that he would need a few days to consider the offer carefully.

Broadcasts to Ireland organised by the Irland-Redaktion came from the Rundfunkhaus (radio centre) Berlin in Masurenallee. The Irland-Redaktion operated from two rooms at the rear of the building. Two of the organisers were Adolf Mahr and Hans Hartmann. Mahr had come to Ireland in the 1920s to take up a post at the National Museum in Dublin. He became a permanent and pensionable member of the Irish Civil Service and Director of the National Museum in 1934, a post personally approved by Éamon de Valera. In 1933, Mahr became a member of the Nazi party and was their leader in Dublin. He was also a member of the Royal Irish Academy. However, although a Nazi, he counted amongst his friends the artist Oskar Kokoschka whom the Nazis reviled.

Hans Hartmann was given a job at the museum under Mahr who sent him to the Folklore Department at Earlsfort Terrace, Dublin. He mastered Gaelic in less than two years. Both men attended the swastika festooned Nazi parties in the Gresham Hotel, Dublin, in December 1937 and 1939. Hartmann played Santa Claus for the German children. When Mahr hastily left Ireland via Cobh for Hamburg in July 1939, Garda Special Branch were intercepting and copying a letter to his Dublin address, 37 Waterloo Place.

The first talk from Berlin Rundfunkhaus, on December 1939, was in Gaelic and lasted for 15 minutes. It was given by Ludwig Muhlhausen. The Irish government was pleased with the international recognition for the Irish language. Muhlhausen had visited Ireland in the late 1920s on many occasions and had given seminar lectures at University College Cork in 1929. His study of Donegal and Kerry Gaelic dialects gave him a good pronunciation for broadcasting. Among Hartmann's talks *as gaeilge* was a potted history of the Nazi Party and Hitler's rise to power. He quoted chunks from Wolfe Tone's diary. Otherwise broadcasts were in English. Muhlhausen supported "a united Ireland" when on 15 December 1940 he exhorted: "stand firm against the English now, and the whole of Ireland will at last be free. God bless and save Ireland."[1]

From Stuart's decision to broadcast it may seem as if he had become fully pro-German. He has commented that: "Being in Germany was one thing, lecturing at Berlin University was bad enough – but going over to the other side of the street?" Another comment reveals that he "somehow felt the necessity to broadcast". Deep down it was a decision taken because he sensed that Germany would lose the war and he would be with the losers in their utter perdition. He repeated this to me on a number of occasions. This may seem like wallowing deliberately with the outcasts – except that no one sees the Nazis as outcasts. It is not easy to understand Stuart's pursuit of being the dissident outcast and outsider; his only exemption clause is that he was not a member of the Nazi Party, unlike the millions of Germans who were. I have met people who said to me, "How could you consort with that vile supporter of such a regime?" In my twenties it was something I never questioned. In later years I realised that those who condemned Stuart for broadcasting were entitled to their viewpoint. Even after I read the transcripts of Stuart's broadcasts from Berlin I did not feel like breaking our friendship, no more than when I read Ezra Pound's hideous anti-Semitic broadcasts on Rome radio during the same period did I lose my admiration for Pound's poetry.

Stuart gave a test broadcast on 9 June 1940 entitled "The Modern Novelist and Society". The tone is pugnacious about his alienation in mercantile society, the evils of materialism and money. There is a nod towards embracing the new social forms of Germany and an attack on Steinbeck's novel *The Grapes of Wrath* (1939) which he didn't consider a great work of art. He began broadcasting more regularly from August 1942 onwards, aided by Madeleine.[2] The broadcasts are trenchantly anti-British within a staunch nationalist and militant Irish Republican tradition: "It is because of the dynamiters of the last century, and not because of the men who condemned them, that we survive." He repeatedly affirms his devotion to Pearse, claiming that: "As soon as I had written a talk I asked myself if there was anything in it contrary to Pearse's outlook; if there was, I tore it up and wrote another." And not only Pearse; he is equally devoted to the other leaders of the 1916 Rising, and, not least, the War of Independence heroes: Cathal Brugha, Liam Lynch and Michael Collins. His obsession with the unfinished business of unifying Ireland, referred to in the broadcasts, was as intense as de Valera's credo on that subject, except that Stuart supported the bombing campaign by the IRA in England during the war. Neither is de Valera beyond his praise, nor the Catholic Primate of all Ireland, Cardinal MacRory.

His appeals for a united Ireland might easily have been quoted in leading articles in *An Phoblacht*: "Ulster will once again be free Irish soil." He looks forward to a great sporting event to be held "outside Belfast to celebrate the return of the six counties", and says that "Ulster is Irish as much as Connaught or Munster". While he does not support coercion of the Northern Unionists, he dares to suggest that "it is of no importance that the Tricolour should fly from the City Hall in Belfast instead of the Union Jack". There are pro-German statements in support of the city of Danzig being reclaimed by the Reich. He singles out the bravery of the ordinary soldier: "I am glad to be living among such people." However, he states that he is not casting disparagement on the average British soldier. He states that the inspiration for all German soldiers is "rooted in one man, Hitler" and adds, that he was "completely fired by enthusiasm" when he first heard about the German leader before coming to Berlin.

Stuart's vociferous anti-Democratic diatribe may sound somewhat contradictory: "The Axis leaders do not shout about the Commandments or religion or humanity." His overall viewpoint can best be summed up in his hatred of the Allies' statements that the war was a "crusade for liberty, humanity and idealism against the forces of aggression and barbarism". He is most virulent in detesting "this heresy of commercial Christianity from the United States which gives successful businessmen a solid respectability". Repeatedly, he condemns Churchill and Roosevelt. His vituperative attacks on the socio-economic realities of life would remain an abiding concern of his fiction, in novels such as *The Chariot* and his last work of fiction, *King David Dances*. This, in a nutshell, embodies part of his political position, but I feel it is unjust to pigeonhole him since he would never express any definite politics and was strident about his apolitical affiliations. Stuart continually claimed that he never accepted the consumerist socio-economic reality and could be quite dogmatic on this point. He wanted an ideal world, some sort of paradise on earth, rather than accept humanity's evolved reality of banks, institutions, private property and the democratic structures. In this he was a revolutionary intellectual to some extent, but not an anarchist. If he had inclinations towards violent anarchy I would have disapproved strongly, but he never voiced such opinions to me.

In 1947 he would reflect in his diary: "Perhaps I was wrong to speak, perhaps it was identifying myself too much with the horrors of Nazism and it was a later realisation of this that made me refuse to speak further. Of course in one sense better I had kept clear of the whole business, but had I done so, had I not suffered I would not have come to my present knowledge." When I quoted this, he agreed with its sentiment, stating that he was fundamentally artistically driven; no other consideration was ever of as much importance to him. It is not accurate to judge or analyse the artist from the human dimension, he added, that would be to exclude the artistic impulse, obsession and primary drive of a committed writer and artist.

At the outset there was desperation in the Nazi propaganda network when it needed to increase broadcasts to neutral Ireland. A student of Stuart's, Hilda Poepping, was a broadcaster at the Irland-Redaktion. Susan Hilton also joined Hartmann's team. Stuart remembers that Susan Hilton drank to excess because of severe depression. When Stuart begged Churchill over the radio for clemency for IRA prisoners about to be hanged in Belfast, the German Ambassador Hempel sent him a favourable message: "Your radio comments had a good effect" (*güte wirkung*). Stuart openly opposed the arrival of the United States troops in Northern Ireland in 1942: "As an Ulsterman it is galling to me that a large number of foreign troops are today occupying that corner of our country." The arrival of United States troops meant the end of any possibility of a German invasion of Ireland. When Stuart referred to the refusal of the Department of External Affairs in Dublin to renew his Irish passport, Hartmann censored this comment from the broadcast. The broadcasts, less than ten minutes in duration, were monitored by both British and Irish governments and classified as pro-German. The Irish Intelligence Service, perhaps his only regular listening audience, found many of them were not possible to record owing to faulty sound and static interference.

During Stuart's period of broadcasting, the Irland-Redaktion moved to smaller rooms at 77 Kaiserdamm. Stuart told me about Irishman John O'Reilly, who was the only member of the Mahr-Hartmann team to become a spy for Germany. He was parachuted into Ireland and captured with his Telefunken transmitter in a brown suitcase and £300. In fact, it was his father, Bernard, who handed his son over to the Irish police for a reward of £500. British Intelligence had tipped off the Irish Intelligence Services of O'Reilly's arrival. He was taken to Arbour Hill prison but escaped, was recaptured and finally released after the war. His father had invested the reward money and with this O'Reilly also reclaimed the £300 which he was given by the Nazis and bought a pub in Parkgate Street in Dublin. He is an interesting contrast to Stuart as regards having avoided vilification. Stuart was afraid of O'Reilly in Berlin. "He was a pretty nasty character. I was very suspicious of him because he could well have been a double agent." O'Reilly's place on the broadcast team was filled by Liam Mullally who had been teaching English at the Berlitz. Mullally had found himself in Hungary at the outbreak of the war and, unable to get back to Ireland, ended up in Berlin.

In January 1943, at the request of Frederick Boland of the Department of External Affairs in Dublin, William Warnock of the Irish Legation, Berlin, had his secretary Eileen Walsh deliver Irish newspapers to Stuart. He was also given access to Radio Éireann in order to keep up with news from home so that his broadcasts might show balance. Warnock, Walsh and Stuart often met for a game of golf which Stuart said was always a strange outing in the midst of the war. When news of the siege of Stalingrad reached Berlin, Stuart broadcast the following:

> I speak to Berlin University students every week about Ireland. Today I spoke of Liam Lynch and Cathal Brugha, of Yeats and Synge and Pearse, for a nation's soul is revealed in its soldiers and poets. I would refer again to Stalingrad. The

> Irish would understand what the German people felt. This has moved Germany more than any other event of the war, for while such victories as the Fall of Paris might be attributed to the perfection of the German war machine, this is a triumph of flesh and blood.

The tone of this is unmistakable but also perplexing since the surrender of Field Marshal von Paulus made Stalingrad into a kind of Battle of Waterloo for the Nazis. Just as Napoleon's Grand Army was defeated outside Moscow in 1812, the Germans at Stalingrad met with a crushing defeat. Hitler felt betrayed by his generals and could not understand how von Paulus did not choose suicide over blatant betrayal.

Prior to the general election of 1943, one of Stuart's broadcasts became party political in content. Frederick Boland in Dublin cabled Warnock in Berlin: "Francis Stuart has been advising people to vote against Fine Gael." However, Fine Gael did not poll well in the election and the de Valera government was returned to power. Hardly with Stuart's help! A broadcast of May 1943 has often been attributed to Stuart, but the British monitoring services believed it to be by an English-Redaktion announcer, Norman Baillie-Stewart: "Go over to the Germans or to the Italians and I can promise you that you will be received as friends." Norman Baillie-Stewart also called on troops of nationalist sympathy stationed in Northern Ireland to mutiny.

Towards the end of 1943, owing to the intense bombing raids over Berlin, Stuart and Madeleine, with Hans Hartmann and family, moved to Luxembourg. At their new broadcast centre in the Villa Louvigny, they were joined by Johann Mikele who became a friend. Stuart obeyed orders that the broadcast must announce itself as coming from Berlin: "I have the greatest suspicion and dislike for all politicians and, so far as I come under their notice at all, they have the same suspicion and dislike for me." There is an unwieldy tone to many of the broadcasts, and despite their intense interest as historical documents they make for dull reading compared to his novels.

One of his last broadcasts, on 8 January 1944, concludes: "Until Dublin becomes a much better place for the average working family to live in than Belfast, we lose more than half the force of our claim to Belfast." He recalled for me a time when he refused to broadcast any further because of self-disgust. Mahr sent him back to Berlin with

Madeleine. They were to report to the Rundfunkhaus. When they refused they were threatened with arrest and deportation to a prison camp. Stuart's passport was seized. They were lucky compared to other broadcasters, Sonja Kowanka and Susan Hilton, who were deported to concentration camps for refusing to broadcast. Stuart told me that after the war, Susan Hilton was arrested by the British and sent to Holloway prison for 18 months. The last broadcast from Bremen by the Irland-Redaktion was in May 1945, by which time Hitler and Goebbels, the Propaganda Minister, were both dead. Hartmann read the news in Irish and ended the short bulletin with a John McCormack recording of "Come Back to Erin".

Mahr and Muhlhausen were interned without trial after the war. Mahr was ill-treated and released by the Allies in 1946. He died in Bonn in 1951. Muhlhausen died in 1948. He had joined the SS in 1941 and this meant he left prison at the hands of the Allies "physically and spiritually destroyed". Among others, Norman Baillie-Stewart served five years in prison. John Amery, accused of attempting to recruit an SS unit from among British POWs, was hanged five days before William Joyce, "Lord Haw-Haw", at Wandsworth. The fact that Joyce was born in New York did not save him since he had claimed the status of a British subject when applying for a passport before the war. He was found guilty of treason on a technicality. Hartmann fled after the final broadcast and was apprehended. Questioned by British Secret Service agents, he was never arrested. He worked at Gottingen and later rose to the Chair of Philology at Hamburg University. He was a visitor to Ireland in the 1960s in search of sound recordings for his archive in Germany.

Stuart's broadcasts require occasional further comment where relevant in the chronology of his Berlin years.[3] In all, he made at least 100 broadcasts between 1942 and 1944. Transcripts of two-thirds survive and many of these are incomplete because of poor radio reception. Irish Intelligence (G2) usually forwarded copies of the broadcasts to the Department of External Affairs. The BBC monitored his broadcasts also and made verbatim transcripts of some but at some stage it appears that they deemed his content only worthy of compressed versions or third-person summaries.

15

Final Years in Berlin

IN THE SPRING OF 1942, MADELEINE'S sister Trautchen began a romance with a German soldier that resulted in her pregnancy. Frau Meissner ordered her out of the family apartment. Madeleine argued with her mother over this and eventually moved in to Pension Naumann with Stuart. The incident caused a family rift. Madeleine told me that she considered her mother a narrow-minded Catholic and strongly objected to being used as an emotional crutch to take the place of her dead father. Stuart celebrated his fortieth birthday with Frank Ryan, Helmut Clissmann and Madeleine at a restaurant called Stocklers. He had received news that had lifted his spirits, about the imminent serialisation of the novel *The Coloured Dome* that had been passed by the censor for publication in the German newspaper, *Die Woche*. However, a diary of the time records a different mood: "I came here and was plunged into another kind of whirlpool."[1]

He began lectures at the University on D.H. Lawrence's *The Plumed Serpent*, a novel set in Mexico. Lawrence's hatred of mental conceptions divorced from deep emotional truth struck the right note for Stuart who had found in William Blake's writings antipathy to the same kind of mental idealism. He explained to the students – who listened more for the pronunciation of his English than the content of the lectures – that mental concepts were like "flowers in a vase, without roots ... What was vital was Lawrence's vision of consciousness which was pre-mental."[2] Stuart re-read Keats and told me that he found a lot to ponder in poems such as *Ode To Psyche*. Lawrence and Blake awoke in him the creative urge and he began a novel under the working title of "Winter Song". He claimed a quantum breakthrough as a *modus scribendi* in the autumn of 1942, which he called "emotional creation", and his spiritual quest continued: "What is God (or Truth)?", "The purpose of true art is to reveal the truth."[3]

When he sent some of the novel to the Ministry of Propaganda where Joseph Goebbels presided, he discovered that the Nazis believed in their own "official Truth". He told me that this marked a turning point for him about being a passive foreign national and for days afterwards he felt stranded in Berlin, except for his deep involvement with Madeleine. The novel was deemed unacceptable for publication and this led him to have no illusions about Nazi totalitarianism when it came to freedom of speech. The manuscript has never been found. He stopped writing the novel and, when Madeleine next introduced him on the radio with the words: "And now this is Francis Stuart", he began: "Not that I have any desire to join the ranks of the propagandists. Being neutral does not mean to remain unaffected by, or insensitive to events that are going to determine the sort of civilisation that is about to develop in Europe."[4] He said he was in Germany of his own free will, having left Ireland, like millions of emigrants, to earn a living.

In August 1942 there began the protracted situation concerning his passport. During the remainder of the war, passport number C7277 would become familiar if not notorious to the Irish Legation in Berlin, The Department of External Affairs in Dublin and later on at the Irish Legation in Paris. He returned to the Legation (*Irische Gesandtschaft*) in Drakestrasse at the end of the month to be told by Con Cremin that he was on the passport blacklist in Dublin, "I explained to Mr Stuart that he had, as a national, no inherent right to receive a passport and that the government is free to act in regard to passports as it sees fit, taking account of the circumstances".[5] Colonel Dan Bryan of G2 at the Phoenix Park, having examined the circumstances, recommended refusing passport renewal. Stuart's only recourse was to seek advice from the German authorities who speedily furnished him with a foreigner's passport, since he could hardly be without identity papers.

Stuart and Madeleine were able to avail of a week in Vienna because of their services at the Rundfunkhaus. Before leaving Berlin, he introduced her to his translator Frau Weiland. They stayed at the Hotel Koënig von Ungarn in Vienna and went to the races in Freudenau. In a three-horse race, Madeleine backed a loser and started to cry. He comforted her with stories of winners and losers. Then he made her laugh with a shortened version of the race between the pig and the horse in *The Great Squire*. They went on to Baden-Baden for the remainder of the week.

On his return to Berlin, thoughts of his children haunted him and he planned to send Ian birthday greetings over the airwaves at the beginning of October. He would be 16-years-old. In Laragh, the household was able to hear some of his talks but it also depended on reception and the quality of their crystal radio set which often hissed and became loaded with static. The voice of Stuart could also be disturbing and sound so far away that everyone tended to avoid listening if at all possible, since Lily and Iseult found themselves worrying for his safety. Ian did not hear mention of his birthday on Berlin radio because he was in boarding school. However, on one occasion, a study supervisor had him escorted to a recreation room where he did hear his father on the radio. Kay's reaction to the broadcasts at the time meant she began asking the postman for a letter "from my father in Berlin". Her mother and grandmother, whom she called "Ninny", tried to dispel the child's disappointment since no letter ever came from Stuart until years later.

Meanwhile Frank Ryan, who had consistently refused to broadcast, continually associated with an anti-Semite who later took part in the genocide in Czechoslovakia. This was Dr Edmund Veesenmayer. Ryan called him Vau. Veesenmayer is not just an arbitrary character in this account. He met with the Irish minister, Leopold Kerney, in Madrid on several occasions prior to Germany's defeat in Russia. Kerney was acting on behalf of de Valera whose longings for the uniting of Ireland were fed by the possibility of a German invasion. Clissmann also met Kerney who suggested that, if a German invasion of Ireland might still take place, Ireland was prepared to forego neutrality in favour of the Reich. Ryan was deemed to be the go-between or liaison, and certainly de Valera was continuously informed through Kerney about the meetings with Clissmann and Veesenmayer.

Ryan hoped that if Germany was victorious he would be given a high-ranking position. He teased Stuart, expecting from him a loyalty to the Reich similar to his own. He was pleased with the broadcast in December 1942 in which Stuart expressed the view that "it seemed to me at least preferable to be ruled by one man whose sincerity for the welfare of his people could not be doubted, than by a gang whose only concern was the market price of various commodities in the world market".[6] Stuart had made yet another pro-Hitler statement. The "gang" referred to are the democratic nations: Britain, the United States and her allies. He had attacked democratic financing and financial institutions in the way Ezra Pound was attacking them over Rome radio during the same period. Stuart's tone is less quirky, acerbic and zany, and more importantly, is without anti-Semitic content, unlike Pound who claimed that Hitler was another Joan of Arc. Pound wrote various letters to William Joyce (Lord Haw-Haw), but Joyce never sent more than a brief reply. Stuart was in favour of some kind of alternative social and political structure but, on this occasion, praised the Nazi regime while Jews were being transported from ghettos in many occupied capitals of Europe, including Berlin, to the gas chambers in Auschwitz, Birkenau, Treblinka and Sobibor. Did he know? And if he did, should he have stopped broadcasting and fled Germany? To these questions there was only one answer from Stuart. He did not know, he did not flee. To many of his critics this is unforgivable. What did the greater mass of the Germans know? Eugene Kogon, who survived the Buchenwald camp, opines in *Der SS Staat*: "outside the concrete fact of their existence, almost nothing." The real answer is that almost everyone knew and State terrorism ensured that dissenters against Nazism were given "special treatment".

Stuart finds his harshest critics among those who condemn him for his years in Germany and for broadcasting in the pay of the Third Reich. At the time, Cyril Connolly, the eminent critic, wrote about the broadcasts in *Picture Post*: "One or two may believe in the freedom and prosperity promised to the Celtic races by Hitler and Ireland's Haw-Haw, Francis Stuart."[7] I asked if he had seen Connolly's condemnation at the time and he said no, that was impossible because such publications were almost impossible to find in Berlin. In subsequent radio talks Stuart mentioned the Glens of Antrim and his homesickness. Early in 1943 he clarified his detestation of "nauseating war propaganda" and went on to decry Roosevelt. When the German campaign on the Eastern front was becoming a kind of Napoleonic disaster, one which would mark in Churchill's phrase "not the beginning of the end but the end of the beginning", the change in Stuart's tone resulted in his having his passport confiscated by the Nazis.

By 1943 there were nightly bombing raids on Berlin. The winter brought Siberian snows. It seemed like a providential damnation of the Germans on top of their defeat in Russia. Casualties and deaths among civilians were beginning to break down the defiant German egotism. The Herrenvolk who rose up with their Führer's hubris were discovering that they were not superhuman. Madeleine was worried about her finals, the Staatsexamen. Frank Ryan had a stroke and his life became more difficult. He had long since been snubbed by the German authorities and deprived of their previous hospitality, such as a lavish apartment and food coupons. Now he began to hate the Nazis and Stuart found letters of Ryan's that were critical of the Reich, which he destroyed, in order to save him being sent to prison or a firing squad. In his new apartment block, Ryan met Hilda Lubbert, a pharmacist, who fell for him. Ryan mainly encouraged her advances since she could get him medicine, Stuart told me. He had previously tried to have an affair with Madeleine's sister, Margarete, but to no avail.

Róisín Ní Mheara came back into their lives, causing jealousy on Madeleine's part. Stuart was involved in a love triangle again and told me that, in darker moments, he thought of his abandoned children. He longed to send a letter to Ireland, but this was in vain since letters could not be posted from Berlin. Madeleine heard from her sister Gretel about conditions in Hamburg where she worked as a nurse. Gretel had had a breakdown at the sight of death and maiming, caused by firestorms after area-bombing when thousands upon thousands of corpses and bits of corpses lay in the devastated city or were buried under fallen rubble. As already briefly mentioned, in August Stuart went with Madeleine to Luxembourg where they were both used in the propaganda machine of the Nazis on the radio. Stuart was granted leave of absence from his university duties. In Luxembourg, he was intimidated by some SS officers and, becoming drunk, found the courage to utter pro-Russian slogans, such as "Heil Moscow".[8] This was dangerous at a time when Germany was facing defeat but he admitted that his patience was running out. He grew tired of the broadcasts with their endless emendations and corrections by the censors. He was kept on because the Germans wanted to give the impression that broadcasting from "Berlin" was continuing as usual.

When he returned with Madeleine to Berlin in November (because of her studies), they noticed the ashen-faced citizens who were daily bombed into fear, anxiety, insomnia and starvation. The Reich, that had boasted that it would last a thousand years, was to collapse in months. I can still hear Stuart's tone of voice, one of mocking outrage – "the Reich". Similarly, he would say in a rare use of punning, "the furore" instead of the Führer.

Madeleine's twenty-eighth birthday in November 1943 was a night they would never forget. Stuart and she told me this one evening, which I still remember vividly as dusk was falling. Her birthday was a quiet gathering with meagre rations shared by Trautchen and her boyfriend Martin. Everyone found it difficult not to talk about the destruction of buildings along miles and miles of the nearby streets, and the darkness each night in the city that grew darker progressively until the spotlights were turned on to illuminate enemy aircraft for the artillery to shoot at. Suddenly the sirens started wailing, followed by approaching aircraft – a sound familiar to Berliners.

They waited in fear. Soon there were aircraft over the Wilmersdorf sector of the city. There was a thunderous rain of bombs that obliterated their sense of time. They found themselves huddled in a state of shock and terror in the cellar. The building next door was bombed. Explosive sounds were followed by the fall of rubble and dust between further detonations and explosions. Stuart, with Martin, climbed up to the roof of their building and saw sights that would become part of his novels *Redemption* and *Victors and Vanquished*. A war was in progress where aggressor and defender were in conflict with each other, utilising as much might as was needed to win or perish. This was Stuart's definition of a war which he constantly reiterated to me. The sights of such destruction haunted him always to the point of breakdown and madness, he added. Berliners were dying under the torrent of bombs. RAF pilots who had been shot down plunged to a fiery death in the inferno below. In an instant Stuart received intimations that there is no such thing as a just war and realised he was a neutral outsider, that however untenable his position might seem he would uphold the position.

Meanwhile, back in Luxembourg, his final broadcasts before Christmas of 1943 were more in his control simply because the Nazis were losing the war and the bureaucracy was weakening: "If I don't speak anymore it will be because I can no longer say what I want, what I think is the truth."[9] They were requisitioned a room at the Praiser Hof and Stuart, as on previous Christmases, missed Ian and Kay desperately. His telling of this was utterly genuine since he loved his children. He wondered how everyone was in Laragh Castle. His homesickness developed into crisis proportions while Madeleine flirted with the hotel proprietor, Monsieur Petit, and wangled a roast goose out of him on Christmas Eve as well as a bottle of champagne. Monsieur Petit brought Madeleine into the wine cellar and began discussing how the world was falling apart or so it seemed. When he suggested they have sex, she evaded him. In their hotel room, Stuart showed her a new poem that he had written while she was gone, entitled "Ireland". When she read it they felt like celebrating.

> Over you falls the sea-light, festive yet pale
> As though from the trees hung candles alight in a gale
> To fill with shadows your days, as the distant beat
> Of waves fill the lonely width of many a western street.
> Bare and grey and hung with berries of mountain ash,
> Drifting through the ages with tilted fields awash,
> Steeped with your few lost lights in the long Atlantic dark,
> Sea-birds' shelter, our shelter and ark.[10]

When they returned to Berlin in the new year of 1944, they realised that everyone lived for the moonlit nights because this meant the bombers would not come over. Frank Ryan, scared as usual of going into air-raid shelters, had moved to Johannisbergensh and from there reached Dresden in an ambulance by joining the leagues of ambulances which were becoming the main motorised traffic out of Berlin once roads could be cleared. The city was becoming a heap of rubble with a few standing ruins, like the ancient cities of Pompeii and Herculaneum. Stuart and Madeleine moved to Pension Naumann and prayed that they might survive the nightly bombing. Their nearest air-raid bunker was at the Bahnhof Zoo in the Tiergarten. Uncannily, it was overcrowded during air raids despite the rising toll of deaths.

For many Germans, hysteria replaced the years of euphoric Hitlermania, but German national radio still broadcast propaganda, such as "the Reich is free from enemy planes!".[11] By March, air raids were in daylight and it became clear to even the staunchest of fanatics that the end was coming. On Hitler's birthday a Nazi banner proclaimed, "We greet the first worker of Germany – Adolf Hitler". Graffiti along one street proclaimed, "Our walls may break, but never our hearts". Madeleine took the exams and gained her degree, with Stuart's help in preparing for the philosophy questions. In May, during some of the first daylight raids, the Englische Seminar was levelled by bombs and Stuart's lecturing job was over. Obviously, his salary was also stopped. The Irish Legation in Drakestrasse had been bombed the previous November and along with it a fat file on Stuart. Cornelius Cremin had replaced William Warnock and Stuart sought him out in temporary accommodation, hoping for favourable treatment in getting his passport renewed.

Cremin wrote to Frederick Boland in Dublin mentioning the threats Stuart was receiving from German authorities: if he refused to recommence broadcasting, he would be arrested. Early in May, his foreigner's passport had been seized by the Gestapo officials who came expressly for it from their headquarters in Alexanderplatz. Boland contacted Colonel Dan Bryan of G2 who replied in an official manner, at first recommending refusal of a passport because Stuart, "misled your Department when going to Berlin";[12] then Bryan, taking account of Stuart's possible internment in a concentration camp, said, "you may consider issuing him with a passport with suitable limitations on its validity". The matter did not end there. Boland sought higher authority and replied to Berlin at the end of May in code: "Stuart's passport should not be renewed stop For your confidential information he is regarded as having forfeited any claims to our Diplomatic protection by unneutral and disloyal activity."[13]

As Stuart rejoiced in Madeleine's exam results, he received a return-to-sender letter meant for his daughter Kay in Laragh. It had been censored by the Nazis and was officially stamped *Ausland Brief Politizei*. Again he had to fight despair and hope to survive to see Ian and Kay in the future, but when he could not tell. These he admitted to me were some of his darkest days in Berlin – the whole episode seemed like immense folly except for finding Madeleine and their relationship together. Just as many were beginning to slip through the city's dubiously held military checkpoints, Frank Ryan returned from the sanatorium in Dresden with his friend, Hilda Lubbert, the pharmacist who was prolonging his life as he fought against pneumonia, stomach ulcers and fluctuating temperatures. Ludicrously,

Stuart offered to marry Madeleine and get her across the border into neutral Switzerland. It was one way of saving her life, perhaps. Meanwhile, Ryan sought for a passport on the black market and prepared to go to Denmark with Hilda.

Stuart brought him the news of the Allied landings in Normandy. Ryan's health deteriorated and, having struggled back by train to Dresden, he became delirious and died in the sanatorium at Konigspark on 10 June 1944. He was 42 years old. The cause of death was syphilis. Stuart, Madeleine, Budge Clissmann and Hilda Lubbert witnessed his burial in Loschwitz cemetery after a requiem Mass for the dead. As Ryan was laid to rest on the banks of the Elbe, Stuart and Madeleine could not have known that he would be reburied in Ireland 35 years later in 1979 or that they would also be there.

Maddeningly, the Berlin summer was glorious as Madeleine read Dostoevsky. Slave workers from the East cleared hills of rubble to maintain some kind of road system among the ruins, she told me. The whole city looked like a lunar landscape. Photographed together in the park around this time, she looks very tanned and so does Stuart. As they left the park, gossip about the advancing Russian armies made them hurry their steps. They did not have to flee Berlin that quickly in July 1944. However, the armies of Eisenhower and Montgomery were sweeping ruthlessly and systematically through France and Belgium. Paris was liberated at the end of August. Allied armies reached the Rhine the following spring.

Meanwhile, Stuart was looking for a travel pass. His plan was to get as far as possible out of Berlin and then go anywhere away from advancing armies – Russian, American, British, French, Canadian, Australian. He lied about being married to Madeleine when applying for a temporary pass that might get them far as Landsberg in Bavaria. As a farewell to Berlin, Stuart wrote a mystical poem, "The Trees in the Square". They boarded a train at Anhalter Bahnhof in September. They did not acknowledge Martin, Trautchen's boyfriend, who was an officer in the Bahnhofspolizei and had got them their tickets. Madeleine thought again of the heartbreaking farewells between herself and Trautchen the night before. Madeleine's papers declared that she was Stuart's secretary and they would return to Berlin in 48 hours, train transport permitting. When they arrived in to Munich, Madeleine managed to argue for a ticket admitting them to the bomb-damaged Schiller Hotel. The hotel was dilapidated but it was a refuge. Sunbathing in the Englishche Garten the following afternoon they were awoken from sleep by American bombers. The sirens whined and they saw the sky above the Alps thronged with aircraft. They rushed into the air-raid bunker beneath the Gallery of Modern Art.

They survived further bombing. What, one might ask, if Stuart had been a civilian casualty in Germany in 1944? What would have been his legacy as a novelist? The biographical details would have ended here and *The Great Squire* would have been his last novel. After three nights they were asked to leave the hotel. They hauled their belongings from one town to another, returning to Munich a month later. A room became vacant in Pension Exquisite, Luitpolderstrasse 10, in the Schwabing district, and Madeleine was relieved to get it, she said. Stuart wrote to Cremin at the Irish Legation, relocated to Salzburg at the Oesterreichischer Hof after the levelling of their headquarters in Drakestrasse 3, Berlin W 35:

> Since the last bombing, water is scarce, except what comes through the roof! I would like to go to Bregenz too, with my secretary, Fraulein Meissner, and even if accommodation is difficult to get I would prefer to come there and chance finding something rather than remain here.[14]

Stuart bought a ring on the black market from a woman, paying her 1,500 marks. It had a gold ingot on its silver band. He told me about this many times. Otherwise, their finances were managed by Madeleine who was eager to ensure that they had at least enough travel ration cards, *Essensmarken*. They befriended a restaurant-owner, Frau Rüger, who would help them out later. Madeleine borrowed library books, Meister Eckhardt, the fourteenth-century German mystic, and also Rainer Maria Rilke's *Duino Elegies*. It would be unfair to impute that Stuart influenced Madeleine's reading because this is untrue. The situation was entirely different from that of Stuart and Iseult, early on in their marriage, when she introduced him to the mystical writers who would become important in his spiritual development. With Stuart and Madeleine there was a parallel intellectual life in terms of shared interest when it came to spiritual reading. Their age difference was irrelevant, as it is in such matters of spiritual quest where both persons are in union rather than at strife. Jotting down a note for her birthday, he felt "all suffering and dangers are made up for. My beloved Schumpel, my love, my little Hare, my angel along the path to the Truth".[15]

However, they were also beginning to suffer from near starvation and lack of hygiene, always longing for a shower even without soap. When there was no food available they soon saw how useless the *Essenmarken* were against a background of freezing temperatures, as fireballs engulfed Munich when aircraft continued saturation bombing. Stuart began brooding on death and destruction and found that Rilke was similarly obsessed in his poems. It became part of his developing sense of being a novelist as witness to the civilian's war. H comments in *Black List*, "Not that he felt any resentment against those who were doing the bombing".[16] Rather he contemplated what it meant to be killed by a bomb:

> This psyche, as the consciousness thought of itself, imagination's unique locale, its beautiful pattern of roots in the deoxyribonucleic acid, drawing up its "vast ideas" from the deep past, could it be annulled, reduced to a spot of slime on a collapsing wall?[17]

Their Christmas Eve meal was a mixture of mashed potatoes and offal, known as *gröstl*. In their pension room there was no electricity due to bomb damage, so Madeleine lit a candle behind a transparent nativity scene and they sang *Stille Nacht*. Wrapping themselves up as tightly as possible on the narrow bed they tried to sleep, half on the alert for another air raid. Because of the lack of food, their energy levels were low. Outside their window, bombed out trains lay among misshapen bombed out tracks, and beyond lay the ruination of the city.[18]

They found a battered copy of the New Testament and Madeleine read passages from the German in translation for Stuart. When she felt in good form she played melodies on a harmonica and told him about her hopes of reaching a promised land after the war. Madeleine was fond of recounting this story to me. Her belief in their survival kept her going, she added. In the new year, with the devastating bombing of Dresden, especially in February 1945, refugees began teeming into Munich. There was systematic streamlining of these refugees and Madeleine narrowly escaped selection for munitions work. Instead, she was co-opted to a Dolmetscher Schüle, many of which were set up, awaiting the Allies, in order to make the Germans seem "friendly". The imminent influx of post-war bureaucracies would need interpreters, so she got on well at the school. With the uncertainties surrounding their lives, Stuart became restless. He considered returning to Berlin and being a witness to the conquest of the city, but gave up on this idea after meeting refugees who had recently fled from there.

They made Bregenz their next goal. It is situated under the Santis mountains close to the Swiss border; their more desperate need was of getting official documents in Bregenz at the Irish Legation. Bregenz became their watchword. Madeleine was anxious on the night before leaving Munich. When she fell asleep she had a dream about herself and Stuart following a star, Sirius, over hills and valleys. The star stopped near a whitewashed house and this would become their home. Such a dream was a gift from heaven, she told me. Stuart knew by heart the final poem written by Keats with the opening line: "Bright Star would I were steadfast as thou art." This seemed to him another interpretation of her dream since death was everywhere. Daily life meant the sight of corpses, burnt or charred or dismembered and Stuart recalled that no one acknowledged these corpses; even burial squads worked as if they were clearing objects rather than dead people. No one wanted to admit to death on such a vast scale, he said. Fervently, Madeleine saw herself and Stuart travelling under some guiding star like the Magi.[19] At least this was in her more elevated states of mind, but actual conditions easily changed her mood. She was a volatile woman, fiery and passionate even when I knew her in her sixties.

16

Refugee Couple

AGAIN LET ME EMPHASISE THAT THIS account is based on various sources, but it was primarily the Stuarts who told me the story of their flight from Berlin and the ensuing months of deprivation and hazardous existence. Francis and Madeleine did have a definite *frisson* of the rapture involved in being survivors, but this was tempered by their traumatic terms of imprisonment that is also part of this time in their lives. I extracted the core events from what they told me. My endless curiosity never met with any rebuke from them and if I was intrusive perhaps the naïvety was mine but in retrospect it is useful that my probing was prolonged and intensive, despite what must have been the lack of propriety on my part. They would not have spoken of these matters if they did not want to and there must have been a certain level of unburdening on their part also in telling me.

Stuart and Madeleine set out from Munich on 1 March 1945 in fear and anxiety, clinging to their mutual belief that it was all part of an exodus like the Jews of the Old Testament leaving Egypt and trusting in the hope of a promised land. From what I gathered, Madeleine's fervent belief in their ultimate survival became a powerful force that Stuart also came to believe in. It was very much a case of her leading and him following, but sometimes it was the other way round, as happened on the road to Kempten in Southern German.

Before leaving Munich, Stuart was ordered by Bahnhofspolizei to put his luggage that he had labelled for Lindau into storage. Madeleine's travel pass only allowed her a 70-kilometre journey to Kaufbeuren. When the train finally appeared it had no windowpanes, just cardboard. It was a draughty journey that got worse after Kaufbeuren. They panicked and left the train for no reason as it slowed down. Just as they began walking, heavy rain started to fall. The rain turned to sleet and a terrific storm blew up. Ten kilometres of walking brought them to a wood. There was some solace in the frugal picnic lunch that Frau Rüger had given them before leaving Munich. Madeleine became utterly despondent because she was soaking wet, tired, hungry and debilitated. The sound of a lorry (not a military one or they would have hidden) aroused Stuart who marched out onto the road. The driver saw his hand signal and stopped. He offered him the picnic lunch including the precious wine, and they got as far as Kempten, 30 kilometres further on. At Kempten, a signpost to Bregenz (in Austria near the Swiss border) made it seem so far away that they decided to try the railway again. After many delays and the misery of a sleepless night at the station, they finally got on a train that was delayed to avoid air raids. They arrived in Bregenz filled with dread because they had no travel documents. Stuart recalled that Bregenz had been his final stop on the way to Berlin in January 1940 and this reminded him of saying goodbye to Kay and Ian five years earlier. His wife and children, always at the back of his mind and tugging at his conscience, seemed remote and far away.

Madeleine would never forget that Bregenz became for her and Stuart a "city of so much later pain and heartbreak, as no other place had ever in store for us". After desperate searching they found Con Cremin, the Irish Chargé d'Affaires, with his family at the hotel Weisses Kreuz which had become the new address of the Irish Legation. Stuart was expecting to trade on a recent favour he had done for Cremin. He was his official source earlier in the year when the death of Frank Ryan needed positive confirmation for the Department of External Affairs in Dublin. Stuart replied to many letters from Cremin stating that Ryan had died under the name Frank Rickard in Dresden, in letters that had been seen by de Valera. [1] Meanwhile Cremin fed them, which was immediately welcome. The food was heavenly to the dishevelled pair, and the wine made up for the bottle given to the driver who brought them to Kempten. A full meal with dessert, Apfelstrudel. Real coffee. During lunch they got confused by Cremin's conversation about Baillie-Steward because of fatigue and exhaustion. Stuart and Madeleine thought they heard Cremin mention that Herr von Schonbeck wanted to help Stuart, but it seems they misunderstood. There was also the difficulty of getting Madeleine out through any German frontier. This had to be faced. As a Polish-German she would be stopped and scrutinised even with sufficient documentation. When they visited von Schonbeck, the German realised their confusion over Baillie-Steward, the pro-Nazi former Captain of the Scots Guards.

Bregenz, like many other frontier towns and cities, was full of refugees. Many wanted to see the other side of Lake Constance, in other words get into Switzerland. The Swiss borders were shut like the Garden of Eden against Stuart and Madeline, or so it seemed, they admitted. It was almost impossible to gain entry. On 5 March they boarded a train for Tuttlingen. This was dangerous because of constant air raids and, even though they were travelling by night, blackouts in the train did not ensure survival against Allied bombing. The train stopped outside Tuttlingen for no reason that they could discover. They slept for a while from exhaustion. Then Madeleine woke Stuart. She remembered that she had a friend in Tuttlingen.

When they found the place and knocked, the house was occupied by another family who did know her friend but they said she had gone to Berlin. The family were the Liebermanns who took a dislike to Stuart, thinking that he would bring them bad luck when the Allies arrived. They must have sensed his forebodings of doom. A month with the Liebermann family was stretching things a bit; however, they lasted that long. There were terrible squabbles at the end, and they were literally thrown out of the house. Passing through Bregenz, Stuart went to see Con Cremin again who had news from Dublin refusing them Swiss transit visas. Like gypsies they moved to the woods around Lake Constance since the weather seemed to be improving. They had to sleep rough and used their rucksacks as pillows. Stuart woke one morning and palpably felt his children close by, such was his longing to see them. His daughter Kay, he would find out later, during the war years, had often pestered the local postman in Laragh, expecting a letter from her father but she never received one. Tormented by his absent children, he wrote a few lines:

> They played 'till the dusk of summer in the wood
> By the stream full of boulders under the hill
> And now like a shadow and hell within my blood
> Their cries and the wood in the dusk are throbbing still[2]

The town of Lindau became the central point of their wanderings. Stuart was miraculously reunited with his heavy suitcase, but had to haul it around a lot because loitering in a frontier zone like Lindau would bring suspicious inquiries. The town was under military control and in a state of confusion; German rearguard troops were defending their country in the certainty of surrender any day. At night Lake Constance flashed with tantalising lights from the Swiss side, while in Lindau they passed signs for cruises across, dating from happier pre-war days. How they might escape across to Switzerland became their fantasy.

They depended for indoor shelter on the Wartesaal, a hall for refugees which was checked and rechecked by security police. Unless you had a ticket to travel the next day, you were liable for arrest. Stuart was arrested one night without a ticket and mercifully released next day. The Germans had a motley horde of refugees to marshal and did so without compassion as an army humiliated to the rank of custodians. Military morale was kept high from rigorous habits of discipline. Some thought Germany might still win the war with the fervour of former years but Stuart admitted that fanatical Nazis were becoming rarer as the inevitability of defeat loomed.

After a day in Dornbirn (across the border in Austria) Madeleine gained entry into a German refugee camp in Lindau. Here she stored the suitcase to avoid having it on their hands. She was then issued with ration cards and, best of all, some nights could smuggle Stuart in. Otherwise he had to sleep anywhere he could find, usually outdoors. One morning, as he walked back through the woods around Lake Constance, he was stopped by a German patrol. In the distance was the sound of French artillery. A soldier inspected Stuart's papers. Stuart said he was an Irish citizen and declared his neutrality. The soldier left Stuart with a corporal pointing a machine gun at him and went off to an officer who was in a nearby billet. The officer returned and wanted to meet the Irishman because he had read a book by Ernie O'Malley, *On Another Man's Wound*. Stuart told him that he had fought on the same side with O'Malley in Ireland. The officer chatted with Stuart for a while and then shouted orders that he was to be let go on his way unimpeded. This was one of those incidents that Stuart always marvelled at and repeated in awe and wonder.

He returned to meet with Madeleine in Lindau. They decided to go across the Swiss border at Feldkirch (Austria). She tried but was unsuccessful. Stuart could have gone through; instead he mumbled about getting papers for (Madeleine) *his wife*. In the woods they attempted to forge her name into the unmarked section of a passport bought on the black market and next day re-queued as a married couple. The forgery was easily discovered and they were not allowed into Switzerland. They moved away from the queue and sat by the wire fence within earshot of the barking dogs and the Swiss guards on the other side. Once more in Dornbirn (Austria), she begged for shelter and a room from a woman whose son was a German soldier at the front. Frau Fussenegger was a caretaker in a bank and gave her son's room to Madeleine. One day they began to discuss the Bible, relating it to their present lives. Madeleine's room had its own entrance on the ground floor of the bank, and Stuart could sneak in. When Frau Fussenegger caught him she said nothing.

The Allied French armies were a day or so away. The Germans opened up the stores in Dornbirn and fed the refugees as never before with bread, cheese, flour and sugar. The Germans did not want their rations to fall into the hands of the enemy. They hoped that well-fed refugees would enhance their profile as a surrendering army. Days later when everyone had had a feast by comparison with previous rations, the town was festooned in the white flags of surrender. Stuart recalled that his forty-third birthday marked the final shrinking of the Nazi empire that had once stretched from the Caucasus to the Atlantic and remained only a narrow corridor in the heart of Germany, about a hundred miles wide.

It was also the day of Hitler's marriage to Eva Braun. The following afternoon, in their private room in the air-raid shelter below the Chancellery in Berlin, Eva Braun swallowed a phial of cyanide and Hitler shot himself through the mouth with his Luger pistol. His death was marked by the last broadcast of Nazi propaganda; the war was over a week later. In *Black List, Section H* Stuart recreates his mood at the time relating to Hitler's death: "He tried to gauge the degree of despair that had preceded the suicide; despair and disaster fascinated H in direct ratio to his recoil from moral jubilation and victory." According to one of Hitler's secretaries, Hanna Reich, she saw the Führer hours before the end with tears in his eyes saying, "every wrong has already been done to me", and "If the German people are incapable of victory, they are unworthy to live".

The news of Hitler's suicide on 30 April 1945 is changed by Stuart for artistic and fictional purposes in *Black List, Section H* to 29 April. "Today, his birthday, Walpurgis Night, and he'd an idea – though nobody had ever said so – the anniversary of his father's death."[3] This is strange because Stuart's father's headstone actually reads: "Who departed this life 14th August." The fictional alteration of the dates is revealing and may indicate Stuart's trauma in linking the suicides of Hitler, his father and his own birthday. H asks: "Had Hitler been capable of sinking, at the very last, to the incommunicable darkness of the irredeemably lost?" And this question calls up the parallel notion:

> What could a human being in that unique and terrible situation not have achieved, outside all norms of experience, by a profound acceptance of his own ruin, so horrible and irreversible because it had involved millions of others? Instead of preparing himself for the humanly inconceivable, saving miracle he had almost certainly spent his last hours accusing his own suffering people of betrayal.[4]

Hitler's last hours and final decision became part of Stuart's imaginative landscape. "The German leader had an old woman's sucked-in mouth and a way of clasping his pudgy hands in front of him as if he wanted to tuck them under an apron."[5] This is how Hitler is described elsewhere in *Black List, Section H.* In *Faillandia* (1985) the central character wonders:

> what would have happened if Hitler, in full consciousness of the calamity he had brought on millions of people and on himself, (because at this mysterious level, the decisive events are personal) and accepting his utter humiliation, had bowed himself to the blood-soaked rubble and publicly proclaimed his guilt, like Raskolnikov in *Crime and Punishment.* He wouldn't have been "saved" in a political or worldly sense, nor would the millions of his victims have been brought back to life, but Gideon believed, something would have happened to turn the blood-stained tide, and the peace that came to his part of the world would have been one nearer the hopes of the survivors.[6]

Associating his father's suicide with Hitler's is stark and very strange, so it is compelling to cite another reference to Stuart's father in *Black List, Section H* that begins:

> When he thought of his father, as he did with a frequency that he couldn't explain, he believed, that had there not been this uncrossable expanse of time between them he could have

> shared in his father's despair. Not being sure in what it had consisted, this was, he saw, a somewhat doubtful conclusion, but at least he could have accompanied this being whom he felt so close to and familiar with to the room in the tile house in Townsville, Australia, that he kept having glimpses of during his own states of inner misery.[7]

What is immediately noticeable is that even at that time Stuart was still deprived of the known facts, since his father had not been confined in an asylum in Townsville but in Sydney. It also shows his preference for imaginative impressions of events over the so-called "actual facts".

One other reference completes the father theme. A voice comes through H's imagination about the agony of severe thirst. The voice compels him to formulate a speech for it:

> "I want nothing, no posthumous rehabilitation even in your thoughts. I deny and abolish everything that happened to me in my life and don't wish you to think that it, even less my death, had any point at all". Whose despair was he receiving intimations of? His father's? Lane's [the fictional name for Jim Phelan]? Christ's?[8]

When the French arrived in Dornbirn, food shortages were severe. Stuart and Madeleine told me that from here on they lived by miracle and luck when it came to food. Their daily nourishment was some leek soup and a little bread or boiled potatoes with a few onions, or thick barley soup. They went to Mass, read the Psalms and found spiritual nourishment in their plight. They also slept long hours dreaming of happier times in their lives, waking each day to the present difficult situation. Often their sleep was interrupted by the chimes of the clock in the market square. Stuart dreamt of home a lot and thought of leaving Madeleine. He could arrange for her to come to Laragh once he reached the vantage point of Ireland, he thought. A French officer they befriended sometimes gave them cigarettes and this was a form of currency to buy food. The officer advised them to marry and avail themselves of a visa for Switzerland. When Stuart put their case to a British colonel in Lindau the opinion was less optimistic.

Incidentally, Stuart's cousin, Robert Stewart-Moore, spent three and a half years of the war as a POW in Lamsdorf, situated 50 kilometres from Auschwitz. Stewart-Moore of the Royal Australian Air Force had been shot down over Germany, crashed in the Elbe River and managed to get out of his airplane underwater. Although Stuart and he never met, his Australian cousin marks a strong contrast to the way Stuart spent the war.

In mid-July, Iseult received an official card from the Red Cross in Geneva with Stuart's signature and a tick in the box beside the printed words "I am well". His address was Bahnhofstr 2, Dornbirn, Vorarlberg, Austria.[10] Iseult consulted with her mother and half-brother, Seán MacBride. At the end of July she wrote to Frederick Boland at the Department of External Affairs enclosing the card from the Red Cross signed by Stuart and suggested in her letter, "it may be of help to get my husband repatriated".[11] So began a frequent correspondence between her and Boland. They also had many meetings at Boland's office in Iveagh House in Dublin.

Frau Fussenegger gave Stuart and Madeleine a room in the attic. Here Madeleine hung a few picture-prints. One, a Cézanne, *Les Bories,* and *Glenmalure* by Paul Henry, which reminded Stuart of his homeland. There was also a drawing of a tramp which represented his present status; he drew it for Madeleine to make her laugh. They were thankful to be alive after the previous months of bombings and starvation, shock and hardship. Their life entered a period of simplicity in the small attic room with a bed, some food, sensual love and the deeper love for each other. Their lovemaking from the start had achieved what William Blake called "lineaments of gratified desire". They both had the same unashamed impatience for lovemaking. When they learned Psalms by heart and verses from *The Song of Songs* a mystical marriage became a reality for them. In *Black List* there is a telling remark: "It was as if they'd been lovemaking for years."[12] They had soared beyond the Mosaic laws of adultery to a higher union of spiritual and physical love. This was their mutual philosophy and spirituality of healing love, they said.

The summer weather was unbearably hot. Stuart longed for further communication with Laragh whenever Iseult, Ian and Kay came into his mind. He had had no news from home for years and his previous letters had been returned due to the postal blackout between Nazi-occupied Europe and the British Isles. He tried to get visas for himself and Madeleine in Dornbirn and when this failed he decided to go to Paris. He wanted to try to get her into Ireland as a refugee.

Weeks passed before he got a place on a convoy of buses. Eventually it was a Jewish couple going to Strasburg who helped him. Stuart listened to their story of survival from a concentration camp and used what he heard in his novel *Victors and Vanquished*. They parted, and Madeleine said she hoped this would be only a time of preparation for the future. He boarded a train in Strasburg and arrived in Paris on 14 August. He recalled seeing a transvestite with red-painted fingernails as he walked through the Gard du Nord. His ambivalent feelings towards the celebrations in free Paris lost any vestige of festivity at the Irish Legation when he was told that he might not be welcome in Ireland. He asked about bringing a friend home (Madeleine) and was told that she would have no chance of entering the country.

The Department of External Affairs in Dublin had a list of persons suspected of supporting the Nazi regime. Besides, Seán MacBride had found Stuart's German residency embarrassing. MacBride's political ambitions had to survive his half-sister Iseult's public debacle over the Goertz affair and the Stephen Held trial. As Stuart sat in the Irish Legation, he began to understand the official line that would be taken concerning his time in Germany. He was obviously seen as a belligerent. Before leaving the building he queued for repatriation money. Days later he found out about the blacklist of persons who had supported the Axis powers that appeared in an American newspaper. Ezra Pound and Lord Haw-Haw appeared on the blacklist, along with his own name. He told me that he feared for his life.

Meanwhile, in Dublin, Boland requested a report on Stuart from the Head of the G2 Military Intelligence, Colonel Dan Bryan. His comments were also sent to de Valera with a headline on the letter: "Francis Stuart, late of Berlin". Colonel Bryan reported that Stuart "was almost certainly concerned with the dispatch of certain German agents who arrived in this country in 1940 intent on purposes inimical to our neutrality and security".[13] The report included mention of Goertz's and Seán MacBride's activities: "When he was Director of Intelligence for the IRA he was largely responsible for their contacts with the Germans."[14] MacBride's contact with Helmut Clissmann was also mentioned, as was Stuart's relationship to MacBride through marriage. The report expresses the wish to find legal evidence in support of Stuart's alleged pro-German activities. Frederick Boland sent a communiqué to Paris stating that: 'Stuart should not assume from the fact of our agreeing to transmit this £15 to him that he enjoys Irish diplomatic protection or that his conduct in 1940, at a particularly dangerous moment of our history, has been forgotten to him."[15] Iseult had given the money to Boland for her husband.

Boland contacted Seán Murphy at the Irish Legation and asked him to interview Stuart. Murphy reported back to Boland by letter at the end of August, saying that Stuart claimed that he had never made anti-British propaganda, but agreed that it could have been taken as such. He had also told Murphy that he did not want to fall into the hands of the British and that he could reply to the Irish police about the parachutist (Goertz). His use of the word "parachutist" indicates his fear of using the word spy.

In *Black List*, H replies to his interrogator Captain Manville:

> Whatever the motives for my coming here (Germany), and they were complex and far from pure, I've begun to realise that it's here in the company of the guilty that with my peculiar and, if you like, flawed kind of imagination, I belong. The situation I've involved myself in, however disastrous for my reputation, and perhaps because it is disastrous, gives me a chance of becoming the only sort of writer it's in my power to be.[16]

Stuart's use of the word "guilty" is not in the judicial sense. Ezra Pound, the one-time lover of Iseult who figures in *Black List*, had broadcast on Rome radio during the war. Stuart's comments can be read as a revelation of himself:

> I believe that Ezra Pound's violent involvement in political ideology was primarily a means, largely instinctive and subconscious, of deepening his alienation as an artist, he being the kind of writer who requires isolation, even condemnation, from and by his society to reach the peaks of which he is capable. Pound was conscious of the overlapping concept of the artist and criminal. He had an instinct that his poetic destiny involved social ostracism. It was Pound's subconscious urge to become an outcast, so seemingly irrational and self-destructive which impelled him to churn out his wartime broadcasts.[17]

The implication of this comment on Pound is one we discussed on many occasions. Stuart agreed with me when I put it to him that what he had said about Pound might equally apply to himself. He did not believe that he was an actual criminal, but he was capable of imagining himself a criminal at various stages of his life. This expansiveness of the imagination was essential for his art, in depicting such characters in fiction. It also held perils for his conduct, sanity and wellbeing. Pound, unlike Stuart, was indicted for treason and, through an expert lawyer, Julien Cornell, pleaded insanity which saved the poet's life. It remains a debatable point as to whether he was insane; some of the examining psychiatrists adjudged him so. Pound had a mental breakdown after the war and spoke twice during his trial, "I never did believe in fascism, God damn it"; "I'm opposed to fascism." He was sent for 13 years to St Elizabeth's in Washington, a cavernous asylum housing 7,000 inmates. The indictment against Pound was dropped in 1958. On his release and return to Italy, he commented to reporters, "All America is an insane asylum".

Pound sent a letter (undated) to Stuart who had offered to send him one of his novels, *Redemption*.

> St Elizabeth's Hospital
> Washington DC
>
> Francis –
>
> Thanks. Have unslakable thirst for news. Will be glad to try a novel but I'm seldom able to finish one. Always glad to read up prosody.
>
> Cordial regards,
>
> E. P.

Stuart had a copy of the American edition of *Redemption* sent from his New York publisher Devin Adair to St Elizabeth's Hospital, but never heard any more from Pound. Stuart sold the letter to an American university in the 1960s. He told me that Yeats once said Pound referred to Stuart as "the ancient mariner" after Coleridge's poem. I often felt this was quite an accurate assessment of Stuart.[18]

Meanwhile in Paris in the summer of 1945, Stuart could only afford a room in a dingy hotel and felt slightly ridiculous in the floppy yellow pantaloons that were all he could afford. Hotel Copernic was uncomfortably shabby. He visited some pre-war haunts and found an English language teacher who offered to share his teaching schedule. Then, calling at the Irish Legation looking for a reply to a letter to Laragh, he was handed a letter from Róisín Ní Mheara. She had written to him c/o Légation D'Irlande. They met and she talked about longing to return to Berlin and asked him to join her. When he told her about Madeleine she was upset and they did not meet again. He wrote to Madeleine from the hotel and, on the 29 August, boarded a train to Strasburg. He was not permitted to cross the Austrian border into Dornbirn and waited for days in the hopes of finding a way to his beloved. He returned to Paris and got another room at the same hotel. This time he wrote to her explaining his failure to return, stating that in Paris he would ensure his papers were valid and hoped to be reunited with her soon. He wrote to Iseult asking for money. She replied saying that Seán MacBride had given him a coat, but when it arrived it was too small.

Iseult believed the "innocent" references to Madeleine in Stuart's letter. His plans for bringing her to Ireland were not fully clear to her for months. Stuart's actions were those of someone who had left his marriage emotionally and every other way, he admitted to me. To all intents and purposes Madeleine was his "wife". Ian wrote begging him to return home. Kay also, naturally expected her father to return. Ian added how worried Iseult was about everything. She was actually living on the hope of his returning. She planted bulbs and began getting the garden in order. Seán Murphy sent a communiqué to Dublin about Stuart's need of money and by mid-September Boland sent £35 that converted into 200 French francs "for Mr Francis Stuart, an Irish Citizen at present destitute in Paris".[19] Meanwhile Seán MacBride deposited sums of money with Boland over the following three months and inquired how much it would take to keep Stuart in Paris. While MacBride sent in all £75, Iseult sent larger sums which Lily had provided. By the end of the month, the Department of External Affairs in Dublin had renewed Stuart's passport. Seán Murphy grew to admire him and informed Boland by letter: "I think he is a very nice fellow." Boland was in sombre mood: "Stuart's return would certainly lead to publicity in papers like *The Irish Times*, attention would thereby be drawn to any immunity granted, and the British would be unlikely to agree to anything so apt to occasion criticism in Parliament."[20]

Stuart became dependent on visits to Murphy at the Legation on 37 bis Rue de Villejust. It was his way of gaining insight into the situation in Ireland. He told me that he was somewhat oblivious that the debacle was becoming serious. Boland in Dublin and Murphy in Paris were exemplary in terms of their professional expertise in dealing with him, passing on money from home and calming Iseult's fears about her wayward husband. Both diplomats knew well that the official line on the Stuarts was that they had shown pro-German sympathies. However, Boland and Murphy were applying a neutral stance in the post-war situation to these Irish citizens.

Iseult's relationship with Goertz, the German spy, had ended with his capture by the Irish authorities in 1941, a year after his parachute landing in Ireland. It was a sad love story for Iseult. One of the dreams recorded in her diary is of marrying Goertz in Nuremberg with Stuart among the guests along with his girlfriend, "knowing each other's thoughts without words".[21] "Then the wedding was over and we stood outside the Church, my hand on your arm. Life was before us."[22] Her diary comments about Stuart and his soulmate girlfriend are psychic on Iseult's part. Her references to Goertz include, "I can no longer day-dream that some night there might be the noise of a pebble hitting the window-pane".[23] With Goertz in prison in the Curragh, her tone turned to regret: "I have been cowed long enough by the spirits of the flesh and the world. I dare them to say to me: 'When the heart sings it is singing to its mate, therefore you cannot sing.'"[24] After the war Goertz, faced with deportation to Britain in May 1947, poisoned himself in the presence of Irish detectives in the Aliens Office, Dublin Castle, having swallowed a phial of potassium cyanide. When Iseult heard the news of his suicide she wrote in her diary "Que sera, sera". He is buried in the German Cemetery near Glencree, County Wicklow.

Iseult's diary tells everything about her war years: "I felt nearly hopeless. Not resigned."[26] There are many entries on the difficulties of being a parent. Elsewhere in the diary, she mentions that a few words from a beggar become big news for her. On a trip to Dublin from Laragh she found a book on Buddhism which gave her hope after she had failed to rekindle her Christian faith. During the war she had been friendly with Eva Hempel, wife of the German Ambassador, and shared with her a mutual passion for the ancient Sanskrit text *The Bhagavad Gita*, the spiritual song of Lord Krishna. Her son recalled for me many journeys made by Iseult to the Catholic Library in Merrion Square around this time. She read and wrote out copious excerpts from the Gospel of Buddha, the Upanishads, the Dhammapada and various poets such as Whitman and Kabir. She hoped to make a personal anthology for publication. Stuart's study at Laragh Castle became hers in his absence. After two years of study and meditation, she recorded the following: "I left all books aside for the garden. I worked in it as never before."[27] She abandoned her plans to find a publisher for her spiritual writings, seeing it as vanity. Her solitude was filled with loneliness except for Ian and Kay, their grandmother and Gonne. "Today I was quite alone all afternoon. I went up the stairs to fetch my coat. Wet gusty afternoon on the panes. The sound of my steps on the stairs suddenly struck me to the heart. I am trying to write what it was - and I can't. No matter, we know. Suffice it to say it wasn't fear, mostly with some other indefinable striving towards or away from desolation, I am not sure."[28] The final entry in the diary might well be her epitaph: "Only twice in my life has my heart been broken. Such very different things the death of a baby and the defeat of Germany yet both have been worse than all other sorrows."[29]

Her letter to the Hotel Copernic of 17 October 1945 begins "Dear Grim", her pet name for Stuart. The letter concludes:

> But you see, Darling, why I keep reiterating in all my letters that if and when it is possible for you to come home you should do so at once. So long as you must stay abroad they are glad and willing to help, but it would really be an untenable position for you and me if it became possible for you to get home and you refused.[30]

When Stuart wrote for more money she sent it, realising that her threats of "cutting him off" financially would not work. Her reference to "they" means Lily and Seán MacBride. This time he had the money converted to German marks for his next journey. The lure of Laragh could not match his love for Madeleine. Sorrowfully for him this also meant geographical displacement from Ian and Kay who by then were no longer children.

17

Prisoners, and a Wife's Turmoil

BLACK LIST, SECTION H DOES NOT express the turmoil involved in this final decision of Stuart about his wife and children. *Victors and Vanquished* is more revealing, with a brief reunion between husband, wife and daughter. Stuart told me that this was a fictional device. During our meetings Ian Stuart told me that his mother never went to Paris with Kay after the war. Madeleine's diary/memoir, *Manna in the Morning,* is also fairly selective about these months of turmoil. She mentions Frau Fussenegger as her main source of consolation. Madeleine never doubted Stuart's return from Paris. His letters filled her with joy; some made her apprehensive for his safety, but she was sure of his devoted love. Madeleine typed out more Psalms (Nos 40, 121, 126) from the Bible, sewing them together into a little prayer book with a cardboard cover. She prayed for their life together in the future. On 20 August 1945, she wrote in her diary: "I'm allowed to stay here in Austria until the end of December, then have to go back to Germany."[1] As the days turned into weeks she began to despair of seeing him ever again.

While Stuart waited for transit visas in the French capital, he had plenty of time to think how best to further their plans, which seemed a wilful dream at times. He was given official advice about seeking a visa for Madeleine as his Polish fiancée. He sold the gold ring and had the proceeds sent to a bank account in Switzerland, thinking they might go there, since the problems in getting to Ireland, and not least arriving in Laragh, were considerable. Meanwhile he went to the Louvre to see paintings by Cézanne, Giotto and da Vinci. He was glad to hear from Ian who wrote about considering going to a monastery. Stuart replied asking for some clothes. He was feeling healthy again after the previous months of deprivation and though missing

Madeleine greatly, enjoyed his meals in Paris, and the wine, when he could afford it.

In Dornbirn, Frau Fussenegger reproached Madeleine for brooding and staying in all day. Madeleine wrote in her diary, "Darling, where are you, how is it with you? Goodnight."[2] She borrowed a record of Mozart's G Major Mass as soon as Frau Fussenegger purloined a gramophone and also borrowed a book of Verlaine's poems. A letter from Stuart on 10 September sustained her. He felt certain about their reunion in the near future. She began to read more of the books he loved; *Wuthering Heights* (Emily Brontë) and *Autobiography of a Saint* (Saint Thérèse of Lisieux). Stuart was closer to her, arriving in Metz on 31 October, but unsure as to how or when he could get further, owing to travel restrictions and other uncertainties of transport.

When he finally returned to Dornbirn on 8 November, Frau Fussenegger came up to the attic room with his attaché case as a preparation for the excitement. Madeleine rushed downstairs into his arms as he carefully put a food parcel on the stairs. In their room they celebrated with orgiastic lovemaking. They stayed up until five in the morning talking, unable to sleep. Next day Madeleine used a few packets of cigarettes to buy more food in preparation for her birthday which they planned as a thanksgiving celebration. It would be her thirtieth birthday on the 23 November and one that she would never forget because of its horrors.

When the plain-clothes French police arrived on 21 November they were looking for the spy Gerda M. and arrested Madeleine. She had signed her name, Gertrud Magdalena Meissner, on ration cards since the previous July when she had approached the Gendarmerie. She was listed on their files since August as a German professor of languages. Stuart was also wanted for questioning. They dared ask under whose authority the arrest had been ordered and were curtly informed that it was General Dumas, Commander-in-Chief of French Forces in occupied Austria. Stuart and Madeleine put some items into the attaché case and walked down from the attic to the police car. At Bregenz Oberstadt prison they were separated and Madeleine, still retaining some innocence, asked whether they could not be put in a cell together. "Madame, you are not in a hotel," the warder snapped at her in French. The prison building they were in had the gloomy institutional architecture of such places. The entrance was through a portcullis to a three-tiered fortress-like structure with dark corridors, gloomier cells and iron bars on the windows. Doors were slammed shut on each of them and keys cranked and the locks snapped shut.[3]

Interrogations followed over many days but without torture. Stuart would later write of his first impressions of incarceration: "In a cell meant for one, or at most two, we were ten and twelve and we were starving. I remembered that I'd been a writer, but felt I was no longer a writer, that I would never again be a writer. It was a despairing experience, but looking back, I see that the kind of writer I am probably had to reach that complete giving up of his vocation."[4]

The account of their days in captivity is described by Stuart in *The Pillar of Cloud* and the less well-known *The Flowering Cross*. The latter is a more vivid account than any facts that could be given here and will be mentioned in the chronology of his published novels. During her first days of captivity, Madeleine could see Stuart from the barred window of her cell during his hour of exercise when he marched in a circle with other prisoners. He was forbidden to look up at her window, he told me grimly. While no charges were brought against either of them, interrogations continued which would leave both of them mentally scarred. There were other horrors about their confinement as well as the fact that they never knew when it would end. Many of their fellow prisoners grew more and more morose or crazy as their fate was decided during interrogations. Every sound from the interrogation rooms could be heard in Stuart's cell. Military transports came and went with prisoners who were judged to be traitors or collaborators by the interrogation squads. These prisoners were taken away for execution. Stuart told me that he felt that he would be shot and had to manage somehow to live with the choking sense of anguish.

After months, Madeleine had entered the kind of state described by prisoners in Stuart's novels. After further interrogations and a breakdown on her part, she told me, with a look of fear on her face as she remembered her ordeal, that she was no longer suspected of being a spy. In May she was given a promise of early release. Then she was brought with Stuart by transport to Freiburg in Bresgau, not far from the French border in southern Germany. They were detained in a cellar on Beethovenstrasse. It was some consolation that they were allowed to stay together. On 13 July they were released, eight months after their arrest. Their release on Bastille Day was an ironic as well as an official gesture on the part of the French authorities, according to Stuart.

He told me a horrific story about Bregenz prison. In the crowded cell the atmosphere was one of unremitting doom, foetid unsanitary conditions and near starvation. Many of his cellmates were eventually taken for execution either to Paris or Brussels. A fellow prisoner slashed his wrists and was removed from the cell. Deeply disturbing for Stuart, because of his father's death, was when he awoke to find a fellow prisoner had hanged himself during the night. Some of the prisoners decided to conceal the dead man, keeping him propped up as if alive for three days in order to get his food ration. Stuart was living his worst imaginings. He developed a total eczema of the body that added to his miseries. He began to feel like a leper in a lair. The allusion was to the lepers in the Gospels, he added.

In prison Madeleine had been allowed to write two letters, one of them to Stuart's mother. Basil Liddell Hart received a letter from Madeleine in the same month ("Please, please dear sir, help him! Francis Stuart has such a fine and rare soul.").[5] Liddell Hart contacted Sir John Maffey. Liddell Hart, the historian and journalist with *The Times*, had been an admirer of Stuart's pre-war novels, especially *The Angel of Pity* (1935), which was prophetic of the Second World War. Maffey, who had attended Rugby like Stuart, was British Representative to Ireland during the war. His press attaché in Ireland was the poet John Betjeman. Maffey studied the situation and by June of the following year revealed that "Britain was unlikely to prosecute Francis Stuart – all the more so as there is evidence that he broke off relations with the Nazis before the end".[6] In letters to Maffey, Liddell Hart attempted to decrease concern over Stuart's position by keeping it vague. Had Stuart been handed over to the British at this time he would have faced a post-war bureaucracy that had a file on him with additional information from Irish Intelligence. Maffey knew that no final decision had been made on Stuart, as yet, by the British and replied to Liddell Hart, "In May 1940, Goertz landed by parachute in Éire and was harboured by Francis Stuart's wife to whose house he made his way immediately on landing. I need not go into further details as you will understand that to us this case looks pretty bad."[7]

Iseult knew nothing of Stuart's imprisonment until the summer of 1946 when he and Madeleine were transferred to Freiburg from Bregenz. Months earlier, in March, she had written to Boland from Laragh Castle: "I can't shake off an awful sense of apprehension."[8] A letter from Róisín Ní Mheara added to her apprehension, stating,

"He was delighted with your news, and the letters from your children. In spite of all he is steadily writing books, and assured me that much good would come out of his hardship and suffering. I often thought of writing to you, but considered it to be slightly impertinent. I trust you will understand that the present day circumstances may overrule some conventions."[9] Róisín, who had gone to Malmaison in the south of France, concluded her letter, "But I too feel, like dear Francis, that the misery and despair that one has absorbed during these fateful times bind one to those one has shared them with".[10]

When Iseult met MacBride, he advised caution about writing to the address on the card signed by Stuart which she had received from the Red Cross. At the end of May, Foreign Affairs in Dublin contacted Seán Murphy who sent the belated news of his arrest and imprisonment. Boland consulted with a higher authority and telegrammed, "Please take usual measures diplomatic protection".[11] When Stuart was in great danger, Dublin was magnanimously willing to help him. Iseult sent a letter to Boland and asked for a meeting as soon as possible. She did not know how long her husband had been in prison and added: "I read how my old friend, Ezra Pound, was driven insane; yet he always seemed so well balanced but like Francis, a writer and a poet. For such people jail conditions are particularly dangerous."[12] To her great relief she obtained a letter from Stuart and disclosed the contents to Boland:

> He and his former secretary, Gertrude Meissner, were arrested last November, and have been kept in jail since then, he doesn't know why, as no charge has been brought against him and he has done nothing to which the French authorities could take exception.[13]

Her letter clarifies much about their relationship, her fears for his safety and her total misinterpretation of the presence of Madeleine (Gertrud Meissner) in his life. It reveals a lack of self-knowledge on her part and the all too human tendency to think that what she hoped for would happen:

> Francis has no practical sense. Only, about Gertrud Meissner, I feel very worried. You may remember last year I asked you would it be possible to get permission to have her over here, and you told me then nothing had yet been decided about the

> question of refugees from Germany. Apparently she has lost all her people, is homeless and destitute, and Francis is under some great obligation to her. Now, by way of paying it back, he has managed to get her into jail as well as himself. Trying to put myself in his place, I think I would sooner spend the rest of my life in jail than be dragged home into safety and comfort, leaving behind some unfortunate person for whom I was responsible.[14]

Obviously, Iseult felt that Stuart's delays and subterfuge about refusing to return to Ireland sooner had been because of some loyalty between friends in the extremes of war; she still did not know that Stuart had thrown in his lot with Madeleine. Iseult's letter continues:

> Then Lily mentioned she's willing to pay for Gertrud Meissner – "If she can't find work, at the worst she can stay with us." I had always meant to adopt some German child; we can adopt her instead. Please believe me, the very obvious interpretation that could be put on this concern of Francis for her would not be the true one, although I quite see that sounds hardly credible. Francis is so unworldly that he hasn't the sense to see that. But he is quite incapable of hypocrisy, and he wouldn't have written of Gertrud and of the way of the Catholic Church being the only one in the same letter if he was carrying on some silly flirtation.
>
> … so it would be a great kindness for the best possible solution if you would consider seriously this application of mine to let her come over if it is at all possible. [15]

The letter begs further comment concerning what was unknown to Iseult at the time of writing it. Iseult may have thought that if Gertrud (Madeleine) came home to Laragh with Stuart that she could talk her husband out of his "silly flirtation". His mention of Madeleine was a way of beginning to break the news to Iseult about the new special relationship in his life. For Iseult to think of Stuart as "unworldly" reveals a huge gap in her knowledge of him. He had simply been unable to tell the truth to his wife. A central fact of his life was this personal difficult triangle of Iseult-Madeleine-Stuart.

The concluding diplomatic situation went as follows. In Paris, Seán Murphy contacted the French Cachet du Ministère, who duly replied that Stuart had been arrested six months previously for recruiting spies for the Abwehr and broadcasting on German radio. The report stated that Stuart had been released on 13 May (actually July) and transferred to Freiburg and had to report weekly to the military police. Murphy foresaw the gravity of Stuart's situation and cautiously approached the British Military Intelligence division in Paris who said they were not dealing with Stuart's case. Boland reported to Murphy, "I think it would be a correct diagnosis of Mrs Stuart's state of mind to say that she does not want Gertrud Meissner over here but that she is afraid that if Gertrud Meissner cannot come, Francis won't come either, being unwilling to leave her."[16] When Murphy contacted the British Foreign Office in July he was given the complete disclosure that, unless some grave charges were found, "they [the British] will support the view that Stuart should be handed over to us".[17] Murphy made approaches to the French authorities about repatriation.

Boland received a visit from Iseult at the end of August. He already knew about the letter she had received from Stuart, looking for more money which she sent from her bank account to the Department of Foreign Affairs. "Francis is a bad subject for starvation, although he is being so thoroughly aggravating,"[18] she wrote to Boland at the beginning of September. She began sending food parcels to Stuart and Madeleine through the Irish Red Cross at Lincoln Place in Dublin. Boland and Murphy kept their patience in trying to help Stuart to safety through repatriation. Stuart ended his correspondence with Murphy in late September, writing from Schwarzwaldstrasse 2, Freiburg:

> A chara,
>
> In answer to your letter of September 12, while thanking you for your offer of securing permission for me to travel to Ireland, I am writing to say that I do not want to return there at present.
>
> I thank you also for your letter of August 29. I am now trying to have money sent home through Switzerland as you suggest.
>
> Mise le meas,
>
> Francis Stuart.[19]

Iseult contacted Boland asking that Stuart be repatriated "with or without his consent" in order to avoid any further dangers of rearrest. By September, Murphy's endeavours on behalf of Stuart had achieved a deportation order from the French authorities. In November, after family discussions with Seán MacBride and Gonne, Iseult wrote to Boland asking him to withdraw the deportation order. She recanted at the end of the letter, mentioning Lily's illness and asked to have Stuart deported. Stuart's desertion of Iseult had become a reality, but she still wanted him home. Boland wrote to Murphy saying, "I don't know what more we can do at the moment. The 'eternal triangle' factor makes the whole thing tiresome and rather hopeless."[20] Both diplomats were further frustrated because the French made the deportation order official on Stuart at the beginning of November, signed by General Koenig. By January of 1947 arrangements to fly Stuart from Paris to Collinstown, using the balance of monies deposited in his name by Seán MacBride, were operative.

Boland was contacted by Iseult who expressed no particular anxiety about getting Stuart home. Murphy received a disconsolate letter from Boland in mid-January, "Better for us simply to lie low and not do anything unless we are forced into it by pressure from the French authorities. Do you agree?"[21] Stuart had been telling lies to his wife and, to a lesser extent, to Frederick Boland and Seán Murphy, in the obsessive pursuit of a new life with his beloved.

The fine line drawn between traitors, collaborators and the "innocent" drawn in the months after the war might easily have put Stuart on the execution list in Bregenz Prison, as he freely admitted to me and many others who questioned him on this point over the years. His broadcasts have elements of anti-democratic bias and while they are not Nazi propaganda in their totality, a phrase here or there out of context could have been used decisively in support of his execution in court proceedings. The fact that the broadcasts came from Berlin may have been damning enough, whatever their content. Helping Goertz with information about landing in Ireland and providing a safe house with Iseult might also have been damning. Also, Stuart's presence in Berlin, in the pay of the Reich, could easily be twisted to sound like a pro-Nazi position. For many people these facts were conclusive of his absolute Nazi affiliation and sympathy. His birth in Australia might have been construed as making him British, even though he possessed an Irish passport. There can be so many conjectures after the events. Persons were being shot and hung on the flimsiest of Nazi collaborationist connections. In an interview with Naim Attallah in the 1990s, Stuart conjectured, "They could have hanged me, I suppose ..."[22]

In the aftermath of the Nuremberg trials, perhaps Stuart's imprisonment as a suspected pro-Nazi might be seen as unjust. To his detractors, certainly not. However, a brief survey of leading Nazis tried at Nuremburg reveals a wide discrepancy in sentencing policy. Albert Speer, for instance, Hitler's architect as well as Minister for Armaments and Munitions, received a 20-year sentence. Speer would go on to become a much sought-after guest on worldwide TV chat shows after his release. More pertinent is the case of Hans Fritzsche, who worked under Joseph Goebbels as a leading broadcaster arousing popular sentiment for the German war effort. He was acquitted since the broadcasts were not deemed to be an incitement to the committing of atrocities. Legally, if Fritzsche was deemed innocent why not Stuart? Hjalmar Schacht, the central figure in Germany's rearmament, was acquitted. Karl Donitz, commander of the German Navy, got ten years. Besides, Stuart's neutrality put him outside any trial for treason in any country except his own. He would never have been tried for treason in Ireland after the war, but he was wanted by the gardaí. Colonel Dan Bryan of G2 had expected to interview him on his arrival at Collinstown Airport outside Dublin.

Besides, Stuart, unlike the writer Knut Hamsun, for instance, never publicly supported Hitler in print. Hamsun approved of the Nazi occupation of Norway and had a meeting with Hitler that was exploited as propaganda by the Germans. On the death of Hitler, Hamsun wrote a favourable obituary, was charged with treason after the war, tried and had his assets confiscated. He lived in poverty until his death. In Ireland, Frederick Boland of External Affairs begged de Valera not to respond publicly on the death of Adolf Hitler. As it happened, de Valera made an official visit to Dr Hempel, the German Ambassador in Northumberland Road, on 2 May 1945, to express condolence.

18

Freiburg Trilogy

APART FROM THE SITUATION with his family, Stuart recalled for me how he bought some notebooks and pens and began to write in longhand. For Stuart, to have gone from writing *The Great Squire* to *The Pillar of Cloud* was a quantum leap in terms of fiction. When he and Madeleine were released from custody in July 1946 they lived in a small one-roomed flat in Schwarzwaldstrasse no. 2 in Freiburg. Here he began writing *The Pillar of Cloud*. He paused to make a diary entry in mid-August: "It is seldom a writer is given such a plot as this with its roots in his own life, so full of movement, so deep with significance. If I don't make a good novel out of this then I shall never do."[1] The completed manuscript is dated on the final page, 9 October 1947. Under the title, there is a dedication to Madeleine as "Magdalena". They hoped that the novel would find a publisher in the future.

Freiburg is closely surrounded by the Schwarzwald (the "Black Forest"). This provides a backdrop to the novel. It is also the birthplace of Martin Heidegger, who became a big influence on Stuart. His best-known work, *Time and Being*, was published in 1926. Heidegger declared the death of philosophy after the war and published essays on poets such as Trakl, Hölderlin and Keats. At that time, Stuart read these essays, considered to be the epitome of valid criticism. Stuart always encouraged me to read Heidegger, which I did sporadically, becoming absorbed by his *Poetry, Language, Thought*, translated by Albert Hofstadter.

The title *The Pillar of Cloud* might suggest some weighty Old Testament content to anyone who has not read the book. However, Stuart is not evangelical in that sense. Evangelicalism is a symptom of religious obsession and its exponents never appealed to Stuart, who was inclined to see such fervour as religious fanaticism. In the novel, Dominic Malone is a refugee living in a frontier town on the German–Swiss border. In places, the book has an anti-German and pro-French stance: strange, since it was the French authorities who imprisoned Stuart and Madeleine. Dominic believes in a fraternity based on individualism and the type of loving community espoused by Jesus who "was the one prophet who did not promise peace on earth, but destruction and desolation". "He did not preach any revolution or any counter-measures."[2] Jesus "had cut a very small figure compared to the great revolutionaries and conquerors", and "had been destroyed by the moralists and the priests and the professional doers-of-good".[3]

Stuart's engagement with the four horses of the Apocalypse in *The Pillar of Cloud* – war, pestilence, famine and death – seems more God-filled than filled with the absence of a god. What or who is Stuart's God? In many ways this biographical memoir is in search of an answer to the question. Stuart was neither a rigid moralist nor a libertine. Neither should one be over-prescriptive and presume to "explain him and his message". The novel exemplifies his concern with the dissenting and neutral artist's need to be an outcast and the artist's imperative to make art, no matter what has happened in life.

The victims who survive in the *The Pillar of Cloud* are similar to other Holocaust survivors, such as Primo Levi, Elie Wiesel or Roman Polanski. Many of them had no interest in speculations about the nature of evil or whether, if Hitler had perished in the trenches of the First World War, there would have been no Holocaust. Stuart and I often discussed such matters and especially Levi who wrote an account of his years in a concentration camp, *If This is a Man* (1960). His trauma is also given voice in a poem, "The Survivor". Levi committed suicide in 1990. The motive for his suicide, if it is possible to suggest a cause, may have been survivor's guilt, which is the theme of the poem. Levi commented that, "every German must answer for Auschwitz, indeed every man, and after Auschwitz it is no longer permissible to be unarmed". There is in his comment the language of human breakdown, but then again there was also a breakdown of language that followed the war in that some writers felt words could not describe what had happened. Theodore Adorno claimed that poetry was impossible after Auschwitz, yet Benjamin Fondane managed to write in Auschwitz. Stuart told me that he did not believe

Adorno's dictum about the Holocaust marking the end of poetry. Samuel Beckett wrote a four-line poem "Saint Lô" after the war and Czeslaw Milosz wrote far greater poetry in the Jewish ghetto in Warsaw.

Stuart's position on neutrality is summed up in the following: "I have friends and acquaintances who say that the dropping of the atomic bomb was not as monstrous as some of the Nazi's acts because it wasn't racial. But all that is a bit specious, what is racial and what isn't racial. It was an act you can't defend."[4] Stuart remained engaged with the *Book of Job* and other such texts in attempting to understand evil. When Job's wife says "Curse God and die", Job endures even her despair on top of endless calamity in a life lived by a "good" human. Stuart consulted the Bible, among other texts, as a meditation before seeking answers to the problem of evil - this central question of existence.

The Holocaust also had its martyrs such as Maximilian Kolbe and Dietrich Bonhoeffer, both of whose works Stuart discussed with me. Bonhoeffer's execution has tenuous links to the Stuart story. He was tortured and hanged in April 1945 along with other German resistance members, including Admiral Canaris who, as head of the Abwehr, chose Captain Goertz as one of the spies to go to Ireland. Canaris, also friendly with Frank Ryan and less so with Stuart, had latterly joined the German Resistance group who wanted Hitler assassinated. The challenge of Stuart's *The Pillar of Cloud,* he emphasised, is not to explain away the war and the Holocaust but to reveal the visions of new life that sprang from it. Because of its scope and breadth, reactions to the novel must remain deeply personal.

In the throes of writing *The Pillar of Cloud* Stuart admonished himself in his diary entry of 19 February 1947: "All must be fact and nothing invented - characters must not be invented. Now at last I know how to write, how to be myself and the long years of uncertainty as a writer are over."[5] It is dangerously easy to locate Madeleine in the novel, as Halka. Obviously no character in fiction is a replica from life, but the derivation is often ascertainable. Is Lisette, her sister, based on Iseult? These critical identifications may be spurious, except that Stuart mined his life for his writings and freely admitted so in our conversations.

Stuart got another letter of desperation from Iseult with the suggestion that Madeleine should "pack Stuart off". "My God, how little

I want to hurt her," Stuart wrote in his diary. There was news about Lily Stuart who had been ill and in delirium "talking" to her son far off in Freiburg. Then Iseult wrote again about Lily who "was feeling better with a spell of good weather". Stuart celebrated St Patrick's Day reading Tolstoy and D.H. Lawrence's story *The Man Who Loved Islands*. He recalled that during the war, after reading Lawrence, he had an insight into "the struggle in the world and the revelation that this struggle is of no real importance, and that the truth lies in being detached from it and in entering into one's own stillness and darkness." It is worth repeating that he equated Lawrence with Blake, who detested "mental idealism", and indeed for Lawrence mental conceptions were divorced from deep emotional truth. Stuart also hated knowingness and wanted his art to be devoid of ideas and deliberately remain "unknown", clinging to its mystery.

Stuart and Madeleine often told me lovingly about their life at the time as they lived in a small room in a solitary surviving tower block in Freiburg. Stuart was still under surveillance from the French authorities and reporting weekly to the French Securité on Beethovenstrasse 7. He had written a poem after visiting Beethoven's house in Bonn in 1942:

> What desire, what unrest
> to have stood there and known
> the still warm, empty nest
> whence the phoenix had flown.[6]

Freiburg began to haunt Stuart and Madeleine with all the rubble of half-destroyed buildings; only the Cathedral stood looming and defiant. After completing the novel, he found himself seriously debilitated from near starvation. Madeleine became a friend of Frau Piening's, a neighbour whom she named "Mutti" meaning "mother". Stuart, because of ill health, was unable to collect his allotted log supply permitted to a refugee, and unable to chop the wood. When Stuart was ill, Madeleine and Mutti nursed him. The *Stürm und Drang* over the food-parcel situation was something that he had incorporated into the opening of *The Pillar of Cloud* changing, for fictional purposes, the operatives into Germans nor did he name the institution, Caritas, which was an Irish Catholic relief organisation. Around this time they went to a concert. It is mentioned in *Black List* when H hears Chopin's Ballade, Opus 4, introducing him "to new states of perception".[7] Wherever there is vividness of place and event in Stuart's fiction it comes from his direct experience.

Against the desolate Freiburg backdrop, he wrote *The Pillar of Cloud, Redemption* and *The Flowering Cross.* He could work on the novels either at Schwarzwaldstrasse no. 2 or at Frau Piening's nearby flat where there was usually a log fire and a continuous soup pot brewing and bubbling. Frau Piening once went to Caritas with Stuart and Madeleine when they had lost hope of ever receiving a food parcel which had been sent by Ethel Mannin, a former writer friend of Stuart's from his time in 1930s London. Frau Piening argued with the faceless bureaucrats and rescued the parcel for them. She also owned a typewriter on which Madeleine typed Stuart's (notebook) manuscripts of the Freiburg trilogy. Stuart never actually referred to these novels as a trilogy; it was my way of mentioning them in our discussions. He got used to hearing the term, or at least never objected to my using it.

19

Gollancz to the Rescue

WHEN STUART SENT THE MANUSCRIPT of *The Pillar of Cloud* to Victor Gollancz in the bitter cold January of 1948, he was already well into writing another novel, *Redemption.* He had yet to find a publisher, since it seemed that his pre-war London contacts did not want any fiction from him. Still, the splendid isolation was another fruitful source for the writing in progress. A year and a half later, in June 1949, he had completed *The Flowering Cross,* the last in the trilogy, and a few days later, as if in reward, received an exit visa from Freiburg. Possession of this *laissez-passer* meant that Stuart was free to go where he liked for the first time since his arrest in Dornbirn in November 1945, with the subsequent months of imprisonment, and the weekly reporting to the French military police following his release. There remained only to get a *laissez-passer* for Madeleine. Meanwhile, Stuart gave a few public lectures in Freiburg, notably on W.H. Auden.

In January of 1948, Gollancz was surprised to hear from a former author after fifteen years. Their last dealings had been over Stuart's novel *Glory,* which in commercial terms had been a failure, leading Gollancz to drop him. Times had changed. Gollancz was pleased with a war novel from the heart of Germany, as he thought, but on reading the book demanded a second opinion. Stuart thought of his reply as a further delay before the inevitable rejection letter. In mid-June of 1948, Gollancz wrote to Stuart mentioning more delays because he was seeking another reader's opinion. He added a hopeful note, "obviously great faults and the question was whether the merits outweighed them".[1] Gollancz based his judgement on personal experience. He had spent six weeks in Hamburg, Düsseldorf and the Ruhr in the Autumn of 1946. The series of reports that he wrote for the British press provided the basis for his infernal account of the post-war period, *In Darkest Germany* (1947).

In Wimbledon, London, Ethel Mannin was continuing her prolific writing career that would total 100 books. She obtained a press pass and arrived in Freiburg with a hamper in the back seat of an army jeep. Stuart was glad to see that the hamper included a case of wine and they renewed their friendship. Before the war they had had a brief affair, and her arrival was really a crusade to lure him back to London. She wanted to make him into a successful novelist. Ethel, disregarding Madeleine, attempted to bewitch Stuart as before. According to Stuart, she was convinced that in two nights she could re-seduce him and carry her trophy back through Europe.

Ethel was originally from Clapham in London, and as a girl had endured the English class system, becoming a Jarrold's author after years of apprenticeship with the same publishers as a shorthand typist. Early on she had a liaison with the notorious sexologist Norman Haire. She was a dark-haired beauty, hated by many men for her advanced political opinions but admired by the likes of Stuart and Yeats. Her once best-selling romantic novels are consigned to oblivion along with those of J. Strange Winter and Marie Corelli.

Mannin's arrival in Freiburg gave Stuart a momentary status which the war experiences had taught him to accept with caution. The very welcome food and nourishment was the best feast they had had since one of Stuart's interrogators, named Captain George A. in Madeleine's diary, welcomed them as guests at his house. Meanwhile, Ethel laid siege to Stuart, telling him of his self-damning broadcasts in terms as vicious as his previous French interrogators. She left them after a raucous weekend, with nerves fraught on all sides. Reminiscent of the plot in *The Flowering Cross*, a wealthy woman was offering the struggling artist a future of wealth and success engineered through significant connections. How tempted was he to leave a life of struggling poverty with his lover for Ethel Mannin?

Ethel had argued with the Freiburg lovers that Stuart's marriage with Iseult was long over. Her solution was simple: he should get a divorce from his wife. Stuart revealed these details to me and in my opinion might well have been inconsiderate of what he called Ethel's "meddling in his private life", whereas she was actually attempting to extricate him and Madeleine from Germany. Stuart could not divorce Iseult because divorce was not an option at that time in Ireland. In any case, he had never mentally or emotionally faced up to the possibility of a divorce from Iseult. Ethel did not accept Madeleine and belittled her to Stuart behind her back, he told me. Mannin's next book, *German Journey*, did not mention the days she had spent with the two Freiburg refugees. Her disappointment over Stuart was conveyed to Gollancz back in London and influenced his decision. He rejected *The Pillar of Cloud* on 29 June 1947. Stuart had no choice but to try his pre-war contacts in London. Jonathan Cape would give a swifter decision in early July – rejection. Ethel Mannin was convinced that Stuart would remain unpublished because of his wartime broadcasts, and similar news and gossip that circulated in literary London.

He was fortunately well into another novel when he received the rejections of *The Pillar of Cloud*. The search for a publisher would be a familiar pattern throughout his life. Rejection also came for *The Pillar of Cloud* through his agent in America. Forging ahead, Stuart continued with the other novel entitled *Psalm above the Fish Shop*. He told me that he was not capable of churning out war adventure stories in the manner of Cornelius Ryan's *The Longest Day*. He had at last found his real depth as a writer and, despite rejection, completed the trilogy. Mannin again visited Freiburg a year later but by then Gollancz had accepted the novel, retitled *Redemption*, finding it "a finer book". This led to the acceptance of *The Pillar of Cloud*, which went to two editions in 1948 and a third in 1949, the year *Redemption* was published. *Redemption* was republished in New York by Devin Adair. Compton Mackenzie rallied to praise it and, without hesitation, ranked it with Dostoevsky, but tantalisingly for Stuart did not say which novel by the great Russian writer. Mackenzie found it contained classic elements of pity and terror. The favourable comments meant an awful lot to Stuart, he told me. Elizabeth Bowen, reviewing it in the *Tatler*, wrote: "This book may be hated; it cannot be ignored." Stuart was flattered to receive her veto but never became a friend. He said that she smoked too much for his liking and seemed to have a cloud of smoke surrounding her at parties where he found her larger-than-life personality forbidding.

A friend of Madeleine's, Betty Collins, ensured that the manuscripts of both novels reached England safely. Gollancz offered an advance of £75 for *The Pillar of Cloud* and £100 for *Redemption*.

Ethel Mannin disliked *Redemption* and refused to review it. In a letter to Stuart, she wrote: "I don't think I'd like Iseult or Madame to see this book. I wonder if you'll mind if Ian does?" Gonne quickly grasped its autobiographical content, since she felt that Stuart had wilfully abandoned his family in Laragh. It was sad for Iseult, who found in the book a thinly veiled portrait of herself in the character of Nancy. The central character Ezra offers Nancy a triangular relationship with another woman. Here, once and for all, Iseult must have seen that her hopes of having Stuart return were futile. The portrait of Nancy is inexplicable in human terms. Stuart, as an artist in the heat of creation, had only life as the model, while he disregarded the laws of probity and silence. Furthermore his dedication of the novel "To Gertrud Meissner" left no doubt as to the woman he loved. Aunt Janet would be even more unforgiving of her nephew after reading *Redemption*. It is my personal favourite of all of Stuart's work.

While Stuart worked on his trilogy, in Paris Sam Beckett was writing *Molloy*, *Malone Dies* and *The Unnameable*. There is an uncanny similarity between the names Dominic Malone in *The Pillar of Cloud* and Malone, the bedridden geriatric in *Malone Dies*. Beckett too, would override his own wartime experiences and contemplate the human condition. He also made contact with Stuart at this time.

Ezra, the central protagonist in *Redemption*, returns to a provincial Irish town, Altamont, after the war. His infernal accounts of Berlin are some of the finest things in the book. *Redemption* is uniquely subversive in demanding recognition of the life of the murderer while the reader is begrimed with the evil of murder and also evil by implication. Many times in *Redemption* there is reference to "the white Worm, a slug-track across the centuries and the civilisations". By this, Stuart explained that he means the march of evil across time, a theme he can plant in the reader's mind with its ancillary legacy of anxiety, nausea and horror. His work strongly implies that the contemplation of evil is necessary. However, this is also most difficult and dangerous for the imagination. Equally difficult and dangerous is the attempt to judge what is considered evil in others. On this point he was convinced.

Like the poet Rilke, Stuart believes that inside each person there are angels and devils, without positing an anthropomorphic demon of a devil. Such is the power of the white Worm of evil that it thwarts the artist creatively too and not just with a haunting futility that keeps art from brilliance and its best functioning. Just as knowledge of evil engulfs the narrator of *The Angel of Pity* in despair, so Stuart as a writer records his struggle with being himself a purveyor of the white Worm, since nothing, it seems, can evade its influence. But apart from art, confronting the white Worm is the execution of Jesus, the Crucifixion. Stuart is not being rhetorical while asking explicitly if the Crucifixion is one execution among many. If it is, then humanity is left in the power of the white Worm. Hence his work is, among other things, a meditation on the meaning of the Crucifixion. All of this he told me over various discussions about the novel with the sanction that he did not have any definitive explanation of what he had written. I read it in my early twenties and have re-read it more times than any other of his novels except *Black List, Section H*. He would never admit to me which of his works he preferred, but from innuendo I think it was *Redemption*. Our discussions about this novel were quite extensive and I know for certain that its writing was almost of a piece, he said once, with little need for amendment or correction.

Ian Stuart, aged 22, arrived in Freiburg in March of 1949 and was perplexed to see his father in the small room in Schwarzwaldstrasse. It had been ten years since they last met, and there was much to tell and many questions, some difficult to answer on Stuart's part. Ian did not discuss the real feelings of everyone back home or the many unresolved issues around Stuart's apparent desertion of wife and family. Ian rekindled the kind of happiness he had felt with his father in Laragh. He was now a tall man like his father and as handsome, Madeleine remarked to me. Stuart went off to see if he could get a bottle of wine, suggesting that they have a drink together to Ian's manhood. She took quite a fancy to me, Ian informed the present writer in an interview, referring to Madeleine; she was actually flirting with me when my father returned with a bottle of wine.[2]

Ian would begin travelling in Germany, where he met and fell in love with Imogen Werner, daughter of the German writer, Bruno E. Werner. Ian and Imogen were both young artists, sculptors in wood and stone. They began a two-year apprenticeship in Bavaria, taking master classes with the expressionist sculptor, Otto Hitzberger, and then went to Berlin to the *Hochschüle für Bildende Kunste*. In an interview with me, Imogen said that she was captivated by Ian's brooding silences and his unconventional personality. They were both religious searchers and embarked on a romance. Hitzberger, like Werner, had been blacklisted by the Nazi regime and lived precariously during the war. Was Ian subconsciously following directly in his father's footsteps, making art the main business of his life and falling in love with a German woman? When I put this to him, he said it was purely a coincidence. An uncanny coincidence, he admitted.

In mid-June of 1949, Ian returned to Freiburg with Kay who, at the age of 17, was soon to begin her final year at Loreto Convent in Bray. Kay found Madeleine's welcome overpowering. Father and daughter had a special reunion. Stuart found it a great shock meeting with his two children who had become adults. His years of lost fatherhood were also their loss. But they were all deeply joyful as well. Madeleine found that her love for Stuart drew her also to love Kay and Ian with a love that became deeper as they spent the week together. The Freiburg visit was a precious time for Kay and Ian who tried to understand the changes in their lives. They witnessed Stuart's bonds with Madeleine that revealed to them the end of his marriage with their mother. This registered in sadness and a need to accept him because he was their father. At the same time, they felt resentment against him.

They knew their mother's sufferings and her longing for Stuart's return over the previous ten years. Stuart's letters, usually a source of relief and distress all at once, had recently contained a request for his return to Laragh on condition that Madeleine came with him. However, this was beyond Iseult's endurance. Stuart had found Old Testament models for his proposed harmonious polygamy. He had chosen Madeleine by refusing to return to Ireland in 1945, but his decision went back further than that. Agonising in a Paris hotel after the war, he realised that it was highly unlikely that the relationship with Madeleine would end four years after it had begun. At other times he told me that, even in Berlin, he realised that their relationship would last.

When Ian and Imogen Werner completed their apprenticeship in woodcarving and sculpture in Germany, it was as husband and wife that they later returned to Laragh. According to Ian, Kay became slightly jealous of Imogen because she now had Ian's full attention. Iseult was very happy to receive Imogen into the household at

Laragh Castle after their honeymoon in Germany. Imogen settled into the Irish way of life and was able to confide in Iseult, whom she found gentle, generous and always softly spoken. However, Imogen's mother had grave reservations about her leaving Germany for a foreign country with a foreign religion and a foreign language. Later Imogen would confide to Iseult that her father, Bruno Werner, looked on Stuart as despicable because he had broadcast from Berlin. Imogen was in a dilemma on hearing in the fullness of time, from Iseult, about Hermann Goertz and their affair. What kind of family had she married into? This question troubled her sometimes, but her love for Ian was deeper than any sense of conflict within herself.

Lily got on well with Imogen, as did Lizzie Merrigan the housemaid. Imogen, on a visit with Ian to Roebuck House, quickly saw that Gonne's vanity was acute, even in old age. Imogen told me this. Life at the castle in Laragh continued, with Lily providing an annual stipend from her dividends. The food was somewhat medieval according to Imogen's account, country butter, home made bread, milk, vegetables from the garden, chicken, rabbit and few dinners with guests, when Lizzie Merrigan would wear a starched cap and apron over her dark house-clothes while serving from a side table in the otherwise seldom-used dining room. Meanwhile Ian and Imogen set up workshops in the spacious outhouses and on Sundays put out a sign offering sculpture for sale. Lily would happily tend to what few customers called, since the Stuarts, including Iseult, lay low on Sundays to avoid anyone who might call. Lily had become the spokesperson, as it were, at Laragh Castle.

The Flowering Cross is the final novel in the Freiburg trilogy. It was completed in the summer of 1949. Shortly afterwards, Stuart finally left Freiburg for Paris and a period of renewed success as a writer in the French capital. *The Flowering Cross* bears its religious symbolism lightly. It is peppered with appropriate reference to the Gospels and Solomon's *The Song of Songs*. The latter is used for its sensual and erotic content, while use of the Gospels reflects Stuart's continuing preoccupation with his own private religious quest. There is also reference to Amedeo Modigliani, the Italian-Jewish artist famous for his paintings and eccentric behaviour caused by drug and alcohol addiction. Stuart had become obsessed with his paintings and also with the work of another Jewish painter, Chaim Soutine. The novel is tragic in tone; it pivots around a suicide and an abortion, though these are by no means the main events. If the novel is to be read as autobiography, then the triangular relationship of Stuart, Madeleine and Ethel Mannin comes to mind.

In *The Flowering Cross*, Louis Clancy, a French-Canadian sculptor, returns after the war to Armandville in France, where he is arrested. In prison he makes contact with a blind female prisoner, Alyse. His artistic credo is suitable to post-World War Two: "There's nothing left for the artist," he says, "but to give up all the old pretences and show the world as it is. The real criminal, too, is simply someone who has given up all the old pretences and sees evil as it is and isn't afraid to make use of it. They both deal in reality. The criminal goes through the same hell as the artist."[3] Stuart echoes the work of Jean Genet here, particularly *The Thief's Journal*.

Stuart fell ill before completing *The Flowering Cross*. The harmony of their life together as a couple meant that Madeleine did not bicker with him for working too hard. She could have rebuked him for forging ahead and writing three novels in rapid succession, but her love shone through in knowing that he had to write, even when he would have preferred to live. He asked her if he was putting the long periods of writing in notebooks above their relationship. Madeleine indulged him and said, no, she wanted him to recover his strength and have more calm and patience for his work. Were the demands made on her for typing his manuscripts not excessive? I asked. She told me that she enjoyed helping him in any little way because she loved him. At the rate of seven or eight pages a day, she typed the manuscript of *Redemption* in a month. Otherwise, she went begging for fat to make him fried bread. Her despair at not being able to improve his diet was miraculously relieved by the arrival of a food parcel. There was real coffee, powdered milk, sugar, tins of meat, chocolate and cigarettes that were useful in trading for other available food.

Generally favourable reviews followed the publication of *The Pillar of Cloud* in 1948 and this also helped Stuart's recovery to full health, he recalled ironically. He was also relieved when the Security Police in Freiburg gave him clearance to leave. Basil Liddell Hart could not guarantee Stuart a warm welcome on English shores. Liddell Hart had received confusing information from Maffey who held a British Secret Service file on Stuart. It was in January 1949 that Liddell Hart wrote about refusal of domicile for Stuart and

Madeleine in England, "while they would be anxious to drop the action against you over the broadcasts, it is more than can be expected that they should provide you with asylum here".[3] Liddell Hart circulated copies of *The Pillar of Cloud* with marked-up passages to Home Office officials which eased the official pro-Nazi labelling of Stuart in that quarter.

Victor Gollancz, a Jew who might have been otherwise hostile, had become Stuart's publisher once more and completely understood his position, if not his idiosyncratic theology. When Gollancz read the manuscript of *The Flowering Cross* he wrote to him saying, "the trouble is that real Christianity – Blake's sort of Christianity – is quite out of fashion today".[4] Gollancz preferred *Redemption* to *The Pillar of Cloud* and also sent Stuart news of the high praise lavished on it by Compton Mackenzie and others in London. However, England was not an option for the Freiburg refugees.

Part Three

1950–1974

The farthest he was carried away from the light of creation into the darkest, vilest recesses, the truer, if he ever came back, would be his vision. — Francis Stuart, *Victors and Vanquished*

It's easier to believe in a God of chance than a God of love. — Francis Stuart, *Memorial*

You compromise with this society by writing commentaries on it, creating people who fit its ideas of what fictional characters should be: close relatives of those in works already safely established as literature. — Francis Stuart, *Memorial*

20

Paris

DURING HIS FINAL DAYS IN FREIBURG, Stuart met Jerry Nellhaus, an American aid worker and Quaker. Nellhaus proved to be a godsend who would take the manuscript of *The Flowering Cross* to Paris for mailing to Gollancz in London. As a gesture of fatherly affection, Stuart added the dedication "to Ian Stuart", acknowledging his son in the novel whose central character is a sculptor. Madeleine and Stuart parted on 2 July 1949. As they kissed goodbye he hoped she would find the patience to await a letter with good news. She rented a room in Freiburg and braced herself in the glorious summer weather for life without her lover.

In Paris, Stuart visited Jerry Nellhaus who was living on the Avenue de Breteuil, caretaking a house for a Hungarian-Jewish family. The owner of the house, Ladislas Dormandi, had left Hungary with his wife Olga and daughter Judith, when the Hitler regime came to power in the mid-1930s. He was a novelist who would win the Prix Cazes in 1954 for his Gallimard-published *Pas Si Fou*. When the Dormandis returned, they immediately liked Stuart. It was a lasting friendship with some minor disagreements over the years. Olga suggested that Stuart stay at a hotel in the university quarter until she could prepare the attic for him. Ladislas wanted to sponsor Madeleine so that she could come to Paris by pretending to be their servant. By 28 July Stuart had filled out many application forms and Madeleine was full of impatience, fearing sometimes that he might return to Ireland. Eventually, she received a *carte de résident ordinaire* and official papers saying that she was the maid to Ladislas and Olga Dormandi. This sort of fraternity was prevalent, according to Stuart, in the immediate post-War years and he found it suited his transformed personality living a new life with Madeleine, sharing a house and not being a couple on their own.

Their reunion in Paris was at the Gard du Nord on 19 August. Stuart stood with a bunch of white carnations waiting for her train. His good news included mention that Gollancz was interested in publishing *The Flowering Cross*. She was also glad to hear that at the house on Avenue de Breteuil there was a cat, Sophie. Like Stuart, she would retain a lifelong passion for cats. Stuart had not told her that *The Flowering Cross* had been accepted with some reservations. Gollancz was again beginning to wonder about Stuart as a novelist. That autumn in Paris, Madeleine took on the burden of cleaning jobs for friends of Olga Dormandi. A chance meeting between Stuart and Sam Beckett led to a later visit by Beckett who, Madeleine recalled, brought them new potatoes which were very welcome. Another visitor was the poet John Montague who commented that "Stuart was kind and generous to me with what little he had". The prolific writer John Lodwick, having read Stuart's post-war novels, asked Gollancz for his address and sought him out. They would become lasting friends. Lodwick, who had been something of a war hero as a paratrooper with the SAS, thought that Stuart's publishing fortunes were somewhat like those of James Joyce, who in 1922 found a publisher for *Ulysses*. Stuart began to find favour with French publishers. Paul-André Lesort of Editions du Seuil organised a French translation by Thérèse Aubray of *The Pillar of Cloud* entitled *La Colonne de Feu* with Editions du Seuil who also published Heinrich Böll. The French edition was a considerable critical success, receiving many notices, Stuart told me, including *Le Figaro, Le Combat, Le Monde, l'Esprit, Mercure de France, la Croix* and many more. He was favourably compared with Tolstoy, Dostoevsky and Graham Greene.

The publication of the novel in Paris made it possible for them to holiday in Versailles at Paul-André Lesort's villa. Gollancz came to Paris and held a dinner in their honour. He insisted that Madeleine sat next to him and fussed over her, hoping she would enjoy the meal and the dessert, zabaglione. After the meal, as he was leaving with his wife and daughter, he kissed Madeleine on the hand. In November, at the launch of *La Colonne de Feu*, the novelist François Mauriac arrived at 59 Rue de Babylone where the publisher held a party. Stuart, who had read and admired *La Pharisienne,* said as much to the French author who graciously replied, "Touché, touché."[1] Stuart loved to talk about this meeting because it had great personal significance. The night of the party was a double celebration since it was Madeleine's birthday. Later on in the year, Lesort lost the legal battle to publish an edition of *Redemption*, translated by Annie Brière, to the more prestigious Gallimard. Stuart was pleased for the novel, he told me, but not for Lesort who had originally come to his aid in Paris. As a Gallimard writer, Stuart was being promoted with Kafka, Hemingway, D.H. Lawrence, William Faulkner and Henry Miller to the French reading public. The previous year he had enjoyed reading Miller's *Tropic of Capricorn*, while Kafka and Lawrence would always remain among his favourite writers.[2]

There was a further bonanza on the publishing front when Devin Adair took an option for a United States edition of *Redemption*. Gallimard parties began to include Stuart and Madeleine on their guest list. Liam O'Flaherty arrived with his friend Kitty Tailer and wined and dined them at Le Flore and Le Dôme. O'Flaherty was writing a novel, to be published the following year by Gollancz, about the 1916 Rising, entitled *Insurrection*. At Longchamps, Stuart and O'Flaherty backed Tantième, only to see the horse pipped at the post by Scratch. As veterans of the track they were certain that the result was incorrect. There being no photo-finish, the official result was a steward's decision. Stuart's opinion found a vehement supporter in the jockey of the "losing" horse who cursed the steward's decision. A year later, Tantième beat Scratch in the Prix de l'Arc de Triomphe of 1950. Another day, on their way to the racetrack, Madeleine found a thousand-franc note. Was this another sign of change and luck in their lives? When she caressed a stray cat at ground level she found a five-hundred-franc note. O'Flaherty thought she must be a white witch.

Throughout this period of relative peace following their ordeals since leaving Germany, they began to prosper by meagre standards. They attended many parties related to the literary scene, but Stuart admitted to me his low tolerance for such a milieu in any city. He then began to tire of Paris, he said. Their friendship with Ladislas and Olga suffered from the communality imposed by sharing a house together. Somehow, the lure of Paris was rapidly disappearing for him as he wrote everyday in the attic with its view overlooking the roofs and skyline of the city. Between rambling in haunts that he knew since his twenties, and writing, he had begun to read Proust's

À La Recherche du Temps Perdu to fire his own work. Otherwise, he told me, a stagnation began to set in in his life.

Ethel Mannin came over from London at Christmas. Away from Ladislas and Olga, she told them how they might move to London when Stuart expressed a wish to leave Paris. He even had a plan to go to Venezuela at the time, he told me. Stuart hesitated in making plans to move to London for personal reasons, because of Ethel. He did not want to involve himself in a triangular relationship that he felt would be the natural consequence of their moving to live with her in England. Yet he had happily envisaged a *ménage à trois* involving Iseult, Madeleine and himself at Laragh? Another reason was his reading a copy of Mannin's bestselling novel *Late Have I Loved Thee* (1948), which she had sent him, loosely based on Stuart's life. The central character in the book is Francis Sable, successful writer in pre-war London, Paris and Europe. When his beloved that he meets in Germany has died, he enters a community of Jesuits in Clongowes Wood, in post-war Ireland, and dies. Stuart disliked this portrayal and the moralising tone of the book, he told me but he did not comment too adversely on it to Ethel.

Meanwhile, he and Madeleine felt that they could no longer stay in Paris. Yet, he wanted to finish his novel before moving anywhere. They went on holiday to Dennville, returning via Lisieux to make a personal pilgrimage. All of his life he would feel close to Saint Thérèse. In the new year there was further contact from Iseult. She had already given their address to Florrie Salkeld who had sent other Irish news that Stuart always loved to receive. This time it was not good news: Iseult was ailing with angina and Lily had had a stroke.

Stuart decided to return to Ireland. He was exhilarated by the Aer Lingus flight from Paris via Abbeville-Dunsfold-Woodley-Nevin and then to Dublin. The sky was clear as they were leaving Le Bourget for an England that was under heavy snow as the plane flew at 8,500 feet with a mean speed of 200 mph. The Irish Sea blew up a storm and passengers were ordered to fasten their seat belts. The landing was hazardous on a sleety runway but it was, Stuart recalled, professionally handled. He was delighted to see four hares running across the aerodrome in the half dusk. His return after eleven years is evoked in the opening of *Good Friday's Daughter*. The bus from the airport was delayed because of snow and slush on the roads. His meeting with Kay was wonderful, he said to me. They booked into the Standard

Hotel in Harcourt Street overnight because of bad road conditions. She told him all the news and about how she drove to the university every day. Kay, just turned twenty, mentioned her advances in studying archaeology and could not then tell of her resentment against him as a father. She had felt deeply abandoned when he went to Berlin. Her application to study would be rewarded with an honours BA including German and Spanish. Stuart was impatient to see his mother.

When he got to Laragh the following day he discovered that Lily was not fatally ill. She was delighted to see him and the usual barriers to communication were temporarily broken down, he recalled. However, their talk was of a very general nature but unusually warm, for once. A nurse was calling on Lily on a regular basis and Iseult still had a maid to help in the house. There were fraught discussions when Iseult mentioned that she wanted Stuart to sign over his half of Laragh Castle. She assumed that his recently successful novels meant financial security. He admitted that he had received £100 pounds advance for *Redemption* but nowhere near that amount for the other two. He stressed the uncertainty of his earnings, the cramped accommodation in Paris and emphasised his impending homelessness. It was, in retrospect, an unhappy family get-together, doomed from the start anyway because of the past, he said. He mentioned bringing Madeleine to Ireland through a German family, the Holts, who might agree to give her work as a domestic. Writing a letter to her in Paris he addressed the envelope to Mme Gertrude Meissner rather than Mme Stuart as he had done from the hotel in Dublin. He was conscious of gossip developing in the village. He said in the letter that he was missing her and felt a great emptiness with Iseult. To his surprise, Iseult did not mind when a letter arrived from Madeleine. Meanwhile Stuart was delighted to see Ian and his wife, Imogen, settled into the household; it made him feel that Iseult and his mother were less isolated. Workmen had made some changes and mended the roof of Laragh Castle. What had been the kitchen area in the vicinity of the chimney brace was relocated to the back of the house beyond the stone staircase, occupying a new extended lean-to kitchen. However, the stone floor still retained an icy atmosphere, the porch walls dripped and books in the drawing-room had damp blotches on them. The place was unbearably cold with the snow that held for the week, he said, vividly recalling that time for me. [3]

His visit home confirmed a huge decision. It would not be possible to move to Laragh with Madeleine even though Iseult seemed to be somewhat in favour of it. Otherwise, Lily, Ian and Kay were quite reasonable about the situation if he were to return with Madeleine to Dublin. Iseult contacted Seán MacBride who did not favour Stuart's returning with Madeleine. It is extremely likely that MacBride as Foreign Minister would have blocked their return by refusing the necessary documentation for Madeleine, according to Stuart who said he did not apply to his department at this time. When this news reached her in Paris she naturally assumed that Stuart was being lured home and felt that she might be dropped as his companion and lover. He was, after all, still a married man with two grown-up children. She saw herself as his mistress and wrote irately telling him so, but added the demand that she must be much more. Stuart replied, chiding her jealousy and reiterating his love for her, with the rejoinder, "weren't the true loves mistresses rather than wives?"[4]

However, Madeleine felt abandoned and could see none of the heat of passion in his cold, factual letters from Laragh. He wrote, addressing a letter to Sophie the cat in a secret language, asking Madeleine to calm down for her Tiger! He somehow managed to get through the long days at Laragh Castle. By his own account he was glad to leave, owing to uncomfortable feelings of alienation. He had also emotionally left his family behind more than a decade previously, even before the second journey to Berlin. Confirmation of the irreversibility of the past with Iseult struck him with the full force of reality. There was also the unresolved situation of Laragh Castle. Legally, he might still be able to claim a share of it. However, he did not seek advice on the matter at this time.

Passing through London, he stayed with Ethel Mannin and visited Gollancz, accepting the publisher's editing of the novel because it was about to be sent to the printers and would be published weeks later. Communications between him and Madeleine experienced further difficulties when he wrote from Ethel's house, "Oak Cottage", Wimbledon. She wrote a fiery letter back telling him that they were finished and that their love had died. Madeleine, always uneasy about Stuart's friendship with Ethel, now reached unprecedented levels of jealousy and she wrote another letter saying that she would never contact him again. He had expressed intentions about exploring the possibility of their moving to London. Madeleine's jealousy and possessiveness forced her to give Stuart an ultimatum, stating that she wanted all of her Tiger or none of him. She also feared Ethel's need to take control of people's lives and generally felt that he was highly malleable under such conditions. She told me this privately. Within days he returned to Paris and they made up their lover's quarrel, even though he thought her reaction chaotic and deranged. He then realised that Madeleine's love was such that, in extremes, she lost control of herself. She was a highly passionate woman. He had a powerful theme for a new novel.

In Paris, Ladislas Dormandi criticised *The Flowering Cross* during a celebratory dinner. Meanwhile, Stuart impulsively tried to get Madeleine into Ireland but was refused. He never blamed Seán MacBride for this, but was never willing to say very much about him at all to me. I presumed he did not care for him at all. He just froze over at any mention of MacBride.

Imogen and Ian took over as heads of the household in Laragh. The MacBrides at Roebuck House became removed from everyone at Laragh Castle. Ian felt, without disparagement, that they, the Stuarts were the poor cousins and, as is the case with many families, as he and Kay grew older they became more estranged from their cousins, Tiernan MacBride and his sister, Anna. There was also the factor that Seán MacBride's public career did not need skeletons like their father in the family closet. Even the presence of Gonne maintained bygone IRA sympathies close to those of MacBride's former mainstream Republican activism. His mother's image in post-war Ireland was linked with her being Yeats's beloved, while Gonne's activist and militant political days were more safely in the past. Gonne became resolutely anti-Stuart towards the end of her life.

Many years later, Geoffrey Elborn requested an interview from Seán MacBride who refused, saying: "Francis Stuart treated Iseult disgracefully and I will have nothing to do with you."[5] The present biographer encountered a similar reaction when, at first, Imogen Stuart, by then the estranged former wife of Ian Stuart, expressed a reluctance to be interviewed: "As I always felt very loyal to my mother-in-law, Iseult Stuart, I made a point of not getting involved in his life [Francis Stuart's]."

21

Hard Times in London

STUART WANTED TO LEAVE PARIS; IT HAD worked its magic for him at that time and he had had enough. It would continue to be one of his spiritual homes, but in the present situation it was not a happy one. He spent weeks trying to persuade Madeleine to move to London. When the offer from Ethel Mannin was accepted, they began packing their belongings. Stuart decided to leave his papers and manuscripts with Dormandi to lighten his luggage. Just before they said goodbye, Olga Dormandi gave Madeleine a going-away present of the cat. This act of Olga's ensured that the parting was friendlier than it might have been. However, what was left behind of Stuart's papers and letters later went missing, including the manuscript of *Redemption*. Also missing was another novel entitled *Danny Boy* that had been quickly written during the Paris period, and sent in the summer of 1950 to Sheila Hodges. She had found it mystifying, as did Gollancz who finally rejected it, dashing Stuart's and Madeleine's hopes of a windfall.

His other novel, *Good Friday's Daughter*, written in Paris in 1949, has many Joycean echoes. Stuart had reread Joyce before writing the novel, he admitted. The style lacks the vigour of the Freiburg trilogy. However, the theme of prison and execution are strongly presented in the book which otherwise keeps these dark matters as a subplot. *Good Friday's Daughter* can be said to have parallels in the triangle of Iseult, Stuart and Madeleine. This is, naturally for Stuart, the emotionally explosive off-centre of the plot. He had not purged the experience of war as yet, nor had he reconciled his new life with his old life as far as his conscience was concerned. The story is intriguing for its in-depth study of lovers and there may even be a hint of disapproval in the depiction of the madness of lovers. With singular devotion to what obsessed him, he wrote the novel without thinking of either Gollancz or his reading public. At this juncture, one can say that he was only being true to his vision, and another descent into the hell of his personal subject matter was certainly the right path to take. One might add that his courage never faltered.

Stuart and Madeleine's decision to go to London was eventually reached simply because they could not get to Ireland. Britain seemed as close as they could manage at that time. On the 2 May 1951, Madeleine's application to enter Britain was turned down again. Meanwhile Ethel Mannin was willing to vouch on official forms that Madeleine would be her domestic at "Oak Cottage" in Wimbledon. The Olga Dormandi method of moving Madeleine across frontiers would not prove effective this time. The Aliens Department of the Home Office in High Holborn sent on the conditions under which they could enter Great Britain. They also needed papers for the cat. On arrival they had to register with the police and keep them informed of any change of address. They would be issued with identity cards and, as aliens, expected to have them always on their person. Madeleine was forbidden a work permit; neither could she legally carry on any business or professional activities, a restriction that was not lifted until three years later. Stuart was in an ambiguous position, expected to live on his earnings as a novelist. They faced the prospect of finding work as illegals and were prepared to accept the anxiety and daily trepidation involved in such a furtive existence with the possibility of deportation if they were caught. They set out for London without hope of any sort of friendly welcome from state officialdom.[1]

With their arrival on 18 June came further letters to and from Iseult. Stuart hoped to obtain money from his mother's trust fund but well remembered being refused, he told me. Meanwhile, in Dublin, the July issue of *Envoy* published an appreciation of his works including the Freiburg trilogy. The critic David H. Greene provided a substantial essay of sober praise and assessment with a single censure: "*The Great Squire* I have not been able to read."[2] In Wimbledon, Ethel could not abide cats, so Madeleine put her cat into a cattery in Hackbridge. Soon they left Ethel's house and began a life very like the one described in *The Chariot,* at their first flat in London, 101 Warwick Road.

Stuart took a break from writing *The Chariot* in November when Brian Hurst, the film-maker, invited him to go on a jaunt to Europe. Hurst was looking for castles as possible locations for a film script that he was developing, and Stuart hoped he might get some money if asked to work on the script. It was an erratic journey at the whim of Hurst, who paid all expenses. They stayed in Amsterdam for two nights and then went on to Munich. For Stuart it was a strange return to the city that he had last seen devastated by bombing. Munich had been modernised, he added, it was as if the war had been hidden away. Hurst hired a car and they drove to exhaustion point in search of locations. It was a crazy method, Stuart told me, expecting to find exotic locations that would instantly inspire a film script. At the Hotel Vier Jahreszeiten on Maximilianstrasse, Hurst developed chronic indigestion from the frantic rushing about. Soon, he wanted to go to France as his allotted budget was running low.

Madeleine almost starved in the flat in Warwick Road. She was afraid to touch their emergency savings of a treasured £20 note. She toyed with the idea of going to White City and placing a few careful bets, bearing Stuart's gambling credo in mind about never bringing much money to such a venue and always keeping the bets very low. Instead she moped around and distracted herself by reading Dostoevsky's *The Possessed* that overwhelmed her, as previously it had overwhelmed Stuart. In Paris, Stuart longed carnally for Madeleine and grew frustrated with Hurst's mad dash across Europe. They arrived back in London a week after they had left, without any script outline, and the project was shelved. There was some good news, however; his trilogy had finally been translated into French with the latest, *Good Friday's Daughter,* becoming *La Fille du Vendredi Saint* in a translation by Chris Marker and dedicated to Victor Gollancz. Stuart was reviewed in the French press and journals such as *Critique.*

In May of 1952 they went to Epsom. It was Madeleine's first-ever Derby day and one she would never forget. Stuart backed the winner, Tulyar, and, as it happened, Charlie Smirke, a hero of theirs, rode his third Derby winner that day. *The Chariot,* published in the following year, 1953, would contain a vivid description of the Derby. It is dedicated "To Magdalena once more", and strongly reflects their early life in London. It is a decidedly Irish novel in the mode of Flann O'Brien and Samuel Beckett's *Murphy,* where nothing of consequence happens to the characters, yet they capture attention for themselves.

The central character is a writer named Amos Selby. Among his published works is *The Nature and Habits of Bees*. Although *The Chariot* is very funny in places, the themes of hardship and poverty cast a cold light over the whole story. The epigraph is from Blake's *Jerusalem*. 30a Collingham Gardens was the flat at which he wrote *The Chariot* but they soon moved flat again.

The conclusion of *The Chariot* resembled the situation of Stuart and Madeleine in their rented room at 4 Sinclair Gardens (Shepherd's Bush) at Christmas of 1952. They were expected to be festive on Madeleine's bonus from her cleaning job that would hardly have fattened the cat, she told me. Stuart was gloomily awaiting an advance from the German edition of *The Pillar of Cloud* which had recently been translated by Heinz Ohff. On Christmas Eve, he contacted the bank that had received a draft from Heidelberg. Drei Brucken, the publisher, would issue *Die Wolkensaule* the following year. He collected the money and rushed out before the shops closed and bought Madeleine a bracelet. They had enough change left over for a Christmas feast by their standards and still had ten shillings to go dog racing at White City on Boxing Day.

In the new year a letter came from new-found friends Mary and Ron Hall in Exeter who had enjoyed reading *The Chariot*. Meanwhile, Stuart began to reap some financial benefit from translations of his work. *Redemption* had been translated into German the previous year by Elizabeth Juhasz and Maximiliane Fischer-Ledenice. *The Chariot* was due from Editions du Seuil in a translation by Suzanne Voyenne entitled *La Porte d'espérance*. Editions du Seuil had previously published *La Fille du Vendredi* (*Good Friday's Daughter*), *Le Baptême de la Nuit* (*The Flowering Cross*) and *La Colonne de Feu* (*The Pillar of Cloud*). Gallimard, who published a French edition of *Redemption,* would also bring out *Le Pigeon Irlandais* in 1954. Stuart's work would by then be familiar to readers of the literary pages of the French press such as *Figaro*.

None of this, however, amounted to absolute financial security. Stuart would write his next novel while working the night shift in the Geological Museum in Kensington, not unlike William Faulkner who wrote *As I Lay Dying* while working as a night-stoker. Occasionally, he wore a green ribbon on the lapel of his uniform to assert his nationality. When I suggested that this meant he was miserable in London, he replied, "We had hard times in London in the fifties". Stuart's night-shift experience would cast a gloss on one of the novels of this period which has some archaeological references of an imaginative and cosmic nature. When Gollancz read the manuscript he wrote back saying: "The English are becoming as bad as the Americans in their failure to understand your basic attitude to life, which is the only one that corresponds to reality." What Stuart did not know was that, in a private in-house memo. Gollancz wrote: "He is incapable of approaching a novel as a piece of craftsmanship, to be understood for the pleasure of the craft (or to pay the rent): he must be conveying his vision."[3] *The Pilgrimage* was completed at their flat in Sinclair Gardens. The many changes of flat were the result of an effort to find one with some comfort, since they found all of them dingy and depressing, Madeleine told me.

For the last time Iseult exchanged letters with Stuart. Gonne had died in April of 1953 and Iseult was bitterly hurt at not hearing from him. Stuart was haranguing Iseult about money matters due to the plight of working to earn his living and feeling the added physical strains of writing as well. Madeleine was being exploited, as some cleaners were, working long hours at menial rates, seldom doing rewarding work and nearly always dirty work. Her accent often went against her in post-war London where she was thought of as a German. Madeleine often told me that their years in London were unbearably hard.

Iseult soon had to become realistic about her own health. She had also lost a battle of wills. Her diary tells a sad story. Random entries are clear about her state of mind. "I have never more utterly succumbed to the powers of disintegration."[4] "Oh but I am devoured with anxiety and loneliness." Meanwhile her plans for publishing an anthology of religious thought and precepts had never got beyond the notebook stage and remains in manuscript with Ian Stuart. It exceeds a hundred pages and has a contents page. Short essay-length chapters are based on the Gospels, the Gospel of Buddha, Confucius, Lao Tzu, Plato, Plotinus, Epictetus, Eckhart and others. Her sources are similar to Stuart's at various stages of his life. Iseult writes in her diary: "I discovered that failure is more dangerous to integrity than idleness." Her gleanings from Buddhism and Christianity reveal a lifetime spent in devotional reading and meditation. She transcribed countless lines from Buddhist texts to aid her journey towards understanding and peace.

She sought sleep, using pills, and was unable ever to break the ingrained habit of smoking. "Which has more strength, habit or a mental concept? From experience it would seem habit." A typical diary entry mentions Stuart's absence: "It has been a bad thing for her [Kay] your going away and losing all interest in her." In another letter to Stuart she mentions Kay, "There's such a deep sweetness and sense of humour about her, death never seems so close."

When *The Chariot* was published, the reviews were unanimously hostile. Sales were poor and Stuart, not unlike the hero of the novel, took up sorting mail as Christmas approached. Luckily Madeleine managed to save and buy a tiny wireless set. They could hardly ever afford to buy any wine or beer from the off-sales close to their flat, she told me. Iseult was expecting Stuart to visit them in Laragh and explained that she would give him money if he got sick: "If you are at any time seriously stuck for money for your health, for instance, let me know at once."

In her last letter to Stuart she expressed a desire to read his latest novel, *The Chariot*. Then she became seriously ill. Facing her death she changed for the worse, spiritually. Ian found minding and consoling her tested his own levels of patience and endurance. Her pride found it hard to bend in acceptance of death. Whatever she clung to was a mixture of the Christianity of her youth and early womanhood, and the Buddhist doctrines she had followed latterly. In her late twenties she had confided to Arthur Symons in Paris her belief in immortality and in reincarnation. "If I didn't believe in this," she said, "I might kill myself tomorrow."[5]

When approaches on her behalf by Ian to a local priest in Laragh forbade cremation, she became more rebellious and demanded that her final resting-place be left unmarked by any headstone. Instead, she begged Ian to plant a silver birch tree on her grave. In previous years when her heart disease was bad, she had gone to Dublin and lain in bed with her mother. After weeks of suffering, Iseult died peacefully in Laragh Castle of a coronary thrombosis. She had endured the disease for three years. Ian sent a telegram to his father in London. It was 22 March 1954. Ian was 28, Kay 23. Ian wrote to the Hempels: "I think in the end she was not so terrified of death as she used to be and she never realised in the end that she was dying. Kay was sleeping beside her and did not know."

Stuart came off the night shift at the Geological Museum in Kensington and made his way back to the shabby Sinclair Gardens flat. He was on the next mail boat from Holyhead and, having arrived in Dublin, travelled to St Kevin's Church at Glendalough by bus. At Laragh Castle he spent a sleepless night in his old room awaiting the funeral Mass at ten the next morning. Ian recalled his father repeating how he had found happiness with Madeleine, which might not have been the ideal time to tell his son.[7] Iseult's nameplate on the coffin had a misspelling, yet in mythology there are many spellings of the name. As Stuart stood beside her coffin, a bunch of daffodils caught his attention. He could not feel anything like grief or sorrow. By his own admission he was missing Madeleine.[6] After the burial in a grave inside the gate of the cemetery, a short distance from the round tower in Glendalough, the small crowd filled him with unease and he took his leave to return to London. I often found this account of his somewhat discordant but Stuart never embroidered facts, hoping to be as accurate as possible. He would not have gone in for some gesture of reconciliation at Iseult's funeral with Ian and Kay if it was not in his heart, he added.

Madeleine and he went about organising their wedding ceremony in Holy Trinity, Brook Green, Hammersmith. Ethel Mannin and a friend would be the witnesses. On Good Friday, they went to church, and on 28 April they were married. Madeleine wore black in deference to Iseult's death, but she also wore a garland of white blossoms and held a corsage. Stuart was 52 and she was 38. They had been together for 14 years. The honeymoon, almost straight out of the novel *The Chariot,* started with the big race at Newmarket, the 2,000 Guineas. By chance, luck or mystical blessing, Madeleine backed a two-year-old filly, Bride Elect, which won easily in the last race. By traditional standards it was a short honeymoon. They returned to their flat exhausted and he had to change into his uniform for work at the museum.

In September they moved to a two-room flat, with toilet and kitchen, at 63 Barking Road. Their few belongings included a mattress. Their view was of the cranes and passing ships of the nearby Albert Dock. Madeleine, as a married woman, found her work status altered. She gave up cleaning jobs and went to work in a department store, Courtaulds. At weekends they explored Portobello market, buying bargain lots of vegetables, an occasional bottle of wine and whenever possible an item of furniture to alter the bareness of the flat. Otherwise, going racing continued as one of their abiding passions. They matured fully as man and wife and Stuart was able to reflect on his days at Laragh without any sense of loss for the obvious comforts, the pastoral setting, a home with children; in truth he had been a kind of down-at-heel aristocrat in Ireland, but in London was poor and just about getting by in rented rooms. He confided to me that frugal living had given him greater peace than his previous situations except that the jobs he had to do were often laborious. He began another novel that was in part influenced by memories of Iseult. It was written on night shift in a short period of time: less than two months, he told me. The main setting is Lourdes and questions about religious belief are central. The novel is dedicated "To my wife, Magdalene".

The Pilgrimage has many parallels with his first novel, *Women and God*. It is not that strange for an author to return to a theme treated previously. *The Pilgrimage* fits well into the four novels between the end of the Freiburg trilogy and *Black List, Section H*. It is a commendable performance. The Catholic element is foremost. However, Stuart's Catholicism, as should be clear by now, was far from orthodox. Some may even think he is deliberately being heretical in the novel. The book's sensational juxtaposition of the sacred and the profane found favourable if uncomprehending reviewers, according to what Stuart told me. For Stuart, the paradox lay in how close the sacred was to the profane.

22

Return to Ireland

GOLLANCZ WROTE WITH NEWS OF *Good Friday's Daughter* that reached a German edition in 1955. He thought *The Pilgrimage* "[the] best of all your post war novels" and was not worried about Stuart's moderate sales, keeping ever hopeful that "one of these days you will certainly come into your own". Meanwhile, Stuart held onto his meagre clerk's job with Mutual Finance Ltd in Regent Street, earning the princely sum of £6. 10s a week.

With time off from their jobs, Stuart and Madeleine set out for an Irish holiday and to sort out the Laragh estate with Ian and Lily. Stuart was hoping to get a share of the sale price from the castle and to give up clerking. They arrived in Dun Laoghaire in July. Madeleine seemed to have fallen in love again, this time with Ireland. Their journey began in Dean's Grange Cemetery at Dolores's grave, Stuart's daughter who died in March 1921 from meningitis. When they found the grave with its capstone and a cross in relief under a yew tree, the moment was crowned with a decision to make their home in Ireland. After a few days in Dublin they went by bus to County Wicklow. At Glendalough, in the Royal Hotel, the owner and many of the staff remembered him. After lunch they visited Iseult's grave. When they began walking up the hill from the hotel towards Laragh Castle it began to rain heavily so they went back to the hotel and the owner leant them coats. When they finally arrived at the castle, Lily, recovering from a hip operation, was sitting in her wheelchair with a sun umbrella and insisted it had not rained at all.

Lily shook hands with Madeleine when Stuart introduced her. According to Madeleine, the meeting was friendly but not very warm. After all the years of wondering what Madeleine looked like, Lily could now see for herself. Madeleine immediately found it strange that Lily called her son by the name of Harry. Ian, Imogen and their daughter Aoibheann were very welcoming to her. Later on, Ian drove them to see the Upper Lake in Glendalough as the evening mist clung about the trees on the sloping valleys surrounding the lake. In the days that followed there was much to talk about. Understandably, the occasion was also marred by a presiding sadness about the past.

Stuart and Madeleine spent a happier time at the races with Peter Marron and Liam O'Flaherty. Among other sights and scenes, they visited Goff's Bloodstock Sales before leaving Dublin. Their departure meant a send-off at the boat from the artist Cecil Salkeld who had been drinking. Madeleine thought he was "an old pompous prig".[1] Salkeld became something of a liability since they had to lift him to his car and hope he would drive back slowly and safely into the city, as they rushed away so as not to miss the boat. The trip had been a dark odyssey through the past for Stuart and a first visit to what would become a new homeland for Madeleine. When they arrived back in London they felt very despondent, if not slightly depressed.

Madeleine picked herself up and set about looking for a new job. With her translation skills she was taken on part time at Barclays Bank, working two weeks on, two weeks off. Kay visited from Oxford in October and they went to see a film, *The King and I*. When she visited again in September, Stuart was glad of a break from his latest novel. Father and daughter went to the galleries. There was also a Georges Braque exhibition and all three went to see it. At the British Museum they were drawn to the Rock Crystal Skull, a specimen of fifteenth-century Aztec art. Kay told him that she had begun painting watercolours. She had also met a professor of German from Leicester University, Patrick Bridgwater, who she would soon marry. Ian arrived in London shortly after Kay's visit, bringing Aoibheann with him, and they stayed a few days. After the death of Iseult the previous year, the visit of Stuart and Madeleine to Laragh, and the responding visits from Ian and Kay, marked a new beginning for everyone. Madeleine booked tickets for *The Diary of Anne Frank* at the Phoenix Theatre on Charing Cross Road. When Ian arrived home, Lily decided to send Madeleine and Stuart a Christmas card.

Stuart was in a quandary; he wanted to get out of London but was loath to leave good friends such as Brian Hurst, Ron Hall, Mary Hall and the artist, Ted Lacey. Similarly they had developed a fondness for certain places like Soho market, Kew Gardens and Greenwich Park. Indecision and trepidation about moving to Ireland was diffused somewhat as he worked on a new novel, *Victors and Vanquished,* set in Berlin, which can be read as a prelude to *Black List, Section H.* This he freely admitted to me and said he felt perfect validity using his experience in Germany once again. On 25 January 1957 there was a telegram from Madeleine's sister Margarete in Berlin telling of the death of their mother. Madeleine tried to organise a travel visa, but the procedures to get into East Germany under the Communist regime forced her to abandon the idea. A letter from her sister was some consolation, recounting, as it did, their mother's mention of Madeleine shortly before dying as her "all and only one" and adding that "everything was forgiven and forgotten". Madeleine said to me that she felt that she had left her mother for Stuart in Berlin without healing the breach between daughter and mother.

In August Kay stayed with them again, this time accompanied by Patrick Bridgwater, on their way to Ireland. *Victors and Vanquished,* set in wartime Berlin, had been completed that month. Stuart relaxed with the *Sporting Life,* planning to place some careful bets as Madeleine began typing out the manuscript from his notebooks. Stuart always wrote his novels in longhand, even when I knew him. He would use a typewriter for letters, or in many instances dictate to Madeleine. She suggested that he read Thomas Mann's *The Magic Mountain,* but Stuart wanted a break from literature. Madeleine wrapped the typed manuscript and delivered it to Gollancz and they went to celebrate at the Cutty Sark in Greenwich instead of at their usual local, the Tidal Tavern in the Docklands. In the autumn Kay came for another holiday and her promises to look after the cats set their minds at ease, so they set out for Ireland. At the races in Dundalk, in full view of the Mourne Mountains, they read an advertisement in the local paper: "Cottage, at The Reask, Dunshaughlin, County Meath, for sale by auction Sept 23rd." Life's ironies and coincidences were at work again. Would Stuart end up living with Madeleine not far from Shallon, County Meath where some of his boyhood years were spent on his return from Australia as an infant?

They went south from Dundalk on their way to visit Lily. She was frail but otherwise healthy enough, having survived another winter. They then set out to look for the house mentioned in the newspaper advert. Dunshaughlin was not far from Dublin and they found the Reask (*riasc* in Gaelic means "a marsh") with the help of a taxi driver. The cottage had no toilet and no water. There were two rooms and a kitchen, and an outside shed that adjoined the cottage. There were some trees and hedging down to the wide-barred front gate which looked onto the road. It was on a half-acre of land and located four miles from the village. They were excited about the prospect of bidding for it. Meanwhile they went racing at the Phoenix Park.

On their visit to Laragh, Lily looked older, using her walking stick, but she made a big effort and went with them to the Royal Hotel in Glendalough and paid for the tea, sandwiches and cake. However, the talk was mainly about Kay's impending marriage and Lily's foreboding about the consequences. Back in Dublin, they visited Cecil Salkeld who invited them into O'Brien's pub near Leeson Street Bridge, where they found themselves in the company of some Irish writers; Brendan Behan and Flann O'Brien in particular. One drink led to another, as is the Irish custom on such reunions, and the whole evening was so carefree that they nearly missed the boat to Holyhead.[2]

Peter Marron, Stuart's eccentric friend, attended the auction in September, held by Ambrose Steen & Son in Navan, County Meath. They had instructed him on how high to bid. Marron went to £300 and a deposit of £75 was accepted in surety of full payment. They longed to leave London, but worked on so that their new start in Ireland would have sufficient money to make it a success. Their idea at that stage was to try and live self-sufficiently off the land. Madeleine was still with Barclays Bank and Stuart took a job as storekeeper on the docks, having been a mail-sorter, a packer in Harrods and a clerk with a finance company. He had left the job at the museum in Kensington. In October, a greatly relieved Madeleine resigned from her job at the Lombard Street Offices of Barclays Bank.

In November a letter from Kay troubled Stuart and Madeleine who read and reread it. She did not want to marry Patrick Bridgwater. After much discussion for nights on end, they felt relief for her sake at what seemed the correct decision. Their Christmas was quiet, sending a few cards bought at the British Museum to family and friends. Madeleine made the flat festive, lit candles and sang the hymns they used to sing in Freiburg and Dornbirn. On Boxing Day they went into their neighbour's flat and watched the racing on television. Gollancz made contact to say that *Victors and Vanquished* would be published in April and Stuart replied telling him of their definite move to Ireland and enclosing the address. Madeleine would always remember it as a very exciting Christmas because of their expectations about Ireland.

Kay wrote in January saying that she was pregnant and expecting the baby in August. The news made Madeleine return to her previous periods of anguish in London about wanting a child herself, but Stuart did not want any more children. It was not something which ever threatened their relationship, but it had often preoccupied Madeleine. As before, they avoided a confrontation on the matter since they both understood their divergent views. She discussed with Stuart the possibility of adopting Kay's child, seeing it as her last "chance". Then, Kay and Patrick arrived to stay in March and appeared united and happily looking forward to parenthood. Stuart was relieved and Madeleine kept a good face on things for the sake of the young couple.

The preparations for the move to Ireland seemed at first a domestic nightmare but, in the light of previous adventures, they remained resolutely calm, Madeleine told me. Over Easter they packed and British Rail collected their belongings on 16 April. Stuart and Madeleine arrived in Dublin on their fourth wedding anniversary, 28 April 1958. Madeleine had become an Irish citizen the previous February through the good offices of the poet Valentin Iremonger at the Embassy in London.

Peter Marron took them to breakfast at the Shelbourne Hotel in Dublin with his girlfriend, Maeve. It was too early for a drink – not even Guinness which was then 8d a pint. Phoning about the time of arrival of the furniture led to a happy coincidence; if they caught a bus both events would coincide. They shopped quickly in Dunshaughlin and then a taxi drove them to the cottage just as the furniture van arrived and with it the postman who was looking for Francis Stuart. There were letters from Gollancz and Ted Lacey, and copies of *Victors and Vanquished*. Madeleine set her cats down and surveyed what she called her promised land: the Reask. She had seen it all in a dream during their flight from Berlin when she was in Munich. This was a day she could recreate at will whenever I asked her. It gave validity to Stuart and her, she said, admitting to feelings of confusion and guilt over the years about Stuart and Iseult and their children. She believed in these signs and portents, as if their union was destined and blessed. Stuart had been away from Ireland for close on 20 years, apart from a few brief visits. He told me that he was not daunted at the prospect of being a returned exile, but did not foresee some of the difficulties involved in resettling in Ireland.

Immediately Stuart began renewing contact with former Irish friends. The first to visit, besides Ian and Imogen, were the Glenavys, Gordon and Beatrice, otherwise Lady Glenavy RHA. Beatrice found Madeleine difficult to get on with, but they became friends to the relief of Stuart and Gordon. The summer of their arrival was particularly pleasant and sunny and the Stuarts divided their energies between settling in, sunbathing and painting the rooms that needed brightening up. On their way to Laragh in May they visited Lily at Dr Steeven's Hospital, where she was recovering after breaking her hip. At the beginning of June it was Imogen's birthday and they were invited to a party at Laragh Castle. They bought bicycles and cycled to Laytown Races – a unique racecourse with a seascape background. Stuart met Mick Gleeson, his old buddy and trainer. Gleeson had a horse running, Miss Brogue. They also met Brendan Behan and his wife Beatrice. It proved to be an occasion that led to heavy drinking. The afternoon was deluged with rain and they lost on all bets.

Home at the Reask, they listened to Stuart's *Victors and Vanquished* reviewed on Radio Éireann. The novel was given a short, sharp lashing, Stuart recalled for me. They realised that it would not be a warm homecoming for Stuart or his writings. While he would find a friend in the early years of his return in Benedict Kiely, and to some extent in Francis MacManus, the general reception among other literati was a deliberate cold-shouldering of him. It was a painful blacklisting in his home country and often supported by rumour and gossip. He just had to make the best of it, he told me. This cool reception forced him to meditate on his life in Ireland up to the departure for Berlin, he said. Monk Gibbon, a former acolyte of Yeats, believed, along with others, that Stuart had broadcast from Berlin dressed in a brown shirt and wearing an armband with a swastika. Arland Ussher, who would later become an acquaintance, harboured the notion that Madeleine had been Joseph Goebbels's personal secretary. Fact and myth would remain entangled for decades to come.

Despite his reputation being in tatters and facing what would obviously be a position of outsider in the literary scene, domestic issues needed attention, such as buying a Baby Belling cooker. They planted vegetables, including cauliflower, Brussels sprouts, leeks, celery and turnips. Self-sufficiency became vital to their survival in frugal circumstances. Madeleine liked telling me about their self-sufficiency, showing her first-hand knowledge of such matters. Stuart admitted that this contact with the soil and cultivation had a very helpful effect on him. When I first met him he struck me as being an artist immediately, but also had the look of a medieval gardener, botanist and herbalist. When Lily's birthday came around, they went to visit her in hospital. In September they went to the Ballsbridge yearling sales and dreamed of owning a racehorse. Stuart longed for this, hoping to get back into a world that he was obsessed with as much as writing. The Reask was a constant challenge. Before the winter set in, their roof needed mending and they did the job themselves. After Hallowe'en they had a visit from Frank O'Connor, his wife, Harriet, and their child. The conversation was rather banal, but it was a pleasant enough afternoon according to Stuart.

Victors and Vanquished is dedicated to Peter Marron. Marron was much in awe of Stuart and, on being invited to dinner at the Reask, arrived in an agitated state and in the middle of the meal vomited onto the table. Marron recovered from the embarrassment and remained good friends with the Stuarts. *Victors and Vanquished* is a prototype for the last hundred pages of *Black List, Section H.* Stuart commented to me about a recognisable pattern in his writing. He recognised that a good novel had been followed by a not-so-good second novel and an even worse third novel.

> I am one of those writers who identify themselves closely with their fiction. This has a bearing on the fact that it has been at the start of a creative phase that I have written at my best; it has been out of a pressure of stored living and experiencing.[3]

It may not be sensible to argue with Stuart's aesthetics, but *Victors and Vanquished* is valuable for its evocation of Berlin during the war, even if it was written a decade later. His aesthetic is hardly a valid working method when it comes to *Black List, Section H* which is hugely retrospective – what might be called an authentic, emotional autobiography. It is significant when considering Stuart's novels to remember that, by his own standards, his best work comes "out of a pressure of stored living and experiencing". In other words it is a unity of the life and the work – a private obsession that he harboured and one which we often discussed.

Victors and Vanquished presents a Jewish family, the Kaminskis, during the Holocaust, who are apprehended by the SS, the Geheime Staatspolizei. The thinly disguised portraits of Frank Ryan, Róisín Ní Mheara, Iseult Stuart, Kay Stuart and Francis Stuart make the novel compelling autobiographical fiction.

Having just reached the point at which Stuart and Madeleine settled in Ireland, it might seem a deflection to return to Germany, except that *Victors and Vanquished* deals with crucial issues that have not been mentioned elsewhere. Once more, as in most of his fiction, autobiographical contents are central to the plot. The main character leaves his marriage to go to Berlin: "And Leonore, ever since the death of their first baby, had shown an increasing repulsion for physical intimacy." Stuart told me that, when in Berlin, he soon realised that the sort of writers he liked were no longer available in libraries or bookshops – their works had been burnt by the Nazis. He went on: Thomas Mann and Hermann Hesse were vilified and exiled. Hesse had left Germany to live in Switzerland in protest against militarism after the First World War and was a critic of Hitler and Nazism from the 1930s onwards. Stuart said that he began to reread his novel *Der Steppenwolf* during the writing of *Victors and Vanquished*.

In *Victors and Vanquished* the scenes in Berlin are vivid: "the bare, frosty trees of the Tiergarten, where, among the park benches, were several painted yellow and marked 'Nur fur Jüden'." Isaak Kaminski, a Jewish character in the novel, tells of his premonition of the approaching Holocaust:

> ... the suffering that Jehovah allowed Egyptians, Assyrians, Babylonians, Romans and the rest of them to heap on us. So that time after time we've gone down in a flood of our own blood. And so it is once more. These people have the power to inflict horrors on us because our God has allowed it for our ultimate salvation. What is coming I dimly foresee, and I believe that it is part of the pattern of our history.[4]

Luke Cassidy, the central character in the novel, disagrees: "I can't believe in a God who demands holocausts in atonement."

The reviews of *Victors and Vanquished* were awful as well as damning. Stuart was accused of reusing his experiences of the war. For some who openly disliked him and saw him as a traitor to the Allied cause, democracy and Catholicism, the novel implied self-acquittal. Sales were poor. A year later a United States edition was published by Pennington Press in Cleveland, Ohio, for which Stuart received $510. None of the critics noticed that his title came from Hermann Goering's repeated phrase during the Nuremberg trials, "The victor will always be the judge and the vanquished will always be the accused". Latter day revilers of Stuart may no doubt seize on this as incontrovertible evidence of his emphatic affiliation with Nazism.

Stuart would write three novels at the Reask. One was a comedy, which was taken up by Gollancz; another, which was rejected, was extremely difficult to write and almost disastrous as regards publication. This was *Black List, Section H*, his most famous work. Meanwhile, he wrote a story about a cat.[5] It proved an arduous job to find a magazine that would publish it. When *Good Housekeeping* eventually accepted the story, Stuart abandoned the idea of writing for money ever again, he told me with a wide grin. He was paid over £30.

Stuart completed *Angels of Providence*, sending it to Gollancz in November of 1958. With the novel gone he had an acceptance from Radio Éireann for a radio play, *Strange Guest*, an adaptation of his play produced at the Abbey in 1940. Radio Éireann offered a fee of £30. At the end of the month Stuart and Madeleine went to Bray to visit Peter Marron who took them to see *The Sound of Music*. They hated the film, but Madeleine enjoyed some of the songs. Afterwards on a visit to the White Horse pub, they met Benedict Kiely and got very drunk. On their way back to Meath, they had an awful argument. Next morning they made it up. Madeleine suggested they go to confession, which they did, and also Mass. In December Gollancz wrote, saying how much he liked the novel.

Their first Christmas at the Reask was all they could wish for, Madeleine recalled for me. They went to midnight Mass with a neighbour, Mrs White, and accepted an invitation for tea and Christmas cake at her house afterwards. The Glenavys visited on St Stephen's day and, at the end of December, Peter Marron invited them to Bray for a few days. In 1959 Gallimard sent a cable accepting *Victors and Vanquished* for a future French edition, while Gollancz sent the proofs of *Angels of Providence*. Radio Éireann scheduled the broadcast of *Strange Guest* for mid-January, and Ethel Mannin wrote to say that her husband Reg had died in Adelaide over Christmas. They planted their first apple tree at the end of February, making a ceremony of the occasion with a bottle of Riesling. Stuart was a great celebrant of the *l'heure aperitif* as he called it when I knew him – celebrating all kind of events in his life. He usually preferred to drink alcohol after seven o'clock, but could be flexible on this point if he was in a café, bar or hotel having lunch.

Easter found them fit after much tilling and sowing in the garden. They exchanged Easter eggs and set out for the Grand National at Fairyhouse. Unfortunately, they did not back Zonda, the local horse from Balrath, County Meath, which won the National. By July they had sunflowers outside the kitchen window. Ted Lacey, the artist, visited for two weeks but Madeleine found him insufferable and unappreciative of their fresh vegetables. She resolved that he would never be invited again, having taken their cosy rural retreat for granted. After he left, copies of the United States edition of *Victors and Vanquished* arrived in the post.

Ron Hall came to stay for a holiday. Madeleine told me that she preferred him to the egomaniacal Lacey. However, Stuart argued with her after Ron left. She had liked his company but found him intrusive in their private routine and life, while Stuart had been glad of the extra company. The couple had a blazing row that took days to make up. She told Stuart that she hated his intellectual friends such as Ted and Ron. They also drank too much. Ron Hall had actually passed out after drinking 12 pints of stout in a local pub. She hated the house being filled with endless talk for days, especially talk about books and art. She preferred the near monastic existence they had on their own. When visitors stayed Stuart never went to Mass or sat up with her by the fire reciting the Psalms, she told me.

Angels of Providence was published in August. Dedicated "To Dearest Madeleine", it has an epigraph from William Blake. Blake is one of the poets central to Stuart's work and someone we often discussed. Stuart was proud of the titles for his novels and believed that a title is crucial to any novel, both determining its destiny or otherwise. *Angels of Providence* is light hearted and reminiscent of post-war Ealing comedy films. Much of the story, which is set in Ireland, revolves around waiting for an aged uncle to die so that the next generation can inherit the land, property and money. Once more in this novel, Stuart explored the theme of a triangular relationship which obsessed him but which Iseult never condoned.

In September the Stuarts went to the Dundalk Races and then to Peter Marron in Bray for two weeks. Back at the Reask for the winter, they took turns to read *Dear Theo: An Autobiography of Vincent Van Gogh*. In November Madeleine's sister, Gretel, in Germany, made contact: there was news of Traute's husband, Martin Sonnemann, who had killed himself. Gretel wrote telling them because Traute was in a state of grief. Madeleine began reading the autobiography of St Thérèse of Lisieux, seeking consolation. Stuart was struggling with a novel that became a creative nightmare which was entitled *A Trip Down the River*. He pursued it with much frustration, and told me that at times futility set in but it was soon ready for wrapping up and sending to Gollancz.

Around this time Lily Stuart came to live in the Reask because Laragh Castle had become damp and was closed up temporarily. Ian told me that he found the castle began to haunt him with memories from the past. Arrangements were made for Ian and Imogen to move to Germany with their children. Both would pursue a new life while Ian enjoyed the benefits of a Ford Scholarship in Germany in the company of the abstract painter Patrick Collins and the writer Aidan Higgins. Some of their exploits would end up in fictional guise in Higgins's *Lions of the Grünewald,* where Ian is depicted as the Irish sculptor.

Madeleine set out for Berlin on 21 January 1960 to spend a month with her sister Traute, who was recovering from her husband's suicide. He had a *taschenfabrikation* business (handbag and purse manufacturing) in the Wilmersdorf sector of the city. Madeleine and she were very close, as their voluminous and regular correspondence over the years reveals. Madeleine broke her journey in London and took the opportunity of going to see the Van Goghs at the Tate Gallery. Returning to Berlin was very emotional for her, she said. However, Traute never stopped talking and admitted to being very upset and confused. She told Madeleine that Martin had had an affair that led her to contemplate suicide at the time. Now he was dead and she felt that she wanted to go on maintaining the business. When Madeleine mentioned Stuart's commercially unsuccessful novels, Traute suggested that they come and live in Berlin. It was an option to consider and they spent much of the holiday discussing it.

Meanwhile, at the Reask, Stuart received the manuscript of his latest novel, returned through the post with a short note:

> My dear Francis,
>
> Having published you so long, and in good times and bad, so to speak, I feel horrible about turning down a novel by you.
>
> The fact that book after book of yours has not been in any way "a commercial proposition" has never worried me: I have published them because I have enormously liked them, and I haven't worried a bit about the financial results. But here is a book that I cannot bring myself to like; and that does change things. Behind it all, there is of course your old vision: but this time I can't help feeling that it doesn't come through.
>
> I really am awfully sorry.
>
> Yours ever,
>
> VG[6]

Stuart, on reading this rejection of *A Trip Down the River*, felt like abandoning his new-found home in County Meath, he said to me candidly. Victor Gollancz had stuck with me, he added, through the thick and thin of poor sales after *The Flowering Cross*, but *Angels of Providence* marked the end of our relationship as publisher and author. On and off, they had survived nearly 20 years together, he said, and he always spoke highly of Gollancz. "Good old Gollancz, what a great friend to me," Stuart often repeated. Gollancz never complained about Stuart's uncommercial novels and for this deserves great credit. Stuart realised that he was without a publisher once again. He had met such setbacks before and soldiered on. That is how he put it, but he acknowledged the distress involved. Life can be so fraught, he would say to me when discussing such reversals.

23

Unsettling Times

ANOTHER REACTION TO RECEIVING GOLLANCZ'S letter was that he felt more lonely at the Reask because Madeleine was away in Germany, even though he had the company of his ageing mother. He went on Madeleine's scooter to visit Peter Marron and his partner Maeve at Raheen Park in Bray. Leaving his mother on her own may point to a continuing antipathy and ambivalence towards her. Lily, always fiercely independent, was able to fend for herself somehow and neighbours could be relied on to drop in and see how she fared.

Ian got in touch with Stuart because of Laragh Castle and his efforts to sell it. Eventually Cicily O'Kelly purchased the property and its adjoining ten acres for £4,500. Stuart had sought legal opinion as to reclaiming some of its realisation on the sale price. Ian had already inherited a cottage in Duleek, County Meath, on the death of Aunt Janet. Stuart left Bray and visited Gordon and Beatrice Glenavy at Rockbrook House, but found that they were bickering and did not stay very long. On another day he went to visit Dolores's grave in Dean's Grange Cemetery. He decided to abandon the effort of beginning another novel and instead decided to write a play for theatre. In order to focus on such a project, he began to read Genet's play about perverts, *The Balcony*, Behan's *The Quare Fella* and Sheila Delaney's *A Taste of Honey*. Once more at the Reask, he was still missing Madeleine terribly. Lily was glad to see him back and mentioned a letter that had arrived. It was a tax rebate from England for £48. Then Traute sent him some Deutschmarks from Berlin.

Meanwhile, he awaited yet another letter from Gollancz with advice about his present plight as a writer. It might seem pathetic, but Stuart had written a penultimate letter to him. He was losing patience with his old friend and desperately wanted to find any publisher. A letter arrived instead from Peter Marron with news of a first night at the Gaiety Theatre; a play by their friend Patrick Kirwan, *A Lodging for a Bride.* He stacked a load of turf into the shed as heavy snow began to fall and thought he might have to miss Kirwan's opening night. Kirwan was a friend of Rupert Grayson who had published *The Angel of Pity* in 1935. He was eager to get away so he battled with the weather and got as far as a pub in Dunshaughlin. From there he phoned Peter Kirwan who drove in awful road conditions to collect him. Reaching the city they went to Liam O'Flaherty's flat in Wilton Place. Stuart, Peter and Kitty Tailer attended the play. However, Liam promised to turn up later for the party. Stuart spent the night at the Shelbourne Hotel. Kirwan's play was a flop and when Stuart got back to the Reask the weather was worse than in Dublin, but he was glad to get a letter from Madeleine to say that she would be home in a week. When she arrived he was very happy since he had become unsettled on his own with Lily, he told me. It was always a fraught relationship, he confided to me.

Ethel Mannin wrote from Clifden. Her cottage had been refurbished but she felt depleted, physically and financially, and she still had the Oak Cottage property in London. She was considering selling some signed first editions, including those given to her by Yeats. She invited the Stuarts to stay in her cottage in Clifden whenever they wished. When Lily had to go into hospital for a hip replacement, Stuart arranged everything and was dutiful in visiting her. After the operation, which was successful, she hoped to return to Ian's house because she was feeling irritable being under the same roof as Stuart and Madeleine. Stuart told me that that summer there were arduous labours involved in order to make vital improvements to the cottage.

Ian took Lily to his house for a few weeks and then brought her back to the Reask. It was a difficult moment. Stuart made up the row with Ian over the recent sale of Laragh Castle from which he had received nothing. When Ian had gone Lily announced that it was coming up to Stuart's birthday and she would be giving him a present. She gave him £3, with which Madeleine bought a bottle of wine and a pair of tennis shoes. Lily was not at all happy at the Reask on this occasion. She openly stated that the accommodation, even with some improvements, was too primitive for her. The domestic scene of wife, husband and aged mother/mother-in-law became strained. Lily and

Madeleine were always uneasy in each other's company. Stuart began to argue with his mother over money.

Madeleine unwisely began harassing the old lady, calling her a mean old bitch. Stuart defended his mother and this caused a ferocious argument. Lily vented her true feelings about Madeleine, Stuart's abandonment of Iseult and otherwise highlighted her own dislike of living with them. Madeleine took instant offence, threatened to leave mother and son and go to her sister in Berlin. Lily offered her £25 to pay for the journey. Then, Traute sent 500 marks saying that she could not visit her that summer, without specifying the reason. After days of strife, all three at the Reask realised they would have to start putting up with the situation. Madeleine explained to me that it was saddest of all for Lily since neither of them loved her while they had each other's love. They listened to the Epsom Derby on the radio. Stuart and Madeleine backed the winner, St Paddy, at 7/1, and Lily scolded them for betting. Whether because of Lily's influence or not, they stopped attending Mass, preferring instead to pray at home. The house seethed with a rancorous atmosphere.

Then Lily became ill. As she lingered in Navan Hospital, she hoped that Ian would come and take her back to his house. Stuart said this was impossible because Ian was away. Lily became confused. When her condition worsened, she was anointed. She asked for Ian on Stuart's final visit. As he said goodbye, she asked when Ian would be returning from Berlin. Stuart replied that he did not know when Ian would return. "Nor do I," said Lily. They were her last words to him. She died in the County Infirmary on 28 August 1960. Stuart was devastated when he went to the mortuary to see her laid out. He wept openly, Madeleine told me.

Lily was laid to rest in Kilbrew Cemetery near the Reask. Ian, Imogen and their children came to the funeral and Mass in Curragha Church. Kay also came over from Durham. Stuart and Madeleine were glad to see her and she was the last to leave the Reask. Ethel Mannin wrote a letter of sympathy mentioning her own lack of belief in an afterlife. However, Madeleine saw Lily's death as within the will of God, she said to me.

In December 1960 Gallimard produced a French edition of his recent novel, translated by Marie-Lise Marlière as *Vainqueurs et Vaincus.* But neither this nor Lily's money, a few hundred pounds, Stuart said, could relieve their financial problems, so they mortgaged the house for collateral. They were glad to get away for a while and took up an invitation from the Glenavys for Christmas in Rockbrook House, Rathfarnham, Dublin. At Rockbrook the Glenavys had other guests and over the days they were playing croquet, table tennis, darts and, at night over cocktails, charades. After the Christmas panto in the last week of December they went to the backstage party and met Maureen Potter and Jimmy O'Dea.

Stuart was actually in turmoil. He admitted to me that the return to Ireland, at this time, seemed to be going badly from many perspectives. While they both had recouped their energies in the year and a half since leaving London and their life had its joy and routine, he feared being stuck in a rut. I suggested that maybe Dunshaughlin was too rural and isolated after his experiences in European cities? Stuart said that he was used to rural living and generally settled into it. At that time they both considered moving, but had no definite plan.

When they got home to the Reask in the new year from the Glenavy's they still felt very unsettled. Madeleine, fiery as usual, had to sort out a tiff with one of the neighbours. However, by February they were back at the Glenavys for a weekend, which included a visit to Leopardstown races. True to form Stuart picked the Grand National winner, Nicolaus Silver, at 28/1. At the Reask, one of the cats died, probably as a result of eating rat poison. They gave the animal a ceremonial burial, and a garland of primroses was placed on the grave. In April, feeling uncertain about staying in Dunshaughlin, they decided to use their savings and bought a Ford Popular, a tinny bouncy car, but better than nothing for getting around the hitherto long treks involved in country life. Madeleine considered taking seasonal work in London, but Stuart did not want to live on his own. He needed Madeleine constantly, as always, and particularly since he felt the early stirrings of another book. This dependency of Stuart's was one which he admitted to me but Madeleine said that she did not mind his clinging nature. As far as I was concerned she may have even encouraged it except when she wanted to get away on her own. She had, since the writing of *The Pillar of Cloud*, been a guiding angel for his work. Coincidental with the beginnings of his new novel was her finding a part-time job teaching German in the Vocational School in Navan. There was also a small travel allowance on top of the small salary. Every bit counted since at this time, Stuart told me, and he had to get a loan from Peter Marron.

After their summer car-camping holiday around Ireland, Madeleine began her first year of teaching. Stuart started to write a series of pages about his childhood. The prospect was daunting, he added, getting a few paragraphs as if from nowhere and not knowing where they would lead to. Perhaps nothing would come of it, he conjectured, and found the whole departure an agony. It is usually like that for me until the main thrust of a novel takes over, he added. When that occurs, he explained, the situation seems a bit more in control. The autumn of 1961 was bleak, followed by a freezing rainy winter that forced them to buy a Rayburn for the kitchen. Keeping close to the stove and ensuring that the atmosphere in the kitchen provided ideal writing conditions, he worked slowly on what was to be a desperate gamble to confront once more the trauma of his life, from childhood up to captivity after the Second World War. At Christmas they went to Peter Marron, who almost deafened them with his new-found love of jazz on BBC radio, Stuart recalled. When they were not in Dublin drinking in Davy Byrne's they visited the Glenavys as usual and went to the pantomime "Mother Goose". Madeleine had become a big fan of Maureen Potter. At Leopardstown races they met up with Ian. Stuart hosted a night of feasting and drinking at the Dolphin Hotel where he furtively announced that his play, *Flynn's Last Dive,* was to be produced in London in the spring.

When they returned to the Reask he continued with the novel. It is worth pausing to note his indomitable will and energy, as he once more challenged himself creatively even though he had published 19 novels by the age of 57. What he had begun to write would become *Black List, Section H.* He once told me that it was written without any sense of its being a last book, although it would round off a huge chunk of life lived in awful extremities. Did life at the Reask provide the necessary impetus, albeit not as extreme as Freiburg, which gave birth to *Pillar of Cloud, Redemption* and *The Flowering Cross*? He told me that this compact of past experience was what he had to draw on, and that everything lived, or rather endured. Often when he opened up and responded to such questioning, he would quickly shut down, changing the subject and start to ask me questions about myself. Much as I would talk about myself, I often preferred if he spoke more about what I had asked him, in this case *Black List, Section H,* but in time I got better at probing him for answers to my seemingly endless questions about the novel. He was very patient with me.

At the end of February work on the novel was halted because they went to London. They stayed at Ethel Mannin's house in Wimbledon. Ethel had gone to Cairo to Shepherd's Hotel with a close friend, Irene Beeson. Ethel would soon sell the house, keeping a flat in London but living mainly at the cottage in Clifden, County Galway. Stuart and Ethel always maintained a friendship but it was unequal, he added. She had praised his work on and off, admiring *Victors and Vanquished,* but she was very disapproving of *Redemption.* Stuart generally made no bones of expressing his reservations about her books with the exception of her 1954 novel, *So Tiberius* which he and Madeleine liked because it was a story about a cat. While in London, Madeleine went on an anti-nuclear rally, she told me with her ebullient brazenness when it came to such protest. Otherwise, they visited the many flats and bedsits which had been their former homes. They laughed to find that, below one of their flats at street level, was a betting office. They went to see Chekhov's *The Cherry Orchard.* Stuart visited his agent at Johnson & Co. In West Croydon, he met Derek Martinus, director of *Flynn's Last Dive,* and the three actors, one of whom was Rio Fanning, well known from the TV series *Z Cars.*

Ethel's house was a good base and they needed it to have some time away from the Reask. On 5 March Stuart attended two dress rehearsals at the theatre in Wellesley Road, West Croydon, and the following morning, alone with Madeleine, awoke and began singing the ballad about the Irish patriot Kevin Barry which begins, "In Mountjoy Jail, one Monday morning". The bath at Ethel's was so large that they bathed together and rejuvenated their sensual life. They contacted Kay who arrived for the opening night. Reviews were mixed, but the *Daily Telegraph* and the *Stage* were favourable. They found London more suited to their cosmopolitan natures and dreaded returning to the Reask, Madeleine told me. Stuart wondered if he could quickly write another play but had already begun the novel that awaited him in the dresser drawer at home. They decided to stay for the two weeks of the run and did not get back to Ireland until the last day of March, visiting Deddington in Oxfordshire on the way to Kay and Patrick Bridgwater in Durham. Kay seemed happy in her life, according to Stuart and Madeleine, and Stuart was glad to see his grandchildren, Antonia and Benedict. Kay had a birthday party for Stuart, with his grandchildren, even though it was a month away. When they had to leave the next day, Stuart was very overcome at leaving Kay, feeling that for most of his life he had been saying goodbye to her on occasions such as this.

Back in Ireland they were cheered to see the vegetables thriving. Stuart could often spend a long time talking to me about asparagus, beans, peas and onions or the strawberry crop or how he dug potatoes or harvested rows of onions and hung them in clusters in the shed to dry. I was not averse to such talk as I had dabbled in such pursuits myself and worked in the food-growing industry in East Anglia in my twenties for a few years. Madeleine recalled Stuart's sixtieth birthday as he sat in the sun at the Reask, wearing a white shirt and with a straw hat on his head, he looked like a painting by Cézanne, she said innocently and adoringly. Stuart worked solidly at the novel, even when Traute (Trautchen) came to visit from Berlin in the second week of June and brought a hamper of food. It was like Christmas, Madeleine said, and they were very grateful. Having asked for details of their measurements by letter from Berlin, Traute had brought new shoes and socks for both of them. They took her to Dundalk, Laytown, the Boyne Valley and to Fourknocks, the passage grave with commanding views of both the Wicklow mountains and the Mournes. She was very sad leaving after her week's holiday and cheered herself up saying that sometime she might open a little business near them and buy a cottage in County Meath.

By July, "The Legend of H" was half completed. This was the first title of the manuscript as he struggled to write the novel *Black List, Section H*. It would take four years between stopping and starting, with its impetus waxing and waning throughout the process. In August they stayed in the Glenavy's seaside retreat "Rockall" in Sandycove. Stuart had contracted a viral infection in the bladder and groin and benefited from the sea air. He was soon on the mend and marching up and down the pier at nearby Dun Laoghaire.

When they returned to the Reask, there was a letter from Victor Gollancz, containing a combined royalty cheque and closing balance, amounting to £4. 6s. 5d from the English and French editions of his novels. Stuart did well at the Curragh in September, winning £50 on Attic Vale in the Irish St Leger, and they went to Jammet's restaurant in Dublin on the strength of the winnings. Madeleine, an inveterate hoarder, had kept the menu as a souvenir. At the White Horse pub they heard gossip that Benedict Kiely was in the Silver Spoon, so they joined him for a few drinks.

That summer there was the news of Gordon Glenavy's death after two unsuccessful stomach operations. He had written some despairing letters to Stuart from hospital. Stuart had been one of the few people who got on well with the haughty and reserved Glenavy and admitted that he sorely missed his old racing companion. His son was the writer, Patrick Campbell, known for his wit and his stutter. The Stuarts went to the funeral and stayed a few days with Beatrice Glenavy.

24

Black List, Section H

THE 1960S WOULD SEE THE DEATH OF Brendan Behan in 1964, followed by Flann O'Brien in 1966 and Patrick Kavanagh in 1967. Stuart's respect for all three was unequal; he preferred the writings of O'Brien and Kavanagh over Behan. From this time forward a steady stream of Irish writers would begin to seek out Stuart. In him they would find a towering presence, at once a kind of monarch of Irish letters and, paradoxically, an outsider, unaffiliated, until Aosdána was founded in the 1980s. One of these writers was John McGahern whose novel *The Dark* had been panned in the *Times Literary Supplement* by Anthony Cronin, who would subsequently become a close ally of Stuart's in "the literary village" of Dublin later on. Cronin, mentioning the 1960s, recalled seeing *Redemption* advertised on its publication under the *Sunday Observer* leader page, but that Stuart as an author had been no more than a rumour among the Dublin scene. Cronin had returned from Spain via London and then went to teach at universities in Montana and Iowa, having published a comic novel, entitled *The Life of Riley*. They met for the first time at Behan's funeral while Stuart languished under a tree on the edge of the huge crowd.[1]

Stuart was well aware that since returning to Ireland in the 1960s, his presence in the country was known to the literary establishment if not hugely acknowledged. He and O'Flaherty, his oldest friend, occasionally met at the races but did not seek each other out much for socialising. Otherwise, his former friend was judgemental, writing to Kitty Tailer: "What on earth has he got left apart from Gertrud whom he brought back from Germany as *apologia pro vita sua*, in other words a living proof that he had put away his love for Adolf Hitler and turned his face towards Israel?"[2] In the 1960s, among many friends from England who looked him up was Brian Hurst who passed through Dublin on his way to film *The Playboy of the Western World* in Kerry.

Meanwhile he had worked on what would become his most famous novel. Under the title "The Legend of H", the earlier version of *Black List, Section H* was a slightly longer book because the opening chapters were devoted to H's childhood and because the names of well-known persons like Yeats, Gonne, O'Flaherty, Gollancz and others are barely disguised. Yeats he depicted as "Yardley", a well-known cosmetic at the time, implying a slur on the poet. Otherwise, the latter half of the book was pretty much a penultimate draft of *Black List, Section H* with its tumultuous conclusion showing H returning to French-occupied Austria to face prison with his beloved Halka, in a manner not unlike Stuart's own debacle with Madeleine. By early 1966, the novel was finished in yet another version. Various publishers, who had at one time or another published him, read it, including Gollancz, Jonathan Cape and Collins. Then it was sent to anyone and everyone among London publishers. The negative response was disheartening, but when it seemed to result from the subversive nature of the work Stuart felt he should send it around further. The story of the novel's tortuous journey towards publication was one he outlined to me on various occasions. It had tested his patience to the limits, he admitted. He tried a few more agents; the London firm of David Higham Associates read it and returned it with the comment, "It is too long, and as it is obviously autobiographical there is a danger of libel".[3]

Soon Stuart began to dread the arrival of the postman. The kitchen at the Reask was a long way from the double gate down by the roadside. If the post came while Stuart was outdoors working in the vegetable plot, the sight of the returned manuscript would end the day's chores and the disheartened author would take to brooding, he said. On the occasions when Madeleine was handed the manuscript by the postman, and Stuart was away in the village or maybe dragging ditches as he did for choice bits of firewood, she often felt tempted to conceal it for a day or two, but never did. It had been a difficult year for Madeleine healthwise; she'd had a bad fever in the spring and the local doctor had to be called out on two occasions when Stuart got anxious about her condition, but she was now back to full health.

In May 1966, when Stuart backed out in the car over one of the cats, they abandoned their holiday plans that would have included a fortnight in Ethel Mannin's cottage in Connemara. It was symptomatic of his state of mind, he felt, and said so to me. They were both grief-stricken and Stuart blamed himself for the accident. In the aftermath they moped about for days and were invited for a barbecue in Dublin with Ian, his children and some friends. Madeleine's classes had ended that summer, but she got further teaching work in Garristown for the autumn and set about buying a scooter to get to the school in the mornings. The neighbours said that you could set your watch by her as she passed to and fro each day. She had begun typing out the latest version of the novel during the summer of 1966 on a Remington which Ethel had had reconditioned and sent to Ireland at enormous expense. Stuart insisted on sending Ethel some money for it, he told me.

There was no progress in finding a publisher for the novel when Kay and Patrick Bridgwater and their children, who were holidaying in Balbriggan, called to visit the Reask a year later. In September Madeleine went to Glencree with Stuart and had a headstone cut to mark the cat's grave. She planted cyclamen and snowdrops. Madeleine was as grief-stricken as if she had lost a child. Christmas was quiet and its close was marred by the return of "The Legend of H" from MacDonald, a London publishing house. Madeleine tried to lift Stuart's immediate gloom by saying it was not the fault of the novel. Stuart had to admit that it would never be published. It was all a mistake, he thought at that dark hour, so he said to me. They faced the new year with despair, she over the death of the cat, he over the cat and his novel. Madeleine felt the ache of death and its mystery, and they both sought comfort in the mystics.

They bucked themselves up, looking forward to the racing season. In an effort to forget about his troublesome manuscript, Stuart decided to do some work around the house. He installed an indoor toilet and put up a poster of Joseph Stalin on the inside of the door, by way of a joke. By April they had running water in the house, and their days of going to the well were over. After putting in the toilet he made an entrance to the garage from the house to save them going out in the bad weather for fuel and most of their food, which they kept there in storage. Madeleine continued her teaching and Stuart found the strength of will, as in the past, to dare once more to send off the novel, this time to publishers McGibbon & Kee, who had published the Irish poet, Patrick Kavanagh. They eventually replied in February 1968. It was another rejection, but the editor at McGibbon & Kee, Timothy O'Keeffe, would soon play a role in Stuart's publishing life.

The playwright Tom MacIntyre, who had become friendly with Stuart, read the manuscript. MacIntyre told me over dinner that he voiced his critical opinions to Stuart. He suggested that it was better to use Yeats instead of Yardlay, calling well-known persons by their actual names, and recommended excising a huge chunk of the chapters on childhood. He recalled that once, as he was about to leave, Stuart asked him to stay a while longer. "Are you leaving me to walk down the long dark road on my own?" Stuart wanted to know. To which MacIntyre replied, "I am, because you told me that we all have to walk down the long dark road alone".[4]

That October, Madeleine got a Siamese kitten and also secured more teaching hours at Garristown with the four afternoons in Dunshaughlin. In the same month Stuart did well out of betting and won £52. He began going to a local pub, the Northway House, on Saturdays after the weekly shopping. Then he started to rewrite "The Legend of H", with some minor changes, and sent it off when Madeleine had typed it. After a further rejection from André Deutsch, even with the manuscript retitled "We the Condemned" he did some rewriting and finally entitled it *Black List, Section H*, subtitling it "a memoir in fictional form". That summer they were transfixed before the TV watching the American astronauts landing on the moon. They went to Dublin to the unveiling of Henry Moore's sculpture, dedicated to W.B. Yeats in St Stephen's Green.

The next rejection, significantly enough, was from an Irish publisher, Michael Gill, with the comment, "As a novel the book does not start to exist". However, Gill could not have been further off the mark since two days later *Black List, Section H* was accepted by another publisher. Prior to its acceptance, at long last, Stuart had invited Jerry Natterstad to the Reask after they corresponded by letter early in 1969. Natterstad was writing a thesis on Stuart's novels at Southern Illinois University. He was in his early thirties and had left the United States Air Force for academia. In June and July of 1970 he visited Stuart and Madeleine for a second time. During this visit, Tom MacIntyre was invited to dinner. Natterstad stayed a month and in that time was much taken with both Stuart and Madeleine, and noticed the strong bond in their relationship. Madeleine unashamedly admitted that they "were very much in love like in old times". They drove Jerry to Dublin and also to Glendalough.

Natterstad made application to the Department of Foreign Affairs for access to files held by them on Stuart. Permission was not granted, nor was it granted to Elborn in the 1980s when he applied. These files were finally released to the present biographer in 1998. It was a great moment for me to secure such valuable source material. Stuart himself was very pleased to hear of my good luck and had written a letter to accompany my application to Foreign Affairs.

Meanwhile back in 1970 Stuart showed Jerry Natterstad *Black List, Section H*. He was so impressed by the manuscript that he suggested showing it to the assessor of his thesis, Professor Harry T. Moore. A short extract from the novel had appeared in the literary journal *Atlantis* under the editorship of Derek Mahon. Stuart had been diffident concerning his "doomed" manuscript but eventually handed it over to Natterstad. When Natterstad returned to the United States, Professor Moore, the D.H. Lawrence scholar, read it in due course and recommended that it be published by the Southern Illinois University Press at Carbondale. Vernon Sternberg sent a copy of the publishing agreement to Stuart. Thus his most famous book would see the light of day for the first time.

I first read *Black List, Section H* in the early autumn of 1977 before I met Stuart as mentioned in the introduction. The book struck me with such force that I yearned to know all about Stuart's life and began systematically reading his other novels. For me, as for many others, *Black List, Section H* remains a classic work of Irish literature. We had many conversations about the book and I well remember it going from one edition to another over two decades. The night the Stuarts celebrated its being published by Penguin I was among their guests at a special dinner. Stuart always had a secret love for the book, but was self-conscious about discussing it too much. He had his own theories about it, and these theories were part of his satisfaction that offset the anguish of its slow progress into print. Typical of Stuart, he would tell me that the long duration and waiting was all part of the final outcome. Otherwise, he found it obsessively fascinating and strange that his most successful book had been about the crucial events of his life as if writing the book had brought this situation

Stuart and Madeleine, Dublin, 1955 –
it was Madeleine's first time in Ireland

The house in Dundrum – Stuart and Madeleine
lived here from 1971 onwards

Thérèse Martin (St Thérèse of Lisieux) – Stuart had a lifelong obsession with her

Anthony Cronin and Stuart at the Curragh Races, 1983

Stuart with Tina Neylon at the Leopardstown Races, 1986

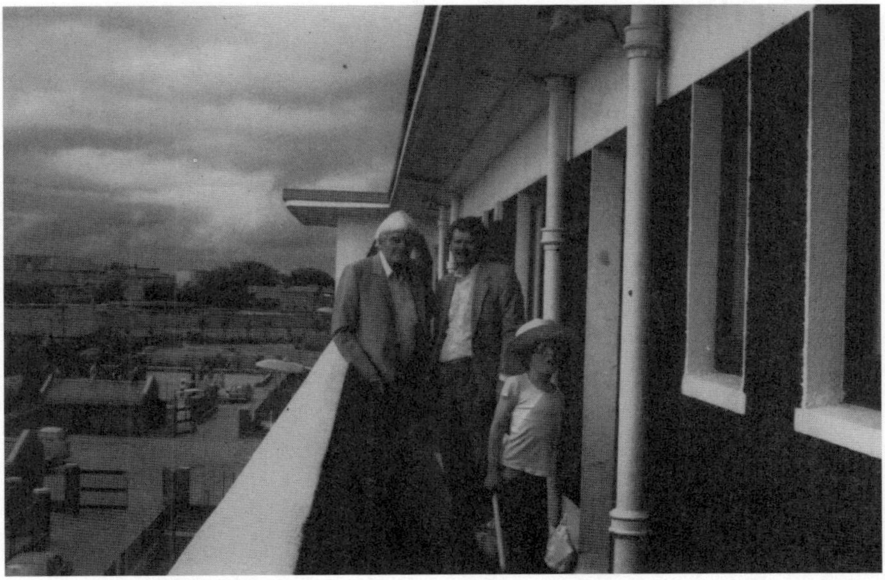

Stuart, Kevin Kiely and Daniel Graham, Fatima Mansions, 1986

Stuart and Madeleine, 1980s

Stuart and Finola with her son and nephew in Galway

Stuart and Finola in Dundrum, 1988

Stuart and Kevin Kiely, Dundrum, 1996

Stuart at 90

Stuart still writing in his mid-nineties

Stuart flanked by Ulick O'Connor (left) and poet Paul Durcan (right) leaving the High Court after his successful libel case against The Irish Times, *June 1999*

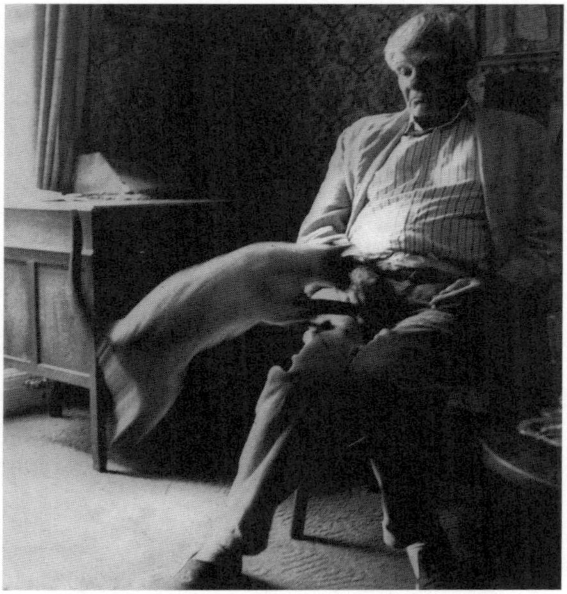

Stuart in his nineties with Min, Dundrum

Stuart aged 95 at his home in Dundrum during the controversies of the late 1990s

Last photograph of Stuart, aged 97 (Colman Doyle)

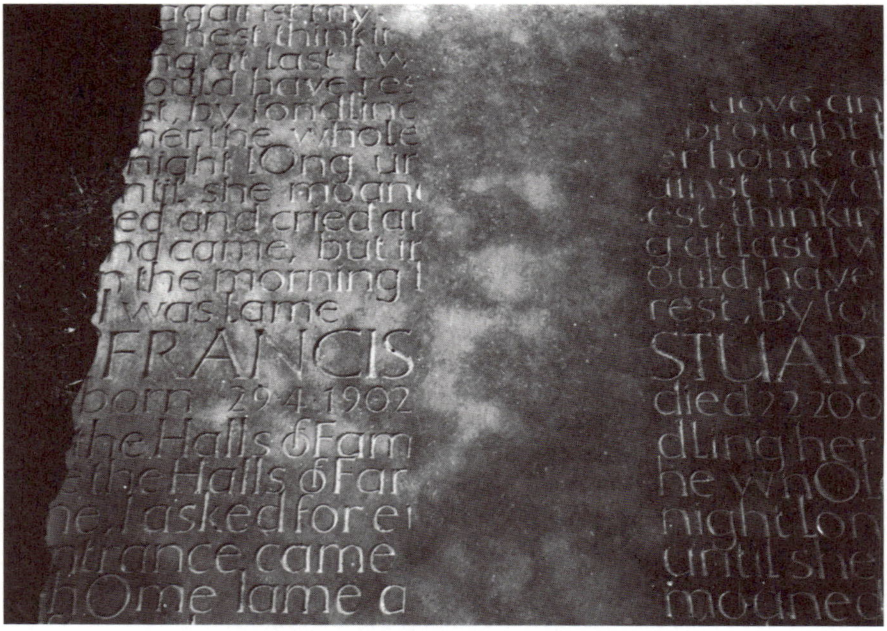

Stuart's gravestone, Fanore, Co Clare

to his attention for the first time. He was also proud of the fact that the novel had such a tortuous route to publication once he could forget his awful despair over the years.

Stuart agreed with my analysis that the use of H for a surrogate of himself in *Black List, Section H* owes something to Franz Kafka, whose central character in *The Trial* is called K. In fact, because of his admiration for Kafka, he was pleased with the comparison. The Czech writer is mentioned in Stuart's novel. The letter "H" is Stuart's literary preserve which relates to his own name, Harry or Henry, and also, coincidentally, to the H in Hitler. It is impossible not to link Stuart with H, he did so himself when discussing the autobiographical content of the novel with me. However, H is not Stuart, nor Stuart H because of the fictional form. One might ask why Stuart did not write it as a conventional autobiography. Because he was a novelist with an unshakeable belief in imaginative fiction over a lifetime of writing. And also because of his concept of fiction, as exemplified in his novels, makes this a key work in attempting to understand his method. There are three references to his father in *Black List, Section H* which could be subtitled "the psyche's secret song". These references have been mentioned in earlier chapters. The suicide of the father preoccupied Stuart throughout his life, and not only during his sixties when he wrote *Black List, Section H.*

I never wished to explain away his novel but, equally so, he never felt that protective of it from criticism. For as long as I knew Stuart, he exuded a detachment from the tortuous history of the composition of *Black List, Section H* and the equally tortuous history of getting it into print. Here follows some critical observations which I put to him concerning the novel and with which he did not disagree. *Black List* is a novel of quest; a portrait of the artist as an adult, not solely from child to adolescent to student, as in Joyce's *A Portrait of the Artist as a Young Man*. Furthermore, H relates directly to Stuart's life, whereas Joyce's masterpiece is a transposition from life into a beautiful artefact. H is not the radical superhero of literary fiction, but the extremely normal character of abundant, diverse and complex life. *Black List* is a selection of life events with omissions for artistic and other purposes because it is not possible to tell all, nor is it necessary, when the imagination can be stimulated to fullness through the psyche's delicate equipment. In *A Hole in the Head* Stuart tried to grapple with this problem, asking of his fiction, "What was dream-within-dream, what plain dream, what drug-induced hallucination, and what [was] the reality at the heart of imagination?"[5] His worst fear was that some of his novels may have been "ingeniously concocted instead of being wrung from the heart".

Black List, Section H reconstructs the events of a life and dares to explain some of its meanings, tendencies and impulses. Part of its achievement is that it avoids the self-consciousness which is the downfall of autobiographical novels. Autobiography is, by its very nature, closer to fiction because of its dependence on memory, which is hopelessly unreliable, and an author can find himself accused of aggrandisement, lying and causing deliberate or unintentional confusion. Stuart had learned some of the pitfalls of autobiography when writing *Things to Live For* (1934). In *Black List, Section H* there is a desperate grasping after the truth of experience based on Goethe's understanding that art is art and not nature. There is an endless humility in presenting H as neither hero nor anti-hero, and great efforts are made to explain motives for action, event and experience in the retrospect of prose narrative. There is also the aspect of Stuart's life compounded and comprehended within the novel.

H is not the Nietzschean superhero; not the spiritually, emotionally and mentally drained Beckettian anti-hero; not the Oblomovian aristocrat drop out; not a decadent, like Frederic Moreau in Flaubert's *The Sentimental Education*, nor the arch-cynic and nihilist *Bel Ami* of Maupassant. In his novel Stuart expanded the Joycean method of autobiographical fiction after the mannered *A Portrait of the Artist as a Young Man.* Joyce was emphatic about the indefinite article of his title: it was "*a* portrait" not "*the* portrait". Oscar Wilde's only novel, by contrast, was *The Picture of Dorian Gray*. However, Stuart could never be at ease with such lush grandiose novels and their titles. Above all, the depiction of H is in direct opposition to such heroes of literary fiction. H is decidedly anti-literary.

Stuart would probe H, his central character, as a 60-year-old novelist, and recreate in *Black List, Section H* an individual tempered by many factors: childhood, soldiering, prison, literary eminence, gambling, sexual adventure, a disastrous marriage, drunkenness, grief, love affairs and war with its destruction of cities and populations. In other ways, he demolishes the "glamour autobiography" by editing the life to suit its fictional counterpart. There are no tall stories. There is no seeking after larger-than-life effects. There are no sojourns or episodes that become too excessive. Stuart, by attempting to give us the formation of a person from inside and out, makes use of incidents from the lives of the saints and martyrs, except that H is closer to criminality than sanctity. Arcane criticism may label H an internal drifter, a Keatsian romantic or a poet such as Shelley who claims to be one of the unacknowledged legislators of the world. H may be guilty of the elevation of victimhood, the untenable position of political neutrality, even moral backsliding. In the words of the poet Carl Rakosi, who comically echoes Shelley's statement about poets, "We are the unacknowledged legislators of the world but we mustn't let it go to our heads".

Despite the rancour of his harshest critics who slight the novel as a devious evasion, a reconstruction of his life and a whitewash of his German period, the great achievement is that H comes to life through the pages. Stuart agreed with me that at one level the novelist who is an artist is only interested in creating a character, depicting an era, what used to be called giving glimpses of a soul; politics, morality, polemics and dogmatism should have no place in such a work of art. Hence, as he often reiterated, anyone who reads *Black List, Section H* seeking an agenda, apology or some self-defence on his part would be misguided.

My own overall view is that the distinct reference to Irish literature in *Black List, Section H* subconsciously takes on Joyce's *A Portrait of the Artist as a Young Man* and proceeds to lower its literary eminence. In the Irish episodes of *Black List* there is a definite lampooning of such literary giants as Shaw, Yeats, Joyce, Synge, AE and others. Behind all this is the unmitigated and unrepentant plea for radical individualism outside any consensus. In other words, H might find himself at ease in the company of Jesus's lepers, or with Socrates, Danton, Robert Emmet, Patrick Pearse. When I suggested this to Stuart, he agreed and said that H is someone who is fairly law-abiding but who is definitely anti-social. Of course, H can only be himself and a surrogate of Stuart, and harmless perhaps except for the dangerous fact of being at large. Whether H is an outcast or traitor, as for Stuart, it is up to each reader to decide for themselves.

Stuart bought Madeleine an opal ring for Christmas and in the new year a couple of advance copies of *Black List, Section H* arrived at the Reask. He signed one in blue ink, "To Madeleine from Francis after twelve years". John Lodwick, the dedicatee of *Black List, Section*

H, was a close friend of Stuart's during the 1950s, a writer, among whose published works is *Somewhere a Voice is Calling*, about a dying cat. Stuart revered Lodwick's other novel, *The Moon through a Dusty Window*, for its depiction of the hero's visit to the grave of his beloved and the prediction of the author's own death. Lodwick died in March 1959 in a car accident. Stuart believed that his death might have caused the personal creative eruption for *Black List, Section H.* [6]

The following year an important article appeared on Stuart in *Hibernia*. The article was written by Hugh Maxton and it noted Stuart's obscurity and lack of a significant reading public. Maxton is the *nom de plume* of W.J. McCormack, who considered *Redemption* and *The Pillar of Cloud* to be the "two outstanding novels since *Ulysses*". He was part of a group of poets, along with John Jordan, Derek Mahon and Hayden Murphy, who became friends with Stuart in the 1970s.

In July, Stuart and Madeleine went to Berlin to visit Traute. Prior to their departure, University College Dublin finalised a contract with him for some lectures starting the following January. After two days journeying, they were enchanted to be together again in Berlin. They stayed with Madeleine's sister Traute, who had a second-floor apartment on Luitpold Strasse 47. The highlight of their visit was finding the room they had first shared at Pension Naumann off Nickolsburger Strasse and finding it still the same apart from some dilapidation. When they saw the linden tree in blossom, their joy was intense. They went bathing in the Wannsee. Madeleine noticed how much weight her sister had put on and, when she stacked up their plates with food, realised that the helpings were much more than they were used to. Traute was over-talkative, which was natural since she was excited to see them, but she never wanted to turn off the TV, which was irritating, Madeleine recalled. Still, they shared and enjoyed Traute's love of good wine. Exploring the city, they could not find the restaurant Nickolsburger Krug where they had first had a meal out together. It was gone. For three weeks, they looked for their previous haunts along familiar streets, but Berlin was much changed. On their return to Ireland in mid-August, Madeleine was thrilled at how well Hugh Maxton had minded the cats at the Reask. He had also bought the Stuarts a present of an illustrated edition of the Psalms and a bottle of Bushmills whiskey.[7]

25

"Culturally and Morally Subversive"

MADELEINE BEGAN A SERIES OF *Thought For The Day* programmes for RTÉ which pleased the critic Mary Lappin. Madeleine enjoyed the experience very much as it gave her an opportunity to talk about the New Testament and the Psalms which had given her spiritual sustenance in Germany during the war and imprisonment. She also went back to her classes at the beginning of the new term that autumn at the technical school in Dunshaughlin. In September the publisher Manesse Verlag sent the contract for the German edition of *The White Hare.*

Meanwhile Stuart wrote what would be his last play, *Who Fears to Speak,* a commission from the Abbey Theatre which proved to be a public scandal. The play, under the intrepid direction of Tomas MacAnna, was withdrawn from rehearsals at the Peacock Theatre, Dublin, in October because of its "propagandist outlook on modern Ireland". MacAnna had fought hard to save it from the directors of the Abbey Theatre, including stalwarts Ernest Blythe, Michael O hAodha and Gabriel Fallon. In protest Stuart returned the fee he had received from the theatre. Interviewed by the *Irish Press,* he said: "I should accept this as one of the hazards of the life of an outspoken writer. But as one who believes that MacSwiney should be sincerely and properly honoured at this time, and not just accorded the usual ritualistic lip-service, I shall do all I can to this end." The play was based on Terence MacSwiney's life and writings. MacSwiney, a revolutionary Sinn Féiner at the turn of the century, had died on hunger strike in Brixton Prison in 1920. The play is Stuart's best work for theatre because of its Brechtian criticism of society. It decries the government, the banks and the Church. The author wrote in a part for himself to carry a gun to the stage at an appropriate moment in the action. There are vivid scenes set in prison when the Spirit of Imagination and the Spirit of Prophecy enter MacSwiney's cell. Patrick Kavanagh is proclaimed as a modern prophet. The play caused a furore of controversy in newspapers and John Mulcahy's *Hibernia*. Maire Ní Thuama wrote a letter of sympathy and support, as did many others, and from this time onwards Stuart began reviewing books occasionally for *Hibernia*. His reviews were of the type that combined insightful preambles and managed to comment on the book under review also as if only by afterthought. These were remarkable and I remember often searching the fortnightly journal to see if he had written something.

A shortened version of *Who Fears to Speak* was read at Liberty Hall on 1 December 1970. Phyllis Ryan did the production, Barry Cassin directed and Éamonn Keane played the part of Terence MacSwiney. On the night of the reading, there was very nearly a riot. The journalist Eamonn McCann voiced dissension from the auditorium. A discussion afterwards was chaired by Professor McHugh of University College Dublin. Stuart claimed that the Abbey Theatre thought the play was supporting violence and because of the eruption of Northern Ireland's sectarian bloodshed it was deemed politically insensitive to stage it. *The Irish Times* was among many newspapers that reviewed the play. Their critic, David Nowlan, felt it was "the sort of play the Abbey should put on". This was also the era of the arms crisis in Dublin, two years after British troops had been sent into Derry and Belfast and not long before "Bloody Sunday" (1972) in Derry and the burning of the British Embassy in Dublin.

Stuart's presence was emerging to the forefront of a one-man counterculture, something he would deny if ever I mentioned it. His belief in literature as a guiding star for society was not always fervent but at the fantasy level he did say that it should be so. He would sometimes admit that, at a subconscious level, there could be a slow attrition that might well up to something beneficial for those who had recourse to literature for spiritual sustenance. Stuart gave a public lecture on freedom at the Mansion House, quoting from MacSwiney's letters: "Comrades, if we twelve go in glorious succession to the grave, the name of Ireland will flash in a tongue of flame through the world and be a sign of hope for all time to every people struggling to be free." Stuart's public persona was seen as being allied to the IRA of the 1970s. He obviously could hardly object to this in the circumstances, but he was also seen as part of the old guard of 1920s Republicanism.

Stuart began to prepare for his Monday seminar lectures, based on Samuel Beckett's trilogy, at University College Dublin. In Beckett's trilogy he found "an experience unique in contemporary literature". A decade later, Beckett would send Stuart a copy of the trilogy, inscribed: "For Francis, affectionately from Sam, Paris 26:10:84." Meanwhile he lectured about the insights he had discovered in Beckett's novels which we also discussed. He preferred *Malone Dies* to *Molloy*. *The Unnameable* seemed to imply a psychosis overcome on Beckett's part and this was not altogether a strange direction for a work of art, he said to me once. As the character Molloy declines: "his inner life becomes more aware and acute so that the moment of death should thus be *the* moment of recognition and peace. The inner centre of consciousness – is death."[1] Stuart acknowledged Beckett's preoccupation with death as healthy once it transcended morbidity or his main effect of *galgenhumor* (gallows humour).

This concentration on death within life was for Stuart the real religious impulse that shadowed his own experience. Whether it derived from his father's suicide, from the death of his daughter Dolores, or the death of others during his early manhood he still could not tell as yet, and he hoped at his age for more years of meditation on the ultimate mystery. We often spoke about death. He feared death, he admitted, but wanted to be conscious for its arrival. He had seen too many people under death sentence who entered excruciating spiritual agonies. This experience was in the Gospels in the agony in the garden, he often said to me. A passage to meditate on, he recommended.

The lectures proved such a success that the university contracted him to deliver some further lectures after the Easter holidays. In the summer, the Stuarts went for a weekend to Malin Head in the Inishowen peninsula, and from there to show Madeleine the Stuart and Montgomery homes of Ballybogey and Benvarden. Passing the Stuart house they saw the roof hidden in a cluster of trees and a sign at the gateway, "No admittance without a permit for fear of fowl-pest". They decided they might return again some day.

Stuart wrote to *The Irish Times* replying to a public query to the newspaper as to why he had never been invited to the Yeats Summer

School in Sligo. His answer referred to Yeats's slur in calling him a dunce in the poem entitled "Why Should Not Old Men Be Mad?" They duly received an invitation to the Yeats Summer School from Professor Augustine Martin. Stuart had already made harsh criticisms of Yeats, O'Casey, AE, Shaw and Joyce, but the magnanimity of Professor Martin was beyond any partisanship in the interests of the wider horizons of literature. Before attending the Summer School, Stuart received a copy of the *Dublin Magazine* with an honourable assessment, he called it, of his novel *The Coloured Dome,* written by the critic H.J. O'Brien. The *Dublin Magazine* was in part a revival of John Ryan's *Envoy*.

The University Library at Carbondale bought a sizeable cache of Stuart's manuscripts, letters and notebooks for an archive. The ensuing windfall of $3,000 would prove decisive in determining the next phase of their lives. Included in Stuart's papers were the manuscript of *Black List, Section H* and an earlier version, which the author explained in a letter to Harry T. Moore:

> differs from the novel as it now stands in tone rather than in construction or "style". As you suggest, as regards these I write fairly spontaneously and without much alteration. But in this case, because the theme was vital to me, and was difficult to get right, I rewrote the book.[2]

Harry T. Moore made the critical comment about the high level of autobiography in Stuart's work that "facts from his life often help illuminate his writings". Compared to the small sum of money which Stuart inherited after the death of his mother, the cheque from the University of Southern Illinois was substantial, he told me, and would enable them to move away from the Reask which had become their deepest wish. The Freiburg trilogy had been their ticket from central Europe in the 1940s, just as *Black List, Section H* would be their ticket out of County Meath in the 1970s. Meanwhile, with interest growing from the Rare Books Room of the Southern Illinois University Library, they began looking for their new home.

Stuart made a trip to Paris in the summer of 1971 in search of manuscripts, including *Redemption,* which he had left behind 20 years before with the publisher, Lesort. However, his attaché case was irrecoverable. This was the piece of luggage he had left Laragh with in January 1940. On his return to the Reask, he was enchanted with

Madeleine, as usual. She had taken in a new pet from the fields. It was a hare. The hare would inspire Stuart to write a novel heralding a new phase, the last of his creative career. Part of his return to Ireland from London in 1959 had included momentous encounters with such animals. He would talk about such animals as companions and great friends. Madeleine and Stuart often talked to me about *Watership Down*, the novel about rabbits by Richard Adams.

Madeleine had applied to the Deutsche Schüle in Clonskeagh, County Dublin for a teaching job. When she was accepted through Helmut Clissmann, it caused them a dilemma about leaving the Reask, which they had once looked on as their ark against the world. The latter was a phrase often used by both of them. However, there was also the recent joint decision about imminent plans to move. Stuart was an active 70-year-old and Madeleine was hale and hearty at 55. She told me that bare subsistence based on tilling and cropping had become too much hard work for them. When they exchanged house with Neil Hickey of Dundrum for a trial period in July, Madeleine realised that commuting to Clonskeagh in the Dublin suburbs from County Meath was no longer viable. Hickey began writing a thesis on some of Stuart's novels. His mother liked the Reask and wished to retire there, finding it a suitable country location. Madeleine and Stuart, with the recent financial gain from the sale of manuscripts and letters plus a small bank loan, bought outright Mrs Hickey's house at 2 Highfield Park, Dundrum, in July 1971 for £6,500.

The house had a front and rear garden, a stream along one side, a view of the Dublin mountains and a sunroom. This was the house where I first met them and enjoyed many further visits. They accomplished the move with gusto and looked forward to their new home. They could still cultivate a garden, but with less labour than was necessary at the Reask. They brought with them the tombstone from the cat's grave and the holly tree from another cat's grave, in what was a very emotional exodus in mid-September. Then Madeleine admitted that the Reask had often made her lonely and melancholy. Besides, she was happy that Stuart was still her husband and they had their abiding love which seemed persistently strong, she said to me. She naturally found the short distance to the Deutsche Schüle easier to negotiate from nearby Dundrum. Their "new" house was a bungalow with dining room, drawing room, study, bedroom, bathroom and kitchen. Stuart divided the sunroom in two with a large space for the hare. They missed the Reask in these early days in Dundrum but felt happy with the house, which suited their needs. Shortly after their arrival, a seven-year-old cat that they had brought with them ran off. Madeleine placed advertisements in newspapers, but to no avail. She was heartbroken as usual over the loss of a pet. I noticed early in our friendship that Madeleine's talk about cats was never trivial, but of such intensity that she treated them as if they were her offspring. She spoke to cats and the other pets that she had with interrogative questions, supplying the answers. Her tone of voice was exactly the same for answering people as for cats. Cats also provided her with great laughter. She saw their moods and mischief as part of the fun of life and believed that they saw things that humans could not see or sense.

When I got to know them first, their years at the Reask seemed to be the safest topic of discussion. After we became friends I found it easier to ask about their Berlin period and subsequent time in Dornbirn, Freiburg, Paris and London. I generally spoke to Stuart about his life with Iseult and his childhood when we were on our own.

They settled into Dundrum, got to know the shops nearby on the corner of Highfield Park and could drive to the Stillorgan shopping centre. Leopardstown racecourse was nearer than before and they could go to Shelbourne Park for dog racing. The weather was remarkably clement late into their first September in the "new house" and they were soon delighted with the move. They went to the Shelbourne Hotel to celebrate the arrival of copies of *Black List, Section H* from the United States. Christmas was quiet as they were still finding their surroundings strange after years of rural life. They put up a Christmas tree and played Edith Piaf on their record player. Vivian Mercier made contact before the launch of *Black List, Section H.*

Stuart told me that the publication of *Black List, Section H* would mark a change in the literary climate for him. Terence de Vere White invited Stuart and Madeleine to dinner. White thought it was Stuart's birthday. The evening was not a great success, especially when the host discovered that his birthday was still four days away. While attending a public reading from the novel that Stuart gave at the Mansion House in Dublin, Ian had walked out in protest and cursed his father. When they visited Ian and his new partner, Anna Buggy in Laragh, Ian had already discovered through gossip and reviews that the treatment of Iseult in the novel was upsetting for him. As the adored only son of Iseult, he was justified in his anger about the negative implications about her in the book, including that she was sexually frigid. It was all literally too close to the bone and when Stuart handed him a copy of the novel as they were leaving, he broke the book's spine and flung it into the muddy track of the laneway outside the house. However, Anna told me that, full of curiosity she had rescued the novel, but soon afterwards decided to burn it in case Ian should find it. Throughout his life Ian understandably wrestled between being able to forgive his father and, at other times, finding it too much to ask. Naturally his loyalties to his mother were far stronger.[3]

Reviews in Ireland were mixed, indicative of the divided reception thereafter in response to Stuart, who gained admirers as well as revilers. John Broderick wrote a wonderful review. Terence de Vere White, literary editor of *The Irish Times,* ridiculed the book, while others such as Mercier reviewed it in *Book World,* Frank Kermode in the *Listener* and Lawrence Durrell in the *New York Times Book Review.* The novel was set for a slow rise of unprecedented success. Praised or damned, nothing could deny it a growing readership.

The house at Highfield Park would become a literary place to visit, however much Stuart would disavow the term "literary". Over the years many Irish writers would seek out the unacknowledged laureate. Some came and went a few times and others became fast friends. Stuart was by no means the over-powering host; Madeleine and he would equally entertain guests together or separately; except when Stuart sequestered himself in the study at the front of the house (also used as the dining room) with some particular friend. In January 1972, W.J. McCormack (Hugh Maxton) wrote in praise of *Black List, Section H.* He found it "compelling". He was among a number of writers who were working on a book about Stuart for Dolmen Press, *A Festschrift for Francis Stuart on His Seventieth Birthday* which was launched at Magee University. McCormack would in time see Stuart as "Yeats's posthumous anti-self", "working out what his mentor had preached" and, in the case of "extreme politics", becoming "active and direct".[4] The implication was that Stuart's decision to go to Berlin after war broke out was a subconscious directive from Yeats. Quite a theory, even damning of Stuart, placing him into the position of dishonour, but it would be unfair not to include such denigration in the interests of balance. If Stuart remains a Nazi by association in the minds of anyone, I will not defend him nor, when we mentioned the topic, did he assert any defence to me. In pugnacious mood, he could quite easily say to me, echoing the Piaf song, "Je ne regrette rien", I regret nothing. Then, he might sip his whiskey and become silent, signalling that the topic was closed on that occasion.

Stuart was unhappy that the *Festschrift* had excluded a poem by Hayden Murphy whose *Broadsheet* would include a few poems of Stuart's. Murphy and Stuart had quickly developed a surrogate son/father relationship over the manuscript of *Memorial*. Murphy, in his capacity as reader for Martin Brian & O'Keeffe and in dealings with Brian Rooney concerning the book, and also *A Hole in the Head*, became someone whom Stuart could trust to see his novels safely into print. He would also read an early version of *King David Dances* that found little response from Rooney and O'Keeffe, and would not see publication until 20 years later in a much revised version. Domestically, Murphy became part of the Stuarts' life, staying for long periods in the house around this time. Being a welcome guest he would stay over while the Stuarts went to Cheltenham every spring. Stuart's devotion to the opening of the flat-racing season meant that Cheltenham was an immovable feast in his life.

Madeleine had recently been made full-time at St Kilian's Deutsche Schüle and was delighted with herself. In April she concluded her broadcasts on RTÉ's *Thought for the Day*. The garden to the back and front of the house had suddenly sprung to life. They had "inherited" a half-dozen apple trees, forsythia and flowering red currant bushes, while the daffodils planted on their arrival had bloomed, along with the anemone from the Reask. With some contradictions in their love/hate relationship with gardening, they still needed the outlet, as they admitted to me, especially since moving to the suburbs.

Stuart went with Madeleine to have his birthday at Bill and Sheelagh Hickey's in Derry. For the last weeks of August, he went to Europe with Ted Dolan of RTÉ to make a film with two cameramen and a TV administrator. His first stop was Zurich, then on to Freiburg for a visit to the room at 2 Schwartzwaldstrasse where he had lived with Madeleine. However, he found the rest of the town, rebuilt since the Second World War, unrecognisable. He then travelled to Berlin where he contacted Madeleine's sister from his room in Hotel Am Zoo on Kurfürstendam. In between filming around the city at the Wannsee, Nikolsburger Platz, the Reichstag and Mariendorf, he visited Traute who, as usual, talked non-stop. Her chattering was something that made Madeleine and he howl with laughter. He was delighted to see Berlin, but witnessed a horrible car accident that shook him deeply. He explained to me that such an event always plunged him into various modes of meditation on the occurrence almost to the point of torture. Was he inclined to see signs and portents? When I suggested such a pattern to him he could be duplicitous and deny the fact.

Back home in Ireland he was contacted by Vernon Sternberg of the Southern Illinois University Press who had placed *Black List, Section H* with Martin Brian & O'Keeffe of London. This London publishing house could not republish the novel so soon after its first edition from Southern Illinois University Press, and were considering another novel of Stuart's which they accepted in December of 1972. Stuart had a new publisher and was entering two more decades as an active novelist, poet, and, though he would deny the title whenever I suggested it, leading underground figure among Irish writers. In disgruntled mood he would say that even a minor politician looms larger in Irish consciousness than any writer.

The novel accepted by Stuart's new publisher, Martin Brian & O'Keeffe, was *Memorial,* begun in April 1970 and completed the following year. The writing of the novel had been interrupted by the completion of his play, *Who Fears to Speak. Memorial* is one of his major novels. It is dedicated "To M, with love" and is a public exposure in fictional form of a sexual infidelity to Madeleine, but one that did not destroy the relationship. It is not possible to speculate whether the novel developed out of the fallow years after the writing of *Black List, Section H,* the impetus of moving to a new house, or the use of a cottage on Innisboffin, since the novel is set on an island. All of these factors could be claimed to initiate the process of writing, which from what Stuart told me was always speedy in his case. If a novel got held up during the writing, he would lay it aside until the creative process recommenced. He would use an ordinary cheap biro and a school copybook and was not averse to using a pencil to get a first draft written. Generally he was not an assiduous editor, never wishing to alter his first impulsive draft; hence a lot of his writing is exactly as he first wrote it.

Similarly it might be conjectured that had Stuart never written another novel after *Black List, Section H,* his final creative phase would have been a great loss to his total output. Occasional comment on these later novels affords a final analysis of his work for my purposes; however, a more in-depth exploration of these works would go beyond the scope of this book. In his later novels he completely debunked the subterfuge of creating a central character and found new scope in the use of self-absorbed personae of himself, evoked through the transparency of fact, fiction, fantasy and imagination.

There is a crisis at the heart of Stuart's final creative phase that began in his seventies. If Stuart is going to have a profoundly depressing effect on any reader it will be a religious depression, and not one that any orthodoxy will easily enshrine. He began writing in the way Jesus was writing, in the sand. The second part of *Memorial* is suffused by imagery of the Last Supper and New Testament. In conversation with me, Stuart often spoke of his special feelings for *Memorial* since it is not fiction. It all happened. However, when asked to identify the girl student involved, he was unusually reticent and unwilling to reveal her identity. "I cannot tell you everything," he said. "Life cannot tell you everything."

Memorial, published in October 1973 during something of a press furore, may well be Stuart's reply to Nabokov's *Lolita,* since both novels explore a relationship between an older man and a schoolgirl. Nabokov wrote about orgasm in a sublime and holy manner in a novella, *The Enchanter*. This was a novel Stuart mentioned with great praise in our discussions. In *Memorial*, Sugrue, the old lecher, is on an island when a school tour arrives and he meets a schoolgirl, Hera Friedlander, who had been institutionalised for attempted suicide. Her wrists bear the imprints of slashes. She may represent Christ and innocence, which are features of the hares, *lepus timide hibernice,* in the novel. She is a Christlike figure or a hare wounded in the coursing of life. In Christian iconography, the hare is sometimes used as an image of God in the Trinity. Stuart often discussed the poet William Cowper with me, adding that the poet's convalescence from temporary insanity was helped by the company of hares.

There is some explicit writing about sex in *Memorial*. The characters are in a state of crisis, like every main character in Stuart's mature fiction. For Stuart, to be alive is to be in a state of crisis. The narrator takes his revelations from anywhere, including a hangover: "I see them as one of the ways that people like us, not perhaps destined for greater illuminations, gain some insights."[5] And of course with greater urgency in these final novels the problem of God appears. "It's easier to believe in a God of chance," Sugrue claims, "than a God of love." Stuart became preoccupied with the writings of the philosopher, Martin Heidegger during this period of his life.

It is also the novel in which James Joyce is derided. "I couldn't love a girl who'd heard of Joyce," says the central character, Fintan Sugrue, who shares Stuart's initials F.S. When I asked him what he demanded from his art, he answered me quite dogmatically: "An art made from trance, contemplation, insights and dreaming." He wanted to articulate some invisible states where language is a key for opening the imagination. His art demands its own excessive weakness in order to avoid an art that verges on propaganda. Or art close to advertising. Close to political cant. Close to the certitudes of gossip. Close to comfort. Too close to comfort. He quoted Kafka: "Neither is there any room for fear of suffering or for the interpretation of suffering as merit." This is also quoted in *Black List, Section H.*

While awaiting the book's publication, Stuart and Madeleine went to Clifden and Connemara in July. The hare had died and Stuart thought Madeleine must get away quickly from Dublin. This sort of stricken panic always weakened them individually, but also kept them close and while in such a state they actually looked like hunted refugees. It gave me a glimpse of what they could have looked like on the hazardous route from Berlin to Freiburg in 1945. They went to Innisboffin and stayed with Tom MacIntyre and his American friend, Deborah Tall, who revelled in their island retreat. Another guest was Vincent Dowling, the Abbey Theatre director. It was a time of relaxation for the five of them except when they engaged in the serious sport of fishing. Madeleine caught two fish and was delighted that Tom had "set her up", as it were, with the catch. MacIntyre had, out of necessity, become an expert forager along the seashores of the island, a topic that the Stuarts would discuss with interest, recalling their own foraging when they lived in County Meath. MacIntyre told me how he saved them, during one of those sudden changes in the tides, when he managed to navigate the well-worn curragh back to calmer waters and, with great relief, to a safe haven and dry land. Stuart and Madeleine stayed at the Clifden Bay Hotel on the mainland after their visit to Innisboffin. When they returned to Dundrum there was a royalty cheque from Stuart's publisher and one from RTÉ because of a repeat of the documentary about his years in Berlin.

Memorial, which had proven faulty in the binding, was deferred until October from its earlier promised publication date of August. Advance copies of the novel were seized at Cork on arrival from London and sent to Dublin for scrutiny by customs. The *Irish Independent* carried the story, saying that Stuart would hope to give a public reading from the book if it was banned. He corresponded with Conor Cruise O'Brien who replied, in his capacity as government minister, explaining the hold-up by the Irish postal authorities because of unpaid VAT. Among others who reviewed the novel was Kevin Casey on RTÉ radio. Writing to Stuart in November as the furore died down, Casey conveyed greetings also from Eavan Boland and praised him for avoiding "the easy options of conventional moral judgments". Eavan was the daughter of Frederick Boland to whom Iseult had written in the 1940s concerning her vagrant husband.

Part Four

1975–2000

If society honours the poet, he's tempted to say what those in authority expect from him. They wouldn't have honoured him otherwise, would they? But the poet will only come out with the sort of truth that it's his task to express when he lacks all honour and acclaim. Oh no, no honours, no prizes, or he's lost! — Francis Stuart, *Black List, Section H*

Any consensus, I believe, is a threat to the imaginative writer, even if it is a very liberal consensus; any attitudes or ideologies that, at a given moment, take over a large section of society are bound to stifle one. There's bound to be a confrontation between them and the sort of imaginative writer I try to be. — Francis Stuart, *A Hole in the Head*

The origin of life appears at the moment to be almost a miracle, so many are the conditions which would have had to have been satisfied to get it going. — Francis Crick, *Life Itself*

26

A Hole in the Head

Bucknell University Press, in the person of James F. Carens, commissioned Jerry Natterstad to compile a short biography of Stuart. Natterstad's thesis on Stuart's novels had brought about the publication of *Black List, Section H*; the circumstances are outlined in chapter 24. The Irish Writers series from Bucknell University Press published Natterstad's short book on Stuart in 1974.

The house at 2 Highfield Park was close to the high walls of the Central Mental Asylum in Dundrum. It was a building that always caught one's attention when visiting Stuart with its portcullis gate and otherwise fortress-like high walls. It seemed strangely appropriate that Stuart lived here like some intermediary between the "normal" world and an institution for the insane. Once more his life confronted him with crucial themes indicative of the continuing struggle over the inner chaos that is the artist's experience awaiting insight and vision. Escaping from the cul-de-sac that a heavily autobiographical novel like *Black List* was for an imaginative writer, he had written *Memorial* (1973) which contained very few events by way of a conventional plot, focusing instead on the narrator's psyche in confrontation with reality as he uniquely perceived it. *Black List* was the novel that changed his direction and enabled his future development as a writer, he freely admitted to me. Now he would start another novel early in 1974, of which the critic Maurice Harmon asserts that Stuart "puts himself into his books, into the central character, with all his passions, shame, hope, regrets".[1] Harmon sees this final phase as purely experimental, "creating heroes who suffer from mental and emotional disasters, who undergo breakdown, who have been treated by modern drugs and in addition are given to sex and alcohol".[2] Stuart, in some respects, reflects a large part of life for modern people in these novels.

Just as Flann O'Brien was rediscovered in middle age by a London maverick publisher in the 1960s, so the same person would become Stuart's sole publisher for ten years on into the 1980s. This was Timothy O'Keeffe, an Oxford graduate, born in Kinsale, who had worked for the London publishers of Hutchinson under the dynamic Robert Lusty before moving to MacGibbon and Kee. O'Keeffe, who had also been a soldier with the British Army, later became a complex and disturbed character not unlike many of Stuart's creations, but before all this happened he was infamous as the publisher of singular works by Flann O'Brien, Patrick Kavanagh and Francis Stuart. O'Keeffe re-established Stuart under the banner of Martin Brian & O'Keeffe, a small publisher in Museum Street, London and by some extraordinary coincidence across the street from the corner pub The Plough which is mentioned in *Black List, Section H*. I met O'Keeffe in this pub for lunch in 1979 and afterwards visited his publisher's office. He was involved in preparing Hugh MacDiarmid's poems for publication, but I noticed how much O'Keeffe revered Stuart. In time, O'Keeffe would also republish two of the Freiburg trilogy, *The Pillar of Cloud* and *Redemption*. On Stuart's prompting he disregarded *The Flowering Cross* in favour of a re-issue of *Black List, Section H* in the following year, 1975.

Meanwhile, in 1974, Stuart concluded his translation of Christian de la Mazière's *Le Rêveur Casqué*. De la Mazière had the kind of background that appealed to Stuart's sense of contradiction. De la Mazière, as his name indicates, was born an aristocrat, the son of a French colonel who joined the French division of the Waffen SS after the fall of France. As a collaborator, he was tried by the French authorities in 1945 and sentenced to five years in prison; he was very lucky not to have been executed. Stuart's introduction commends the text for "the revelation of a human psyche under extremes of isolation and threat", and adds that "the *hero* is not always on the 'right' side and that the 'traitor' can act out of an integrity that others who are completely loyal may lack".[3] Stuart is challenging the judgemental impulse in those who claim the moral high ground. His translation was published by Allan Wingate and entitled *Ashes of Honour*.

In mid-August 1974 Stuart and Madeleine drove to Sligo, first to Drumcliffe churchyard where they went to Yeats's grave. Afterwards, in the Imperial Hotel in Sligo town, they met John Kelly of the Yeats Summer School, Mary Lappin, and Michael and Edna Longley. They stayed up talking and drinking until two in the morning. In the following days, Stuart gave a lecture on Yeats which John Broderick found to be exceptional. He told Stuart so and also spoke of his grief over the recent death of his mother that had coincided with his fiftieth birthday. After a drive to see the surrounding beauty spots with Broderick, they were joined by the poet James Simmons, who sang for them. It was another night of festivities at the Yeats Summer School. When they got home to Dundrum, Bill and Sheelagh Hickey from Derry were there, having stayed in the house. As usual Madeleine was happy to allow friends use their house. A week later they went to visit Edward Maguire who had proposed to paint a portrait of Stuart.

Grace Plunkett painted a portrait of Stuart in the 1930s which has since gone missing. At least Stuart told me so. Ted Lacey's pencil portrait of 1959 was followed by Thomas Ryan's portrait of March 1971, which has a sculptural technique. One of the best-known portraits is by Edward Maguire, who began working on a portrait of Stuart in the autumn of 1974. The painting shows the writer sitting on a rocking chair before a small-framed window. Outside are cabbage-like leaves, and within Stuart's snowy hair, matching bushy eyebrows, pale face and gleaming white shirt. The portrait also suggests Stuart as a prisoner, impassive, facing an interrogation lamp with a look of resignation for what lies in store. Neil Shawcross would produce a somewhat Churchillian-looking Stuart using an oblique parody of the style of Bacon. There is no cigar, but a rabbit sits on his lap and a cat at his feet. The Jack Crabtree portrait found its way on to the cover of the Penguin edition of *Black List Section H* in the 1990s. However, Stuart conveyed his disapproval of it to the publisher. Crabtree has, in fact, made 25 separate studies of his subject which together constitute a significant achievement in portraiture.

The crisis that is foreshadowed in *Memorial* bears its dangerous fruit in his next novel, *A Hole in the Head,* finally completed in 1976 after three years of intermittent work. Stuart moved to Sligo and also to Belfast during periods when he felt the material might be improved with a change of location. Madeleine feared he was being unfaithful to her and, threateningly, left a note in her diary saying that in the event of her death she wished her personal goods and belongings to be sold and the proceeds to go to the animals. It was a fraught time for them both, a crisis on both sides obliquely reflected in the book. Stuart himself refused to provide me with tittle-tattle or gossip about what may or may not have happened, only saying that such upheavals are common to many couples, for once diminishing his special and unique relationship with Madeleine which he otherwise ceaselessly praised. What may explain his behaviour, if hardly excuse it, was the personal crisis reflected in the novel. Madeleine, however, was certain about his having another brief affair, which rocked their hitherto solid and long lasting loving relationship, though not to its foundations.

He was awarded a bursary of £750 by the Northern Arts Council and returned for a reconciliation with a simple bracelet in rainbow colours. They also bought a car, a Sunbeam Vogue, trading in the Ford Escort against the purchase price. The depth of their love was stronger than any dalliance on his part, and Madeleine forgave him. His Belfast visits, in part reflected in the novel, are significant since the second half of the book is set there. Brian Turner, of the Ulster Museum, played a part in providing Stuart with access to more remote parts of the city that he did not know very well.

The central character in the novel is undergoing a psychosis that is relieved in part by his volunteering to become hostage in a siege situation in Northern Ireland. This, and a fiery love affair, brings about his return to sanity. The central impulse for the book is the narrator's muse, Emily Brontë, whom he talks to in his delusional state. He is hospitalised at a French clinic and then flies to Ireland with Brontë to another clinic. The first part is a study of madness. For Stuart, madness is an equally valid picture of reality. The novel may also have been influenced by Evelyn Waugh's *The Ordeal of Gilbert Pinfold* and Malcolm Lowry's *Under the Volcano,* both of which, by chance, Stuart was reading around this time, he admitted. The second part is set in Belfast, renamed Belbury. Some of the graffiti of the city invades the narrative:

> No time for stripping
> As the bombs go bang
> Just hug me closer
> And fuck me as I am[4]

Up the Republic!
Up the Queen!
Up the Orange!
Up the Green!
Up mutual understanding!
Up our Liberty!
Up a united island!
And you up me![5]

Up Saville Lane he'll surely lead
His unresisting Lil.
For him there are two nightly kicks:
Either to fuck or kill[6]

The novel is dedicated to Timothy O'Keeffe and there is something prophetic in that too. Both *Memorial* and *A Hole in the Head* dare go as close to deranged prose as comprehension will bear. Also, Stuart had neglected two huge areas of exploration in the novels that preceded *Memorial,* he told me, and wanted to make an exploration of the interior world that is created by adding to or interfering with the particles of the brain either through alcohol, drugs or altered states of consciousness.

A Hole in the Head was a success in critical terms because of the contemporary nature of its subject. He was interviewed in the local press, was a panellist on the RTÉ book programme *Folio,* and would later become the subject of a special programme with its presenter Patrick Gallagher. Meanwhile he wrote a column in John Mulcahy's controversial fortnightly broadsheet, *Hibernia,* beginning in March 1976. Kevin Casey gave over a whole book programme on RTÉ radio to interviewing Stuart about the novel. I heard this interview at the time and still remember being struck by the veracity of Stuart's voice, it being the first time I'd ever heard him. I would meet him for the first time the following year at University College Galway as outlined in the introduction. The novel led many new readers to discover his other work and increased his stature in Irish literature. A host of critics and writers praised the novel: Victoria Glendenning in the *Times Literary Supplement*; Oswell Blackston in the *Tribune*; John Mellors of the *Listener*; Martin Goff, the *Daily Telegraph*; Nuala O'Faolain, the *Sunday Press;* Myra Blumberg, *The Times* and Denis Johnston, *The Irish Times.*

After a visit from another friend, Alice Murnane, Stuart and Madeleine spent a weekend with Ian, who had moved in permanently to Laragh House, which is on higher ground than nearby Laragh Castle. He now lived with Anna Buggy. They had moved in together as a couple in the early 1970s on the break-up of Ian's marriage with Imogen Stuart. Their marriage had foundered because of his affair with Anna Buggy, a student friend of his second daughter, Siobhán, who attended the Sacred Heart School in Monkstown. When Ian had at first attempted to include Anna in a *ménage-à-trois* with Imogen, his wife made an effort to go along with it, but eventually left him. Seemingly, both father and son had unfulfilled desires for polygamy during their lives. Madeleine thought Anna was too young for Ian and did not understand their bohemian lifestyle. Nevertheless, the relationship between the foursome developed well over the succeeding years.

In April, Stuart set out on a trip to London, taking in Belfast on the return journey to Dublin. He went to London for the launch of the second impression of *Black List, Section H*, and stayed with his publisher, Timothy O'Keeffe at 78 Coleraine Road. Most of their days were spent on a publicity foray with the *Guardian*, *Times Literary Supplement* and other literary editors. Stuart missed Madeleine and felt the party launch was a minor event without her. He now realised that the more he was about in the world, the less quiet and composure he found in people. He longed to return to his haven with Madeleine and their intimate sensual life, he told me. However, the novel was consolidating his reputation and, with O'Keeffe backing him fully for any new book he might write, he could feel more secure as a writer than in the dark days when he lost his then publisher Victor Gollancz.

Back from Belfast he was the subject of a TV programme introduced by Anthony Cronin. Stuart was seen interviewed in the garden at Dundrum with the cat on his lap. This was followed by the book programme (already referred to) presented by the writer Kevin Casey for radio and also recorded at the house in Dundrum. In April, Stuart gave a lecture at the Irish-American Cultural Institute. That summer he received news from the Arts Council in Dublin, through Colm O'Briain, that he had been awarded a bursary of £2,500. Their summer holidays included a few days' stay with Hubert Butler and his wife, Susan, in Kilkenny. The weather was glorious. They went on to Belfast, staying with Ted Hickey of the Ulster Museum and his partner Elizabeth, with whom they felt at ease. They met Andy Tyrie of the Ulster Defence Association at the Europa Hotel. Andy drank vodkas with bitter lemon and told of his views on the problems in the province. He felt Ulster would become an independent state and that the sectarian war would continue.[7]

Days later, Michael and Enda Longley took them to dinner at the Wellington and the pre-12 July Orange celebrations in Sandy Row. Madeleine experienced the Lambeg drums, which put the fear of God into her, she told me, and she thought the bonfires were eerie yet very impressive. On the Twelfth they watched the Orange Lodge parades passing along the Lisburn Road. Afterwards they went for lunch to friends of Ted Hickey and Elizabeth at Marlborough Park, where the food was excellent. The following day, in the Ulster Museum, they saw a drawing of Stuart by Edward Maguire. The highlight of their visit was a trip to Ballybogey and Benvarden where Annette Montgomery, Stuart's cousin, showed them around. They made a brief visit to the Stuarts' residence, hoping to make contact with either Stella or Sybil, daughters of Stuart's Uncle Wallace, but found nobody at home. They returned to Dundrum on 14 July and on the journey Madeleine probed Stuart about his father's suicide, but he did not know the complete facts.

Following the publication of *A Hole in the Head* by Martin Brian & O'Keeffe, there was a United States edition from The Longship Press, Nantucket, Massachusetts a year later in 1977. This came about through a visit to Ireland by William Vorm. Vorm's sister, Sheila Taylor, invited Stuart and Madeleine to stay in their villa in Gstaad, Switzerland. Stuart had been favoured by the Arts Councils both in Belfast and Dublin with a writer's bursary prior to the writing of the novel. He began another novel in the villa at Gstaad after visiting Auvers-sur-Oise where Vincent van Gogh had committed suicide. It would take three years until the completion of *The High Consistory* in 1979.

27

US Tour, a New Academy for Artists

WRITING IN THE *CRANE BAG* IN THE SPRING of 1977, Stuart commented: "Writers in Ireland are much in the position Spanish and Portuguese ones were under Franco and Salazar, or those in the United States under Johnson and Nixon. To my knowledge none of our best writers have [sic] ever been asked to Áras an Uachtaráin." It was all part of Stuart's polemical exercises, he told me on one of my Sunday afternoon visits to Dundrum. He was preparing to travel to the United States in a few weeks.

Stuart had been invited on a lecture tour involving a schedule that was punishing for a 75-year-old, taking in all the major cities of the east coast. Madeleine was going to miss him, she said. He insisted that her "old burning tiger", which she always called him in private, was not burning as brightly as before. Still, he didn't fear the lectures, just the travel and meeting strangers without her by his side. It was an adventure that he braced himself for and he was full of news when he got back. He told me that the trip began with unforeseen delays at Dublin Airport but he managed to get out of Ireland on a flight to Glasgow with the hopes of a connection through Prestwick for Kennedy Airport, New York. By chance he met a friend, Tom Delaney, on the flight to Scotland, and they passed some of the tedious hours drinking at the airport together. On arrival in New York, he stayed overnight in Manhattan, returning the next day to the airport for the flight to wintry Halifax. He enjoyed seeing the restored sectors of the old town and, despite inhibitions with strangers, got on well with who ever he met, finding them pleasantly unhurried in their approach to life. After a lecture at the university, where he received a plaque rewarding his contribution to literature, he flew to Boston. At the airport he waited for hours because two Ghanaian students had got lost in traffic on their way to collect him. At least, that was their story when they found the somewhat bored and disconsolate Stuart waiting for them. He was taken to a number of festive events, it being St Patrick's day, but was surprised at the sobriety among the academics he met in Boston.

He stayed a night with his biographer, Jerry Natterstad, in Springfield, Massachusetts; everywhere was snowbound. From there he went on to St Paul, Minnesota, where he had time to play a relaxing game of pool with a friend, Richard Ryan. Next on to Omaha and then Chicago where he entered into the spirit of his tour but also felt somewhat like a performing animal in a circus, he told me. During free time in Chicago, he went to the galleries to study the Cézannes, Gauguins and Van Goghs, the best collections he had ever seen outside Paris. We were able to discuss this since I knew these galleries from my travels. A meeting with poet James Liddy was a welcome relief from being among strangers, he said. Liddy had come all the way from Milwaukee to hear Stuart speak, but found himself held up at the entrance to the lecture theatre because his clothes were deemed shabby. Stuart spoke up for Liddy and quickly had him admitted. The weather improved by the time he got to Washington and he began to find the short stays with families, which was part of the itinerary, very tiresome. He was also flagging when it came to the lecture schedule. He told me that he would write notes, but feeling diffident would tend to improvise when it came to the lecture; not a good method in any public speech, neither for the speaker or the audience, he added.

He flew from Albany to Pittsburgh and once more, by chance, met Tom Delaney on his way to Oneonta in upstate New York. The sylvan pastoral outskirts of Pittsburgh made for some relief and his temporary lodging was near a wood where he saw possums, raccoons, deer and foxes. Before leaving the United States he met with John McGahern and his wife Madeleine. McGahern had known Stuart since the 1960s and had travelled through Europe, with periods in Majorca, Helsinki and Berlin as well as his long time place of residence at Foxfield, County Leitrim. Stuart's last nights were spent in the Stanhope Hotel along Fifth Avenue at 81st Street but he was aching to return to Madeleine, he added.

He flew to Paris to meet William Vorm in mid-September and stayed with William in his top-floor apartment, otherwise enjoying old Parisian haunts. In a telegram to Madeleine, announcing his arrival in Dublin he signed himself, Colonel Stuart, part of their private code. In October he took up an invitation to address a seminar of young writers at University College Galway and to take part in a panel lecture on "The Writer and the Politician" at the Literary Society of the college. It was at this event, outlined in the introduction, that I first met Stuart. During the first dinner I ever had with him and Madeleine in Dundrum, I elaborated my theory about *A Hole in the Head* which they listened to and afterwards he gave me a signed copy. As I left that night, it was the third time I had met with Stuart; he and Madeleine invited me to visit whenever I wanted to, as long as I phoned in advance. So began for me our great friendship.

Paul Durcan, a very close friend of the Stuarts, visited them a lot and would always send postcards when out of the country. He sent Stuart a catalogue from an exhibition of the Jewish artist, Ronald Kitaj. In November of 1978 Stuart was invited to lecture at University College Cork. In the expectation of his new novel, *The High Consistory*, appearing in print, he referred to the work of Kitaj because the central character in the book was a painter. Kitaj's work was obsessed with attempting to achieve a "scripture-like spirit" in his paintings which was gained through endurance and anguish. The artist said of himself, "Nothing is well with me and never has been".

Dermot Bolger, with experience as a librarian, had recently founded Raven Arts Press (1979). Funded solely by the Arts Council, it also incorporated an arts centre in central Dublin. Bolger would publish himself and other emerging writers, adding Anthony Cronin and Stuart to the list. Colm O'Briain and Lawrence Cassidy of the Arts Council in Dublin also helped Stuart. From 1980, Stuart received a three-year bursary amounting to £9,000. Another artist, Patrick Collins, would also benefit from this patronage by the Irish state and these three-year bursaries are reputed to have heralded the introduction of Aosdána, "an affiliation of artists in all disciplines set up by the Irish Arts Council, with government backing and approval". Aosdána was the brainchild of politician Charles J. Haughey and writer Anthony Cronin. Cronin became cultural adviser to the Taoiseach C.J. Haughey in the early 1980s when Fianna Fáil came to power and state legislation brought Aosdána into being. Stuart was elected a member of Aosdána after its foundation.

There are two features of Aosdána: one is its self-electing function of members, the other is that the elected assembly never goes over a certain number in the various disciplines of music, visual art and literature. Stuart, who became a fully paid member, was often disparaging about the institution and spoke of his discomfort with it. He admitted to me that it compromised his position as an artist, but he needed the stipend, which is what he called the *cnuas* (an annual salary paid to many of the members of Aosdána). He told me that Denis Johnston was equally uncomfortable about being a member and when someone who was new to the assembly asked whether they could sign "member of Aosdána" after their name, Johnston commented ironically, "Why not just sign yourself MA?" Stuart found this funny and he often repeated the anecdote.

Cronin made great claims for Samuel Beckett's acceptance of Aosdána's highest award of merit, known as "being made a *saoi*", the Irish word for "a wise person". He saw it as a coup for the institution, which it was indeed, when Beckett joined. Privately Stuart said he believed that Beckett had been hoodwinked into the institution, giving me his version of the event. At first, Stuart said, Beckett refused to attend a ceremony that was to be arranged at Áras an Uachtaráin in the Phoenix Park. When Beckett nominated a relative of his living in Dublin as recipient of the award in his absence, the preparations were shelved. For some time the award was not conferred on Beckett because of the disappointment for the organisers, since it had been hoped his attendance would make the public occasion a cultural event. When eventually the award was re-offered and Beckett accepted, "through Aosdána he was making his peace with Ireland," according to Cronin, "its mere institution had altered the relationship of the country to its artists for ever and the bad old days of censorship and semi-starvation were now over".[1] Beckett sent a letter to Adrian Munnelly, Registrar of Aosdána: "The news of my election to the dignity of *saoi* has moved me deeply."[2] He did not come to Dublin from Paris and was sent a torque, the token symbol ceremonially presented to a *saoi*. At the ceremony, Stuart read a tribute to Beckett that was later published in *Cara*, the Aer Lingus in-flight magazine. Beckett's niece sent her uncle a copy of it and he responded by writing Stuart a friendly note with an open invitation to visit him in Paris.

When Deirdre Bair's biography of Samuel Beckett appeared in 1978, I remember visiting Stuart at the time. He had been sent the hefty looking tome, the first full-length biography on Beckett, for review, but was deterred from writing anything about it, he said. This led to a discussion of Beckett, most of it very favourable until he added, "You know he accepted the *croix de guerre*?" I just nodded, but Stuart stared intensely, making me momentarily uneasy, a condition unusual for me in his company. "Oh did he?" I responded, picking up on his tone of censure. "He did," said Stuart, "And the less Beckett he." Stuart emphatically loathed hearing about any artist that he considered worthy of the title accepting any sort of public honour or award.

In the year that followed, Stuart went on to explore some of the questions raised by the concept of a collective body of creative persons and other relevant issues about academies of the arts in *The High Consistory*. His first experience of such institutions was with Yeats's Irish Academy of Letters that conferred their poetry award on him involving a symbolic crown of bay leaves. *The High Consistory* is a book that owes something to *Black List*. It might glibly be retitled "Black List Section H Revisited". It is also a third attempt at "autobiography" and important in the Stuart *oeuvre* for the reflection and emphasis it places on certain parts of his life and writings. "I still think it is my best, or equal-best to *Black List* novel," he commented after sending it to Timothy O'Keeffe in London. A further comment at the time reveals his abandonment of character creation as if the whole concept is alien to the process of making fiction. "It is quite different; no 'real' people are in it, though a kind of model could be pointed to for almost all the characters."

The conditions for writing *The High Consistory* were somewhat arduous. Stuart had fallen from a tree in the garden as he was lopping off branches. It was early January of 1979. Madeleine was distraught and had an ambulance rush him to St Vincent's Hospital. Stuart was released the same day, but the hospital visit engulfed him in past thoughts of admission to prison, he told me. The leg injury would eventually require a hip replacement and convalescence in his suburban house. *The High Consistory* may appear to be the work of a writer ploughing the same furrow as before. However, it is daring in its fictional manipulation, if not occasionally a burlesque of events in Stuart's life. Each diary entry chapter is haphazard in the chronology of the life of the central character Grimes, who is obviously a replica of the author. "In the early spring of 1940 I was asked by Eduard Hempel, the German Ambassador accredited to my native land, if I would be interested in doing a portrait of Hitler." [3] The dramatis personae include: Iseult Stuart, Henry Irwin Stuart, Libertas Schultze-Boysen (the anti-Nazi saboteur executed by the Gestapo in 1942), Robert Banim (alias the American poet Robert Lowell), Julio Bailey (alias the Irish writer John Jordan) and the usual references to Stuart's muses, St Thérèse of Lisieux, Emily Brontë and Vincent van Gogh.

There are fantasy sequences; with Pearse and Connolly during the 1916 Rising; in Churchill's house in London in 1940; and in Berlin where two British secret service agents shadow the central character and ask about his "collaboration with the Nazi authorities". He meets people who will get him an interview with Hitler, the daughter of General von Milch, and Gerda Christian, Hitler's private secretary. Stuart told me that he once had a meal with her. St Thérèse of Lisieux appears in a vision to the central character and he asks her for the name of the horse that will win at Chantilly.

There is a comic interlude about James Joyce's waistcoat that is brought to an arts festival as a relic. The portrayal of Robert Lowell in the novel casts a shadow over the conventional biography of Lowell by Jonathan Raban. Stuart met Lowell at dinner in Garech Browne's hunting lodge in Luggala, County Wicklow. Stuart told me that he could well believe that Lowell displayed periods of wild extrovert behaviour followed by deep traumatic eclipse. According to a well-known Irish poet who wants to remain anonymous, Lowell admitted to drinking *eau de cologne* during his stay at a Dublin hotel. Lowell was prone to mental instability and derangement in the tradition of Berryman, Plath, Poe, Baudelaire and Rimbaud. He fascinated Stuart, who often discussed him and his poetry with me. He satisfied a criterion for Stuart that poets include the animal kingdom among their poetry in some insightful work. This is what he told me. The fact that Lowell was "disturbed" was something of great significance for Stuart. He demanded such personality as a hallmark of poethood, but was not too dogmatic on this point.

O'Keeffe would not publish *The High Consistory* until 1981, by which time his publishing business was in debt and thereafter ceased to exist. Thus Stuart was without a publisher once again which was nothing new in his long career. After its publication in London, it was reissued in the United States by William Vorm of the Longship Press. The novel was widely reviewed in Ireland, London and in the United States. I reviewed it for a national newspaper. Stuart also enjoyed hearing comments from close friends. John Wheale of the University of Warwick thought the novel a masterpiece. He had written a study of Stuart's post-war novels entitled "Redemption in the work of Francis Stuart". John Jordan wrote admiring the book. Seán Dunne wrote from Cork sending a poem, "For Francis Stuart on his seventy-ninth birthday". This would become one of the many poems written for Stuart by other writers. Bernard Loughlin, director of the Tyrone Guthrie Centre, the artist's retreat in County Monaghan, invited him for a period of seclusion, but received a grateful but negative reply. Tommy Smith, the publican, was full of praise for the novel when Stuart, with Madeleine, visited Grogan's Pub in Dublin shortly after publication. Madeleine was celebrating too. She had qualified for a pension the previous year and so retired from the Deutsche Schüle after ten years of fruitful service where her approach to teaching young children was unique in its sensitivity. Meanwhile, Stuart was sought out for seasonal interviews, photographed at the Phoenix Park races and featured on the cover of *Books Ireland.*

As 1982 dawned he was facing his eightieth birthday. He and Madeleine had a private celebration at their house. Among the guests were long-standing friends John and Nuala Mulcahy, Anthony and Thérèse Cronin, Garech Browne, Patrick Gallagher, Thomas Kilroy, Richard Ryan and Katherine Maloney, the widow of Patrick Kavanagh, who brought a present of a portrait of the poet. It was also a busy time in literary Dublin – the Joyce centenary year. On RTÉ radio, Stuart was interviewed before his birthday on 29 April: "As a writer," he declared, "I would hope to be as vulnerable as the people I write for." He explained the difficulty of finding a new language to explain his unrelenting creative needs, their victories, defeats, joys and ongoing turmoil. He gave the impression of making unceasing demands upon himself to be continuously subversive and revolutionary in wanting change in society for the common good. Raven Arts Press reissued *We Have Kept the Faith* with new and selected poems introduced by Anthony Cronin. Paul Durcan wrote a long poem, "Ark of the North", which praised Stuart's poem "Ireland" written in Berlin in 1944. Both books were launched during a public birthday celebration at the Peacock Theatre in Dublin. Derek Bell, the harpist, played music in his honour. Garech Browne, director of Claddagh Records, organised a sound recording of Stuart. The title of the record/cassette was *Alternative Government*. One side presents extracts from his writings and the other is a lecture that serves as a general introduction to his work. Richard Ryan was the recording editor for Claddagh Records on the project.

The Taoiseach Charles J. Haughey and his wife Maureen invited Stuart and Madeleine to attend a function in Dublin Castle that opened the Joyce festivities. Stuart put aside his antipathy to Joyce and attended the event that was marked by near hysteria, such was the strong feeling in Dublin in the centenary year of Joyce's birth. When the Gala Poetry Reading took place at the Mansion House a few nights later on 18 June, another event of the festival, Stuart was not present to hear Sir William Empson, Jorge Luis Borges, Robert Sabatier and Sorley MacLean, amongst other poets. Stuart had published a repudiation of Joyce in *Minority Report*. This further exemplified his rejection of Joyce in *The High Consistory* and he had consistently damned Joyce since *Black List, Section H.*

Stuart would consolidate his position in an interview later with Bill Lazenbatt: "In one sense our greatest novel, *Ulysses*, was a non-believer's book, I think, adamantly so. But I would say that I believe that belief is essential. You can be a writer without it, but whether you can be a prophet, I don't know. Writing is a prophecy."[4] The morning after the Gala Poetry Reading in the Mansion House, Stuart was brought to the Shelbourne Hotel for a meeting with the Argentinean writer, Jorge Luis Borges. He presented Borges with a translation of *Redemption.* When Borges mentioned Yeats as being as great a poet as William Blake, Stuart went silent. In *Black List,* when H has fallen in love with Iseult, he is soon aware of "the magic of Yeats's shadowy world enclosing them before he had the strength to make her aware of his own". However, the meeting was special for Stuart, who commented on Borges's humility. "Is it not reassuring to think of such people on this earth, for which reason, if no other, it may be spared as Nineveh would have been had it contained one just soul." Stuart's comment grants such a writer as Borges a high place in society. *In Dublin* magazine published some of their conversation in the issue of 24 June in an article entitled "Books and The Night".

Later in the year, Stuart took a break from writing a column for *In Dublin* magazine and went to Europe. As on previous summers, he and Madeleine holidayed with Sheila Taylor and Bill Vorm at their villa in Gstaad, Switzerland. On their return journey through France they visited the Abbaye de Lerins, Cannes, for a few days' meditation and spiritual renewal. In October Stuart was the invited speaker at the Douglas Hyde Gallery, Dublin, when Co-op Books were launching plays by Bernard Farrell and Stewart Parker. Also launched were *Captives* by F.D. Sheridan and the present writer's first novel *Quintesse*. Stuart showed his support and encouragement for new writers on the literary scene by speaking at some book launches. For instance, Co-op published Neil Jordan's story collection, *Night in Tunisia*, and he spoke at the launch of Jordan's first novel *The Past*.

Kay Allen, a bookseller in Avoca, began to collect Stuart's novels and other books and asked him to sign them. The year 1982 saw the acceptance of *Black List, Section H* by Penguin Books, through the good offices of Timothy Binding who was about to leave the firm for Picador. The first edition sold extremely well, with pre-publication sales reaching 5,000 copies. In 1984 he got an Allied Irish Banks Award for Literature and met Mary Ladky who was writing a thesis on "The Visionary Aesthetic: Francis Stuart's *Black List, Section H* and its Literary Antecedents". That year he also presented Poet's Choice on RTÉ radio, reading from Keats, Borges, Ernest Dowson, T.S. Eliot, Stephen Spender, Thomas MacGreevy and the United States poet, James Dickey.

Apart from the public events, typically Stuart would not be tamed and contributed an ideologically unpopular introduction to an anthology of poetry, *After the War is Over* (1984), published by the Raven Arts Press in protest against Ronald Reagan's visit to Ireland. In it he recalled the meeting with Borges, "the memory of whom still sustains me". He listed former world VIPs who had visited Ireland: J.F. Kennedy, Princess Grace of Monaco, Pope John Paul II, Henry Kissinger "responsible for the bombing to death of thousands of civilians in South East Asia, whom we saw on television being warmly embraced by the wife of the Taoiseach". Stuart knew that the amount of bombs dropped on Hanoi during the Vietnam War exceeded the tonnage dropped on Dresden in the Second World War. Ironically, the anthology was dedicated to Ronald Reagan. Stuart concluded, "As a judge of world affairs with the power of life and death over hundreds of millions, it is hard to conceive of somebody less desirable". Reagan would also find some official protest against his visit when he came to address both houses of the Irish Government and a few elected representatives walked out of the chamber when the United States leader entered.

Timothy O'Keeffe, who had moved to a new address in Coleraine Road in London, was by then a struggling small publisher. He would never publish another Stuart novel, but availed himself of a bi-publishing deal with Raven Arts Press for *States of Mind* which had extracts from Stuart's *Things to Live For: Notes for an Autobiography*. Some of his *Berlin Diary* was included and, intriguingly, an advance extract from *Faillandia*. This was proof of the rumours of another novel which I knew to be true from visits to him. Once more his notebooks in the desk drawer of the living room were filling up with the evolving book. And there were many new readers since the re-publication of *Black List, Section H* by Penguin. By the end of 1984 a bio-film on Stuart was completed by Ian Bruce of Octagon films based on *Black List, Section H.* The Irish actor T.P. McKenna read extracts from the novel. Stuart was interviewed on camera at his home in Dundrum by Carlo Gébler, with Madeleine in the background and also their cat and hare. There is also a racing sequence filmed at Leopardstown in which their friend Anthony Cronin lines up in the stand with Stuart and Madeleine to watch a race.

Since giving up her teaching at the Deutsche Schüle, Madeleine set to work editing her diaries and they were published in 1984 under the title *Manna in the Morning*. The *Sunday Press* and other newspapers heralded and lauded the wife of Stuart on the publication of the book. In the past she had been somewhat reviled and was latterly publicly celebrated. Madeleine could also be heard on radio occasionally and was continuously entertaining select friends and visitors at Dundrum. In June, Stuart agreed to give a talk at the local library in Dundrum that was organised by Joan Ann Lloyd. In July, Brian Maguire, chairman of the Independent Artists, invited him to open their exhibition, which was scheduled for September. Then, on 7 September Liam O'Flaherty died, leaving Stuart as the doyen of Irish letters. The comments about his old mentor and friend were affectionate, if critically unfavourable: "The thing about O'Flaherty," said Stuart, "was his fine untamed spirit that never really got into his writing." It was the suppression of O'Flaherty's novel *The Puritan* which had prompted Yeats to found an Irish Academy of Letters. Over Christmas, Stuart forgot about the contradictions he saw in Aosdána and which he had articulated regarding academies for the arts in *The High Consistory* and instead began rereading *Crime and Punishment* (Dostoevsky). He still found it "a really glorious book", he told me on my next visit to Dundrum. For Stuart Dostoevsky was always a major figure.

28

Loss of the Beloved

STUART COMPLETED THE NOVEL *Faillandia* in 1982 and through Raven Arts Press sought for a London publisher but to no avail. Chatto & Windus rejected it in November of that year. During that season I remember we met at a gala dinner in a private house in Monkstown and Stuart told me that he did not care about the difficulties with finding a publisher. He had been through this kind of rigmarole in the past. It will be published eventually, he said calmly. Prophetically, the novel alluded to the death of the central character's wife in the opening page followed by his speedy remarriage. This echoed Stuart's past life when Iseult died in the 1950s and he married Madeleine. However, as he wrote the novel he could not have known that it foretold the death of Madeleine and his third marriage, still in the remote future. *Faillandia* was published by Raven Arts with Arts Council funding in 1985.

Suddenly, Madeleine was stricken with cancer, detected after her debilities during their European holiday that year. She would die a year later at home in Dundrum. Madeleine, who might have expected to outlive Stuart, worried about him as he got older, especially after his fall from the tree in the garden. In the autumn of 1985, they were approached by Geoffrey Elborn who wished to write a biography of Stuart. Over dinner in the Shelbourne they found Elborn, the genial Scot, suitable and he duly set to work on his ambitious project. Then, in March 1986, Stuart and Madeleine accepted an invitation to take part in "Irish Week" sponsored by the University of Nova Scotia. Their stay was hampered somewhat by heavy snow; however, Stuart managed to give some talks and readings from his work. Madeleine found conditions very comfortable during their stay in the Lord Nelson Hotel, she told me. When they returned to Dublin they hoped to have courage for what faced them because of Madeleine's serious illness. I remember she told me about her fatal illness on one of my visits when she offered me wine and refused any herself. She was also convivial and enjoyed a glass or two of wine but suddenly mentioned that she could not drink alcohol anymore.

Elborn moved in with the Stuarts during this period. Madeleine was confined to bed during the summer of 1986 while Elborn worked daily on the book. During her illness she maintained a stoical calm sustained by her faith. Stuart tried to cope with the fact of his beloved's dying by reading Nadezha Mandelstam's *Hope against Hope* and *Hope Abandoned* about life with the Russian poet, Osip Mandelstam, who died in the Kolyma Mines Labour camp under the Stalinist terror of the 1930s. As the sunflowers outside the windows grew to their full height Madeleine weakened but not before she had an insight that a stray cat that came to her for food would not return. The cat never did return. Madeleine still had her cat, Manna, and the rabbit called Gard du Nord as a reminder of her reunion with Stuart in Paris in September 1949. Her last days were eased by morphine and Stuart and Elborn were with her night and day. She died peacefully in her seventy-first year on 18 August while in a coma. She was cremated in Glasnevin, Dublin. The attendance was that of close friends and the event was kept private even though it was reported in the main newspapers. Her last wish was for a secular funeral with the Beethoven E flat Quartet as solemn music. One might have expected a reading from *The Song of Songs* or *The Psalms.* However, such were exclusively for her private times of prayer alone or with Stuart.

I remember being in Dundrum with Stuart and Elborn on the day after Madeleine's cremation. Stuart was in good condition considering Madeleine's death; if anything Geoffrey Elborn was as stricken with grief. Geoffrey, who saw me to the door, said that Stuart would be alright but that he had been weeping a lot in private, and hoped Stuart would not hear him. I could well imagine, such was Madeleine's embrace of so many of us. She could be mother, sister, friend, confidant and a lot more. In the weeks after her death Stuart received scores of letters of sympathy from Ireland, England, Europe and North America. Naturally his daughter Kay was among the correspondents. Sheila Taylor of the Longship Press noted Madeleine's final holidays in both the Villa Toscana, Cannes and at Gstaad. Sheila recalled her quoting Kierkegaard: "I despair, therefore I am capable of the Good."[1] Madeleine seemed continually joyous in her latter years and seemed to have only once had doubts about her love for Stuart: "Francis has been my whole life and now I feel so dependent I feel I am an incompetent idiot, I cannot even buy a railway ticket by myself."[2] However, she admitted this with a hearty laugh. She was the great woman always by his side since 1940. In many ways she had been the making of him. Never very haughty, she craved wide recognition for his writings many of which she had brought to manuscript condition from Stuart's handwritten notebooks. Once she said to me, Francis is a true writer otherwise he would never have overcome the hardship of it. Madeleine's life was lived completely in loving Stuart, and in that was concealed and revealed in the mystery of love.

One visitor who missed her funeral was Tina Neylon; yet a bit of a godsend in that she arrived the day after from Cork, and also stayed with Stuart in his first days of grief and greatest need. She stayed over a week and made sure his friend from the racetrack, Mattie O'Neill, organised a few distracting sojourns. Neylon had known Madeleine and named her daughter Eve Madeleine in 1982. The Stuarts had invited her to stay with them during her pregnancy because of difficult personal circumstances. She first met Stuart in the late 1970s with Dr Andrew Carpenter of University College Dublin. However, Tina's main allegiances were with University College Cork. Her real connection with Stuart was through his novels that she had found in the public library at Miltown Malbay, County Cork she told me, in the Martin Brian & O'Keeffe editions. Stuart was glad of her company and she remembered when he and Madeleine had gone on holidays in the summer of 1979, she stayed and minded the house for them with her son Mikaela. She also recalled how Madeleine had said to her in the presence of Stuart once, "When I die, will you look after my lovely Francis?"[3]

As Elborn worked at the biography, Stuart began writing an essay that would clarify some of his views and present his picture of reality. He still felt obsessed enough to write on that difficult subject: What is the meaning of life? Does God exist? If so what kind of God? Madeleine and Iseult would again dominate these later works with some personal hints which give a fuller understanding of their lives.

Faillandia found disapproval from even liberal critics – such is the fear of radical change from the democratically entrenched. Similarly,

Huxley's *Brave New World* and Orwell's *1984* remain close reflections of evolving society, prophetic in their warnings, piercing in their satire and ultimately a flattering image of capitalist-democracy. So how could Stuart's utopia improve on these or take on Thomas More's *Utopia,* a book that has been interpreted as a precursor to doctrinaire Communism?

In *Faillandia* Gideon Spokane, former editor of a weekly entitled *The Tablet of Stone* returns for his wife's funeral to Failland - or Ireland - during a public referendum on adultery. On arrival he finds a job with an underground newspaper, "Faillandia". It is difficult not to associate Iseult Stuart with Lydia and Kay Stuart with Laura in the novel. Who can determine what conglomerate amorphous material goes into the make-up of any character in any novel? Stuart said this to me once. In every respect, character in a Stuart novel from this period is at best a very tenuous construct. One can read his fiction as almost completely against character construction beyond the limits that Samuel Beckett went to in the final volume of his trilogy, *The Unnameable,* where the disembodied anti-hero becomes "another discarded fictional identity of the ultimate author". Stuart was in some agreement about the validity of this method of Beckett's, he said during our discussions.

I distinctly remember Stuart's unresolved conscience in matters relating to Iseult. He was prone to guilt about the desertion even fifty years later. I mentioned the Bible letter of St Paul to him: "God has called us to peace" (1 Cor 7:15). He nodded disconsolately. He never appeared to me to be shrouded in guilt but wanted to contemplate whatever messages came from that source and to consider whether these might be useful and healthy, he said. This also came from his lack of a definitively prescriptive morality. Nor should the impression be given of a man living in a morbid weaving and unweaving of his past. Far from it, he realised the virtue of remaining or trying to remain without anxiety and calm about the future. This was what he said.

I asked him many questions - if he believed in self-forgiveness? Did he believe that he could escape the White Worm referred to in his novel *Redemption*? If not, did this make him a Calvinist who believed that one cannot avoid evil? He had no rational answers, he added, it is very difficult to judge degrees of personal culpability for evil, but the rational mind usually knows it through a bad conscience. Stuart may well have believed that the desertion of Iseult was evil, albeit on a small scale. He never admitted such but his sorrow over it was intermittent. He grappled with the big questions and to do this he said that it was fitting to judge oneself but to acknowledge that one is capable of so little. I asked him if his theology led on to predestination, which posits a God with foreknowledge of each human's fate? Or was his a God who gives humans the power of complete and total free will, such as was Hitler's to act as he wished, and Stuart's also. The God of Calvin implies blaming God for the evil in the world. Nietzsche, confronted with the problem of evil, made God responsible for "a sum-total of pain and inconsistency which would debase the entire value of being born". This concept for Nietzsche led on to atheism, which Stuart rejected. To my various questions on God Stuart was never prescriptive. Nor would Stuart accept the position of Dostoevsky's Ivan Karamazov who suffered the negation of a complete view of life's realities by dwelling on the sufferings and deaths of life's innocent victims, including children. Stuart said to me, that it is not fitting or wise to endlessly walk behind the funeral of humankind.

The problem of evil is discussed in *Faillandia*. In the novel the monk Frère Emanuel is based on a Dutch theologian Edward Schillebeeckx, so Stuart told me when I asked. The Romans are seen as the precursors of the Nazi regime with slavery, conquest of neighbouring countries and a holocaust of slaves worked to death and crucifixions. The meaning of life includes for the main characters in the novel the fact that even God's chosen son is condemned to death. At the end of the novel there is some resolution in that "apparent failure was a part of all great endeavours if they were ultimately to bear fruit". This is also why the book closes with the dejected followers of Jesus walking to Emmaus when they meet a stranger who turns out to be a manifestation of Jesus. The journey away from defeat is, according to Stuart, the beginning of the journey towards finding meaning in life.

Some writers referred to in *Faillandia* are also mentioned in *The Pillar of Cloud*, showing Stuart's continued loyalty to Robert Brasillach, Boris Wildé and Benjamin Fondane – French poets who were executed. In the case of Brasillach (1909-1945), he was shot by firing squad after De Gaulle rejected a petition for clemency signed by leading French writers Paul Valéry and François Mauriac. The Irish poet, Patrick Pearse, shot by the British in Dublin in 1916, is mentioned and the Japanese novelist Yukio Mishima who committed ritual suicide in Tokyo in 1970 "because of his country's consumerist degradation". Writers are expected to discover "alternative concepts and new insights". Genet, the French writer is seen as a more valid sexual being than Joyce whose "sexual fantasies were those accompanying masturbation, and they intensify the isolation that characterises his loveless masterpiece" (*Ulysses*). It is not only Joyce whom Stuart censures as usual. From *Black List, Section H* onwards Stuart was in revolt against the giants of the literary revival. No one is spared the lash: Yeats, Joyce, Shaw, George Russell (AE), O'Flaherty, O'Connor. Less than a decade earlier in "The Soft Centre of Irish Writing" (1976) he had written a manifesto encapsulating some of his concepts about imaginative literature and attacking the Irish Academy of Letters which "became another small institution defending establishment art and subscribing to whatever is the literary equivalent of the political tenet of not rocking the boat".

For Yeats and Shaw the academy was founded on solid principles some of which were outlined in their original manifesto: "our sole defence lies in the authority of our utterance. This, at least, is by no means negligible, for in Ireland there is still a deep respect for intellectual and poetic quality. In so far as we represent that quality we can count on a consideration beyond all proportion to our numbers, but we cannot exercise our influence unless we have an organ through which we can address the public, or appeal collectively and unanimously to the Government." Stuart rejected such a collective and did not feel unanimity with all of his contemporaries. However a contradiction would enter his ideology as a new Academy of the Arts (Aosdána) loomed on the horizon in the 1980s.

29

"Theology Not Philosophy"

I OFTEN CONSIDERED OVER THE YEARS, as our discussions intensified and also my reading and studies, how I would attempt to jot down a brief outline of Stuart's personal theology. This chapter provides a respite to make such a comment before charting the final years of his life.

One of the books that Madeleine Stuart was devoted to at the end of her life was *Jesus* by Edward Schillebeeckx. This book also influenced Stuart and through them I found myself locating a cheap edition of what was a bulky theological tract and soon read it with fascination and delight. Published in the 1970s, it would land its author in trouble with the Congregation for the Doctrine of Faith. Stuart and Madeleine became deeply attached to this dissident theological text. When Madeleine died without recourse to a cleric or minister of the faith, on 18 August 1986, Stuart dealt with the pain of his grief, spurred on by recent correspondence in the letters page of *The Irish Times*, by rereading the Schillebeeckx book. It became the impetus for his essay about the nature of reality, *The Abandoned Snail Shell*, which takes its title from the Surrealist poet, David Gascoyne. The essay attempts to confront pain, death and evil. "Faced with the problem of evil, neither philosophy nor theology has anything to say. Nor, come to that, has physics or astronomy."[1] The essay also takes its impetus from Stuart's preoccupation with Jesus and women, and with Jesus and the Agony in the Garden. "Confronted with what can be imagined as the totality of evil," he writes, "the resistance of Jesus was tested to breaking point."[2]

Among many letters to me from Stuart is one disavowing much of *The Abandoned Snail Shell*: "[It] took me a bit out of orbit and it is only Section 9, or last page, that I feel fully committed to."[3] However, it is a key work. It refers to his novel *Redemption* and is a fuller explication of his own theology which in retrospect he regretted committing to print in a polemical manner.

Schillebeeckx's *Jesus* is proof that theology is mystical without being mystifying. When Stuart writes, "Psychic health depends on liberation from assumptions imposed from outside, and in which the truth about ourselves and our real needs is known,"[4] he reiterates the vision that pain and disaster are necessary to the subconscious in order to be prepared, "for registering signals from reality".[5] One can ignore the use of "our" since he is telling the truth as he struggles to define it. There is much emphasis on the apparent failure of Jesus. The essay moves quickly through the life of Jesus up to the crucifixion. The Gospel, in its basic framework, is a biography containing four versions of the life of Jesus. The death of Jesus is prefigured by an incident when Mary Magdalene anoints his feet with costly oil, having washed them with her tears. This event with Mary Magdalene is no mere biographical incident. Jesus foretold that this event would not be left out when his life was recorded for the future. Stuart adds that Jesus "welcomed her understanding of what was ever at the back of his thoughts".[6] Stuart implies both death and sensuality. Mary Magdalene was "the woman perhaps closest to him".[7] The love story of Jesus and Mary, the greatest love story in all history perhaps, remained a sweet balm among Stuart's realms of contemplation at the edges of his novels, he said. Near the end of his life, Stuart wrote: "I have the Gospel women in mind, or in the subconscious, when depicting the main female characters in my fiction." This feature is adapted from characters such as Sonia, the prostitute in Dostoevsky's *Crime and Punishment*. Dostoevsky based Sonia on Mary Magdalene from the Gospels. She is also highly significant in Stuart's fiction as the harlot friend of Jesus.

Stuart's Jesus is unique, like that of many other writers from the evangelists on, through Ludwig Feuerbach, Ernest Renan and Albert Schweitzer. Stuart was aware of the Gnostic texts such as the *Gospel of Philip* and the *Gospel of Mary Magdalene*, found in Egypt in 1943 two years before the more famous discovery of the Dead Sea Scrolls at Qumran. Dan Brown's *The Da Vinci Code* (2003) makes use of material from the latter gospel, showing how Mary Magdalene was excluded from the inner circle which dogmatised the secondary role of women throughout the history of Christianity. "And Peter said, 'Did the Saviour really speak with a woman without our knowledge? Are we to turn about and all listen to her? Did he prefer her to us?'" Brown's novel also depicts the Vatican's further loss of authority amongst its supposedly devout flock because of extreme sects seizing power within the church, such as Opus Dei. The *Gospel of Philip* contains the following: "The companion of the Saviour is Mary Magdalene. But Christ loved her more than all the disciples and used to kiss her often on the mouth." Just as the Dead Sea Scrolls provided additional proof of the authenticity of Jesus, so also do the Gnostic Gospels, with variations in some details of his life from the historically dominant four Gospel accounts in the New Testament.

The image of Jesus has been recreated by ancient historians such as Tacitus, Suetonius and Pliny the Younger, and poets such as Christopher Marlowe who presumed a homosexual Jesus because of his special relationship with the apostle John. Oscar Wilde found the archetype of the artist in Jesus. Dostoevsky and Bernard Shaw found an ultimate anarchic critic of society. Legions of believers recognised Jesus as God. Schillebeeckx found disfavour with the Vatican and the then Cardinal Joseph Ratzinger, watchdog for deviation from orthodox Catholic theology. The book that Schillebeeckx wrote, challenges Roman Catholic dogma from the Council of Chalcedon in AD 451 up to the present times. The Council of Chalcedon defined the divine and human natures of Christ. Two centuries earlier the Church had excommunicated Arius for stressing the humanity of Jesus. Church teaching emphasises that Jesus is both Son of God and Son of Man. Schillebeeckx, by emphasising the humanity of Jesus, found himself under investigation by the Roman Catholic Church and was publicly humiliated. In modern times the Church no longer burns its heretics, as happened with Giordano Bruno and Girolamo Savonarola among others in the middle ages, but it expresses its disapproval and where possible bans "suspect" theologians from teaching at Catholic institutions. Such has been the fate in the past of some thinkers and theologians including Pierre Teilhard de Chardin and Hans Küng. Stuart emphasised his inherent interest in theology over philosophy. Theologically speaking, and as far as I can gauge, Stuart was not Catholic in his theology; indeed his belief structure was not that of the reformed churches. What was his position, then?

He is careful to point out in the essay: "I have left to one side the all-powerful God of the triumphalist-orientated Church."[8] In keeping with the tenor of his vision, he goes on: "The religion offered by Jesus in the Gospels is evidently one for individuals and not for collective or institutional man."[9] "As Carl Jung and other psychologists have recognised, a large proportion of people live in a state of weak or semi-consciousness, and these require a less personal spirituality." This is in keeping with a familiar phrase of Stuart's in conversation. Stuart expected the artist to give everything in exchange for an ultimate confrontation with reality and out of this would come the art. There could be no compromise. Stuart's standards were Olympian, but as I heard such dictates from him, I realised that he had been touched by the fire of so many of the great writers of the twentieth century.

The Abandoned Snail Shell gets its title because of the place where Jesus was crucified – "Golgotha (a place of skulls, or the abandoned shells of consciousness)".[10] Schillebeeckx is a theologian who challenges the very core of traditional Christianity by his particular focus on the resurrection of Jesus. He takes the first "appearance" of Jesus to Mary Magdalene in John 20:

> Only with Jesus's death is his life-story, in so far as his "person" is concerned, at an end; only then can our account of Jesus begin.[11]

Schillebeeckx naturally found favour with Stuart and Madeleine when he presented a radical Jesus:

> Jesus's practice of deliberately keeping company with sinners and others who were officially beyond the pale, thus extending to them the offer of salvation, was to give offence to the official representatives of the nation, it was an explosive sort of conduct.[12]

Schillebeeckx is almost bland in his characterisation of the death of Jesus as an execution of a just man wrongly accused and wrongly crucified. Schillebeeckx joins the increasing band of liberation theologians who question the bodily resurrection of Jesus:

> The resurrection in its eschatological "eventuality" is after all nowhere recounted in the New Testament; nor of course could it be, because it no longer forms part of our mundane, human

> history; it is, qua reality, meta-empirical and meta-historical: "eschatological."[13]

The latter, he defines "as everything to do with the ultimate". He concentrates on the appearances of the risen Christ or "the Easter experience". By implication, the raising of Lazarus and all post-crucifixion narratives in the Gospels are mystical. This shifts the experience directly to the sorts of writings which Stuart himself spent years studying in Glencree during the early years of his marriage to Iseult. Such reading and study may achieve the intensity which the experience of Jesus renders actual rather than virtual. Mystical writers tend not to exude evangelicalism which is often too melodramatic, rhetorical and homiletic. Mystical experience *ipso facto* is not prescriptive. Mystical writers such as Stuart categorically deny any such affirmation.

Schillebeeckx is quietly emphatic about the resurrection, even resorting to symbolism from Egyptology, including the phoenix burning back into life from its ashes. The resurrection, for Schillebeeckx, is a "manifestation" and "vision" when Jesus "makes himself seen" and bestows the peace which surpasses understanding. Schillebeeckx does not specify whether this is visual or auditory, as is mentioned in the experience of Mary Magdalene who was first to experience the phenomenon of the risen Christ. Elsewhere, Schillebeeckx implies that a physical resurrection would be located in time and a small number of people would then have to recount their experience which, in a generation or two, would have been pushed back to the realm of myth. This also ties in with the Mandelstam poem quoted by Stuart in the essay and also in his novel *Faillandia*, where he cites the first recognition of the risen Christ by a woman, which links her with Eve in Eden.

> To be first to meet the risen,
> And we should trespass to demand caresses of them,
> And to part from them is beyond our strength

In this he is close to the Gnostic interpretation of Genesis where God, Adam, Eve and the Serpent represent different parts of a single being – a quaternity that does not exclude the Divine. The Trinity of Father, Son and Holy Spirit seems to exclude humanity, who seek the divinity that is outside, whereas the kingdom of heaven is within, according to what Jesus said to his followers.

Schillebeeckx points out that the Gospel narrative is not a literal one, but is written in a secret mystical language, which is porous, fluid and capable, as Stuart says, of planting a seed in any consciousness, so the meeting on the road to Emmaus is not some actual reappearance of Christ to two disciples but an experience which is not communicable, such was its impact. It is a vision where reality is removed and a revelation occurs, with all the disturbing aspects that implies. It is the ultimate shock, which renews life because it brings the longed-for glimpse into the heart of reality. For Stuart this type of experience is most likely to occur in the presence of the lover awakening her partner to the transcendent but also can be a manifestation of pain and is, in any event, uniquely individual. All of what is here I am piecing together from many discussions that we had on these matters. Stuart also speaks of there being a master touch in the writing of the Gospels, which exalts them above the hand of mere authors.

Stuart's *The Abandoned Snail Shell* stresses the unique place of women in the Gospels and, if one looks closely enough, women have central prominence, except for Jesus or an ultra-feminist version, if it existed, which sees Jesus a daughter of God. Feminist theologians believe that the absence of women in the account of the Last Supper shows some censorship on the part of early editors of the Gospels. The great concern of most Gospel readers, who are not orthodox but who begin reading the Gospels as part of their spiritual journey, is how much has been tampered with by early churchmen for the sake of institutionalising the church. And if there are spurious dogmas falsely attributed to Jesus, what about omissions in the Bible, such as the material in the Gnostic Gospels? Elaine Pagels's *Beyond Belief: The Secret Gospel of Thomas* (2003) contrasts the canonical Gospel of John with that of Thomas and cites the well-known depiction of the latter as "Doubting Thomas". Her exegesis shows how Irenaeus, among other early church leaders, championed the Gospel of John, deeming that of Thomas to be heretical.

Stuart told me that he could abide such omissions in the belief that the outlines of the four accounts by the Evangelists are diluted so that contemplation of any scene or section will fill the psyche, regardless of what might be excluded or has been rendered apocryphal in the text by the Roman Catholic church. In other words, he looked towards the spirit of the text rather than the alleged total accuracy of chapter and verse. In some ways he saw the Gospels like the work of "a super-Tolstoy" with many characters, some presented for no more than a paragraph, a few for three or four lines or verses, but each character made singular, no matter how brief their entrance and exit. Here at last was what he saw as the miracle of character creation in a written text that could represent a viable depiction of reality.

Schillebeeckx is not triumphalist in his text:

> In bearing it [the crucifixion] Jesus was able to give point to what was pointless - death, and even to gear it into his immediate proffer of salvation. Obviously, the negativity of death was a thing that Jesus filled inwardly with his Abba experience and therein with his love for people, his prophetic loving service "unto death".[14]

Jesus cried out to God the Father using the Hebrew word for "Daddy" or "Papa" that is "Abba". Schillebeeckx goes on to expound the loss of God, the abandonment of Jesus by God at the very moment of physical and mental torture on the cross which also became the moment of spiritual terror. This spiritual terror was called the dark night of the soul by St John of the Cross.

It may be worth repeating that Stuart's contemplation of the crucifixion was a central theme, since Jesus, who proclaimed himself to be the Son of God, was publicly executed and, not least, with two criminals, giving the event an added social reality. The cowardly disciples represent humanity who can contemplate neither his agonies in the garden, hence they fall asleep, nor his subsequent execution, from which they run away. The profundity of this situation is the religious aspect in many of Stuart's novels: meditations on the pre-execution scenes of a party or supper at which the victim has full premonition of what will happen but endures the mental torture of anxiety, dread, doom and sorrow in the Garden of Gethesemane, followed by arrest, torture, imprisonment, trial, verdict and summary execution.

30

Paris – Proposal, Dublin – Wedding

AROUND THE TIME THE *The Abandoned Snail Shell* was completed, Stuart rekindled a former acquaintance with a young artist, Finola Graham. Her life before meeting Stuart could easily have been adapted from an amalgamation of his heroines. They met in the grounds of St Kilian's Deutsche Schüle in Dublin when her car broke down. This happened on the sports day, which annoyed her boss Helmut Clissmann, she told me. Madeleine Stuart worked at the same school and briefly knew Finola, who taught art. The school held an exhibition of her work in 1976. She was born in 1945 in Castletroy, Limerick, and attended Laurel Hill School, also the Alma Mater of novelist Kate O'Brien. Her father was the local doctor who allowed his daughter to set off for Paris where she was an *au pair* for six months before applying for entrance to the Musée des Beaux Arts. With the security of a scholarship in 1966, her life in Paris improved.

She became the lover of Basim, a political exile from Iraq, became pregnant and gave birth to twins, who died. It was 1968. Basim got her message and returned to see her while she fought to regain full health at the apartment of a good friend, Brigitte Chaveau. Just as she had painted a portrait of her father when he was dying, she now began a still life based on her deceased infants.

As art teacher at Clondalkin Technical School in 1970, she wanted the school to have some murals and frescoes and that caused tension with the management. Nude drawing classes also caused a confrontation when she set up an exhibition of students' work. The press became involved. Elgy Gillespie did an article in *The Irish Times*; Trevor Danker in the *Sunday Independent*; The poet Michael Hartnett gave a talk in the school and referred to Clondalkin's phallic Round Tower.

Hartnett pleaded for common sense, as did the journalist Liam Hourican. However, Finola was dismissed.

On a visit to Paris she met Yoshio Sato, a painter who later died of cancer. Back in Ireland with Colm Crone, she rented a house in Fanore, County Clare (owned by the Bishop of Galway, Dr Eamonn Casey) and founded "Fanore Mosaics". Colm produced some of his finest work in sculpture, but otherwise sought relief in alcohol. Finola, who had been to Stuart's house once for lunch in the early 1980s while Madeline was alive, wrote to him with photographs of recent work, asking him to nominate her for Aosdána. Stuart made contact and agreed to put her name forward, having seen some of her work at the St Kilian's Deutsche Schüle exhibition. However, when selections came round she did not gain enough votes and was not offered membership.

Colm Crone was still dealing with his artistic demons and their relationship became difficult. Finola gave birth to a healthy son, Daniel, in 1982. In 1986 she moved into a flat in Fatima Mansions. She read Stuart's novel *Faillandia* and wrote to him. Stuart invited her to lunch at Dundrum, where he was living on his own. She gave him the impression that she was vulnerable and weak, which she was not, she told me over a series of interviews. In fact she was making a life on her own with her son and a few friends. However, she did find it hard to manage on a low income, she admitted to me. At their first lunch, in Dundrum, Stuart could not eat the fish that she brought. When she phoned later asking about a sharp knife left behind, they both felt that it was a bad omen.[1]

She read other Stuart novels, *A Hole in the Head, The High Consistory* and *Redemption,* where she found the concept of a communal life, such as Stuart had in mind for Madeleine, Iseult and himself, to be implausible. They began seeing each other on a weekly basis. Stuart would get a number 17 bus from Dundrum to Fatima Mansions. She would visit him and Min, the cat, in Dundrum. She did not accept his paternalism, while he found nothing wrong in seeing her as vulnerable and in need of protection. He looked up to her and began reaching out to her. Max, the vicious Alsatian, a couple of doors from her flat, soon got used to the tall figure of Stuart on regular visits.

When Finola suggested a visit to Paris, Stuart was delighted. They stayed with her longtime friend, Brigitte Chauveau. Liam and Patricia Hourican travelled from Brussels and everyone went to dinner. The restaurant where they wished to book a table was full and Patricia Hourican informed the maitre d'hôtel that among their party was Ireland's greatest living writer. Suddenly they were admitted with much politesse. Among the guests at the Left Bank Brasserie Lipp was Marcello Mastroianni, who spent the evening amazed at Stuart's head. "*Quelle tête*!" the Italian film actor kept repeating.[2] He was not the first person to remark on this over the years. After the meal everyone squeezed into Hourican's station wagon and drove up the Quai St Michèle – the wrong way on the bus lane. When the car hit a bollard and one of the tyres burst, everyone had to get out and push it off the street. Then it started to snow. Stuart left them and walked off with Brigitte. As Finola walked home alone later, he got out of a taxi with Brigitte. It was a kind of reunion after a fracas, yet perhaps it presaged another bad omen. Stuart and Finola walked to Montmartre and chatted as the snow fell, each aware of private memories of previous sojourns in Paris. They began discussing the possibility of having a life together.

A day later, Stuart went to visit Sam Beckett. Beckett did not encourage Stuart's offer to visit him at the apartment in the Boulevard Saint-Jacques. Beckett lived a semi-reclusive life, separate from his wife Suzanne. Stuart found the meeting chilly at first and then both writers reached some understanding. Beckett admitted that his days were filled with trivia. It was a meeting between a prophet of despair and a prophet of hope, although Beckett and Stuart paradoxically held both visions. The meeting transcended arts and politics, focusing on the vanity of the world, he said. They dismissed the notion of themselves as stalwarts in the vanguard after Joyce, Yeats, Synge, Moore, Shaw, O'Casey and others. Clearly nothing seemed to matter for both of them.[3] Beckett would die two years later, just months after his wife, Suzanne. He spent his last years in a municipal old people's home, Tiers Temps. His room looked out on to a courtyard in which stood a single tree. It might easily have been the stage setting of *Waiting for Godot*.

On their return to Dublin, Stuart and Finola decided to spend a few days with his friend Tina Neylon, curator and administrator at Richard Wood's Fota House and Wildlife Park outside Cork City. The visit coincided with the launch of a novella, *The Lost Notebook,* by the poet John Montague. The book was dedicated to Stuart even though Montague affectionately summed him up for me as a "disturber of the peace". After the launch at the Triskel Arts Centre, a festive dinner at the Oyster Tavern was continued chez Montague at Grattan Hill. Unfortunately Stuart found himself entering upon a hostile argument with one of the guests, the sculptor John Burke, whom he accused of flirting with Finola. However, Stuart had many friends in Cork. These included the writer Seán Dunne and his partner, Trish, with whom he felt close affinity and, to a lesser extent, figures from the literary scene such as the poet and academic Seán Lucy. It was rumoured that Stuart and Tina might have made a match, and he had considered proposing to her until Finola came on to the scene. Tina knew that she and Stuart had a special relationship but she was never in love with him, whatever romantic notions he may have harboured about her.[4]

Stuart and Finola spent an otherwise quiet week at Fota House during which they were fully indulged by Tina, as a couple rumoured as soon to marry. She was not unhappy to see them leave, she told me, since she had found they were somewhat too self-indulgent. She thought Finola had extravagant tastes, not least for expensive clothes, was self-centred and demanded pampering from everyone, including Stuart. Stuart at this time seemed to dote on Finola who frolicked in the bath for him, which Tina felt breached their otherwise normal decorum as guests.

Back in Dublin to mark Stuart's eighty-fifth birthday in 1987 his theological essay was launched in the Winding Stair Bookshop and many writers came to pay homage, including Conleth O'Connor, Anthony Cronin and Paul Durcan. I remember the night as typical of the era and Stuart seemed somewhat accepting of and was even enjoying the experience. When I next visited, he showed me a letter from Paris. It was from Beckett, "Dear Francis, many thanks for *The Abandoned Snail Shell.* It was good seeing you again at last. Affectionately. Sam." *The Abandoned Snail Shell* was published by Raven Arts Press, and was widely reviewed. Stuart was interviewed on Andy O'Mahony's book programme on RTÉ radio. At 85 years of age, he had no advice to give except "perhaps never sink into some sort of complacency". He gave a brief reading of his poems in Trinity College at which John Banville read from *The Book of Evidence.* Cronin and Durcan and others read poems. Stuart received much acclaim, as was usual at public occasions in the 1980s. For his great age he was still strong and healthy, but required a hip replacement that was postponed for a very good reason: his impending marriage to Finola.

The wedding took place on 29 December 1987 at St Francis Xavier's, Gardiner Street, Dublin. Stuart wore a silver sheened suit and Finola a kimono. The atmosphere afterwards was both festive and confused in that some guests disapproved of their marrying. Dissenting voices pointed to the age gap and felt either party might have married for the wrong reasons. Was Stuart merely seeking a nursemaid for his old age? Or indulging an old man's fancy for a younger woman? Was Finola, a struggling artist, making a career-move marriage? One female guest was even heard inquiring how could a man of 85 physically satisfy a woman like Finola, less than half of his age. I remember there was a lot of conflicting energies that morning, but I looked forward to the occasion since Stuart would have a partner in life once more.

The night before the wedding Geoffrey Elborn heard an awful quarrel that led him to believe that, as a couple, they were far from the bliss of lovers.[5] Meanwhile, on the wedding day itself, the house in Dundrum swelled with people to celebrate with Stuart and Finola. Among the guests were John Jordan, Anthony Cronin, Nuala O'Faolain and Nell McCafferty, who was matron of honour. During the wedding celebration party an incident occurred between Mattie O'Neill, a long-standing friend of Stuart's, who got into a dispute with Gerard Barry, the composer, who then knocked O'Neill down with one punch. The situation was fraught, since Barry was an ordinary guest, whereas Mattie O'Neill in Dublin parlance "went back a long way". He had first met Stuart years before at Frank Ryan's reinterment in Ireland in 1978 and thereafter idolised Stuart. They also shared bygone Republican roots. Like Stuart, Mattie had been a prisoner in the Curragh during the Civil War. During that time Mattie revered Máirtín Ó Cadhain who taught him fluent Gaelic. Later he would idolise Brendan Behan and be the main speaker at Behan's funeral at Glasnevin in Dublin. However, the fight did not mar the occasion and the bride and groom were toasted before they left for a night at the Shelbourne Hotel. I was very hopeful for Stuart and Finola and their future together, and wished them well as did many others before they left the house in Dundrum.

In January Stuart went to Cappagh Hospital for a hip replacement and brought along Dostoevsky's *The Devils* to pass the time. I visited him and he said that the hospital, no matter how kind the staff, reminded him of prison and that he could not abide any institution. It was the same with hotels, he added. On his return to Dundrum he began a new novel, just as Elborn was completing the biography *Francis Stuart: A Life*. Stuart became a part of Finola's life and this helped to stabilise the early years of her son, Daniel. A collection of poems was published by Raven Arts to mark his eighty-sixth birthday, entitled *Night Pilot*, which included "A Writer's Farewell". The opening lines are as follows:

> Bury me in Fatima Mansions
> Between the wire and the wall.[6]

I first saw the poem when it appeared in *The Irish Times*. He seemed to have found a mythological urban shrine in Finola and Fatima Mansions for some months. The relationship, however, would not be a marriage in the traditional sense, as will be seen. In the meantime, Stuart, as a wedding present, offered to organise the building of a studio for her at the house in Dundrum, according to her design, and bought her a present of a restored Morris Minor, sprayed yellow according to her wishes. Later in the year he gave a talk at Coleraine University. The university had recently bought a sizeable cache of manuscripts (Stuart's) together with Kennys Bookshop in Galway. They also bought letters to Stuart from various literary persons and others, which would go to creating an archive at the university. Professor Robert Welch, as prime mover of this, saw to it that Stuart received an early emolument of £6,666, a third of the monies paid to Kennys.

In 1989, Finola's mother died and she began to spend periods in the house at Fanore in County Clare with Daniel, away from Dundrum, because Stuart found being a stepfather to a seven-year-old difficult at his age. Then she set about buying her house from Dr Eamonn Casey, whose involvement with an American, Annie Murphy, had come to the knowledge of the newspapers and would later be told in a subsequent book *Forbidden Fruit*. Annie had conceived a son while she was a guest at the Bishop's Palace recovering from a nervous breakdown. That year Stuart went to the Oxford Ireland Festival in England. Back in Dublin, as a member of Aosdána, he was the only one who refused to vote on a pro-Salman Rushdie motion against the threat of Rushdie's execution. A *fatwa* from the hierarchy of Islam, through its Iranian leader, the Ayatollah Khomeini, declared an open contract to murder Rushdie, whose novel *The Satanic Verses* was seen as blasphemous. On one of my visits to Dundrum, Stuart explained his stance on the situation as not wishing any harm to befall the author of *The Satanic Verses* but that he did not want to disavow those elements of Revelation in the Koran which he favoured.[7] Typical of him to have an individual and original position on everything, I thought. When I mentioned that I had read Rushdie's novel, he asked me to talk about it but when I offered him a loan of the book, he declined. We had leant each other some books over the years, usually novels, and our regular meetings meant that each of us could return the book in question when finished reading it.

31

Last Novel, Public Controversy

IT WAS REMARKABLE TO RECEIVE an invitation to the launch of Stuart's twenty-fifth novel, *A Compendium of Lovers,* simply because of his age and seemingly unending ability to write. He was 88 that year. The book was launched at a private occasion in Books Upstairs, College Green, Dublin along with the biography *Francis Stuart: A Life* by Elborn. On publication, the biography was heavily criticised for its shortcomings by Nuala O'Faolain who interviewed Elborn.

To all intents and purposes Stuart and Finola began living apart: Stuart in Dundrum, and Finola in Fanore in the west of Ireland. His life suddenly grew solitary except for his chocolate-point Siamese cat, Min, for whom he wrote:

> She cannot read
> She cannot write
> She cannot bark
> She will not bite
> My dear companion day and night[1]

Finola drove from County Clare occasionally to stay with Stuart. Her son Daniel found his schooling divided between the *gaelscoil* in Inchicore, Dublin and the national school in Fanore. On short visits to Dublin, Finola could get little use from the studio at Dundrum that had been completed in 1990. Stuart was disappointed that the studio that had been made for her at his expense was not being used, he told me. Her later visits tended to be on occasions when he was attending public functions. In fact, their relationship was undergoing a transformation.

Stuart, who was able to cook and care for himself, still engaged a manservant and, supported by a few loyal friends, entered a period of seclusion. He began revising a short final work of fiction, *King David Dances,* and whenever the spirit moved him, he wrote some poems. This year would see him featured in the *Field Day Anthology of Irish Writing,* with a lengthy extract from *Redemption*. However, he had entered a period when every anthology editor wanted to include some of his writings. He became friendly with Hugo Hamilton whose work he admired, and kept in touch with other contemporaries such as Derek Mahon. Mahon described Stuart to me as a moral somnambulist and secular mystic. Brendan Kennelly remembered going with Stuart to Mountjoy Gaol to meet with prisoners at a writing class organised by Vincent Sammon. Stuart's former prison experiences meant that he was immediately able to communicate on a meaningful level with those he met "inside".

In 1991, he and Finola attended the Pankowi Literary Festival in East Berlin. Once more he visited places in Berlin, a few of which remained unchanged from fifty years before. When Stuart was asked by younger writers if he was aware of the Jewish Holocaust in Berlin during the Second World War, he said, "yes". "And what was your reaction?" someone else inquired, to which Stuart replied, "I was too busy looking for the next crust of bread".[2]

A Compendium of Lovers (1990) is not a recounting of his past life, as some wags jibed, but rather a novel that comes close to being a science-fiction book. He had already, in *The High Consistory* and in The *Abandoned Snail Shell,* discussed astrophysics and speculations about the cosmos. Stuart told me that he supported Fred Hoyle's theory stated in *Faces of the Universe* that "before this cosmos there was another". Stuart was opposed to the Stephen Hawking theory of a single Big Bang that began Creation, which will eventually collapse into a black hole and nothingness will once more prevail. He could be quite dogmatic on the issue and we had many discussions of this nature. This nothingness, which Stuart told me he was able to *see* imaginatively, is close to the speculation of Martin Heidegger: "What if there was nothing at all, but since there is – why, but there need not have been a single iota of the Creation in its good and evil splendour and effulgence ... Given the natural law relating to inertia, there may have been nothing, no cosmos, no creation."[3] Heidegger's concept is akin to Thomas Aquinas and one of his proofs for the existence of God: "And if there had ever been nothing, nothing would now exist.

For no thing can bring itself into existence. But it is clear as a matter of fact that there are things."[4]

Stuart explained this theory, attributing it to a phrase in the Gospels, "Heaven and earth shall pass away, but my word shall not pass away." (Matt. 24:25; Mark 12:31; Luke 21:33). He was still searching and reading diverse material in the last decade of his life, for example Keith Floyd, United States psychologist, who contends that consciousness "creates the appearance of the brain, matter, space, time and all the rest". In *A Compendium of Lovers* Stuart writes, "Our bodies are formed out of material forged aeons ago in the hearts of exploding stars",[5] He told me once that there existed in deep space a hot black sun whose fiery side was incapable in its present trajectory of shedding its rays on us. The ellipse traced in the heavens by our earth's orbit around the sun approximates to the size of the Black Sun. If the rays of the Black Sun are ever shone upon the earth it would cause the annihilation of our planet. This may be reminiscent of the Revelation to John, known as the Book of Revelation, though Stuart was dismissive of the book's apocalyptic content. He mentioned, in a comic aside, an invented scene where his brain and imagination are entered in a competition. His brain, he conjectured, would get a recommendation, whereas his imagination would get first prize.

It is little wonder that *A Compendium of Lovers* discusses visitors from outer space and a reinterpretation of Noah's ark as spaceship, not merely a floating zoo. The Bible depicts a vision in Ezek. 1: 4-28 which has been interpreted as describing a spaceship and aliens. Stuart's novel refers to ancient temples that still have carvings or engravings in rock of "solar barques".

The novel brings together every relationship Stuart had in a blend of fact, fiction, reality, fantasy and make-believe. It is studded with reference to lovers: Osip and Nazehda Mandelstam, Mayakovsky and Lissik, Anthony and Cleopatra ("I am not entirely at ease with them"),[6] Keats and Fanny Brawne, Jesus and Mary Magdalene, Raskolnikov and Sonia (characters in Dostoevsky's *Crime and Punishment*) and "Emily Brontë, with whom I recorded, in the third person, my own fictional relationship in a novel called *A Hole in the Head*".

The problem of God comes up: "What the great chemist, physicist and mathematician had tried for was an escape from his own divine isolation, not a loveless solitude, but solitude none the less." Is there a God? Stuart poses the ultimate question. In *Black List*, quoting from Dostoevsky, H restates the ultimate, "All is allowable is only true if there's no God". Stuart's work depicts this quest for a God who may or may not exist. For him this was the knife-edge of reality. Is there a God? Either answer implies a different yet still grievous responsibility for humans. Without God the suffering, evil and pain of existence must be faced and is often beyond endurance. With God the suffering, evil and pain of existence must be faced and always kept close to God. Stuart admitted to me that he did not believe in a personal God and implied that only God knows about God.

This subject brought his discussions with me into obscure and diffuse areas of thought. For instance, Berdyaev's remark about Dostoevsky: "If the world consisted wholly and uniquely of goodness and righteousness there would be no need for God, for the world itself would be God. God is, because evil is. And that means that God is because freedom is." Those who cannot address their questions directly to Stuart will find some of his answers in *A Compendium of Lovers*. When I asked him who were the greatest minds of the century, he answered that in his opinion the three prophets of the age were Einstein, Wittgenstein and Heidegger – "two Germans, an Austrian, two of them Jews."[7]

In March of 1991 Finola's exhibition of paintings would sow the seeds of a major controversy for Stuart that would smoulder throughout the decade. I remember the exhibition well: the opening itself was a very festive occasion. However, before the exhibition in the Duke St Gallery, Dublin, Stuart had sent an invitation to Kevin Myers, well known for his "Irishman's Diary" in *The Irish Times*. The invitation was intended to mark the anniversary of a party Stuart had hosted in the Hotel Kaiserhof in Berlin on St Patrick's Day 1940. Incidentally, the Kaiserhof was Hitler's favourite hotel in Berlin. Myers's next diary in *The Irish Times* linked the Nazi atrocities against the Jews with Stuart because of his years in Berlin, the implication being that his residency was one long party. Shortly afterwards *The Irish Times* published in its letters page a comment from Prionsias Mac Aonghusa who demanded "an immediate and major apology" to Stuart. While Stuart sought legal advice about Myers's condemnation of him, he had also recently discovered that his nomination for the honour of *saoi* had been turned down by Aosdána. Ignominy, obloquy and continued vilification seemed to pursue him in public, he said to me at our next meeting, but not in any self-pitying manner. However, he found it amusing that his former Republican mentor, Peadar O'Donnell, had not received the necessary majority of votes to be honoured as a *saoi* either. "The old rebel from Donegal," he added, chuckling.

From now on Stuart would carry on a long-distance marriage with Finola, and faced old age. Yet he had the blessing of robust health. I asked him how was he so healthy for his age? I attribute it to the good wines which I drank when I could get them, he said as he poured me a drink. There was a special public birthday celebration at the Peppercanister Church in Mount Street, Dublin for his ninetieth birthday in April 1992. Stuart was photographed by Russell Banks outside McGrattan's restaurant with Finola and her son, Daniel. He was interviewed by Joe Duffy for RTÉ Radio. Questioned about his father, he gave the usual answer of having little knowledge about him. Asked if he had ever considered suicide himself, he said no. Generally the interview became lighter in tone with mention of his being barred from a pub in Dundrum which, in any event, he rarely went into, preferring to drink at home. I always welcomed the glass of wine he would offer me at his house, but knew the whiskey would eventually make an appearance, making for a formidable evening's drinking. Anyone who ever drank with him can testify to his capacity to consume considerable amounts of drink, but not on a daily basis. He was dependent on friends calling, he told me during my visits, and many did drop in on him. Lawrence Cassidy of the Arts Council, Anthony Cronin, Ulick O'Connor, Lucille Redmond, Nuala O'Faolain and Dermot Bolger who was founding a successor publishing house to Raven Arts Press with Edwin Higel, named New Island Books.

In 1994 this house would reissue *Redemption, The Pillar of Cloud* and the poetry collection, *We Have Kept the Faith: Poems 1918–1992*. Critics such as Augustine Martin in *The Irish Times* and Anthony Cronin in the *Sunday Independent* reviewed both novels and agreed on their major significance. Similarly, Hugo Hamilton, in praising *The Pillar of Cloud,* understood the alien status given to Stuart because of his own Irish/German parentage. Colin Smythe and Raven Arts Press had jointly reissued *Memorial* in 1984. By 1994 many of Stuart's pre-war novels would be listed in *Modern First Editions* edited by Michael Cole. These included *Women and God,* priced £175; *Pigeon Irish,* priced £95; *Glory,* priced £95; *Try the Sky,* priced £95. The possibility of a complete set of Stuart's novels being reissued – all 25 of them – may seem remote but with the consistent reprints of *Black List, Section H* along with a demand for a handful of his other novels, the probability may become actual. Stuart was diffident about this, he told me, because he could at last see that his work getting into print had followed an almost unfathomable pattern, one that he still contemplated with great puzzlement. He also said that he did not mind the different levels of his work, having published bad novels as well as his best.

In the winter of 1992 he joined a dozen other Irish writers taking part in a festival of literature at Grenoble. He was one of the oldest living writers in Europe as the 1990s rolled on. By 1993 he had stopped considering Fanore as a place to visit, finding the journey too long. By then Finola's visits to Dundrum were infrequent, but she could be guaranteed to come to Dublin if Stuart was attending a public occasion since he was inundated with invitations. I often met him at various public venues; sometimes looking very well, but occasionally looking his age, slightly stooped and walking slowly but always revived by a few glasses of wine. Late in December came news of the death of Timothy O'Keeffe, but Stuart lacked the energy to go to England for the funeral, he told me. O'Keeffe had gone into an eclipse of the mind before his death, Stuart said to me, in praising his very loyal London publisher and good friend.

His daughter Kay made contact in these years by letters from Durham where she lived with her husband Patrick Bridgwater. Their children, Antonia, Ben and Christina, were grown up by then. She was developing a similar disease structure to her mother, Iseult. Confronting the illness meant also confronting her past. In retrospect, she realised that she had not been as close to her mother as Ian was, while her relationship with Stuart was marred by his long-distance fatherhood. In latter years, Kay hoped that Bridgwater would buy her a cottage in Wales but that never happened. Travelling alone in England, she had had an affair.

She now tried to convey her "feelings of abandonment and desolation" to her father. She began a diary as an *aide-mémoire,* but time was running out for her. She read the Elborn biography cursorily as a further part of her rediscovery of the past and concluded that her father had tried hard to make full emotional contact with her mother, but failed because of Iseult's depressive neurosis. She forgave his abandonment of her, his only daughter, finding it impossible to explain, and concluded that part of the cause might reside in "the mystery hanging over [his] father's death".[8] When she sent him a watercolour of birds picking at rotten pears in the garden at her home, Springwell Cottage, in the summer of 1993, she had less than a year to live. Ian went to her side in her final illness as he had done with his mother. Kay died of heart disease and is buried in Durham. Stuart was too old to make the journey. Kay had suffered through the absence of a father during the formative years of her life. When Stuart went to Berlin in 1940 she was nine years old. When they next met she was 17 and thereafter communications and short periods together were infrequent. She had latterly insisted on being called Kay Stuart Bridgwater to emphasise the link with her father whom she had found so distant and obsessively present in her interior life, and yet so difficult to understand.

I know personally that Stuart went though very dark thoughts about Kay; he could never think happily about her in such a mood. It was a particular torment to him how she had been in some ways deprived of a father through the trajectory of his life. There was also the inexplicable, as he called it – his own lack of a father and yet as a father himself, his own daughter had also lived or rather endured a similar absence in her life along with the gnawing father obsession. Kay's plight was one of his great sorrows.

32

More Controversy

STUART WOULD PUBLISH A SLIM VOLUME of poems in 1995, entitled *Arrow of Anguish*. The title comes from a line in Kipling's poem, "The Rabbi's Song". This collection includes a companion piece to his much-anthologised poem "Ireland". The new poem was less adulatory than the first one:

> Ireland, I abhor thee
> From Liffey to the Lea
> With your only passion greed
> And cars your only heaven,
> Endless chat about their speed.[1]

The poems were welcome and included homage to Louis MacNiece. The volume is dedicated to Madeleine and in a newspaper interview with Eileen Battersby of *The Irish Times* he said: "In all my long life I have loved two women, Iseult and Madeleine." This seemed to exclude Finola Graham, I put to him at a meeting around that time. However, following a new edition of *Black List, Section H* from the Lilliput Press, he inscribed a copy for his wife, "to dearest Finola with all my love, May 1995 several decades after the (real) events in this narrative occurred."

Critics swooped with another reissue of the novel and adverse criticism highlighted what Jason Cowley of the *Observer* called "the darkness of the life". Cowley accepted Stuart's claim that he had never written "an anti-Semitic word", but not everyone was as forgiving. Chris Petit, in the *Guardian,* ranked him alongside Primo Levi, the Italian-Jewish writer who survived Auschwitz, and Louis-Ferdinand Céline, author of the sublimely pessimistic novel *Voyage au bout de la nuit,* seeing all three authors as dealing with the human psyche "under extremes of isolation and threat" – the phrase is Stuart's. Stuart kept four framed photographs on a window ledge in the sunroom in Dundrum that he was proud of showing to visitors: one of his father, one of Madeleine and himself, one of St Thérèse of Lisieux and one of Céline.

The publication of a new novella in 1996, his final publication, coincided with his public honour as a *saoi* by Aosdána on 21 October. The ceremony took place at the offices of the Arts Council following confusion about the date on the first occasion when the administration neglected to invite the President of Ireland, Mary Robinson, who was to give the award. The award of *saoi* involves presenting the awardee with a genuine gold torque, a replica of an ancient Celtic necklet. In keeping with the pronouncements of H, the central character in *Black List, Section H*, in an interview with Naim Attallah Stuart replied to the question: "Aren't you pleased that you are being honoured?" by saying: "Not especially, no. I don't consider it a great honour, but I will go along with it."[2] In the above-mentioned interview with Battersby of *The Irish Times*, he further amplified events from his life:

> I went to Germany for work and stayed there because I had a job and also of course because my marriage had gone wrong. There is always the impression that I married this older woman and it was awful. That marriage lasted one way or the other for twenty years, poor Iseult, between myself and her mother, she had a hard time. Whatever she saw in me remains a mystery. When I first saw her at George Russell's house, I thought she was Maud Gonne. Iseult's beauty was far softer than her mother's. By the time I met Mrs MacBride she was quite haggard.

As I began to read such interviews I could see that he had to accept the divided public image conferred on him, whereas his private life was very different as hopefully has been revealed in cameo here.

His membership of Aosdána was brought into question a year later, which resulted in a public controversy that lasted for months. At the assembly of Aosdána on Wednesday 26 November 1996, Máire Cruise O'Brien, otherwise known as Maire Mhac an tSaoi, the Gaelic poet, proposed a motion for Stuart's removal from Aosdána. Her reasons stemmed from his appearance on a Channel 4 documentary concerning the Holocaust. During the documentary its presenter, Simon Sebag-Montefiore, interviewed him about his residency in Germany during the Second World War, implying that this was anti-Semitic. Aidan Higgins (Member of Aosdána) supported Máire Cruise O'Brien's motion and her husband, Dr Conor Cruise O'Brien, the political ideologist, commentator and author, was also present. The charges against Stuart, whether or not he was a racist, were neither proved nor disproved at the meeting. In any event the meeting of Aosdána on that occasion ended because the room in which it took place was available only for a limited period. Members voted on the motion that Stuart be asked to resign for his alleged racism against Jews. With 14 abstentions, 70 opposed and only a handful in favour, the motion was dropped. Máire Cruise O'Brien, the proposer, resigned from Aosdána as a matter of principle. The debacle would continue unabated with commentators and critics either attacking or defending him.

Máire Cruise O'Brien had many issues with Stuart and not least with Aosdána finding "that no one in the secretariat was willing, or perhaps competent to conduct business in Irish – in spite of the Celtic Revival terminology in which the organisation clothed its proceedings".[3] Her bigger agenda was cogently anti-Stuart. Cruise O'Brien's position is a good one to cite as compounding the anti-Stuart position. She is indisputably a gifted poet, Gaelic scholar and translator. While she did not want to deprive Stuart of his annual stipend from Aosdána, she felt the assembly had awarded "its highest distinction to someone who unrepentantly chuckles over his role as wartime propagandist for Nazi Germany".[4] She was virulent: "We have bestowed the highest honour at our disposal on an unrepentant – indeed gloating – racist."[5] She extrapolated on Stuart, "insofar as he expresses any sympathy for Jews, it is their supposed criminality".[6] In *Black List, Section H* she found a "consistent sado-masochism"[7], agreeing with Brendan Barrington who wrote *The Wartime Broadcasts of Francis Stuart 1942–1944* (Lilliput Press) which has a scathing anti-Stuart polemic as introduction.

Back in 1971, Harry T. Moore, who proposed publication of *Black List, Section H,* commented in his preface to the first edition, "Stuart indeed never seems to have been anti-Semitic". Moore goes on to say, "He made a few radio broadcasts from Germany to Ireland, more in the manner of P.G. Wodehouse than of Ezra Pound".[8] (Wodehouse was exonerated by the British in the 1940s and made a KBE in the 1970s). The following supports Moore's claims and is from *Black List, Section H:*

> Jews struck H as having an admirably skilful way of handling the messy, jagged edged, broken mechanics of life, piecing together and straightening out what they could and making the best of what they couldn't. Concepts of perfection and abstract ideals were things they didn't indulge in, which was partly what made them reliable critics both of society and art, and, at times, original artists themselves.[9]

What could be added to this are the further comments of H in *Black List* when he explores Iseult's "attitude" to Jews and which are discussed in Chapter Ten.

Following this extraordinary meeting of Aosdána in 1997, and the press coverage, letters were published in *The Irish Times* for weeks afterwards, many of them condemning Stuart. On my visits throughout this period, Stuart would allude to the latest "sally", or talk about how "the barrage has commenced". If someone was defending him, he would say, "Did you see 'so and so' fire a volley back?" Other newspapers, such as the *Sunday Independent,* carried articles in his favour, refuting the remotest possibility of his being a racist. Louis Lentin, the film and documentary maker, vehemently accused Stuart of anti-Semitism, while writers such as Paul Durcan, Anthony Cronin and Colm Tóibín believed that calling Stuart a racist was incorrect and unjust. Other commentators believed that Stuart's residence in Germany under the Third Reich rendered him a collaborator. A continuous press furore about Stuart and anti-Semitism made the news from November until January of 1998. After this period he made a statement on national radio and in the newspapers, acknowledging the menace of Hitler and his evil doings. A suitably penitent Stuart was photographed in the press repudiating any imputed tendencies to anti-Semitism by utterly denying any such tendencies in his person or his writings.

Along with this, other critics of him believe that, taking into account his stance as outcast and outsider, he should never have become a member of Aosdána. He claimed that his reasons for accepting were financially motivated and that he always disapproved of academies for the arts. In *Black List, Section H,* H says to Iseult:

> If society honours the poet, he's tempted to say what those in authority expect from him. They wouldn't have honoured him otherwise, would they? But the poet will only come out with the sort of truth that it's his task to express when he lacks all honour and acclaim. Oh no, no honours, no prizes, or he's lost!

Similarly on the dust jacket of *A Hole in the Head* (US edition) he is quoted:

> Any consensus, I believe, is a threat to the imaginative writer, even if it is a very liberal consensus; any attitudes or ideologies that, at a given moment, take over a large section of society are bound to stifle one. There's bound to be a confrontation between them and the sort of imaginative writer I try to be.

Ciaran Benson of the Arts Council remarked during this period of controversy on "issues of contamination of art by association with ideologies of violence". He goes on:

> Only by understanding the supremely social and dialogical nature of individual consciousness can we understand how we have come to protect the artistic nature and the intellectual voice, be it maverick, mendacious, marvellous or mad.[10]

Benson does not specify whether Stuart fits the category of each (or any) of the four m-words. His statement is an example of an Arts Council member joining the ideological debate. A full engagement with that debate here would mean too lengthy a digression, if not the starting point for a completely different book. Yet the issue requires some comment. Whether Stuart is anti-Semitic or not is a very important question. His critics and admirers find themselves entrenched in opposing ideological camps. Another issue is the extent to which Aosdána is responsible for maintaining a particular political stance in the arts. Aosdána is a collective body of artists with obvious influence who decide which artists are to be representative of the State. Does this selective state-sponsored body of artists give equal autonomy to every artist in the State? Perhaps members and future members of Aosdána will come under similar scrutiny to Stuart concerning their political, moral and other affiliations.

There is the further question as to whether Aosdána's institutional framework is ideal and sufficiently vital for any group of artists. Is the very concept of an institution for artists alien to the notion of the artist? Stuart admitted that he thought the answer was a definite "yes". Aosdána can and does have a clotting influence on some of its members who become pensioned off by it and creatively barren. Then there is the contentious issue of those who are artists but are not members and whether they feel brave enough to criticise an institution to which they may secretly hope to gain admittance. Aosdána is also seen as an effective civil service for artists, while this very idea is repugnant to a minority of artists who genuinely do not want to become members, such as John Banville, who left Aosdána, and the poet Thomas Kinsella, who made the following comment in an interview: "there are individual members in the various media whom I greatly respect, but the membership as a whole is indiscriminate and filled out with people of no real talent, so that I see no point in membership as a mark of reputation or quality."[11]

Late in 1997, while the furore over his membership of Aosdána raised by Máire Cruise O'Brien was at its height, Stuart had left his house in Dundrum for a retirement home in Glenageary, County Dublin named Altadore. Here he sat out the first part of the newspaper furore and soon moved to another retirement home in Dundrum, which was coincidentally named Altamont. Altamont is also the name of the fictional Irish town in his novel *Redemption*. In both homes he kept his cat close by him day and night. However, the cat's presence was barely tolerated by matrons and staff at both institutions, he said to me during my visits. When guests called, he offered them Bushmills whiskey or Schooner Sherry, a drink that had recently become his favourite. While Finola considered that moving him to Fanore would be possible, her house there would need provision of facilities for an aged person whose ability to walk was becoming more impaired. She therefore considered having the house in County Clare enlarged with a room for him. Ian Stuart eventually rescued his father from retirement homes in January 1998 and brought him to Laragh from where Stuart had set out almost 50 years previously for Berlin. Stuart had come full circle, as it were.[12]

One need not read too much significance into the return of the father to the son's house. The situation was domestic and familial, I recall, and also strangely moving to witness. Stuart had returned "home". He had found many other homes during his life but, on this occasion at Laragh, felt that time might be running out both for him and his cat, he said to me. He lived in the annexe of Laragh House with a view of Laragh village, not far from the castle with haunting memories of Iseult and their life there in the 1920s and 1930s. Laragh House was a combined venture between Ian and his second wife, Anna Buggy Stuart. Stuart settled into the regime, fully alert for his age and inclined to worry about his limping cat, but otherwise oblivious of the infirmities of old age. His bedside books I noticed were the Gospels, in the Fontana paperback edition, *Good News for Modern Man,* a selection of Heidegger's writings, and *The Oxford Book of English Verse,* edited by Arthur Quiller-Couch. He was lively, and eager some days for a short spell of exercise, Ian told me. Glad of visitors, he awaited his ninety-sixth birthday that was planned for Fanore if a suitable apartment was ready; otherwise it would be held at Laragh.

Ian, while well into middle age himself, held his father in fitting love and affection. He refrained from making any favourable comment about his father's *Black List, Section H* and remained particularly hostile to it because of its depiction of his mother. However, he admired his father's poems. He worked, when able, on his own woodcarvings and other sculpture. He had found favour as an artist in Ireland as early as 1962 when James White, Director of the National Gallery, hailed him as "a sculptor of our time". His conviction for possession of cannabis in Holland in 1994 meant adverse publicity, though he was sentenced in absentia. He felt this biased certain galleries in Dublin from exhibiting his more recent work.

Ian was interested in preparing a selection of his mother's writings for publication. While Stuart was staying at Laragh, he got hold of Iseult's diary and began tearing it up into pieces until Ian rescued it. The diary was still just about readable, but needed careful handling to sellotape the many torn pages together.[13] The fact that Stuart should attempt to destroy it revealed the power of Iseult to haunt him and his private thoughts. Her presence does not, however, permeate the pages of *King David Dances* (1996).

King David Dances is a novella dedicated "For Madeleine in Memoriam". It is a fictional story about a friend from Stuart's past, Lodsi Dormandi. Madeleine and Stuart lived with Dormandi, his wife and daughter in Paris for over a year until their move to London in 1951. In the novella, Dormandi becomes a fictional mask for Stuart to write a "Song of Songs and, at times, Dirge of Dirges". *King David Dances* is set in Jerusalem and this gives Stuart licence to refer to and quote from the Old Testament prophets. Lodzi enters a crisis, because of the loss of his cat, Sabrina, and the state of the world. His interest in Martin Heidegger ("I'm in awe of him") parallels Stuart's own.[14] Heidegger's birth in Messkirch, in the Black Forest, also the place of his death, is close to Dornbirn where the Fusseneggers (who also appear in the novella) helped Stuart and Madeleine when they were refugees. While Heidegger made public declarations in support of Hitler for some months in the 1930s, as rector of Marburg University, he refused to allow the works of Jewish thinkers such as Husserl and Bergson to be struck off the philosophy course. Stuart was excited by Heidegger's comments about the conquest of death, "death did not establish an impenetrable frontier," according to the German philosopher. Stuart himself, when interviewed by Naim Attallah, said: "It's beyond me to say yes or no to an afterlife. There is no point in doing so. In my long life I have had some very intense memories of far back happenings, and I can't see them being erased completely, even after I die."[15]

Heidegger reveals himself as a philosopher who was actually a frustrated poet. Stuart remarked on this in discussions with me, particularly when one reads Heidegger's study of Hölderlin's poem "Heimkunft". His writings on Stephan George, Celan and Rilke brought him to the conclusion that some poems were "a life-long meditation on death and dialogue with the dead", leading to the postulation that "death was a vital part of Being but also that loneliness, that normally dull angst that waxes and wanes, comes from our shutting off of the dead". Stuart adopted this concept of contemplating humanity as an outpost of the null in a key phrase of Heidegger's: "It is only by reason of the wonder – that is to say, through the manifestation of the Nothing – that there arises the 'Why'?" Stuart told me that this capitalised "Why" went beyond any nihilism in Heidegger's thought. I admit that these are not easy concepts to grasp, but since they preoccupied Stuart they need to be included.

The critique of the consumer society reaches its peak for Stuart and this is one of the great strengths of the novella. The narrative is compelling in its description of an obsessional cat lover in pursuit of his lost cat. When he questions himself about life, the answer is, "We are here to 'tend the miracle', by which I mean treasure what is given, including the pain, provided it doesn't exceed our nervous and mental endurance".[16] I remember once I asked Stuart, "Why are we here?" His reply was, "We are here to tend the miracle". Stuart's personal emphasis to me at our many meetings related to Martin Heidegger. Not the Heidegger lured by the power of National Socialism, he was careful to add. He believed that Heidegger became a National Socialist in order to attempt to cope with his inner chaos. Stuart defiantly singled out the man's writings without regard to his political affiliations, which he said was a desperately mistaken phase in his life.

He often recommended Heidegger to me since the philosopher had been responsible for certain personal insights which he had achieved. Stuart told me that the union of reality and imagination in the psyche produces fiction as the best vehicle to reflect the experience of what it means to be alive. Pure reason does not have the ability to reflect reality with any great accuracy.

33

County Clare

MEANWHILE, STUART'S NINETY-SIXTH birthday approached with no definite plans by his son Ian who continued to house his father. Finola's visits from Clare were almost weekly as she administered the renting of rooms at Stuart's Dundrum house. These years had found Daniel, Finola's son, enjoying a better relationship with his stepfather, Francis Stuart.

RTÉ screened a documentary made by Ted Dolan to coincide with his birthday. In the late 1960s, Dolan had made another film when Stuart was asked to revisit Berlin. The programme, screened in 1998 and advertised as "Francis Stuart; Portrait of H", was actually titled *Undercover*. Besides documentary facts of Stuart's life, the content was already well publicised through the hostility to Stuart by former Aosdána member, Máire Cruise O'Brien. Stuart was supported by many friends, all members of Aosdána: Bill McCormack (Hugh Maxton), Anthony Cronin, Paul Durcan and Dermot Bolger.

On 2 May in *The Irish Times* Eddie Holt commented on the programme in general and noted that Máire Cruise O'Brien's attempt to have "Francis 'Germany Calling, Germany Calling' Stuart expelled from the club was like seeing Irish McCarthyism fail. The club is, of course, a self-perpetuating elite, suspiciously fond of its self-generated gravitas and cod symbolism." Stuart's life once more infringed on public affairs of State since he had become a protagonist from the position of outsider, or traitor as his detractors viewed him.

Stuart could not accept an invitation to the Arts Council headquarters on the 1 May 1998 for reasons of age. The great occasion was Seamus Heaney's receiving the honour of *saoi* from Aosdána. Having discussed this situation at Laragh House with me, Stuart handed over a copy of *The Oxford Book of English Verse* with the words: "Here, take this, if you need it, I don't want it." He had cheerful, if censorious, comments on Quiller-Couch's prefaces to the book. When reminded that he had a copy of the *Oxford Book of English Verse* with some other belongings in his attaché case on leaving Berlin with Madeleine in September 1944, he said: "Maybe when your biography is published I will read about my life and my writings. Since I've told you about all my life, I've forgotten lots of it." He laughed and then looked out of the window at the trees and when he did not say anymore, it was time to thank him, say goodbye and go.[1]

Domestic matters in Laragh made his continued residence with Ian and Anna untenable so that, at the start of June, Finola moved him back to the house in Dundrum. Ian had also been the witness of Stuart's critical faculty. When Ian showed him a piece of his woodcarving, Stuart retorted: "Take away that thing, it's grotesque." For all that, Ian felt a deep bond with Stuart and remarked to me: "I wouldn't run down my father, the poor old thing." Stuart had lived for five months with Ian and Anna and they found him beyond their care long term. He could still walk with the help of a Zimmer frame. Sometimes, more daringly, he walked using only a stick. At his age, he could still dress and undress himself. His shaving difficulties were solved with an electric razor.[2]

He readjusted to the house in Dundrum, happy in the knowledge that his cat was still well and limped behind him wherever he went. At nights Stuart and the cat slept together. When Finola left for Fanore in County Clare to inquire locally about accommodation for Stuart, her son Daniel and a cousin stayed in Dundrum. Daniel cooked Stuart his daily porridge, made to a specific consistency with cream poured on top. Stuart was visited by Ulick O'Connor, Patrick Cooney of the *Independent* and Paul Durcan, and I stayed a few days to show an early draft of this book for critical comment. Stuart was pleased that I would keep my promise to complete the book as a mark of our friendship. Around this time, Judge Patrick McCartan offered to bring Stuart into his household in Wicklow and while the arrangement appealed to Stuart, it did not come to pass.

Stuart was quite evasive when a health nurse arrived with questions about his hygiene. When asked if he ate his breakfast each morning, he replied, "What do you think I do with my breakfast?" He recalled for the nurse his next-door neighbour's comments when she had read about his life during the recent controversy: "Oh Francis," she said, "I never knew you were such a gad-about!" In mid-June, Stuart complained, with good humour, about the wallpaper in the sitting room where most of his daytime hours were spent. Next morning, when he made his cautious way into the room, he found it brightened with white paint rolled over the wallpaper during the night by myself and my partner, Maeve McCarthy. Stuart, on seeing the zealous actions of his guests, felt that to have taken him literally was an overreaction, but he was not in the least put out by our alterations to his room.

On 13 August Finola packed his clothes and a few books and set off for Fanore with Stuart holding the cat on his lap. Outside the town of Moate the exhaust pipe of her yellow Morris Minor snapped, bringing them to a noisy halt with sparks flying into the wind. They alerted a local garage and got towed into town. Finola asked Stuart to bide his time with the cat and the newspaper. Meanwhile the parts of the damaged pipe were brought into the garage for welding. In the midst of the work Finola and the mechanic heard someone approaching. Stuart was making his way into the hazardous interior of the garage workshop, limping and prodding the Zimmer frame ahead of his faltering steps, followed by the cat.[3] The mechanics began talking about engines and cars. Stuart was delighted, telling them about his motorcycle from the days of the Black and Tan war before he progressed to a Peugeot, an Opel, and then a Buick before the outbreak the Second World War.

Fanore is on the west coast of Clare with a view of the Aran Islands when the day is clear. Stuart's apartment had a view of the islands. Closer in, the sandy beach was fringed in black rock and, on tempestuous days, washed in mountainous waves that rolled in from the Atlantic. He was in fact six kilometres from the village in the townland of Crumlin, which is ten kilometres from Lisdoonvarna and 18 kilometres from Ballyvaughan. It seemed strange that here, more than likely, he would end his natural life – in fact an extraordinary life which spanned the century, beginning with that notorious movement since known as the Celtic Twilight, and concluding with that economic boom known as the Celtic Tiger. Nothing linked Stuart to Clare except that his wife lived a mile away and visited daily. Otherwise he was looked in on by Christina O'Connor, a retired nurse, and her husband, Ambrose, whose house adjoined the apartment. Here in the outer limits of Ireland he would end his days. I made a number of visits and, because there was an extra room, was able to stay with him. He had some of his novels, including a first edition of *Redemption*, published by Gollancz with a quotation from Compton Mackenzie on the yellow fly cover. *The White Hare*, his novel of the 1930s, opens in this part of Ireland and ends with Hylla Canavan mourning the loss of her lover in a shipwreck. Stuart walked without the Zimmer frame, an adventurer to the end. His consumption of Schooner sherry decreased as he settled into Fanore, but the porridge and cream remained a necessity.

Here he began a diary, writing a header on consecutive pages, "most secret and confidential", which reflected his final preoccupations and thought patterns. When I asked some remaining questions on visits during autumn of 1998, he said that his days were spent in enforced contemplation, which was most desirable since, if he had his life to live over again, he might have chosen to be a contemplative monk in an enclosed order. Another day he said: "I'm an Australian sometimes. Then I feel Meath is my home and also North Antrim." His infrequent jottings in the diary mentioned repeatedly the need of a clock and his worries about the cat. Numerous times his wife supplied him with a clock that he broke, perhaps from boredom, she said to me. His notes included a title for a new novel, "The Cat's Silent Planet". His thoughts ranged from thinking about favourite drinks and favourite menus, including steak tartare, to the pending libel suit against Kevin Myers and *The Irish Times*.[4]

Often in his mind were, "my dear, dear lost ones: among whom Madeleine, Iseult". He reiterated how he had come to value Finola very much and kept her portrait of him at the apartment, along with his son Ian's ink drawing of a horse. His religious contemplation included repeating the short prayers – "Bestow on us, O Lord, a gentle, contrite, wondering and tender heart"; "I look up to the hills whence comes my strength,"; "Before Abraham was I AM," – and his guiding principle of abandonment to divine providence. To be with him in those days was almost more extraordinary than at any other time in our friendship because often his silences were to me immensely peaceful. I had stopped my endless questions and talk as we entered a different realm of friendship. He could still have his sleep disturbed by nightmares, he confided in me one morning over breakfast as we looked out at the sea. He had frightening dreams about being arrested, firing squads and other executions or vast tableaux of mass destruction of human life from the war. He sometimes wondered whether, with little or no conversation or company, day in day out, his lifestyle would be endurable. Before Christmas, cards arrived from constant friends and Finola bought him a book, *Visions of Heaven: The Mysteries of the Universe Revealed by the Hubble Space Telescope,* by Tom Wilkie and Mark Rosselli. Christmas also brought news from Paris in a letter sent by Jean-Pierre Sicre of Éditions Phébus about arrangements for a French translation of *Black List, Section H*. Ambrose O'Connor put up coloured lights on a tree outside his window for a festive touch.

In the new year of 1999 he was invited by Counsellor Richard Conroy of the Dun Laoghaire Poetry Now Festival to come as special guest. In March he was booked into the nearby Hotel Pierre and duly arrived by train and taxi. The poet, nearing his ninety-seventh birthday, was helped to the rostrum where he made no speeches but read a few poems, amongst them, "The Great":

> The great are not great now, the good are not good
> All who are named, who appear in the eye of day
> Are touched by the rot, are lipped and lapped by the flood
> Of our downfall. Black is the hidden ray
> Of the good and great in our time. Unknown
> Are their voices, their faces are turned, do not shine.[5]

Before reading his much-anthologised poem "Ireland", he admitted he was well and truly sick and tired of it. After the poetry reading, a crowd of us, including Anthony Cronin and Patrick Galvin, went back to his hotel for a celebration. I found it extraordinary to be carousing with a writer in his late nineties - my friend Francis Stuart.

When he braved the return journey to his apartment in Fanore, his diary notes continued with the following: "Mystery I'd like to have cleared? Suicide of my father." His ninety-seventh birthday was a subdued affair at Fanore. Finola bought a bottle of champagne and insisted on making some kind of a party. Patrick Cooney had a feature in the *Guardian* on Stuart that almost coincided with the birthday. The Cooney piece had become synonymous with the constant press attention given to him, part of the relentless quest for an understanding of the man and the enigma. Visitors included Paul Durcan, Ulick O'Connor with Judge Pat McCartan, Anthony Cronin with Anne Haverty. Maeve McCarthy visited and made preparations to paint a final portrait of him which was completed the following year and exhibited at the RHA in May 1999. For some reason it hung next to the Archbishop of Dublin, Desmond Connell, in the gallery at Ely Place.

In mid-June he was at the High Court in Dublin for the libel action against *The Irish Times*. Prior to the court hearing he visited his barrister, Adrian Hardiman SC. Both journeys from Fanore to Dublin were made easier by a chauffeur-driven Mercedes provided by local people for Stuart, Finola and Christina O'Connor. When the case went to court, senior council for *The Irish Times*, Mr John Gordon, retracted in full the remarks made by Kevin Myers in "The Irishman's Diary" of October 1997 which had suggested that Stuart's writings contained anti-Semitism. The libel was settled with Justice Peter Kelly's intervention in favour of Stuart who, outside the Four Courts after the half-hour proceedings, told RTÉ's Colm Connolly that he felt redeemed. He could also expect damages of between £10,000 and £20,000. Newspapers in Ireland and England reported the event. The London *Independent* referred to the situation as "one of the most bitter literary rows of recent years".

Not long after returning to Fanore he fell and was rushed to hospital in Galway. In casualty he was found to be in shock but had broken no bones. A week later he was back in his apartment in cheery mood, remarking on the by now familiar view of what he called "the united islands of Aran". His life once more entered the near monastic daily routine with the added stricture of moving about with the Zimmer frame. He drank less sherry and remained quite isolated but for Finola's visits. His appearance in the newspapers and on TV over the libel action brought some curious locals, but soon again his solitary life resumed. He longed to hear the music of the spheres again which he said he had heard, but, meanwhile, in moments of fantasy, he hoped to go to one of the Aran Islands with his cat and a crate of sherry.

In July the translator of *Black List, Section H,* Isabelle Chapman, wrote from Paris enclosing a sample of her version of *Liste Noir*, published eventually by Éditions Phébus in 2000. Stuart was pleased at the prospect of a French edition of his most famous novel. In August, he fell out of bed in an attempt to reach a pen on his bedside table. Though still able to dress and undress himself, his daily routine began to depend more and more on the energies of his wife and Christina O'Connor. From then on his days at Fanore were spent in a prolonged isolation which led him, in moments of weary gloom, to look on the place as the darkest side of the moon, he told me one night over our pale sherries.[6]

In October 1999 more controversy hit the headlines in the *Sunday Independent* when Anthony Cronin and Dr Conor Cruise O'Brien publicly debated Stuart and anti-Semitism, on this occasion with reference to his novel *Julie*. Dr O'Brien referred to a thesis by Dr Raymond Burke that claimed that Goldberg, a character in the novel, was portrayed in a negative manner. Cronin maintained that Goldberg was, in fact, treated with much sympathy in the novel. I decided to make a neutral comment which was printed by the *Sunday Independent* the following week. Stuart himself, well used to controversy, held his silence as the millennium approached, certain of the continuing unfolding of his destiny. That was the way he put it in our discussions.

Meanwhile he wrote: "I wait each day with nothing to do but live in imposed contemplation for the final revelation at Fanore." Occasionally he made notes in huge childish handwriting, the sentences often incomplete. One of the final entries he wrote was, "a great privilege to be living now". It is easy to imagine in the swirl of his thought that the people mentioned in his life and writings floated in and out of his memories and into his dreams, including Iseult and Madeleine and a man on horseback – a jackaroo herding sheep in Queensland, Australia during a drought. The man is Henry Irwin Stuart. He is beset by heat and fatigue. His misery becomes agonised as the horse turns and he is facing the sun. The horse – the image is apocalyptic, dramatic, fictional, imaginary and real – rears because of its rider's tremendous fear and anxiety. The shouting of Henry Irwin Stuart is lost as thousands of sheep surround him. Then begins the journey to the asylum and, with his spirit broken and with approaching insanity, he chooses to die by his own hand. The next scene is the long sea voyage from Australia to London. Among the passengers are Lily, Nellie Farren and an infant affectionately known as Harry who was christened Henry Francis Montgomery Stuart.

34

A New Century

BY THE AUTUMN OF 1999 STUART'S residence in the apartment at Fanore alongside the O'Connors was putting a great strain on all concerned. It was not so much the cold spell, with which he could cope because of central heating, but his inability to walk and his stubborn resistance to using sticks or the Zimmer frame. By this stage it was apparent that his sense of place was forsaking him and that he was entering the early stages of senility. A local priest, Father Michael Reilly, visited regularly to give him Holy Communion and soon realised that he had a profound interest in the Gospels. Meanwhile, the health nurse, Kathleen Malone, surveyed the situation and recommended that Stuart be moved to a nursing home or hospital for a fortnight, in order to give the carers some respite.

Nurse Malone found Stuart a place in a nursing home in the first week of December and he waited for an ambulance to take him to Ennis where he would be under the care and attention of Dr Boland and the nursing staff. For the last time he would see the yard at the O'Connors with their crowing rooster, clucking chickens and especially the peacock who sometimes went into the apartment when Stuart called him. This peacock was wont to stalk the French doors at different times each day, tapping with its beak on the glass much to Stuart's delight. When Christina had new chicks hatching, she would bring them in to show him and he would ask her to lay them down beside his stove near the heat. Stuart, according to Christina, was always content with simple things like his breakfast and having the fire lit to augment the central heating. "A fire was like a crock of gold to him," she said to me.

When the ambulance arrived, nobody thought he was leaving Fanore for the last time. He was put into Unit Four at St Joseph's

Hospital on the Lifford Road in Ennis. To say he was happy there would be incorrect. When Christina had asked him once in Fanore if he was happy, he replied, "Happy? I'm happy nowhere." However, he had to settle into the hospital ward which he shared with seven others, none as old as he, but all aged and ailing. In the fortnight before Christmas he was in good health as Christina discovered on her weekly visits. Finola, too, noticed the difference and immediately wanted to bring him back to the apartment in Fanore. Nurse Malone advised against it since he was incontinent and bedridden. With the onset of Christmas, Stuart contracted the flu bug. On the advent of the millennium there was a serious flu epidemic. Hospitals began to feel the pressure on bed space, Ennis no less than other places.

Stuart's Christmas and New Year were spent in the clutches of the virus and he began to deteriorate, as could be expected for a man of his age, 97. In a home video made by Ambrose O'Connor, Christina's husband, he predicted that he would live to be 98. Give or take a few weeks, he was correct in his final prediction. Tina Neylon visited him on the last Sunday in January and noticed his weight loss and increasing debility. While he recognised her immediately and gave his wonderful smile of recognition, his speech was inaudible, she told me. When Christina visited the following Monday she was so taken aback that she had to face the fact that he was declining rapidly. Christina was invited by a nurse to feed Stuart but she was wary because the virus had entered his lungs. When he took some food and immediately vomited it up, his pallor changed to ashen grey. Then he erupted in such a coughing fit that she felt he might die.

The following day Finola and Christina visited with the cat and stayed all night by his bedside. The cat snuggled in beside her master. When Christina was leaving, the nurse said she would enquire as to how the cat might be looked after at the hospital, so that Stuart could have his pet nearby. No sooner had they got back to Fanore than the hospital phoned to say he was sinking fast. When they arrived, Stuart was very weak and they put the cat in beside him. Around four in the morning his breathing was very loud and strained and Finola held his hand. His eyes were closed. After half past four his breathing became so soft and gentle that they looked on him with less trepidation. Suddenly his pallor changed and just on his last breath he opened his eyes so wide, as if at last he had seen something revelatory, Christina told me. His face and features shone in a peaceful repose as he died, she said. It was ten to five on 2 February 2002.

On the confirmation of death he was brought to the mortuary and later that day moved to Finola's house in Fanore. The cat found him strange as he was laid out on a bed in the living room downstairs, which faced the Atlantic and its pounding waves. The cat licked his face and eventually curled up on the end of the bed. Next day, despite Christina's offer to take care of the cat for the remainder of its life, Finola contacted the vet in Ennistymon who came and put it to sleep. Then it too was placed in the bed beside its master.[1]

As soon as I heard the news, I travelled west from my flat in Dublin. Slowly the news filtered out to the press and media. Stuart's death was announced nationwide and beyond. A wake was organised for Thursday night in Finola's house with food and drink. She wanted the party atmosphere of a well-behaved gathering in order to give him a good send-off. Many locals called in to see Stuart laid out in his brown shroud, looking like an abbot, with the cat tucked under his arm in the white bed linen. People sat and talked in the rooms and at eight o'clock went to St Patrick's Church for prayers. All except Ian, who stayed with his dead father. Father Reilly was perplexed at the fact that the remains were not brought to the church. However, he officiated and announced the funeral details for the following morning.

Next morning in the very bracing cold, a small procession walked behind the hearse, including Finola, Stuart's stepson Daniel, Stuart's son Ian and his wife, Anna, children and grandchildren and other mourners. The church was overcrowded and packed to the door. Ashling Drury Byrne, the cellist, played the music and Father Reilly said Mass at one o'clock. The President Mrs McAleese was represented by her aide-de-camp, Commandant Dermot O'Connor, and the Taoiseach Mr Ahern by his aide-de-camp, Captain Michael Kiernan.

Stuart's descendants were headed by Ian, Anna and his granddaughters and grandsons. The main tributes and speeches were by writer friends and acquaintances from Aosdána. Offertory gifts were brought to the altar in procession and laid on the coffin, including some of Stuart's novels, bread and wine, his field glasses and the cat basket. Ulick O'Connor read a poem and recalled his friend's seraphic smile. Nell McCafferty recalled Stuart's love for Madeleine, and commented on the horrors he had witnessed in his life. She had been Finola's bridesmaid at their wedding and remembered Stuart's fondness for steak tartare and wine, his love of cats and his deep need for the love of a woman. Paul Durcan read from Keats's "Ode to a Nightingale", a favourite of Stuart's. Anne Haverty read her poem written to Stuart. Anthony Cronin quoted from the novel *Redemption* and from Stuart's poem, "The Great". Finola referred to her art exhibition note written by Stuart and read Auden's love poem, "Lullaby".

The scene was sombre, but not tearful, in the yard outside the church, as friends met, having travelled from various parts of Ireland and abroad. The hearse moved off in slow procession for the longish journey to Craggagh cemetery, past the Burren Riding School where a posse of horses lined up along the fence as if at the start of a race. The coffin was shouldered along the uneven terrain of the cemetery to the shallow graveside that faces the Atlantic Ocean. I was one of those who lifted the coffin. Father Reilly recited prayers for the repose of the soul of the deceased. Stuart's poem "Ireland" was recited by Lara, his granddaughter, and laments were played on the flute as the coffin was lowered and the grave filled in. Here, finally, Stuart was laid to rest.

A small crowd gathered in O'Donoghue's pub across from Craggagh Post Office, not far from the cemetery. Meanwhile Finola's sisters, Moira and Nora, helped to feed the multitude who arrived from the pub. Over the course of the night people discussed the enigma of Stuart's life and his writings. Some thought his life was like some lengthy Russian novel with all its journeys and intense twists and turns of events. But there were still questions about Stuart, including his burial with the cat: Did it reflect some ancient Egyptian rite? They talked of his seemingly haphazard ending in Fanore, a town he had never been connected with except for in the last year of his life as its oldest and most famous citizen; of his life in the cities of Dublin, London, Paris and Berlin. There were perceived portents: even in the date of his death, 2/2/2000; and in a village rather than a city, a village whose name in Gaelic, *fáinne ór,* means the golden ring; and in the day of his death, 2 February, a legendary birthday in Irish literature, that of his old adversary, James Joyce.

His son Ian could shed some light on his father's life by saying that as a writer he had been obsessed with art beyond everything else. Others found this an unacceptable excuse for the excesses of his life. Some said that he was more obsessed with theology and the mysteries of religion. Many felt that his Berlin years would never erase the slur of fascism and the Third Reich which contaminated his reputation as a writer. Everyone knew people who considered him a villain and a traitor. While arguments were put in favour of his being chiefly a poet, others felt his greatest achievement was as a novelist and many believed that he had blended both into what was best in his books.

As the night wore on for the revellers at the wake of Francis Stuart, the debate and the controversy continued: how he had witnessed the breakdown of civilisation during the Irish Civil War and the Second World War, glimpsing the full release of evil into Europe by the Nazis, and yet his spirit had never given in to pessimism, far from it, since many found humour, solace and counsel in his friendship. When some mourners began to leave and return to their own lives, naturally saddened at his loss, a few stayed over with Finola who, the next day, went to Galway for the opening of her exhibition at the Logan gallery.

Days later *The Irish Times* gave his place of death, incorrectly, as Finola's house in Fanore, thus lending further credence to Stuart's dictum that all writing tends towards fiction and every picture of reality is ultimately depicted in fictional terms.

Works by Francis Stuart

Novels

(Translations of novels into French, German, Hungarian, Italian and Spanish are here abbreviated: TF, TG, TH, TI, TS. They are referred to in the text appropriately.)

We Have Kept the Faith, Oak Press, Dublin, 1923

Women and God, Jonathan Cape, London, 1931

Pigeon Irish, Gollancz, London, 1932; Macmillan, New York, 1932 (TF)

The Coloured Dome, Gollancz, London, 1932; Macmillan, New York, 1933

Try the Sky, Gollancz, London, 1933; Macmillan, New York, 1933

Glory, Gollancz, London, 1933; Macmillan, New York, 1933

Things to Live For: Notes for an Autobiography, Jonathan Cape, London, 1934; Macmillan, New York, 1935

In Search of Love, Collins, London, 1935; Macmillan, New York, 1935

The Angel of Pity, Grayson and Grayson, London, 1935

The White Hare, Collins, London, 1936; Macmillan, New York, 1936 (TG)

The Bridge, Collins, London, 1937 (TG) (TI)

Julie, Collins, London, 1938; Knopf, New York, 1938

The Great Squire, Collins, London, 1939 (TH) (TS)

Der Fall Casement, Hamburg, Hanseatische, translated by Ruth Weiland, 1940

The Pillar of Cloud, Gollancz, London, 1948; Martin Brian & O'Keeffe, London, 1974; New Island Books, Dublin, 1996 (TG) (TF)

Redemption, Gollancz, London, 1949; Devin-Adair, New York, 1950; Martin Brian & O' Keeffe, London, 1974; New Island Books, Dublin, 1994 (TG) (TF)

The Flowering Cross, Gollancz, London, 1950 (TF)

Good Friday's Daughter, Gollancz, London, 1952 (TF)

The Chariot, Gollancz, London, 1953 (TF)

The Pilgrimage, Gollancz, London, 1955

Victors and Vanquished, Gollancz, London, 1958; Pennington Press, Cleveland, 1959

Angels of Providence, Gollancz, London, 1959

Black List, Section H, Southern Illinois University Press, 1971; Martin Brian & O'Keeffe, London, 1975; Penguin Books, London, 1982; Lilliput Press, Dublin, 1995; Penguin Books, London, 1996 (TF)

Memorial, Martin Brian & O'Keeffe, London, 1973; Raven Arts Press (Dublin)/Colin Symthe (England), 1984

A Hole in the Head, Martin Brian & O'Keeffe, London, 1977; Longship Press, USA, 1977

The High Consistory, Martin Brian & O'Keeffe, London, 1981

We Have Kept the Faith: New and Selected Poems, Raven Arts Press, Dublin, 1982

States of Mind, Raven Arts Press (Dublin)/Colin Smythe (England), 1984

Faillandia, Raven Arts Press, Dublin, 1985

The Abandoned Snail Shell, Raven Arts Press, Dublin, 1987

Night Pilot, Raven Arts Press, Dublin, 1988

A Compendium of Lovers, Raven Arts Press, Dublin, 1990

Arrow of Anguish, New Island Books, Dublin, 1995

King David Dances, New Island Books, Dublin, 1996

Pamphlets

Nationality and Culture, Sinn Féin Árd Chomhairle, Dublin, 1924

Mystics and Mysticism, Catholic Truth Society of Ireland, Dublin, 1929

Racing for Pleasure and Profit in Ireland and Elsewhere, Talbot Press, Dublin, 1937

Plays

Men Crowd Me Round, Abbey Theatre, Dublin, 1933

Glory, Arts Theatre Club, London, 1936

Strange Guests, Abbey Theatre, Dublin, 1940

Flynn's Last Dive, Pembroke Theatre, London, 1962

Who Fears to Speak, Liberty Hall, Dublin, 1970

Selected Articles

"A Note on Jacob Boehme", *To-morrow,* editors Stuart/Salkeld, 1924

"In the Hour Before Dawn", *To-morrow,* editors Stuart/Salkeld, 1924

"Frank Ryan in Germany", *The Bell,* November, 1950

"Frank Ryan in Germany " (Part II), *The Bell,* December, 1950

"Selection from Berlin Diary", *Journal of Irish Studies,* January, 1976

"Berlin in the Rare Oul' Times", *Irish Press,* 1 September 1989

Select Bibliography

After the War is Over (Introduction by Francis Stuart), Raven Arts Press, Dublin, 1984

Alldritt, Keith, *W.B. Yeats: The man and the milieu*, John Murray, London, 1997

Allegro, J.M., *The Dead Sea Scrolls,* Penguin, 1957

Attallah, Naim, *In Conversation with,* Quartet Books, London, 1998

Autobiography of a Saint: Thérèse of Lisieux, translated by Ronald Knox, Harvill, 1958

Barrington, Brendan (ed), *The Wartime Broadcasts of Francis Stuart 1942-1944*, Lilliput, 2000

Beaumont, Barbara, *The Road from Decadence, Selected Letters of J.K. Huysmans,* The Athlone Press Ltd, 1989

Beckett, Samuel, *Disjecta Miscellaneous Writings and a Dramatic Fragment,* John Calder, 1983

Bewley, Charles, *Memoirs of a Wild Goose,* Lilliput, 1989

Bonhoeffer, Dietrich, *Letter & Papers from Prison,* Fontana Books, 1969

Brett, C.E.B., *Buildings of County Antrim*, Ulster Architectural Heritage Society with Ulster Historical Foundation, 1996

Brown, Dan, *The Da Vinci Code*, Bantam, 2003

Bullock, Alan, *Hitler: A study in tyranny,* Penguin, 1990

Burke's Landed Gentry of Ireland, 1958

Cardozo, Nancy, *Maud Gonne,* New Amsterdam, 1990

Carpenter, Humphrey, *A Serious Character: The Life of Ezra Pound*, Faber & Faber, London, 1988

Carroll, Joseph T., *Ireland in the War Years 1939-1945*, David & Charles Ltd, 1975

Clarke, Charles, *The Ballyhivistock Manuscript Revisted 2003* (unpublished family history)

Cole, J.A., *Lord Haw-Haw: The Full Story of William Joyce*, Faber & Faber, 1987

Cooper, R.W., *The Nuremberg Trial*, Penguin Books, 1947

Costello, Peter, *Liam O'Flaherty's Ireland*, Wolfhound, Dublin, 1996

Cronin, Anthony, *Heritage Now: Irish Literature in the English Language*, Brandon, 1982

Cronin, Anthony, *Samuel Beckett: The Last Modernist*, HarperCollins, London, 1996

Cronin, Seán, *Frank Ryan: The Search for the Republic*, Repsol Publishing, 1980

Cruise O'Brien, Máire, *The Same Age as the State*, The O'Brien Press, Dublin, 2003

de la Mazière, Christian, *Ashes of Honour*, translated Francis Stuart, Wingate, London, 1975

Deane, Seamus, "Francis Stuart: The Stimulus of Sin", *In Dublin*, 17 December 1982

Dostoevsky, Fyodor, *Crime and Punishment*, translated by David Magarshack Penguin Books, London 1975

Dostoevsky, Fyodor, *The Brothers Karamazov*, translated by David Magarshack, Penguin, London, 1977

Dudley Edwards, Ruth, *Victor Gollancz: A Biography*, Gollancz, 1987

Duggan, John P., *Neutral Ireland and the Third Reich*, Dublin, 1975

Durant, Alan, *Ezra Pound, Identity in Crisis*, Harvester Press UK, 1981

Elborn, Geoffrey, *Francis Stuart: A Life*, Raven Arts Press, 1990

Fallon, Brian, *Imogen Stuart: Sculptor*, Four Courts Press, Dublin, 2002

Fitzgerald, F. Scott, *Tender is the Night*, Penguin Modern Classics, 1980

Foster, R.F., *W.B. Yeats: A Life II. The Arch-Poet*, Oxford, 2003

Foster, R.F., *W.B. Yeats: The Apprentice Mage*, Oxford, 1997

Francis Stuart (obituary) *Irish Times*, 5 February 2000

Francis Stuart (obituary) *The Guardian*, 4 February 2000

Francis Stuart (obituary) *The Independent* (London), 3 February 2000

Francis Stuart (obituary) *The Irish Examiner*, 4 February 2000

Francis Stuart (obituary) *The Scotsman*, 7 February 2000

Francis Stuart (obituary) *The Times*, 3 February 2000

Francis Stuart File A72 (private release by Gary Ansbro of Department of Foreign Affairs (Ireland) from National Archives to the biographer)

Harmon, Maurice, *The Irish Novel in Our Times*, University of Lille, 1976

Hemingway, Ernest, *The Old Man and the Sea*, Jonathan Cape, 1970

Hesse, Hermann, *Steppenwolf*, Penguin, 1965

Hull, Mark M., *Irish Secrets: German Espionage in Wartime Ireland 1939-1945*, Irish Academic Press, Dublin and Portland OR, 2003

Jeffares, A. Norman, Anna MacBride White and Christina Bridgwater, *Letters to W. B. Yeats and Ezra Pound from Iseult Gonne*, Palgrave, London, 2004

Jordan, Anthony J. *The Yeats–MacBride–Gonne Triangle*, Westport Books 2000

Jordan, Anthony J., *Willie Yeats and the Gonne-MacBrides*, Westport Books, 1997

Kavanagh & Rodriguez (translation), *The Ascent of Mount Carmel, Collected Works of St John of the Cross*, Nelson and Sons, US, 1966

Kavanagh & Rodriguez (translation), *The Living Flame of Love, Collected Works of St John of the Cross*, Nelson and Sons, US, 1966

Keats, John, *The Poetical Works*, Henry Frowde, London, 1905

Kelly, A.A., *The Letters of Liam O'Flaherty*, Wolfhound Press, Dublin, 1996

Keogh, Dermot, *Ireland and the Vatican*, Cork University Press, 1995

Kiely, Kevin, *Quintesse*, St Martin's Press, New York, 1985

Lawrence, D.H., *Lady Chatterley's Lover*, Penguin, 1961

Lawrence, D.H., *Women in Love*, Penguin, 1964

Lazenbatt, Bill (editor), *Writing Ulster: Francis Stuart Special Issue* (1996)

Levi, Primo, *If This Is a Man/The Truce*, translated by Stuart Woolf, Abacus, 1987

Lewis, Wyndham, *Tarr*, Penguin, 1982

Macann, Christopher, *Critical Heidegger*, Routledge, 1996

MacBride, Maud Gonne, *A Servant of the Queen: Reminiscences*, Gollancz, London, 1974

Maddox, Brenda *George's Ghosts: a New Life of W.B. Yeats* Picador, 1999

Mannin, Ethel, *Late Have I Loved Thee*, Jarrolds, London, 1948

McCartney, Anne, *Francis Stuart Face to Face: A critical study*, Institute of Irish Studies, Queens University Belfast, 2000

McCormack, W. J. (ed.), *A Festschrift for Francis Stuart on His Seventeenth Birthday*, Dolmen, 1972

Meyers, Jeffrey, *The Enemy: A Biography of Wyndham Lewis*, RKP London, 1980

Molloy, F. C., "The Life and Death of Henry Irwin Stuart", *Irish University Review*, Vol. 16, No. 1, 1986

Natterstad, J. H., *Francis Stuart*, Bucknell University Press, 1974

Ní Chuilleanáin, Eiléan, *As I was among captives: Joseph Campbell's Prison Diary, 1922-1923*, Cork University Press, 2001

Ní Mheara-Vinard, Róisín, *Cé Hí seo Amuigh? Cuimhní Cinn ag Róisín*, Coiscéim, Dublin, 1992

O'Keeffe, Paul, *Some Sort of Genius: A Life of Wyndham Lewis*, Cape, London, 2000

O'Malley, Ernie, *On Another Man's Wound*, Anvil Books, Dublin, 1979

O'Connor, Ulick, *Biographers and the Art of Biography*, Quartet Books, 1991

O'Connor, Ulick, *Brendan Behan*, Hamish Hamilton, 1970

O'Donoghue, David, *Hitler's Irish Voices,* Beyond the Pale Publications, Belfast, 1998

O'Farrell, Padraic, *Who's Who in the Irish War of Independence and Civil War 1916-1923*, Lilliput, 1997

O'Toole, Fintan, "F. Stuart – Up to 90", *The Irish Times*, April, 1992

Pagels, Elaine, *Adam, Eve, and the Serpent*, Penguin Books, 1988

Pagels, Elaine, *Beyond Belief: The Secret Gospel of Thomas*, Vintage Books, New York, 2003

President de Valera; Great Contemporaries Essays, Cassell, London, 1935

Private Diary of Iseult Gonne-Stuart 1940-1949 (Courtesy of Ian Stuart) unpublished

Private Diary of Madeleine Stuart 1958-1975 (Courtesy of Francis Stuart) unpublished

Robinson, Lennox (editor), *Lady Gregory's Journals 1916-1930*, Putnam & Co Ltd., 1946

Sagar, Keith, *D.H. Lawrence: Life into Art*, Penguin, 1985

Schillebeeckx, Edward (translated by Hubert Hoskins), *Jesus: An experiment in Christology*, Collins, London, 1979

Schulberg, Budd, *The Disenchanted*, Allison & Busby, 1993

Shanks, Amanda N., *Rural Aristocracy in Northern Ireland*, Institute of Irish Studies, Queen's University Press, Belfast, 1988

Shirer, William L., *Berlin Diary*, Hamish Hamilton, 1941

Steiner, George, *Heidegger*, Fontana, 1978

Stephen, Enno, *Spies in Ireland*, MacDonald, London, 1965

Stuart, Madeleine, *Manna in the Morning: A Memoir 1940-1958*, Raven Arts Press (Dublin)/Colin Smythe (England), 1984

Symons, Arthur, *The Symbolist Movement in Literature*, E.P. Dutton & Co, New York, 1947

Toland, John, *Hitler*, Wordsworth Editions, 1997

Tytell, John, *Ezra Pound: The Solitary Volcano*, Bloomsbury, 1987

Ussher, Arland, *Journey Through Dread*, Darwen Finlayson Ltd, 1955

Ward, Maisie, *Gilbert Keith Chesterton*, Sheed and Ward, London, 1944

Ward, Margaret, *Maud Gonne, A Life*, Pandora, London, 1993

Welch, Robert, *Changing States: Transformations in Modern Irish Writing*, Routledge, 1993

Welch, Robert, *The Abbey Theatre 1899-1999: Form and Pressure*, Oxford, 1999

Williamson, Claude, *Letters from the Saints*, Catholic Book Club, London, 1958

Yeats Annual No 7, edited by Warwick Gould, Macmillan, London, 1990

Yeats, W.B., *Collected Poems*, The Macmillan Company, 1967

Young, Amy Isabel, *Three Hundred Years in Innishowen*, The Linenhall Press, Belfast, 1929

Chapter Notes and Sources

Not every interview and conversation, of which there were many over many years, is listed in the case of Francis Stuart (F.S.) and Kevin Kiely (K.K.), except for those pertaining to the period 1997–2000. Some interviews by K.K. with contemporaries of Stuart are not listed; there are comments and quotations from such persons in the text. There is reference to interviews with Stuart family members and some close family friends.

Abbreviations used:

F.S. – Francis Stuart

F.G. – Finola Graham, his widow

I.S. – Ian Stuart, his son

A.B. – Anna Buggy Stuart, wife of Ian Stuart

K.K. – Kevin Kiely, biographer

A.F.S.E. – Archive of the Francis Stuart Estate

Introduction

1 Manuscript 17, Reader's Report on *The Pilgrimage,* Francis Stuart Collection, University of Ulster Library.

2 Stuart, Francis, "The Writer and the Politician", *Études Irlandaises* No. 3, 1978, p. 49.

3 Beckett, Samuel, *Disjecta,* Calder, London, 1983, p. 145.

4 Stuart, Francis, *Things To Live For: Notes for an Autobiography,* Cape, London, 1934, p. 191.

5 Pound, Ezra, *The Cantos,* Faber, London, 1975, pp. 520–1.

1. The Australian Tragedy

Further sources for this chapter include: *The Ballyhivistock Manuscript Revisted 2003*, compiled by Charles Clarke, a relative of Stuart's living in New Zealand. It contains a family history and information on the Montgomery and Stuart ancestors (Stuart's mother's and father's people, respectively) from *Burke's Irish Family Records*, 1978 and *Burke's Landed Gentry of Ireland*, 1958. The Stuart ancestors also feature in Amy Isabel Young's *Three Hundred Years in Innishowen*, The Linenhall Press, Belfast, 1929. The homes of Stuart's parents and grandparents are outlined in C.E. Brett's *Buildings of County Antrim.* Also consulted was Amanda N. Shanks's *Rural Aristocracy in Northern Ireland,* Institute of Irish Studies, The Queen's University Press, Belfast, 1988.

Sources for Stuart's early life in the opening chapters include: J.H. Natterstad, *Francis Stuart*, Bucknell University Press, 1974; Geoffrey Elborn, *Francis Stuart: A Life*, The Raven Arts Press, 1990; and the autobiographical novels by Stuart (he used the substance of his life in some of his fiction), especially *Black List, Section H*, Penguin Books, 1996, *The High Consistory*, Martin Brian & O'Keeffe, London, 1981 and other novels referred to in the biography and the notes that follow; also *Things To Live For: Notes for an Autobiography* (Francis Stuart) Jonathan Cape, 1934.

During interviews with K.K. on 19 March 1997, 1 April 1997, 2 June 1997 and 22 June 1997, Stuart asserted the authenticity of material used in Elborn and Natterstad, such as letters to F.R. Higgins, Joseph O'Neill and to Natterstad himself; letters from O'Flaherty, Iseult Stuart, Ethel Mannin and others.

1 Document of Indenture, A.F.S.E.

2 Jane Black's North Queensland Pioneers. Cited in "The Life and Death of Henry Irwin Stuart", F.C. Molloy, *Irish University Review*, Vol. 16, No. 1, 1986.

3 Geoffrey Elborn, *Francis Stuart: A Life*, The Raven Arts Press, 1990, p. 12.

4 ibid, p. 12.

5 Letter from F.C. Molloy, New South Wales, Australia, 25 February 1987.

6 J.H. Natterstad, *Francis Stuart,* Bucknell University Press, 1974, p. 15.

7 F.S. interview with K.K.

8 J.H. Natterstad, *Francis Stuart,* Bucknell University Press, 1974, pp. 14–15.

9 F.S. interview with K.K.

10 Francis Stuart, *The High Consistory,* Martin Brian & O'Keeffe, London, 1981, p. 241.

11 Geoffrey Elborn, *Francis Stuart: A Life,* The Raven Arts Press, 1990, p. 21.

12 J.H. Natterstad, *Francis Stuart,* Bucknell University Press, 1974, p. 16.

13 Geoffrey Elborn, *Francis Stuart: A Life,* The Raven Arts Press, 1990, p. 19.

14 J.H. Natterstad, *Francis Stuart,* Bucknell University Press, 1974, p. 17.

2. Yeats, Maud Gonne and Iseult

See the *Select Bibliography* (p. 335) for further sources on Yeats, Pound, Wyndham Lewis, Maud Gonne, Lady Gregory, Iseult Gonne, Lennox Robinson and others from this period. Interviews by K.K. with Stuart on 28 July 1997, 1 September 1997, 8 September 1997 for material in this and subsequent chapters.

1 The definitive account of the Gonne-MacBride marriage and complex judicial separation process can be found in Anthony J. Jordan's *The Yeats–Gonne–MacBride Triangle,* Westport Books, 2000.

2 Anthony J. Jordan, *Willie Yeats and the Gonne-MacBrides,* Westport Books, 1997, p. 150.

3 Francis Stuart, *Black List, Section H,* Penguin Books, 1996, p. 31.

4 *The Gonne–Yeats Letters 1893–1938,* Edited Anna MacBride & A. Norman Jeffares, Hutchinson, 1992, p. 375

5 W.B. Yeats, *Collected Poems,* The Macmillan Company, 1967, p. 138.

6 Francis Stuart, *Black List, Section H,* Penguin Books, 1996, p. 22.

7 Francis Stuart, *The High Consistory,* Martin Brian & O'Keeffe, London, 1981.

8 Francis Stuart, *Black List, Section H*, Penguin Books, 1996, p. 20.

9 *The Gonne-Yeats Letters 1893–1938*, Anna MacBride & A. Norman Jeffares (eds.), Hutchinson, 1992, p. 402.

10 ibid, p. 403.

11 Francis Stuart, *Black List, Section H*, Penguin Books, 1996, p. 19.

12 W.B. Yeats to Lady Gregory, 1 August 1920, Berg.

13 Roy F. Foster, *W.B. Yeats: A Life Vol. II: The Arch Poet 1915–1939*, Oxford, 2003, p. 171.

3. Soldier and Poet

1 J.H. Natterstad, *Francis Stuart*, Bucknell University Press, 1974, p. 26.

2 *The Gonne–Yeats Letters 1893–1938*, Edited Anna MacBride & A. Norman Jeffares, Hutchinson 1992, p. 426.

3 Francis Stuart, *Things To Live For: Notes for an Autobiography*, Jonathan Cape, 1934, p. 188.

4 Francis Stuart, *Things To Live For: Notes for an Autobiography*, Jonathan Cape, 1934.

5 Francis Stuart, *We Have Kept the Faith: New and Selected Poems*, Raven Arts Press, 1982, p. 12.

5a *As I was Among Captives: Joseph Campbell's Prison Diary, 1922–1923*, ed. Eiléan Ní Chuilleanáin, Cork University Press, 2001, p. 57.

6 F.S. interview with K.K., 28 September 1997.

7 Francis Stuart, *Things To Live For: Notes for an Autobiography*, Jonathan Cape, 1934, p. 212–3.

8 Francis Stuart, *Black List, Section H*, Penguin Books, 1996, p. 137.

9 ibid, p. 138.

10 F.S. quoting Patrick Kavanagh, interview with K.K. 6 October 1997.

11 Francis Stuart, *Black List, Section H*, Penguin Books, 1996, p. 140.

12 Francis Stuart, *Black List, Section H*, Penguin Books, 1996, p. 140.

13 Francis Stuart, *Black List, Section H*, Penguin Books, 1996, p. 111.

14 *Biographers and the Art of Biography*, Ulick O'Connor, Quartet Books 1991, *vide* "To Tell or Not to Tell", pp. 46–58.

15 W.B. Yeats, *Collected Poems*, The Macmillan Company, 1967, p. 333.

16 Francis Stuart, *Night Pilot*, Raven Arts Press, 1988, p. 11.

4. Pamphlets, Poultry and Mysticism

1 *Nationality and Culture*, Sinn Féin Árd Chomhairle, Dublin, 1924, p. 19.

2 *The Letters of Liam O'Flaherty*, edited by A.A. Kelly, Wolfhound Press, Dublin, 1996, p. 263.

3 Francis Stuart and Cecil Salkeld, *Tomorrow*, August, 1924.

4 Maddox, Brenda, *George's Ghosts: A New Life of W.B. Yeats*, Picador, 1999.

5 *Mystics and Mysticism*, Catholic Truth Society of Ireland, Dublin, 1929.

6 *The Living Flame of Love, Collected Works of St John of the Cross*, translated by Kavanagh & Rodriguez, Nelson and Sons, US, 1966, p. 629.

7 *The Ascent of Mount Carmel, Collected Works of St John of the Cross*, translated by Kavanagh & Rodriguez, Nelson and Sons, US, 1966, p. 154.

8 Francis Stuart, *Black List, Section H*, Penguin Books, 1996, p. 142.

5. Pilgrim, Novelist, Hedonist

The commentary on Stuart's novels is based on interviews with Stuart; see bibliography for a selection of critical work on Stuart's novels.

1 Francis Stuart, *Black List, Section H*, Penguin Books, 1996.

2 J.H. Natterstad, *Francis Stuart*, Bucknell University Press, 1974, p. 35.

3 *The Road from Decadence, Selected Letters of J.K. Huysmans*, edited/translated by Barbara Beaumont, The Athlone Press Ltd, 1989.

4 F.S. interview with Naim Attallah, Quartet Books, 1996.

5 Keith Sagar, *D.H. Lawrence: Life into Art*, Penguin, 1985.

6 Francis Stuart, *Black List, Section H*, Penguin Books, 1996.

7 ibid, p. 174.

8 ibid, p. 174.

9 J.H. Natterstad, *Francis Stuart*, Bucknell University Press, 1974, p. 37–8.

6. Some Early Success

1 Ernest Hemingway, *The Old Man and the Sea*, Jonathan Cape, 1970.

2 Arthur Symons, *Studies in Prose and Verse*, Dent, 1904, p. 288.

3 Francis Stuart, *A Compendium of Lovers*, Raven Arts Press, 1990, p. 83.

4 Percy Hutchinson reviewed *Pigeon Irish* in *The New York Times Book Review* 3 July 1932. His comments are glowing over two pages, below a photograph of Stuart, "it will be one of the most widely read of recent novels". Hutchinson would champion Stuart's novels throughout the 1930s in *The New York Times Book Review*: *The Coloured Dome, Try the Sky, Glory, Things to Live For: Notes for an Autobiography, In Search of Love, The White Hare* and *Julie*. Except for some reservations over *In Search of Love*, he seems overwhelmed by Stuart, "half poet, half seer, not to know his work is to neglect the most arresting novelist in many a year"; "... a novelist so far removed from the general run of fiction writers that few of the usual canons apply".

5 Francis Stuart, *Pigeon Irish*, Gollancz, 1932, p. 222.

6 *The Bookman,* August, 1934, Samuel Beckett (under pseudonym Andrew Belis).

7 Geoffrey Elborn, *Francis Stuart: A Life*, The Raven Arts Press, 1990, p. 91-2.

8 ibid, p. 91.

9 *The Letters of Liam O'Flaherty,* edited by A.A. Kelly, Wolfhound Press, Dublin, 1996.

10 Francis Stuart, *The Coloured Dome*, Gollancz, 1932, p. 167.

7. Rejection by Gollancz

1 *The Letters of Liam O'Flaherty,* edited by A.A. Kelly, Wolfhound Press, Dublin, 1996.

2 Francis Stuart, *Try the Sky,* Gollancz, 1933, p. 4.

3 Francis Stuart, *Black List, Section H*, Penguin Books, 1996.

4 Francis Stuart, *Try the Sky,* Gollancz, 1933, p. 161.

5 Bullock, Alan, *Hitler: A study in Tyranny,* Penguin, 1990.

6 F.S. interview with K.K., 27 October 1997.

7 Francis Stuart, *Glory,* Gollancz, 1933, p. 193.

8 *The Letters of Liam O'Flaherty*, A.A. Kelly (ed.), Wolfhound Press, 1996, pp. 268-9.

9 Geoffrey Elborn, *Francis Stuart: A Life*, The Raven Arts Press, 1990, p. 97.

10 Francis Stuart, *Black List, Section H*, Penguin Books, 1996.

8. Cape, Collins, Womanising

Lengthy interview by the biographer with Stuart, 14 November 1997 supplemented material in this and subsequent chapters.

1 Francis Stuart, *Things To Live For: Notes for an Autobiography*, Jonathan Cape, 1934, p. 177.

2 ibid, p. 91.

3 ibid.

4 Geoffrey Elborn, *Francis Stuart: A Life*, The Raven Arts Press, 1990, p. 102.

5 Francis Stuart, *The Angel of Pity*, Grayson and Grayson, London, 1935, p. 57.

6 ibid, p. 284.

9. Pre-War Plots

1 Francis Stuart Diary 10, 20 July 1947. There are eighteen diaries dating from March 1942 to August 1977 in the Francis Stuart Collection at the University of Ulster Library at Coleraine. *Manna in the Morning: A Memoir 1940–1958*, Madeleine Stuart, Raven Arts Press (Dublin)/Colin Smythe (England), 1984 and the Private Diary of Madeleine Stuart 1958–1975 (Courtesy of Francis Stuart), unpublished. All of these sources provide a key structure along with interviews between F.S. and K.K. on 21 November 1997 and 28 November 1997 for verification purposes. It is not feasible to litter the text and notes with superscript and references, hence a suitable selection has been made to acknowledge these important sources.

2 Francis Stuart, *Julie*, Collins London, 1938, p. 25.

3 ibid, p. 121.

4 Geoffrey Elborn, *Francis Stuart: A Life*, The Raven Arts Press, 1990, p. 110.

5 J.H. Natterstad, *Francis Stuart,* Bucknell University Press, 1974, p. 53.

6 Francis Stuart Diary 2. *Vide* note 1 above.

7 Francis Stuart Diary 10. *Vide* note 1 above.

10. German Odyssey

Supplementary sources for this chapter include Mark M. Hull's *Irish Secrets: German Espionage in Wartime Ireland, 1939–1945,* Irish Academic Press, 2003 and Róisín Ní Mheara-Vinard's *Cé Hí seo Amuigh: Cuimhní Cinn ag Róisín,* Coiscéim, 1992. The latter is an account written in Gaelic of Róisín Ní Mheara's period in wartime Berlin.

1 Geoffrey Elborn, *Francis Stuart: A Life,* The Raven Arts Press, 1990, p. 114.

2 J.H. Natterstad, *Francis Stuart,* Bucknell University Press, 1974, p. 55. Natterstad altered his estimation of Stuart decades later, stating that "his collaboration with the Nazi regime had genuine propaganda value for the Germans" (J.H. Natterstad, *Éire–Ireland,* xxvi, no. 4 (Winter 1991), p. 61.

3 Geoffrey Elborn, *Francis Stuart: A Life,* The Raven Arts Press, 1990, p. 113.

4 Francis Stuart, *Black List, Section H,* Penguin Books, 1996, p. 63.

5 Geoffrey Elborn, *Francis Stuart: A Life,* The Raven Arts Press, 1990, p. 115.

6 ibid, p. 116.

7 Letter from Francis Stuart (unpublished) in the Francis Stuart File A72 (private release by Gary Ansbro of Department of Foreign Affairs (Ireland) to K.K.) The file contains copies of letters, telegrams and otherwise vast documentation that provided this biographer with the facts about the official and diplomatic furore surrounding Stuart in Germany during the war years and after. Two previous biographers, as well as other writers on Stuart, were consistently denied access hence this material has never been made public before.

8 Hempel introduced Stuart in the letter as a "genuine friend of contemporary Germany, a very good representative of Irish nationalism and reliable", Microfiche no. 463, December 1939 (Politisches Archiv des Auswärtigen Amts, Bonn, Büro Staatssekretär (Irland).

11. Friends, Lovers, a Spy

1 F.S. interview with K.K., 5 December 1997.

2 ibid.

3 Ernst Woermann, Under-Secretary of State at the Auswärtiges Amt, noted Stuart's comments in an aide-mémoire 26 January 1940 stamped "top secret". Microfiche no. 464 (Politisches Archiv des Auswärtigen Amts, Bonn, Büro Staatssekretär (Irland).

4 Francis Stuart, *Black List, Section H,* Penguin Books, 1996.

5 I.S. interview with K.K. 8 February 1998.

6 Carroll, Joseph T., *Ireland in the War Years 1939–1945,* David & Charles Ltd, 1975, p. 74.

7 ibid, p. 11.

12. Frank Ryan, Operation Dove

1 J.H. Natterstad, *Francis Stuart,* Bucknell University Press, 1974, p. 61.

2 Cronin, Seán, *Frank Ryan: The Search for the Republic,* Repsol Publishing 1980. Cronin's book on Ryan provides the background while interviews with Stuart have added to a hitherto unknown portrait of Ryan.

3 Alan Bullock, *Hitler: A Study in Tyranny,* Penguin, 1990. This informs the greater bulk of the material on Adolf Hitler here. Citations in the biography can easily be sourced in Bullock's annotated index.

13. Madeleine

Interviews with Madeleine Stuart refer to a considerable number of meetings and conversations over twenty years.

1 Madeleine Stuart, interview with K.K. All sources, other than her diaries, come from letters and documents of the A.F.S.E.

2 F.S. interview with K.K., 19 December 1997.

3 ibid.

4 Francis Stuart, *Black List, Section H,* Penguin Books, 1996, p. 348.

5 ibid.

6 ibid.

7 ibid.

8 Francis Stuart, *Things To Live For: Notes for an Autobiography*, Jonathan Cape, 1934, p. 144.

9 Madeleine Stuart in conversation with K.K.

14. Irland-Redaktion, Berlin

1 David O'Donoghue, *Hitler's Irish Voices,* Beyond the Pale Publications, 1998 and Barrington, Brendan (ed.), *The Wartime Broadcasts of Francis Stuart 1942–1944,* Lilliput, 2000. Both are excellent books that provide and inform the material in this chapter along with interviews by K.K. with Stuart himself as protagonist in what for some critics, such as Frank Kermode, is the most intriguing episode of his life. All references easily accessible from Barrington and O'Donohue's indexes.

2 ibid.

3 For full text of broadcasts *vide* Barrington, Brendan (ed.), *The Wartime Broadcasts of Francis Stuart 1942–1944,* Lilliput, 2000. Damien Keane, University of Pennsylvania at Seeley G. Mudd Manuscript Library, Princeton University, USA.

15. Final Years in Berlin

1 Lecture (unpublished) from A.F.S.E.

2 ibid.

3 Francis Stuart Diary 2, 1 October 1942. There are eighteen diaries dating from March 1942 to August 1977 in the Francis Stuart Collection at the University of Ulster Library at Coleraine.

4 For full text of broadcasts *vide* Barrington, Brendan ed., *The Wartime Broadcasts of Francis Stuart 1942–1944,* Lilliput, 2000.

5 Unpublished letter. Source: Francis Stuart File A72 (private release by Gary Ansbro of Department of Foreign Affairs (Ireland) to K.K.) The file contains copies of letters, telegrams and otherwise vast documentation that provided this biographer with the facts about the official and diplomatic furore surrounding Stuart in Germany during the war years and after. Two previous biographers as well as other writers on Stuart were consistently denied access hence this material has never been made public before.

6 *vide* note 4 above.

7 *Picture Post*, 11 April 1942, cited in Geoffrey Elborn, *Francis Stuart: A Life*, The Raven Arts Press, 1990, p. 159.

8 F.S. interview with K.K., 5 January 1998.

9 *vide* note 4 above

10 *We Have Kept the Faith: New and Selected Poems*, Raven Arts Press, Dublin, 1982, p. 35.

11 *Manna in the Morning: A Memoir 1940–1958*, Madeleine Stuart, Raven Arts Press (Dublin)/ Colin Smythe (England), 1984, p. 36.

12 *vide* note 5 above.

13 *vide* note 5 above.

14 Francis Stuart to Con Cremin (unpublished letter). *Vide* note 5 above.

15 Francis Stuart letter to Madeleine Stuart (unpublished letter) A.F.S.E.

16 Francis Stuart, *Black List, Section H*, Penguin Books, 1996.

17 ibid.

18 F.S. interview with K.K., 31 January 1998.

19 *Manna in the Morning: A Memoir 1940–1958*, Madeleine Stuart, Raven Arts Press (Dublin)/Colin Smythe (England), 1984, p. 115.

16. Refugee Couple

1 Francis Stuart File A72 (private release by Gary Ansbro of Department of Foreign Affairs (Ireland) to K.K.). See note 5 to chapter 15.

2 Francis Stuart (unpublished sonnet) A.F.S.E.

3 Francis Stuart, *Black List, Section H*, Penguin Books, 1996, p. 375.

4 ibid, p. 374.

5 ibid, p. 268.

6 Francis Stuart, *Faillandia*, The Raven Arts Press, 1985, p. 318.

7 Francis Stuart, *Black List, Section H*, Penguin Books, 1996, p. 50.

8 ibid, p. 172–3.

9 Jim Phelan (1895–1966) on the anti-Treaty side was imprisoned with Stuart during the Irish Civil War 1922–1923. Stuart loosely based the character Lane on him in *Black List, Section H.* He was fascinated by Phelan, but they lost contact after being released. Phelan

spent long sentences in prisons at Maidstone, Dartmoor and Parkhurst for armed robbery and other crimes up to the late 1930s. He was the author of prison literature including *Lifer* (Peter Davies, London, 1938) and *Jail Journal* (Secker & Warburg, 1940).

10 Postcard from Francis Stuart to Iseult Stuart. See note 1 above for source.

11 Iseult Stuart to Frederick Boland (1904–1988) secretary, Department of External Affairs, 1938-1950 and later president of the UN General Assembly (1960–61). See note 1 above.

12 Francis Stuart, *Black List, Section H*, Penguin Books, 1996.

13 See note 1 above.

14 ibid. Seán MacBride (1904–1988) Son of Major John MacBride and Maud Gonne, half-brother to Iseult Stuart and brother-in-law to Francis Stuart, had a very distinguished career at the Irish Bar, as Dáil Deputy and Minister for External Affairs. Awarded the Nobel Peace Prize in 1974 and the Lenin Peace Prize in 1977 and the American Medal for Justice in 1978.

15 See note 1 above.

16 Francis Stuart, *Black List, Section H*, Penguin Books, 1996.

17 Geoffrey Elborn, *Francis Stuart: A Life*, The Raven Arts Press, 1990, p. 145.

18 F.S. interview with K.K., 5 February 1998.

19 See note 1 above.

20 ibid.

21 Private Diary of Iseult Gonne-Stuart 1940–1949 (Courtesy of Ian Stuart) unpublished.

22 ibid.

23–29 ibid.

30 Unpublished letter from Iseult Stuart to Francis Stuart, cited in Geoffrey Elborn, *Francis Stuart: A Life*, The Raven Arts Press, 1990.

17. Prisoners, a Wife's Turmoil

1 *Manna in the Morning: A Memoir 1940-1958*, Madeleine Stuart, Raven Arts Press (Dublin)/Colin Smythe (England), 1984.

2 ibid, 27 August 1945, p. 65.

3 F.S. interview with K.K., 14 February 1998.

4 Cited in Anne McCartney *Francis Stuart Face to Face: A critical study*, IIS, QUB, 2000 and used in teaching a course on Stuart's novels at the Queen's University in Belfast.

5 For this material relating to the British Ambassador to Éire, Sir John Maffey, Basil Liddel-Hart and Francis Stuart *vide* chapter 11 pp 187–194; Geoffrey Elborn, *Francis Stuart: A Life*, The Raven Arts Press, 1990, p. 191.

6 ibid.

7 ibid.

8 Letter from Róisín Ní Mheara to Iseult Stuart May 1946. *Vide* Francis Stuart File A72 (private release by Gary Ansbro of Department of Foreign Affairs (Ireland) to K.K.)

9–21 All extracts from letters or letters contained in Francis Stuart File A72 (private release by Gary Ansbro of Department of Foreign Affairs (Ireland) to K.K.)

22 Naim Attallah interview with Francis Stuart, Quarter Books, 1996.

18. Freiburg Trilogy

1 Francis Stuart Diary 9, 23 August 1946. There are eighteen diaries dating from March 1942 to August 1977 in the Francis Stuart Collection at the University of Ulster Library at Coleraine.

2 Francis Stuart, *The Pillar of Cloud*, Gollancz, 1948; Martin Brian & O'Keeffe, London, 1973; New Island Books, 1994, p. 131.

3 ibid, p. 142.

4 F.S. interview with Bill Lazenbatt, *Writing Ulster (1996): Francis Stuart Special Issue*, p. 7.

5 Francis Stuart Diary 10, 19 February 1947. *Vide* note 1.

6 *Manna in the Morning: A Memoir 1940–1958*, Madeleine Stuart Raven Arts Press (Dublin)/Colin Smythe (England), 1984, p. 29.

7 Francis Stuart, *Black List, Section H*, Penguin Books, 1996, p. 396.

19. Gollancz to the Rescue

Ethel Mannin's bestselling novel *Late Have I Loved Thee*, Jarrolds, London 1948 is loosely based on Stuart's life. The central character in the book is Francis Sable, successful writer in London, Paris and Europe.

When his beloved dies he enters a community of Jesuits in Clongowes Wood, in post-WWII Ireland, and dies soon after.

1 Geoffrey Elborn, *Francis Stuart: A Life*, The Raven Arts Press, 1990, p. 204.

2 I.S. interview with K.K., 22 March 1998.

3 Geoffrey Elborn, *Francis Stuart: A Life*, The Raven Arts Press, 1990, p. 212.

4 ibid, p. 224.

20. Paris

1 Francis Stuart Diary 14, 24 December 1949. There are eighteen diaries dating from March 1942 to August 1977 in the Francis Stuart Collection at the University of Ulster Library at Coleraine.

2 Francis Stuart Diary 13. See note 2 above.

3 Imogen Stuart interview with K.K., May 1998.

4 Francis Stuart letter to Madeleine Stuart A.F.S.E.

5 Geoffrey Elborn, *Francis Stuart: A Life*, The Raven Arts Press, 1990, p. 7 and Geoffrey Elborn interview with K.K. February 2000.

6 Imogen Stuart letter to K.K. *Vide* Brian Fallon *Imogen Stuart: Sculptor*, Four Courts Press, Dublin, 2002, a biography of Imogen Stuart, born Imogen Werner in Berlin 1927. Her half-Jewish father survived WWII. She married Ian Stuart, Stuart's son in 1951. They separated in 1970 and, apart from periods in Berlin, she has lived in Ireland ever since. Her works in sculpture, mainly in wood, have gained an international reputation.

21. Hard Times in London

1 Madeleine Stuart in conversation with K.K. Also documents in the A.F.S.E.

2 David H. Greene, "The Return of Francis Stuart", *Envoy* 5, 1951.

3 Manuscript 17 reader's report on *The Pilgrimage*, Francis Stuart Collection, University of Ulster at Coleraine, Northern Ireland.

4 Private Diary of Madeleine Stuart 1958–1975 (courtesy of Francis Stuart), unpublished.

5 *Yeats Annual No. 7*, Warwick Gould, editor, Macmillan, 1990, p. 204.

6 F.S. interview with K.K., 22 March 1998.

7 I.S. interview with K.K., 22 March 1998.

22. *Return to Ireland*

1 Madeleine Stuart in conversation with K.K.

2 F.S. interview with K.K., 27 April 1998.

3 Francis Stuart in letter with A.F.S.E and interview with K.K., 18 June 1998.

4 Francis Stuart, *Victors and Vanquished*, Gollancz, London, 1958; Pennington Press, Cleveland, 1959, p. 82.

5 Francis Stuart, "Minoe: A Short Story", *Good Housekeeping*, March 1959.

6 Victor Gollancz to Francis Stuart, 16 February 1960. Manuscript 25, Francis Stuart Collection University of Ulster Library, Coleraine Northern Ireland.

23. *Unsettling Times*

1 F.S. interviews with K.K., 26 June 1998 and 18 July 1998, supported by the private diary of Madeleine Stuart 1958–1975 (courtesy of Francis Stuart), unpublished.

24. *Black List, Section H*

1 Anthony Cronin, poet, writer and founder of the Irish Academy of Writers and Artists - Aosdána - interview with K.K. April 1998.

2 *The Letters of Liam O'Flaherty*, edited by A.A. Kelly, Wolfhound Press, Dublin, 1996, p. 365.

3 Letter in A.F.S.E.

4 Tom MacIntyre, Irish playwright and poet, in interviews with K.K. 1998–1999.

5 Francis Stuart, *A Hole in the Head*, Martin Brian & O'Keeffe, London, 1977; Longship Press, Massachusetts, 1977, p. 13.

6 Francis Stuart, "John Lodwick", unpublished essay, A.F.S.E.

7 Private diary of Madeleine Stuart 1958–1975 (courtesy of Francis Stuart), unpublished.

25. *"Culturally and Morally Subversive"*

1 Francis Stuart lecture, A.F.S.E.

2 Manuscript 52, The Stuart Papers at Carbondale, Southern Illinois University Library.

3 Anna Buggy-Stuart interview with K.K., 22 March 1998 and subsequent telephone interviews.

4 W.J. McCormack, "Francis Stuart", *The Independent* (London), 3 February 2000, p. 6.

5 Francis Stuart, *Memorial*, Martin Brian & O'Keeffe, London, 1973; Raven Arts Press/Colin Smythe, 1984, p. 53.

6 ibid, p. 73.

26. *A Hole in the Head*

1 Maurice Harmon, "The Achievement of Francis Stuart", *Writing Ulster* no. 4, 1996, p. 34.

2 ibid.

3 Christian de la Mazière, *Ashes of Honour* (Translated by Francis Stuart) Wingate, London, 1975, p. 7.

4 Francis Stuart, *A Hole in the Head*, Martin Brian & O'Keeffe, London, 1977; Longship Press, Massachusetts, 1977, p. 175.

5 ibid, p. 176.

6 ibid, p. 179.

7 Private diary of Madeleine Stuart 1958–1975 (courtesy of Francis Stuart) unpublished.

27. *US Tour, a New Academy for Artists*

1 Anthony Cronin, *Samuel Beckett: The Last Modernist,* HarperCollins, London, 1996, p. 576–7.

2 ibid.

3 Francis Stuart, *The High Consistory,* Martin Brian & O'Keeffe, London, 1981, p. 24.

4 Francis Stuart interview with Bill Lazenbatt in *Francis Stuart Special Issue of Writing Ulster 1996,* edited by Bill Lazenbatt, University of Ulster, p. 16.

28. Loss of the Beloved

1 Sheila Taylor to Francis Stuart, letter, A.F.S.E.

2 ibid.

3 Tina Neylon, journalist for the *Irish Examiner,* in interview with K.K., 13 April 1999.

29. "Theology not Philosophy"

1 Francis Stuart, *The Abandoned Snail Shell,* Raven Arts Press, 1987, p. 40.

2 ibid, p. 40.

3 Francis Stuart letter to K.K. in A.F.S.E.

4 Francis Stuart, *The Abandoned Snail Shell,* Raven Arts Press, 1987, p. 42.

5 ibid, p. 43.

6 ibid, p. 43.

7 ibid, p. 45.

8 ibid, p. 49.

9 ibid, p. 60.

10 ibid, p. 71.

11 Edward Schillebeeckx, *Jesus: An Experiment in Christology* (Translated by Hubert Hoskins), Collins, London, 1983, p. 387.

12 ibid, p. 593.

13 ibid, p. 380.

14 ibid, p. 648.

30. Paris—Proposal, Dublin—Wedding

1 Finola Graham interviews with K.K., April, 1998.

2 Rosemary Hartigan in conversation with K.K., February, 2000.

3 F.S. interviews with K.K., 21 July–28 July 1998 at Dundrum, Dublin; 17 September–23 September 1998 at Fanore, County Clare; 18 February–23 February 1999 at Fanore, County Clare.

4 Tina Neylon, journalist for the *Irish Examiner,* in interview with K.K., 13 April 1999.

5 Geoffrey Elborn in interview with K.K., February, 2000.

6 Francis Stuart, *Night Pilot,* Raven Arts Press, 1988, p. 16.

7 F.S. interview with K.K., 15 August–21 August 1999 at Fanore, County Clare and 19 November–23 November 1999.

31. Last Novel, Public Controversy

1 *Books Ireland: New Writing* (ed. Kevin Kiely), November, 1997, p. 302.

2 John Montague in conversation with K.K.

3 Francis Stuart, *A Compendium of Lovers,* Raven Arts Press, 1990, p. 15.

4 F.C. Copleston, *Aquinas,* Pelican, UK, 1970, p. 124.

5 Francis Stuart, *A Compendium of Lovers,* Raven Arts Press, 1990, p. 21.

6 ibid, p. 145.

7 ibid, p. 170.

8 Katherine Stuart to her father, Francis Stuart, letter, A.F.S.E.

32. More Controversy

1 Francis Stuart, *Arrow of Anguish,* New Island Books, Dublin, 1995, p. 18.

2 F.S. interview with Naim Attallah, Quartet Books, 1996.

3 Máire Cruise O'Brien, *The Same Age as the State,* The O'Brien Press, Dublin, 2003, p. 331.

4 ibid, p. 333.

5 ibid, p. 335.

6 ibid, p. 338.

7 ibid, p. 338.

8 Francis Stuart, *Black List, Section H,* Southern Illinois University Press, 1971, Postscript, Harry T. Moore, p. 438.

9 Francis Stuart, *Black List, Section H,* Penguin Books, 1996.

10 "Francis Stuart honoured by Aosdána", *Art Matters* No 24, p. 4, An Information Bulletin of the Arts Council (Ireland).

11 *Poetry Ireland Review* Winter 2002/3 edited by Michael Smith, p. 119.

12 I.S. interview with K.K., 22 March 1998.

13 ibid.

14 Francis Stuart, *King David Dances*, New Island Books, Dublin, 1996, p. 19. The novel contains many quotations from Heidegger and many biographical facts about his life also. Stuart's obsession with his philosophy overflows here. Other works on Heidegger that are drawn on for this chapter include George Steiner, *Heidegger,* Fontana, 1978; *Critical Heidegger,* Christopher Macann, editor, Routledge, 1996.

15 F.S. interview with Naim Attallah, Quartet Books, 1996.

16 Francis Stuart, *King David Dances*, New Island Books, Dublin, 1996, p. 57.

33. County Clare

Interviews mentioned below took place between the biographer and Stuart within the periods: 17 September–23 September 1998, 18 February–23 February 1999, 19 November–23 November 1999.

1 F.S. interview with K.K.

2 Finola Graham, Stuart's widow, in interview with K.K., February, 2000.

3 ibid.

4 F.S. interview with K.K.

5 *We Have Kept the Faith: New and Selected Poems*, Raven Arts Press, Dublin, 1982, p. 6.

6 F.S. interview with K.K.

34. A New Century

See "Chapter Notes and Sources" (p. 341) concerning interviews with contemporaries of Stuart.

1 Ambrose and Christina O'Connor interviews with K.K. February 2000.

Index

About the Author

Kevin Kiely, poet, novelist and critic, was born in Northern Ireland. *Breakfast with Sylvia* (2005) won the Patrick Kavanagh Fellowship for poetry in 2006; *A Horse Called El Dorado* (2005) a Bisto Honour Award for fiction in 2006. An honorary fellow of Iowa University, he has lived and worked in Europe and the United States. He was Editor of *Books Ireland New Writing* 1996–2001, Assistant Editor of *Books Ireland* 2001–2005, and has received a number of Arts Council Bursary-in-Literature Awards: 1980, 1989, 1990, 1998, 1999 and 2004. Radio dramas include *Children of No Importance*, RTÉ, 2000 and *Multiple Indiscretions*, RTÉ, 1997. *Mere Mortals* (1989) was on the Hughes & Hughes Fiction Prize short list in 1990; his first novel, *Quintesse* (1982), was reissued by St Martin's Press, New York in 1985.

He has written for *Hibernia, Irish Examiner, Irish Studies Review, Honest Ulsterman, Fortnight, Books Ireland, The London Magazine, The Irish Book Review, Poetry Ireland Review, The Irish Times* and the *Irish Arts Review*. He is Fulbright Scholar-in-Residence at Boise State University, Idaho, 2007-2008 and completing a PhD on the Woodberry Poetry Room, Harvard University, 1942–1969.

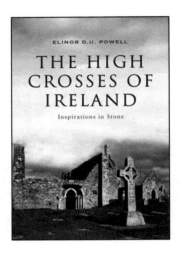

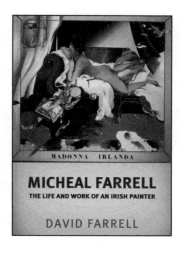

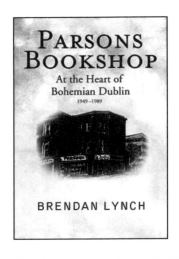